Hazeline

by
Barbara Kidd Lawing

BURKWOOD
Media Group

Burkwood Media Group
P O Box 1772
Albemarle, NC 28001-5704
www.burkwoodmedia.com

Printed in the United States of America

Cover Art by Gayle Halpern

Dedication

This novel is dedicated to the memory of
my mother – Sheila Beatrice Caruth Kidd.

She read fairy tales to her children, and
took me along when she rode the bus
to Charlotte's library.

"Truth hath better deeds than words to grace it."
~Shakespeare, The Two Gentlemen of Verona

AUTHOR'S NOTE

Hazeline's story is set in 1937 – the year electric lines were run in the north end of Mecklenburg County, North Carolina. I am indebted to librarians at Charlotte's main library who researched that detail for me.

The roots of Hazeline's story go back to my early childhood and my grandparents' cotton farm. Cotton had been a reliable moneymaker for decades. When I was a young child my Grandpa, James Barkley Kidd, was still growing cotton, and sharecropper families – who helped with planting and picking – still lived on the farm.

One day when I was perhaps four years old I went with Grandma (Nettie Caldwell Kidd) to the cotton field. She was not usually a picker so the skies must have been cloudy. Once it rained no more cotton could be picked for some while, and I suspect she surmised that her presence would have the pickers giving closer attention to their task. She did pick, and had pinned together a small bag to fit over my shoulder, but I was too enthralled with my new surroundings to pick more than a handful or two.

The pickers lived on Jim and Nettie Kidd's property in sharecropper homes. Years later I moved back to the area and sometimes walked the land where once there had been a cotton farm. To my surprise I found that one of the little houses was still standing. The front door was missing and a tree had fallen across the kitchen. I stood on the rock step and leaned forward to peek inside. The interior seemed too small. Surely a whole family could not have lived in such close quarters.

Each time I tarried at the little house I wondered, *Who lived here?*

At right of the front entrance was an alcove where perhaps husband and wife slept, a space about the size of a double bed. The center of the very small living area was rectangular. Fireplace bricks had tumbled to the hearth. I ventured inside to retrieve one. A handmade brick, one of my treasures.

Kitchens pre-electricity were built at the back, so visualize at right of the fireplace a step up into the kitchen. The outhouse (toilet) was also still standing. I figured some of the youngsters had slept in the crawlspace up near the tin roof in cold weather, and perhaps outside in warm weather. The toilet also was built of wood that had never seen paint, and consisted of one wooden seat with a hole, and a door for privacy.

There had been two or three other sharecropper homes. Those houses never saw running water or electricity. Water had to be hauled from the well which was not close by. I remember the well. It was at the end of what is now Jim Kidd Road. To get to the little houses you went up hill, going north, and over the ridge then a bit more distance, so toting water in a bucket was no small task.

In 1937, in the north end of Mecklenburg County, neither white nor colored folk had electricity, but lines were being run. Other parts of the county already had electric lines. Hazeline's story is set in 1937 so the reader sees one full year, all the seasons – and to remind us of how our lives differ tremendously from those folk of such a short time ago – when no matter who you were you lived per the season of the year. And also lived without modern medicine or transportation.

My first task was to imagine a fictional character – which I did sitting at my dining table with a small group of women who had come to join me in a session of freewriting. I set my sights on imagining a woman who lived in that last still-standing sharecropper house, and in that Sunday writing session did put something to the page in a way she might have spoken.

Shortly after my writer friends departed I stood at my kitchen counter and gazed out the window in the direction of the sharecropper house and said silently, "What is her name? The woman who lives in that little falling down house? What is her name?"

I knew it must be an old-fashioned name. Thought of several options. Then the name of one of my dad's cousins came to mind. I jotted 'Hazel' on a scribble pad and stared at it, feeling not quite ok with it. And soon realized the urge to add i-n-e... *Hazeline*.

****

Those treks I made to the little house were across property that had been Grandpa's farm. He and Grandma had by then left this life, though most of their children were still living. Now all that generation is gone, and many of their descendants still live in the vicinity. I am one of those, and thankful to be close by to what was Jim and Nettie Kidd's farm.

I have put the fictional Robbins family in a house like my grandparents' home, a typical farmhouse of the period – with two big square rooms on the ground floor and two upstairs, and dining room that opened onto the back porch, with kitchen at the rear. Houses pre-electricity (pre-air conditioning) always had the kitchen at the back. Since electricity was not yet available in 1937, even water for the landowners' family had to be carried into the house. There was a wide porch at the front of the house, for resting at the end of the day, and a back porch that ran lengthwise adjacent to the kitchen and dining room.

So, to enter the house you stepped through a screen door that opened to the back porch just in front of the dining room door. The well for drawing water was at the end of the porch, only a few steps from the kitchen.

Remember – no air conditioning, no electricity, and lots of wood to be cut for the cook stove and for heat in the dining room and living area. In winter most bedrooms were without heat and folks slept under many covers. And when you got up during the night you had no heated bathroom, just a metal pot with lid to receive your body's waste. Genteel folk called it a chamber pot. My folk called it 'the pot.'

****

Sharecroppers were wanted help. They received some pay when the cotton was sold. My one clear memory of a cotton field dates to when I was a young child. Most Mecklenburg

County farmers had or soon would quit planting cotton. Government agents came through to urge farmers to quit because with each season the soil became more depleted and the boll weevil a bigger pest.

The sharecroppers were valued laborers. They lived on the farm and cashed in on a portion of the crop's proceeds. They were valued assistants. In wintertime, of course, there was not so much to be done on the farm. Folks spent a lot of time sitting by the fireplace or stove.

Respect between the races as they lived and worked in such close proximity was of course mandatory. The farmer needed the workers, yet would not hesitate to send a family packing if those workers didn't pull their share or did not get along with the rest.

As I began Hazeline's story I interviewed four sharecroppers who had lived on Grandpa's cotton farm. They remembered the child I was in those long ago years. And to my surprise, they lived close by.

I interviewed Puella Morrison, Robert Pharr, and Louise Wilson by phone. Each sounded delighted to talk with me about those olden days.

I had clear memories of Puella Morrison, a lovely woman with a bright smile. She had worked in the cafeteria at my elementary school. In the year when I birthed my first child my little family lived adjacent to the school. I was not aware that Puella still worked at the school cafeteria till one afternoon there came a knock at my door. And there she was, with a small gift for my firstborn.

I was tickled pink to see her. It was a joyful hour, for she remembered when my mother and I arrived in the States. My dad and one of his brothers served in WW2, and soon after the soldiers were delivered to the States the Army sent the big ocean liner back to Europe to deliver to the U.S. wives and children of the soldiers. (The ship can be viewed online.) Since I was an infant, I remember nothing of the journey.

My chief interviewee was Gertrude Bost. Her husband and my dad remained friends long after there were no cotton fields, for they had grown up together on Grandpa's cotton farm. By the time I made contact with Gertie she was a widow. We spent many hours together in her home, only a mile or so from where those long ago cotton fields were. During the time I interviewed her she turned 90. I am sorry I did not complete the novel before she left this world.

When I commented that I couldn't imagine living in one of those tiny little houses Gertie chuckled and murmured, "Oh, it wasn't so bad." One evening I said I wished I knew who had done the laundry for my grandma. She chuckled and said, "Barbara, I did your grandmama's washing." It was a fine moment.

When I had time to think a bit I understood. Washing clothes outdoors in iron pots was just the way things were done then...simply the way things were. When things are a certain way we humans tend to adapt. Her remark soon had me remembering my early childhood, when my family – Mother, Daddy and two young brothers and I – lived for a short time in a house only slightly bigger than Hazeline's.

We had an outdoor toilet, and Mama would fill a round galvanized tub with warm water and give her children a good scrub.

It's sure been a joy to imagine a fictional story built on memories I recall from childhood. My one sadness relates to that lovely stream in the woods, the one Hazeline loves to visit when she needs comfort or wants to express elation. That stream used to be a blessed haven for me. Now it has new owners and big signs that say, 'No trespassing."

I enjoy reading of Hazeline's visits to that stream. I almost feel as though I am there, by the gurgling water and moss-covered rocks. A place of comfort.

****

Pulling together the story of a fictional character and citing accurate details of a long ago way of life required research. Jack Conard, Jr., self-appointed historian of Cornelius, NC, was a huge help. We made a few treks in his Suzuki to outlying counties where we found old houses, still-standing corner stores from early 1900s, old barns and outbuildings, and utensils – things reminiscent of a past pre-electricity. And Jack informed me of a ferry that used to cross the Catawba River and provided a photo from his collection.

I wanted Hazeline's story to be true to the period – so, for example, it was good to come on a butter churn. Or an old car of the period. Jack knew where we could see an old iron bridge, a bit rusty yet still intact, like the one that used to stretch high above McDowell Creek on our historic Beatties Ford Road.

We also came on cooking utensils, trucks, and heavy antique irons like the ones Hazeline uses when ironing. And plows, tractors, early machines, wagons, and fire trucks. It had been years since I had seen a mule or the wooden wagons that mules used to pull. Ride today in those same outlying areas and you will likely find no evidence of life pre-electricity.

Because I grew up on a farm in the fifties and sixties I already knew a whole heap about gardening and canning/preserving food in glass jars, and that cows had to be milked morning and evening, and of horses and geese and the dog that rounded up the cows, and chickens that set on nests and produced eggs.

The women in my early years used wringer washing machines. And 'rinsed out' some underwear or a dishtowel between washings. Pans used for cooking or for rinsing out your underwear were made of metal. There was as yet no plastic.

I watched Grandma sew up dresses and shirts and pillowcases on a machine with a treadle that she rocked back and forth with her foot to make the needle go up and down. And watched her put a worm on a fishing hook then drop the line into the pond and wait for a tug on the line. And each July we trekked down the far side of the hill in the direction of the creek and picked blackberries. We'd return to the house in time for Grandma to prepare 'dinner' – main meal of the day, served at noon. And in the afternoon during warm weather months she was often canning blackberries or corn or beans in canning jars. With strawberries and damsons she made jam. And in autumn we went looking for muscadines, a wild grape, in hopes of picking a few before raccoons got to them. And we grandchildren liked to climb up and sit on the limbs of a mulberry tree.

The milk her sons brought to the house came straight from the cow – unprocessed milk. The cream soon separated and rose to the top. After electric lines were run Grandpa soon bought an electric icebox. And when electric washing machines came on the market, Grandma soon owned one. At that stage, doing the family laundry meant the machine swirled the clothes about in soapy water, then you held each piece of the wash to a machine-turned wringer that squeezed out excess water. Then you were ready to proceed to the clothesline and use clothespins to fasten the wet laundry to the wire.

As you read Hazeline you escape into her era, a time when people lived a slower and simpler life. In good weather, time was spent outdoors or on the porch. The pace of life back then was easier, in rhythm with nature. In the evening maybe, after supper, listen to the news or a radio version of a soap opera. Or sit under the stars. No streetlights – and the sky rich with glistening jewels. And when the full moon brightened the air, the night was magic.

Chapter 1

'Bout soon as I got here I was wantin' to leave. Miz Robbins, she got big comp'ny coming. Her kinfolk. They always does visit in cold weather, 'fore springtime come along with its heap of chores so big yuh can't keep up. Been working at it a few days now, the fire in the cookstove going and me running to and fro 'tween the kitchen and bedrooms—and not once had to go out and carry water. The well right by the kitchen, so I just step out the backdoor and take hold of the pump handle. Don't have to skimp on water not one bit.

I drop another stick of wood in the cookstove. My pound cake soon gon be done. Made one yesterday but forgot to check it in time. One thing 'bout Miz Robbins though, she don't complain 'bout sump'n like that. It my mistake and she know I gon set it right.

Yesterday she got to piddling round in the kitchen and me wishing she'd go on, and all a sudden she pop up and say, "Hazeline, you counting on finding you another husband?"

My heart thumped a few times. I was staring at the wall, seeing the li'l lines on the beadboard—looking right over her head, cause she a li'l woman.

She say, "You dreaming in that direction?"

My throat got a lump in it. I stepped aside and reached up and begun pulling at my hairnet. Knowed I had to keep myself in check, so's not to march right out the door.

Couldn't do that. So I swallowed the lump and took me a deep breath.

"No'm, not dreaming. You ready to hang them curtains?"

Most of the time, he already gone by the time I gets here. Not so today, and I can't help but overhear. I knead my dough hurrieder and hurrieder—louder his voice get.

"Doggone it, wife—what you got up your sleeve now?"

Once they get to arguing, he gets loud and she backs off. Now he saying, "I might just hightail it outta here!"

She say sump'n back, I reckon, then he at it again. I see him clear, likely his hand on his head, smoothing down that hair tha's going a bit thin. Now he be shouting. "That brother of yours ain't no 'count, no 'count a'tall. And all that talk wears me out!"

She prob'ly reminding him they won't stay long. Maybe mention the times his folk come. He get all happy then and hang round the house. Used to be he'd put my Joshua in charge then. Wouldn't surprise me none if'n when these folks come, he tell'em 'at now 'at his foreman ain't here to do the job, he gone have to be out and doing.

"Two nights! Goldarn it, Mabel, you said one!"

So she's agreed to let 'em stay longer. If'n I had to guess I'd bet all this stir-up's 'bout her not asking him. Mister Luther Robbins always do like to play the boss. If I could get up my nerve, I'd speak my mind to him.

There he go, stomping out the dining room door and slamming it shut. My shoulders ease. I's done pummeled this yeast dough way more'n it need. Put it aside to rise, and go see what the missus want me to do next. Long as her comp'ny's here, she gon be wanting me here till way on over in the afternoon—so the mister ain't the only one none too happy 'bout her folks staying a bit longer.

Best grease my pans and wash up these bowls, give her a little time to calm herself. Ain't no wonder she such a unhappy woman. Right pitiful, most of the time. But soon as I think it, sump'n else come to mind. Uh-huh, they was a day.

He'd been hollering and fussing and stomped out— same as he done today. They right often rubbing the other'n the wrong way, so it was some surprise—what she say. Right quick after he was gone she come out by the washpot.

More'n likely my face was showing my sympathy, cause I'd heard him yelling. First thing, she blow out her breath. Then she say, "Does him a world of good to fuss at me a bit."

S'pect my face showed my shock. Might be this little woman was some bit wiser'n I thought.

Joshua yelled at me once. We hadn't been married long. What was it he got so upset about? Don't even know, but I sure r'member how it shocked me, him flying off the handle thataway. Scared me some too, sort'a like all a sudden a mad dog'd showed up.

I smile a bit thinking on it. That day? Why it was more'n fine. I let him storm on a bit, and then set in to giggling. That made him yell the louder and I laughed so hard I doubled over. Truth was, I was just playacting— cause I didn't have no idea what else to do. But right quick, I could see the funny in it. Here this sweet man, my new husband—and him so handsome—and blowing up thataway! It wadn't even me had upset him. And if'n it had been me, still wadn't no reason to carry on like that. Ever after, when we was on the outs, sooner or later one or t'other of us'd come round to the laughing. Guess yuh could say it become our way of breaking the hold of a bad spirit.

"Hazeline!"

Miz Robbins speak so sharp and quick it give me a start. I turn round and almost stumble over the lard bucket.

"We gon need least one, maybe two, more sweets. Whatcha think 'bout
cherry pies?" She set two cans of cherries on the counter.

She be looking thinner'n ever. That ole faded workdress just hanging on her, and her hair all straggly. Most of the time she keep it drawed tight in a bun. Now 'at I be looking at her close I see 'at my boss lady's hair's going gray. Wonder how old she be? Always has figured she's been on this earth just a wee bit longer'n me.

"Miz Robbins, if'n it all the same, I rather make chess pies."

She heave a sigh. "My land, Hazeline. Sometimes you a lot like Luther. No matter what I say, you change it about."

I stand real still. Waiting.

And she say, "But tha's alright. Make the chess." She turns away, out the kitchen door through the dining room. I calls after her. "Miz Robbins, you got one of your headaches comin' on?"

If'n she answer, she don't talk loud enough so's I can hear. A bit later I peep in the front room and there she be—laying flat on her back wit' her eyes closed.

No matter how much time the two of us be's t'gether, we ain't never at the same level. It'd surprise her to know how oftentimes I feel like the one on the higher rung, cause I so often pitying her. She the one said 'I do'—and wit' that she made her bed. Now she got to lie in it.

On over in the afternoon I be hauling my tired self 'cross the pasture, headed for the li'l house, and a strange thought come. What woulda this day been like if'n I was the white woman—and her the colored?

Don't take long to come up wit' the answer. Wouldn't be no dif'rent a'tall. Cause one body'd still be white and the other'n not. If'n I was white I'd be same as her, cause tha's the way white folks be. They done took up all kinds of wrong thinking, so wouldn't nothing be different—'cept I'd be living in the big house, and her in the shack.

****

"Woman, my stomach telling me it ain't been fed in a week. We got anything in the house to eat?" My man. Home from his labor. I'd caught his whistling 'fore he got to the door. His grin was spread ear to ear, and I knowed why.

I was just inside the kitchen where I could see him coming in the front. He hung his cap and jacket on the nails by the door. Joleen was at the kitchen table doing her homework. His grin was for me, I knowed that—and knowed how to read it too. Night be'forewe'd had us a fine ole time. Joleen'd been gone, took her school clothes and stayed over the Sunday night too, so we had all that time to ourselves.

Close on to two-year now since he been gone. When my man left this world, my heart just went right out of me. Even now, seem like all I does is look back and wish things was the way they used to be. Coupla nights ago it dawned on me why that ain't no way to live. A picture crossed my mind. With all this looking back, I might end up like that woman in the Bible. She looked back, and got turned to a pillar of salt.

It be a lot easier to look back than to look ahead. May as well be blind for all the good these eyes be for seeing wha's gon happen—and if'n I can't see wha's gon happen, how I s'posed to know what to do?

Only blind person I ever knowed was one of Mama's brothers. He was a lot older'n her. I never did see him more'n a time or two. His wife'd take him by the arm and lead him along, and when yuh stood in front of him yuh could tell his eyes couldn't see. These eyes of mine work fine for wha's right in front of me, but I be needing to see some months down the road. How I gon tell what to do if'n I can't see?

"Just tell me that now."

I say it loud from the back step and Ole Dog lift a ear. He done lost most of his hearing and don't get about too good neither. I done finished my breakfast, so now it time to feed him and the chickens.

"Ole Dog, a good thing you here, cause if'n yuh wadn't, I'd have to say I be's talking to myself." I chuckle, but the worry don't ease none. More'n likely Mister Luther

Robbins gon decide he want me to move out this li'l house. Then what I gon do?

"Any idea, Ole Dog? Problem be, ain't nobody here to take me by the arm and show me where to go."

Feels kind of strange to feel so blind, cause my eyes be's good. But what I needing now be some magic spectacles—eyeglasses 'at let yuh know wha's down the road a'piece.

Ole Dog gobble down his breakfast. I stand back of the house and look up 'cross the field, say good morning to the day.

A mem'ry come. Joshua was upset and me thinking I oughta cheer him up. Him and Ole Dog was out at the bench and I went traipsing out there. Ole Dog raised his head and looked my way, likely trying to tell me sump'n.

Next thing, Joshua was saying it. "Git on back in the house, woman. Leave us be."

I hurry on, get myself ready to go, pull on my old sweater and tie a kerchief on my head. I pick up my bag wit' a change of clothes and set out, cause today be's Monday. Washday. The day ain't so bad cold, and soon enough I'll have a fire going under the washpot.

Walking along, I decide I likely be needing some greens to eat. A body do need fresh stuff, so reckon I better find me some chickweed. That li'l plant a marvel, way it stay so green in the dead of winter. I bring it almost to a boil, then serve it up alongside some dried beans. Might be just a weed, but it sure help me make it through the winter.

Chapter 2

Gathering kindling. Glad to have a excuse to get out. Cloudy and not too cold, but feel like the weather maybe getting ready to change. I look up in the sky and think of the flying machine. A millionaire, the paper called him. Say he flew a aeroplane from one side of this country to the other.

I chuckle to myself. Which the hardest to b'lieve? The flying all that way? Or that they anybody that rich?

I get to the edge of the woods up on the hill and stand there looking out cross the big field and on past the cedars 'long the fencerow. When spring come, they gon be a heap of a lotta cottonseed going in the ground. If'n Joshua was here, he'd be in charge of the work crew.

Was when this land was cleared that Mister Robbins first put Joshua in charge. Most of the hands worked at it, and worked many a day, cutting trees and trimming 'em and laying 'em to dry. Time would come they'd load 'em on a wagon and haul 'em to the sawmill. Mister Robbins depended on Joshua—for carpentry work too, even the doctoring of the horses and mules.

The day I remembering, they was felling trees and I followed in behind to get the gleanings. Tha's what the Bible call it, in the story of Ruth. She went along behind the harvesting to get grain for her and her mama-in-law.

The time I be's r'membering was late in the year, after the cotton had been picked. I carried along my hatchet, looking to get a good supply of brush. Had in mind to build up another brush pile where the bobwhites might move in. I so love to hear that bird call its name. *Bob-white, bob-white.*

Sound sorta like, all's right, all's right.

Wonder how I remembers so much 'bout that day so long ago? Mister Robbins was always wanting more of the woods cleared so's to grow more cotton. He kept after Joshua, pushing him to make the work go faster. Kept on saying, 'Time is money.'

Don't take long this morning 'fore I got all the kindling my little wagon can hold. Still I linger on a bit. Just stand still. And look. From up here on the high ground I can see far and wide 'cross the fields. In the distance, there the big house, and the barn and sheds, and chicken coop and hog pen. From up here I can see most of the li'l houses too.

Last time the cotton was ready for picking, thought I was gon have to stay wit' Miz Robbins—and wadn't one bit looking forward to that! The picking make my back ache sump'n awful and wear me out till I does wonder if'n I's ever gon get over it, but even tha's better'n being cooped up day after day wit' that sad li'l woman. But, reckon I'd be sad too if'n I had to put up wit' him. He the boss, and wanna make sure ever'body know it.

She was poorly then, and as it turned out she got one of her ole-maid cousins to come stay wit' her. Mister Robbins insisted on it—say I too good a picker to stay in the house. Had me a new straw hat to wear for the picking. A gift from Ruby. Wadn't brand new, was secondhand from Miz Dellinger, her boss lady, so to make it a proper gift Ruby put a new ribbon on it. Red ribbon.

Ever' woman oughta have a friend like Ruby Pharr. She ain't no kin to me, but seem like more'n kin. While I was picking I 'magined her picking in the Dellingers' fields—few miles from here. Her back aching too. Me and Joshua used to rub the other'un's back and shoulders after a day in the field. Ruby's husband never was that kind—and he long gone now, praise be.

Sure feels good to be out in the air. A clear winter day, not so awfully cold, but same as usual my worry keeps nagging at me.

Had a good bowl of grits wit' fresh-churned butter for my breakfast, ain't got no aches nor pains to speak of— but nowadays I just plain lonely. Saturday it be, and plenty to keep me busy. Promised to help wit' some cleaning over at the church, and one of the neighbors has fell sick so I wanna bake sump'n to carry over there.

Rather go back to bed. But that wouldn't do no good. This li'l house ain't much, but where in tarnation will I go if'n I has to leave it?

Well, best get on. Maybe walk down in the woods. Uh-huh, that likely be just the thing. Don't usually go so early in the day.

I soon get my boots and my ole coat and set out. Weather's clear. But the ground's wet. I carry a coupla thick sacks to put across my rock, cause I know I gon be wanting to set a spell. Air fine and crisp, but the ground's wetter'n I thought. Not sure these ole boots gon keep my feet dry.

But awready I feeling some better. 'Fore long the water come in sight, and it just as I thought. Enough water running to make a mighty fine music. My good fortune, living so close to this little branch, and it in a patch of woods kindly outta the way, so usually ain't nobody down here.

First thing…stand real still and look and listen.

Then go downstream a little distance. And tha's when I spot it, over on the other bank. I cross the water, stepping on the rocks, and yessiree—there it be! The bloom come early in the year and don't last long, so I don't often see this li'l beauty. The blossom kinda pink and kinda lavender, and the flower show itself 'fore the leaves come. Look just like a jewel—sprouting up through the brown leaves. Prob'ly got some other name, but I's always heard it called liverleaf.

I hug my coat round me and stand for a bit. This li'l beauty sure worth a bit of admiring. "Awright, li'l flower. You sure fine and I sure pleased to see you, but right now I gon set myself down and listen to the music—listen to water run."

I spread the cover on my rock. A flat black rock, right by the stream. Set myself down and begins listening to the gurgling. The water be's fairly deep and just a'scampering over the rocks.

"Morning, water. Glad to see yuh still here and running along like usual."

I set real still and soon gets to r'membering how I been feeling so outta sorts. Truth be, my life prob'ly 'bout good as it can be right now. Got enough to eat, a roof over my head, and been earning a few dollars—'nough to call myself getting by. Got many a fine mem'ry of my sweet Joshua to keep me comp'ny. And Joleen and her husband, they doing awright.

But this loneliness for my man...it always wit' me. And I ain't never far from the worry 'bout maybe having to leave this farm. I tries to see where I'd go, but don't see no place. I be's like one of them aeroplanes. Wanting to set down, but not finding nowhere to set down.

I set there a bit longer, listening to the gurgling and singing of the branch water, but 'fore long I gets the shivers and says my goodbyes and head up the path. Don't go far 'fore I gets to chuckling at the beech trees. Look like they waving good-bye. A beech tree keep its dead leaves till spring, when the new ones come along and push off the old.

I keep standing for a bit, looking at the brown leaves still on the twig. And hear myself say, "Reckon they's people like that too. Won't make a change till they's pushed to."

Well, said I'd help clean the church, so best get going. First, gather up some cleaning rags. If'n I get there a bit early, can stop by Joshua's grave. And my boy's too. Seem sometimes like I find my comfort talking wit' the dead. Now ain't that sump'n?

****

Monday, but won't be no standing over the washpot this day. Rain just a'pouring. Big racket on the tin roof. I settle in the rocker, sipping at my coffee. Taking it easy.

Rather live easy on a sunny day. But tha's a for-sure pipe dream. Soon's yuh know spring's round the corner, ain't no way yuh can keep up. It be always on your mind, how yuh gotta get all yuh can done while the weather's good. Make hay while the sun shine!

But right now, wit' this raining cats and dogs, might be I could do nothing...if'n I care to. But the worry done caught up wit' me, so setting and taking my ease won't come easy.

Now that I think of it, setting and doing nothing—why tha's doing sump'n. cause even when yuh doing nothing yuh doing sump'n. Now that sound kinda like a riddle. I gets to laughing at my own funny. And Joshua come to mind. He the one knowed how to laugh. Uh-huh! Big fine laugh—fill the whole house! Was the first thing 'at drawed me to him.

May as well set myself down at the machine and get some work done, but first thing, got to move the kerosene lamps. The poor light the worst thing 'bout this li'l house—and tha's saying a lot, cause they a heap 'bout it 'at ain't so good. On a day like this'un, get so dark in here it put yuh in mind of a grave.

Huh—wish I hadn't thought that. Made me shudder. But as a rule, work be a good cure-all and I sure got plenty to do. Three dresses cut and ready. For a cousin to Miz Robbins. She a big woman, so big she prob'ly can't find readymade clothes.

Only thing I has to change be color of the thread—and keep going, cause all of 'em off'n the same pattern. They still a li'l short sleeve jacket to make yet, and I gon have to do some figuring on it. Maybe put in a extra piece up under the arm. Figure on sewing at the machine today, and tomorrow, do the finger work. This first part be's easy—don't have to pay it much mind, so right soon, my head starts to traveling. Going just ever-which-way.

First off, settle on the day Joshua come home wit' Suzy. He'd bought his own mule. But wadn't zactly his. Some of the men 'round had put what they could t'gether to get a mule, but was Joshua's idea and him was to care for it.

I always did like Suzy. She was a lot like the mule 'at pulled the wagon the day they went to the cemetery to bury my boy. We'd been married a coupla years, lived on the Patterson farm in a li'l house 'bout the same as this 'un.

The needle on my machine keep going and going, and me 'magining again what that day must'a been like. The day of the burying I didn't know nothing. The birthing was a hard one. I was lucky to make it through—tha's what the midwife told Joshua. And the doctor they called said the same.

I done pictured it over and over, so when I think back, seem sorta like I was at the cemetery. I see the li'l box wit' the li'l body, and me weeping and weeping. By the time I old and gray I prob'ly won't know I wadn't there, cause I done took it for my mem'ry.

Another Suzy picture pops up. The day she got away and had herself a fine ole time in the Robbins corn patch. That cost Joshua 'bout as much in shame as it done time and money. Joshua a proud man! Got away wit' him, it did, to have to admit to his boss man 'at he couldn't keep his mule up.

I keep going. Put the sleeves in. Put pleats in the skirt. My hands stay busy, my head too. It show me Joleen, 'bout eight year old. Playing in my scrap bag. Asking can she have this, can she have that—and I say she can. Not long after that Joshua get to laughing and laughing. I was busy in the kitchen but I heard him, and went to the backdoor to see. Joleen was wearing the new sunsuit I'd stitched up the day before. I'd fancied it up with rows of rickrack round all the edges.

She'd draped cloth round Suzy's head, over her ears and round her neck. I wondered if'n Suzy bent down and let Joleen do that? But I knowed better. Would'a been her daddy held her up and let her do her work.

A fine mem'ry. The happy swell up in me like a balloon. Seem lately like most of my happiness come from looking back. And that do make sense, cause the past where my heart be. But ever so often I does chide myself. Joleen...she still here, she ain't gone. And Ruby. And Henrietta and Sam. But still, that don't make up the loss. Joshua was the best thing in my life.

A voice come back, say I oughta be ashamed. And I knows what that voice mean. My happiness can set on Joleen. But she got her own life, she a grown woman.

Ouch! Well I be doggone! The needle nicked me. Won't get no more work done on these dresses today, I don't s'pect. I rest 'gainst the chair back and wrap a scrap round my finger. Tears come and my chest goes tight.

When nightfall comes, I still feeling bad. In the grip of some terrible thing that ain't nothing but fear. But it a fear 'at look awful scary.

I was wanting to knock out the three dresses so's I could feel pleased wit' myself. A hard-working woman—tha's Hazeline Morrison! But nowadays, most times, seem like I more often turned toward what once was.

The thought jerks me up. It do seem a blasphemy.

Is all the days ahead gon be like this'un? Me staying busy, earning a few dollars, buying my few things? Been hard lately for me to pray. Hard to say I be's thankful for this lonely life.

Soon as it be good and dark, I crawls in the bed.

Chapter 3

Next thing I know the sky's beginning to show light. Don't remember when I's slept so deep. And right after that thought I get the feeling again. I know its name. *Dread.*

How I does dread the long stretch of days ahead! Don't feel nowhere near ready to die...yet here I be—all on my lonesome. And this sorrow so big it'd wrap round me many a time.

Still cold. And been so much rain of late I couldn't do the Robbins laundry. But, tha's winter. And tha's weather. Yuh can't never tell. Reckon I too much the kind 'at like to keep to a reg'lar schedule.

Ain't no money exchanged, so least it ain't changing the 'mount of money in my li'l change purse. The thought gets me to chuckling. And the chuckle do ease me some, and none too soon! Ain't one bit fond of getting all worked up wit' my thoughts rambling ever-which-away.

Look like the weather might be clearing, so maybe I can do the Robbins washing tomorrow. Sure be a burden when the dirty clothes pile up. Bending over a washboard ain't sump'n yuh wanna be doing for too long a stretch.

Been working wit' my Dutch Boy quilt squares. Make one boy at a time. Stitch the pieces I's cut from my scrapbag onto the backing, then when I get all the squares done I gon pull out my stash of material and hope to find just the right cloth for making the strips 'tween the squares.

I dream of getting it done in secret and lay it by for the time I hope to see, when Joleen and Troy give me a grandchile. Guess I best make two, the other'un a Dutch Girl.

One thing I sure glad of. Troy a town worker. Even bought hisself a car. Look like a rattle-trap, but most of the time it do run. I s'pect he might make a good daddy for my grandbaby. And hope they gon be more'n one—boys 'at grow up to look like him, wit' wide shoulders, and a wee bit tall.

He got his eye on getting ahead. I 'spect it be Joleen putting off the notion of chirren. She wanna be a uptown girl—work a public job and dress in nice clothes. I s'pose getting ahead a alright thing to set yuh sights on, long as yuh don't get obsessed wit' it.

I see'd the pattern for this quilt in the Sears Roebuck catalog. Li'l girl in a dress and bonnet. Yuh couldn't see her face cause her bonnet so big, but I knowed her face was white—so I cut my own pattern, a Dutch Boy, so's to show a bit of his face. He got dark skin, and the quilt's shaping up good. Next thing, gotta figure how to save it good, so's no water leak can stain it, nor no mouse gnaw at it.

Right now I gon set myself down by a winduh and read the *Charlotte News*. Reading oftentimes give the mind sump'n different to think on. Maybe help me set aside this worry 'bout what gon become of me.

Uh-huh. Strange as it do seem, now they just Hazeline Morrison. On her own.

Joshua put in these winduhs. One face east, and one south. Ain't none o' the other sharecropper houses got any windows...just shutters to pull closed over a opening. I pull my chair over so's to catch the last of the daylight. Ain't wanting to burn my kerosene lamp no more'n I has to.

A Saturday it was. He come home wit' two winduhs. Him and Sam had been out gallivanting in Sam's car. Took 'em from a house was gon be tore down. First thing when he come in he say he gon put 'em in this house. And tha's zackly what he done!

This li'l house face east. The front door opens off a tiny porch at ain't much bigger'n a stoop, and that stoop needing some repair. At the back they a outhouse, and a shed and a chicken coop. And a ole hog pen. Since Joshua's been gone, I ain't tried to keep no pig to fatten for the kill. Fat pigs can get pretty mean, so I don't wanna fool with one.

This li'l house and the ones like it on the place, all of 'em made of boards that's weathered to a deep gray. They ain't never see'd no paint. First thing, when yuh come in yuh sees the fireplace and the mantel board. And right by it, the opening to the kitchen.

The kitchen jut out the back, so's the chimney takes the smoke from the cookstove and the fireplace. They a tiny loft too, big enough for 2 or 3 young'uns to crawl up there and sleep, but Joleen never liked going up there by herself. Most all these tiny houses be's way overcrowded, folk packed in like sardines.

This farm the first place Joshua got settled in. He quit thinking 'bout moving on and begun building some. First off, made the lean-to, so's to keep some dry wood handy. And put in a extra door out that way too and built a lean-to, so's we could step right out and grab a armload of firewood.

This li'l house! Don't seem hardly big enough to turn around in, yet somehow or 'nother they been a heap of living up under this tin roof.

A body coming through the front door see first thing, the iron bedstead. Time was, we'd pull a curtain round the bed, so's to have a bit of privacy, but nowadays I don't bother wit' no curtain. The ole bed sleep fair and gon sleep better when I get 'round to filling the ticking wit' some new straw.

Joleen, she slept in the other front corner. I hung a coupla long curtains over that way too. Joshua put up a plenty of hooks for hanging clothes and such. Some of the floorboards still covered wit' a wore-out linoleum rug he come carrying in some long-back day. The pattern was 'bout wore off and the edges raggedy, but it sure better'n plain floorboards for keeping out creepy crawlies.

And I's made a good many plaited rugs. It one of my favorite ways to pass time when it freezing cold outside. I huddle near the fire and take my time, hooking scraps of cloth together. I like figuring which colors fit best together.

By the fireplace they two rocking chairs. Joshua made 'em in a friend's cabinet shop. And a straight chair at my machine. And another'un over in the corner.

They three kerosene lamps, one hanging from a chain close by my Singer sewing machine. And a chifferobe and a trunk—and a jumble of piled up stuff, like this here stack of papers. Ah-ha! This one—the one I been wanting to read.

Miz Robbins saves the papers for me. *The Charlotte News* delivered to their place in the afternoon. Might be I gon find sump'n in this paper for my 'edification.' The thought gets me to chuckling. Mighty big word—one I been thinking on since Sunday last when it come from the mouth of the deacon was standing at the pulpit.

Where I get my edification? Not from no Rev'rend Jones. He got two other churches he serve, so most Sundays our deacons in charge. On his Sundays, I sometimes think 'bout staying home—but I be doggone if I gon let that fool make me miss my churchgoing. Get to dress up some, and see ever'body. Best part's the singing. Raise our voices, make a joyful noise!

****

This a ole paper. Friday, it say, January 1, 1937.

March just 'round the corner—and here I be a'setting and reading 'bout *the first snowblanket of the year.*

"Uh-huh—I sure remembers it!"

Was when I spotted the li'l red fox. Spotted him from right here, from this winduh. He was scouting 'round the edge of them big black rocks at the edge of the field. He dug in the snow a bit, but 'fore long, backed off. I figured he hadn't found nothing, but after a bit he come again. And sure 'nough, he was soon feeding on sump'n. Maybe a mole. That pretty li'l fox stayed right there for some li'l bit. I could see him chewing. And all the while his eyes roving, on the lookout. Was fine to behold! A red fox in the pure white snow.

That snow kept me in two or three days. Didn't do much more'n keep close by the fire. Done a bit of reading, made some lace, baked up a fine egg custard. Made snow cream too. One night I slept so heavy I didn't get up soon enough to tend the fire, so when I come to I was scrunched up like a baby—and chilled to the bone! I pulled the cover over my head and huddled in. Always has been one 'at dread putting my feet out on the cold floor of a morning. Rather sweat any day'n be drawed up wit' cold.

They do be one thing I likes 'bout the cold. Don't have to worry much 'bout bugs. When weather's warm and they's crawling, ain't no way yuh can keep 'em out, cause these li'l houses is crude built.

This newspaper for white folk. But most times I find sump'n in it to tickle my fancy. Like this right here. A big ad, urging ever'body to buy a e-lectric range. Say they not just for people wit' lots of money. And I say, *Huh! What good would a fancy cookstove be in this l'il house? Ain't no 'lectric power here!*

Even the rich folk 'round ain't got no use for such. In Charlotte they got 'lectricity, but ain't no 'lectric lines been run through here yet. Won't be long though, cause now they got sump'n called the CCC—wit' workers somewhere up this way now, setting poles and running wire. I know sure as I be setting here that soon's 'lectric power gets hooked up, Mister Luther Robbins gon be taking hisself to town to buy one of them fancy cookstoves.

If'n I still on this place then…well, it ain't a prospect I care to think on. But they be one thing in my favor. Mister Luther Robbins the kind likely spend money on a tractor, 'stead of sump'n for the house. I heard him say again, just recent, how a mule's a heck more reliable. But one day 'fore long, he gon buy hisself a tractor. Ain't no doubt 'bout that.

What I'd buy, if'n I had 'lectric power and a heap of money, would be this fine Philco radio in a pretty 'console' cabinet. $29.95. Then I'd head over to Efird's, get in on the shoe sale. $3.95. I could use some new garters and stockings too.

Here a ad for Lydia E. Pinkham's pills for women's ailments. If'n her pills cure loneliness and broken hearts, I 'spect this Lydia woman gon end up rich as the Rockefellers.

The paper say Mr. Roosevelt and Eleanor, they stayed home—at the White House, had they selves a quiet New Year's Eve. And some rich lady in Washington give a big party and wore the Hope Diamond, right on her finger! She sure wadn't doing no dishes! Likely don't know how to wash a dish. Reckon she stayed busy just holding out her hand so's ever'body could see that rock shine.

The high entertainment be the ongoing story, Chapter XIX in this paper, 'bout the king over in England marrying a Missus Simpson. She got a divorce—*not once but twice!*

On the front page I find *hunt up the beginning*. I says the words to myself. "Hunt up the beginning." And right behind it, wish I could. My fam'ly surely come from Africa. But where in Africa? And what was we like then?

One day at church—when I'd stopped listening to Rev'rend Jones, I got to wondering if back then we prayed to the same god we be sending up prayers to now. I r'membered what the Bible say. They only one god—so that was the end of that. Guess folk in one place picture God dif'rent 'an folk in other places. But all the praise and complaints—all of 'em go to the same place no matter where they spoke.

Oh well, past time to quit this reading. Time to hunt up some supper.

****

All this long afternoon I's felt like a whirligig. Going round and round. Back when the weather was warm I saw one of Miz Robbins's grandchirren playing wit' a whirligig. Li'l gizmo on a stick and the wind blow it round and round. Tha's how I been feeling, sump'n pushing me.

The weather right warm today and I ain't getting nothing done, so I come out here and set myself down on Joshua's whittling bench.

"Joshua, here I be again, wishing you could tell me what the future gon be like." A big sigh then and I says, "Hadn't never once thought you'd go so soon."

My head drops to my hands and a few tears come, but after a bit I set in to talking again. "Sure wish you could help me. Don't know if'n I should go or stay. Can't picture somewheres else. Ain't never had to think on it, cause I always knowed I'd go wherever you went."

I quit then. Tears burning my eyes, and my stomach curled up in a knot.

Chapter 4

The missus follow the mister out to the porch. Arguing 'bout sump'n or other. She eggs him on—and I can't figure that out. Might be cause they don't talk none a'tall if'n they don't fuss. In warm weather, they set on the front porch a good bit. I do wonder what they talk 'bout then.

He soon gets in his big black car and takes off. Then she come out where I be. I's bent over the washboard. She mutters a few words. I don't even have to hear it all to know what she saying. I's heard it many a time. "He right often putting the cart 'fore the horse."

These overalls done soured, so washing 'em won't likely get rid of the bad smell. They three men live in this two-story house. Two 'bout-growed sons, and the boss man.

Dirtiest clothes in last. Won't be long now finishing up. Most part of this day, worry's been trying to set up in me. I tole it I wadn't gon listen and set right in to humming. Started wit' 'Down by the Riverside' – and kept on, one tune after another, so's the worry couldn't find no room for settling.

Cold and wet. This kinda cold yuh don't get used to. Been many a year I been doing laundry for this fam'ly. Can hardly wait to change into dry clothes. Ain't 'llowed to use the outhouse, and wouldn't wanna change in there no way. When ain't nobody home but Miz Robbins, I slips over to the front room—the 'comp'ny room.' It don't hardly ever see no comp'ny.

A bunch of rumors been flying, rumors I ain't wanting to hear. The talk go one direction—then the other. Folks saying the boss thinking 'bout putting *a fam'ly* in my li'l house, so's to have more workers on the place. I keep pushing the thought away and it keep circling round again. Don't have no idea where I'd go.

I dump the washwater, wit' the hope 'at I can dump these worry-pictures outta my head too. A while ago, got to I thinking 'bout the Abernethy girl. Word be, she expecting a chile—and won't tell who the daddy be. I does wonder what the future gon hold for her. She maybe the oldest of the chirren in the little houses on this cotton farm, and the one she in packed way full. I know what it like...too many in a tiny place. Too many mouths to feed. Some sleep at the head of the bed, other'ns at the foot.

Well...at last! Praise be! Might be now I can shut down this thinking, cause my washday work's done. I soon head out, shivering a bit wit' the cold. Gon get the fire going in the fireplace and set right by it—long as I care to, maybe even till they be coals dying down, then feed it a bit more kindling and it get going again. Always has been one of my favorite pastimes, a hour or more, when the mind go 'long wherever it care to go.

Soon as I catch sight of the Abernethy house I whispers a li'l prayer for the girl. Then soon pass by where the Douglas fam'ly live, then the Gudgers' place. They one more l'il house on the property, up by the edge of the burnt woods. The Ballards lives in it.

Won't be long now. Get my fire going and settle in Joshua's rocking chair—and do not one thing.

****

Next morning I settle at my Singer sewing machine, ready to sew up some curtains. And gets to thinking again 'bout the Abernethy fam'ly. But right soon I says to myself, "They ain't my business."

My business be getting on wit' this work, so I set my foot on the pretty iron scroll of the treadle, rock it back and forth, and there go the needle—up and down, up and down, and 'fore yuh know it—one whole panel's done joined to the other!

Early on, after Joleen was born, I could see how sewing for a fam'ly was gon take a heap of my time if'n I had to make all the stitches by hand. So one Saturday morning early we got us a ride to Charlotte wit' Sam, Joshua's brother, and bought this machine on the time-payment plan. Nowadays, Sam be driving a second-hand car, but that day long ago we rode on a wagon his mule was pulling. And now here I be, still setting at this sewing machine. Had it so long now, it feel kindly like a part of me.

But I does wonder if'n I ever is gonna finish these heavy curtains. Miss Cornelia, one of the Alexander sisters, sent word by Miz Robbins. Wanting me to come over and measure they winduhs. The cloth's what some folks'd call elegant—and that be fitting for the Alexander fam'ly. The mama and daddy done gone on to the next life, but they one son and two daughters 'at' never married and still live on the homeplace. They one more, a sister 'at married a Moore, what lives a short walk from this li'l house. I does a lot of sewing for her.

Both fam'lies what yuh call 'aristocrat.' Time was, both families owned plantations. Then that War 'tween the States come along, and when it was over and done, wadn't none of 'em rich no more.

I held my breath when I tole Miss Cornelia what I'd have to make for sewing up such long, heavy draperies. She a tall skinny woman wit' a head 'at put me in mind of a chicken. Her face drawed up tight and she set in to telling me how much they was 'prepared to pay.'

I knowed she didn't have no clear idea 'bout how long it'd take me to do the sewing, and I has to go back and hang 'em too, so I drawed in my breath and opened my mouth. On my walk over there I'd decided what I had to do. Don't make no sense to work for nothing—may as well set by the fire and take it easy.

Even so, when the time come, I sure did shock myself. Spoke right up, I did. What I bargained for still wadn't enough for so much work. If'n she'd hired a white lady she'd pay more—but Hazeline Morrison, why she 'just a darkie!'

I gets to chuckling. Miss Cornelia didn't like my 'negotiating'—didn't like it not one bit! The nerve of it— that colored woman speaking up so!

Thing of it was, they was sump'n she wadn't understanding.

For Hazeline Morrison, it be a matter of life and death. How I s'posed to make it on my own if'n I can't get a few dollars for my sewing? For just a bit, Miss Cornelia did look a bit flustered. But then she heave a sigh and say, "How soon can yuh have 'em done?"

I tole her I wadn't quite done yet wit' another job—but s'pect I could have 'em ready in two weeks.

"Hmmph," she say. And turned away. She picked up the material from the long table in the dark hallway and come back, holding it out to me. I was out and on my way when she holler from the screendoor, "I'll look for you on that Wednesday then!"

Thing 'at bother me 'bout that tall skinny white woman? Way she looks at me. Seem like she looking at me. But it plain as day she ain't really seeing me. I might as well be a fencepost. Or a statue.

That much material ain't so easy to carry a long distance. I'd took along a burlap sack, and the cloth was wrapped in brown paper, so I dropped the bundle in my sack and slung it over my shoulder and set off walking. More'n a few times along the Neck Road I had to stop and catch my breath. And then the thunder. Close by. I was close on to the Moore property by then, so I picked up my step best I could, crossed the li'l footbridge over the creek, and headed up the path toward home.

The load was heavy, but I knowed I couldn't take no more rest stops. Wouldn't do to let the cloth get wet, so I picked up my step. Might need to find shelter. My left side got to hurting awful bad, but I kept on, and on—and made it home just 'fore the storm broke. I dropped the sack inside the door and leaned ag'in the door, trying to catch my breath.

After a bit I crossed over to the kerosene lamp and lit it, thinking how I soon gon need kerosene. It cost a bit. But the big worry always the same. How to get it here.

All I was wanting was to set myself down and take my ease. Then I thought how good a fresh cup of coffee would be. But soon as I thought it, I remembered I hadn't took the ashes out of the cookstove. I leaned my head 'gainst the opening to the kitchen and moaned. Thought how the job of living's never-ending, and so often hard to deal wit'—even for folks of my kind, ones of us 'at don't wish for nothing more'n a plain and simple life.

Well, that was then. Right now, I's 'bout ready to jump up and down and sing hallelujah. I's got 'bout all these heavy panels joined together—ones for the lining too! Still got hemming and pleating to do, but that the easy part. Do that by hand.

Right now I plumb tired of fooling with these heavy curtains. Gon set myself down by the winduh and mend a brassiere for Joleen. That girl of mine make sure she stay far away from anything to do wit' sewing.

****

Spring really coming on now. Hard to make myself set to work. The lilac bush in bloom and smells divine. Ole pear tree coming out too. Even the little peach tree showing a few flowers, though it don't never bear fruit, least none 'at stay on the tree long enough to ripen. The thought gets me to grinning. Look like—uh-huh, sure look like!— Hazeline Morrison been sticking to the limb 'bout long enough. Ain't rotted yet—so might be time to call her ripe!

I chuckle a bit, but next thing I be remembering the work 'at's waiting for me. Easter Sunday coming round soon and I done sewed up nine Easter dresses. Some of 'em kinda fancy, but the one gon wear the fancy don't never think the extra time it take to sew it mean I oughta earn a li'l more pay.

Prob'ly gon end up telling somebody I can't do hers. Tha's when the poor-mouthing start. 'But Miz Hazeline, I can't afford no store-bought dress. I's had my material— just forgot to get it to yuh. And it a easy pattern!'

Most ever' Easter I wakes up sleepy and has to drag myself off to church. One time, way back, Joshua threatened to carry my sewing machine out and not let me finish the dresses I'd started. Another time, he laid the law down soon as spring begun to show.

We was at the table. Joleen was away and we was still wrapped in the happiness of a night to ourselves and I'd fixed us a fine breakfast. Hot biscuits, country ham, red-eye gravy, eggs over easy, and a fresh-opened jar of the last of my strawberry preserves. I'd been saving it for a special occasion. More'n likely I'd said sump'n 'bout how sweet and slow the morning felt, not like the hurrying I'd have to do to finish my sewing.

Joshua had a spoon raised over the jar of preserves. He stopped the spoon in the air and raised a eyebrow. "Use your common sense, wife. You got good sense—use it!"

I promised I'd be careful not to say yes to more'n I could do. Don't r'member if'n I kept my promise, but I'm tickled pink now—just cause his words showed up. I can hear 'em like it was yesterday.

But seem now like I be needing more'n common sense. This *not knowing*—tha's wha's got me on edge. Is Mister Robbins gon send me packing?

That ain't no little worry. Guess what I be needing now, if'n I can find it, be's 'trust.' The Good Lord will help me.

And courage. Need some of that too. For sure needing that.

****

Just look at that dog. He be eyeing a squirrel. But he ain't chasing no more. Ole Dog. Used to have some other name I reckon, but since he been with us he always been Ole Dog. Me and him, we a pair. Reckon I gon have to start thinking of myself as a ole woman one of these days, but long as they real ole folks around, like Miss Estelle, I can count myself a youngster.

Oughta go see Miss Estelle, I reckon. Don't know what other folks think, but when she come to mind I tend to figure she be one tha's obsessed. All she care 'bout be that good-for-nothing son of hers. The eldest boy. They ain't no doubt—he just ain't no 'count.

Well, Miss Estelle, love for a chile sump'n I can understand. Thank goodness Joleen turned out alright. Only problem be, she don't never seem to have no time for her mama. She prob'ly think them few words she say when she pass by me at church be's enough. I head on back in the house. The day soon gon come to a close and the air's turned chilly. Gon set near the fire and get the lamp going, so's I can see to read the paper.

Too early to eat supper yet, so I settle in—a log on the fire and the funny paper in my lap. First thing, I spot a drawing of some li'l green men. The kind from Mars. I hear folks mention 'em sometimes. Just 'maginary talk, 'bout li'l green people maybe come down here to this planet to visit.

My mind takes off. Wondering what I'd say to folks from Mars. Ain't hard to figure.

'Now these folks over here, they the ones got all the say-so. But these ones over here ain't 'llowed no power. They just s'posed to do what they told. They been fed a promise—the promise that if'n they just be's patient, in the by-and-by ever'thing gon be fine and dandy.'

Well. That 'bout the way of it. We s'posed to lay low and put up with the way things be and keep our hopes set on the hereafter. What I'd say to little green men? Why it wouldn't make no more sense to them'n it do to me. I lay the paper aside and get to humming a ole blues tune.

Next morning I has to pull myself outta bed. Once you get a worry going, you can count on it. It gon steal all your get-up-and-go.

Don't never help, gossip don't. Folks wagging they tongues. 'So-and-so said... and I figured you'd want to know....' Folks round here be saying a woman on her own can't stay in one of these little tenant houses. Most of the houses got six or eight or more packed in. Was Henrietta filled me in 'bout the gossip—and she don't even live round here. So the talk start here and buzz round, get to her ear—and she give it back this way. Traveling talk.

Right now, b'lieve I might fry up some of that cured ham I been saving. Me and Ole Dog have us a feast for breakfast. I sure looking forward to when the weather stays warm and the hens start laying good again. Till then, I mostly eating mush for breakfast. While the cookstove's heating up, I gon take myself out the door and say good morning to the sun. Maybe it have some answers for me.

Chapter 5

Was on my way home from the Robbins household. Passed by the grape arbor and on to the bottom of the hill. Water runs in that low spot this time of year, but I'd made it across wit'out getting my feet wet. Was just after that, goose bumps popped out all over me. I stopped in my tracks. A strange feeling had come over me. I whispered, "Joshua?"

I stood right still for a minute, but nothing happened. So I walked on. In my head a whole parade of mem'ries got to marching by. I clutched my bag tight and set out fast as I could go.

When I reached the gate they was just one picture I was seeing. That morning. Him trying to breathe. There I was in the picture too, watching the life go out of him. And then me, wailing and wailing. But I kept my wailing down. Didn't want it to get loud—cause last thing I wanted was somebody else showing up. First, I had to say my own goodbye. As luck would have it, and I sure said my thanksgivings for it, Joleen wadn't home that morning, had stayed the night wit' one of her cousins.

Wonder why the memory show up today?

I carried myself up the hill fast as my feet could go. When I come in the door I closed it tight and leaned back on it. Had thought if'n I didn't soon make it home I'd just lie down on the ground and start in to weeping. That wouldn't do. Wouldn't do a'tall. If'n they's grieving to be done, I wants to do it on my own.

That morning in my mem'ry be one I aim to keep out of my mind. Don't do not one bit of good to go over it again. My Joshua had done passed through the door leading outta this life. And that meant I'd done stepped on through another door too—the door to this lonely life I be's living now.

The afternoon ain't so very bad cold so I go out and set on his bench. Used to watch him set on it, him doing his whittling. Most of the time had to watch from a distance, cause this bench was his spot. He didn't make nothing, just took his pocketknife in one hand and a short piece of sapling in the other and whittled away. The busyness in his hands, I reckon, helped ease his mind.

Don't no more'n get settled on the bench than here come a pack of stray dogs. Scares me some, but 'fore I know it I be on my feet hollering. "Go on—get out of here!" I wave my arms in the air and holler a few more times – and lo and behold, tha's just what they do!

After a spell I head back in the house and dip the dipper in the bucket and gulp down a bit of water, then take myself out again to watch the evening sky. When dusk settles in I say goodnight to Ole Dog and come on in the house to find a bite for supper. Gonna go to bed early. Be glad to get shed of this day and all those mem'ries it pulled up.

****

Tuesday 'bout midmorning I go out the backdoor carrying my scrap bowl. It near running over wit' potato peelings and such. I carry it a piece from the house and dump it in a clump of weeds then stand real still for a bit, taking in the good air. Off in the west they a dark cloud. More rain coming maybe. They's signs of spring popping out all over. Wildflowers in bloom. And the maple up on the hill showing its buds.

Ain't in no hurry to head back in, so I step along in the other direction, so's to see the sunrise. But that way too, they be gray clouds. And right then, I come to it—how it be time now, time to really look at this dark cloud in my head. It's been there for some while now—and I's knowed it, but just kept sweeping it in a corner.

Don't reckon I can put it off much longer.

I head back in. Too early in the day for so much thinking. And a smile come to me. Uh-huh. Just the thing for me to think on. Ain't often I gets to set a spell and talk wit' Henrietta when they ain't nobody else 'round—but tha's what happened yesterday. Was in the afternoon. She fixed us some coffee and leftover applesauce muffins and we set ourselves down near the fireplace. She had shooed the young'uns away, tole 'em to git, go somewheres else and play. And so it was. Just the two of us. I surprised myself, I did—talking on and on, telling her all my woes.

I finished up wit', "And on top o' all that, ants done set up shop in my kitchen!"

Henrietta's eyes was just a'twinklin' and I could guess why. She ain't used to hearing me go on so. I usually the quiet one—least tha's what folks say. She clucked her tongue. We set and talked a spell longer and I begun to get some sense of what I has to do. Figured it on my own, wit' her putting in the *uh-huhs* and *what thens*. It don't never fail. Time wit' that wise woman always good.

Long as Joshua was here, I knowed where I belonged. He'd be wherever he could find the best work and I'd be right by him. Now I ain't gon say working on this cotton farm's the best yuh could do, but most times Joshua and his bossman did get along right well.

My head been so busy I ain't even noticed the time. Wednesday, the week racing on by. Seem like I no more'n turn 'round a few times 'fore the day coming to a close. When at last I crawl in the bed I lay on my back for a spell and soon make myself a promise. If'n I still living tomorrow, I gon do what I done decided.

Lay awake for a good while after that, till a whippoorwill somewheres close by gets to singing— singing a lullabye. And I begins to get drowsy.

****

Too soon to suit me. Daylight's come and me not one bit ready to think of getting on wit' my plan. But I did promise myself—and this my one chance. If'n I don't do it now, have to wait till next week.

I get myself ready but keep finding another thing to do—and another and another, like I be trying to get out of going. Gon have to hurry now. Might better wait till next week. I stand there by the kitchen table saying all this in my head, but turn quick then and open the door and head out.

"O well," I says to the world. "Ready or not, here I go."

Going to see the man. I know his schedule. Ever' Thursday morning he get in his big black car and leave, off to see his brother. One 'at run a store down on West Trade Street.

I has to walk at a fast clip and keep hoping I not too late. Don't take too long to reach the spot, on the red hill where they's thick trees on both sides. I wanting to get him by hisself, catch him off guard.

This day the weather's alright for driving, but that ain't so when the rains come heavy. It a dirt road 'at comes off the Beatties Ford Road into this farm. Him and his folk made it, and right 'long here they a real steep hill. Call it 'the red hill.' Many a time they ain't been no going out nor no coming in, and more'n once a wagon or a car stuck in the mud.

Right on time, here he come. I flag him down and he stop. I step up 'side the car.

"Hazeline, what the hell you doing out here?"

"Well, sir, I come to speak wit' yuh."

He give a kind of laugh and tip back the bill of his hat. "Is that so? Well then, make it quick. Neil's expecting me."

"Yessir, I don't need much of your time. I just wants to ask what yuh got in mind. Joshua been gone now almost two year, and folks has started talking, saying yuh gon want me to move outta the li'l house—so I figure I best know wha's coming."

I can tell I's surprised him. He don't answer right quick.

"Would be good," he say, "to have a working fam'ly in that house. What you heard makes good sense from a business standpoint."

"So, that be the plan then? I be needing to know, cause if'n that the case I got my own plan to make."

"Your own plan, hunh? And what might that be?"

I start to stuttering. Don't have no plan, not one I can see clear no way. And if'n I did I wouldn't be telling it to him.

He reach up a hand and take hold of one of his suspenders. He got such a look of merriment in his eyes I wants to smack him. That feeling so unlike me it give me a start, so I don't say nothing, just stand there by that big shiny black car and look at the fool behind the wheel. He ain't a handsome man. Too skinny, he be, and his face long and bony.

He rub his chin and look at me wit' some kind of look I don't like. He say, "So you gonna move? Is that it?"

My fingers twiddle at a button near the collar of my shirtwaist. He glares at me like I's done sump'n wrong. This the way wit' him. He good at making the other'n feel guilty. Well, I ain't got nothing to feel guilty 'bout, so I stand up straight as a July cornstalk and my mouth fly open so quick it shocks me.

"I can be outta the house 'fore long. I knows yuh can find somebody else to do yuh washing. And whoever yuh find be there to he'p Miz Robbins wit' the cleaning and cookin'." I be playing his game now. His brow wrinkle up. If'n I was a betting woman I'd bet he's been thinking on having somebody else move in—but now he be thinking 'bout the missus.

His eyes go wide. "Hazeline, if I want you out, I'll inform you. Right now I've got to get on to town." He turns away then and changes the gear, ready to go, but he turns back and says one thing more. "And for your own good, you oughta quit listening to what others say."

And wit' that, off he goes, stirring up a bit of dust and leaving me standing in it—but I be's smiling. I done called his bluff. Don't seem like Miz Robbins got much say-so in that house. But seem to and what is? Why, they horses of a dif'rent color!

****

Saturday morning I snuggle under the quilt a bit longer'n usual. At last I rouse myself and get a fire going in the cookstove. 'fore long I setting myself down to my breakfast. Leftover cornbread heated in a li'l fat in the frying pan and drizzled wit' molasses, and two eggs over easy, and my usual two cups of strong coffee.

Less'n a week till Easter, so I soon get myself going, knowing I gon hurry fast as I can go most of the day long. If only I hadn't said I'd sew up so many dresses. But said it I did. First the thread breaks, then it knot up. And a button goes missing. Even the bobbin don't seem to wanna fit in the slot—my own bobbin in my own machine!

Cross my mind 'at now'd be a good time to be a cussing woman. And tha's when it dawn on me. The problem? Why it be Hazeline Morrison.

Best let the sewing go for now. In the kitchen I spot a wore-out towel I laid out so's to cut some new dishrags. Done that, and was putting a plate in the dish-drain when I heard sump'n. Sound like mebbe somebody stepped on that loose board.

I hurry thataway and spy a young man just out the screen door—a tall young man. His hair cropped close, his eyes big and bright, and his skin that pecan shade so many folks envies.

He saying, "Ma'am, Mister Arthur—uh, he say he knowed your husband, and say your husband had bought some lumber 'fore…"

He stop then, not quite knowing I reckon how to say *'fore he died.*

"Tha's right. He bought some lumber. What else Mister Arthur Henderson have to say?"

The boy hold to his cap and turn it round and round. "He say you might wanna sell the lumber, ma'am—at a good price, I mean. Good price to me, I mean, since you don't have…"

He stop again. Look like he got a habit of starting out wit' his words and getting tripped up on 'em. And all the while still turning his cap. I push the screendoor open and let him in. He be wearing a shirt in need of some mending. Plaid shirt. I always does like seeing a man in a plaid shirt.

Just so happen that while I had the cookstove heated up for fixing two breakfasts—my own and Ole Dog's, I decided to put in some more firewood and stir up a coupla chess pies. I figured they oughta be just about cool enough to cut. 'fore long we was setting at the kitchen table and him telling me he wanting the lumber to make a hog pen—the very reason Joshua got the wood. It's been stacked under the lean-to for a good while now.

He tell his full name but say most folk call him Slim. Say he ain't no relation to Mister Arthur Henderson. But if Arthur sent him this way, tha's enough for me—I be glad to let this boy have the lumber. Was 'bout to tell him go ahead and take it, but he start in talking 'bout how his dollars few but his skill wit' tools be's good and how gladly he'd do some chores for me.

Well, I didn't say it, but he couldn't have said nothing 'at please me more. Joleen's husband be's kind and thoughtful, but I doubt he'd have any idea what to do wit' a hammer and nail.

The pie sealed the deal. He say he be back to get the lumber soon's he can borrow a mule and wagon, and promised to fix the loose board on the porch first thing. And then tole me to think on what else I need doing.

Reckon I was wrong. He ain't no boy. This a man. And seem like a man 'at ain't afraid of work. He hadn't been here more'n a few minutes 'fore I was thinking how he 'bout the age my boy'd be now...if'n he'd lived.

****

Wonder what day it be. Well, lemme look at the calendar, right here on the wall near the backdoor—so le's see. Last date I sure 'bout was washday, and the day after it, then one more...uh-huh, so this be's Thursday. April 8, 1937.

"Okay, Thursday, time to go up in the far pasture and see if'n they might be some creasy greens." This talking to myself done become a habit—but reckon tha's awright. Don't mean I be going crazy. I chew my lip, thinking one more time how never once did I see me coming to this—

this living alone. I sigh real big and shake my head side to side. Can I get used to being on own.

I pull in a big bunch of air and blow it out. "Maybe sometime or 'nother."

The calendar picture for April...a blue-ribbon pig at the county fair? Tha's sure strange, cause this ain't even close to the time of year for the fair. It be toward the end of the year.

Across the top the calendar say, 'Neel's Pharmacy, Huntersville, North Carolina.' Just the place I be needing to go to. Need Vaseline. And Pepto Bismol. My shoulder was sore most of the winter so I done used up all the liniment I bought the day I picked up this free calendar.

First thing, I feed the chickens and gather the few eggs, then pull on my boots. The weather warming some now so I got to be on the lookout for Mr. Snake. They's chiggers too, but they don't bother me much. I soon be stepping along the edge of the woods.

Wish I could picture where Joshua be. So sudden it was that morning, he was gone. Just 'fore daylight. Wadn't even time to say goodbye. Don't know if'n to think of him sleeping—waiting for the Judgment Day—or think of him gone, snuffed out like a candle.

Ain't so sure I b'lieve ever'thing I hears in church. Don't wanna walk no streets of gold. Rather walk right here, heading for the spot where last spring I found a patch of wild greens. This time last year my heart was full of worry. Now I done got up my courage and had my say. And I still amazed. But I did it, spoke right up.

How'd I get up the courage? Ain't a li'l thing to face up to the man wit' all the power. I'd been allowed to stay on a while, uh-huh, cause Miz Robbins depend on me, but all the while I kept wondering when word would come. Go find somewheres else to live. Go find somewheres else. Uh-huh. That was the way of it. And then me shoving the thought down to the ground again.

Wadn't no good rest to be had. On and on, a li'l voice saying what I was afraid to hear.

Then one Monday morning there in the backyard near the well, I was bent over the Robbins washpot, same as usual. Trying to wring water out a pair of bib overalls, wit' my back aching sump'n awful. But up under my breath I was still singing. "Joshua fit the battle of Jericho, Jericho, Jericho! Joshua fit the battle of Jericho and the walls come a'tumblin' down."

All a sudden, felt like they was somebody close by— turned quick and spied a man. He'd sneaked right up on me!

My clothes was wet and I must'a looked a sight. But he wadn't one you'd wanna impress. Scruffy and ragged, he was. Wit' buckteeth. A white man, but awful dirty. Hunting a job. I wouldn't'a hired him. But might be Mister Robbins would decide to take him on and I'd have to give up the li'l house for him and his fam'ly. I knowed Mister Robbins. Knowed he'd rather have more hands to clear more new ground and chop more cotton.

Late that day I took myself down to the woods and like usual settled on my rock. After a bit I say, "Water, you always a help to me—but I has to admit, I feel more a'kin to this rock. I rather stay right where I be. The li'l house, it ain't much, but it do be keeping the mem'ries of my man and the growing up of my girl. Reckon that be reason enough to wanna stay on."

I knowed the water in that little stream flowed all the way to the creek, and the creek carried it on to the river, and the river to a bigger river—and on, a whole bunch farther, all the way to the ocean. Just thinking 'bout the water by me going all that way brightened my spirits. It was then I could see. If'n I had to leave this farm, I'd be zackly like that water—keeping on going, to see where I'd end up.

Ain't no way to say how much better I felt after that.

"Well well," I says. "All this walking to get here, and ain't nothing here. Look like somebody beat me to it, picked all the creasy greens to be had in this spot. Picked it clean. But may as well keep going for a bit. Might be some up on the shoulder near the Beatties Ford Road.

I pass by a field tha's just been plowed and reach down and get a handful of the dirt. Red dirt. Tha's the kind we got here, but where Ruby live—a few miles from here, the dirt's real sandy.

I head on, smiling. Mother Nature make many a kind. Black dirt, brown dirt, light dirt, and more, I s'pect. And she make the folks 'at walk her ground them same colors.

Chapter 6

————————————

End of the week at last, and my wounds 'bout dried up. Wednesday, it was. Day I went over to Miz Moore's. Started out like usual, me saying I was thankful for the new day, and soon as I'd finished the morning chores, started out. It a short walk so I was soon crossing the bound'ry 'tween this farm and the Moore property.

'Fore that War 'tween the States, the Robbins farm and a heap more land, thousands of acres, so I's heard, was the Moore Plantation. Heard it said 'at way on back, it stretched maybe a thousand acres. Heard talk too 'bout ledger books the master kept, noting how much they paid for a slave or when a slave died or was sold away.

As I got close to the house 'bout a dozen guinea hens scurry off, and just then, over near the smokehouse, the peacock decide to spread his feathers. I stopped in my tracks. Ain't often yuh gets to see such, so I just stood there looking. The day did seem a fine one, and I felt blessed.

I moved on to the backdoor and soon was setting on the backporch and waiting while she went and slipped on the dress I'd brung. It fit her fine, and she give me my money and I headed out. I was thinking how it still early in the day so maybe I'd take the long way home. A fine sunny day, so I kept on walking and my spirits rising higher and higher.

A fine thing to be out and about. And in no hurry.

Hazeline

First thing, I decide to go a different way and has to crawl under a fence. I set off but don't get far 'fore I spot that new bull Mr. Robbins bought recent. Big. Shiny. Young black bull. He was turned the other way, feeding on the grass—and I didn't tarry. Quick as I could move I got myself back the way I'd come and soon was setting on the ground on the other side of the fence, chuckling to myself. Most ever' night, right be'foreI head off to sleep, I tells Joshua 'bout my day, so already I was 'magining telling him 'bout my fright when I spotted that new bull.

I kept on and a short while later was moving along by the edge of the burnt woods and spotted a young holly tree. Maybe it'd be one wit' some red berries come Christmastime Well, I figured, might as well take a closer look. And that's when they got me! I took off running, flinging my arms in the air. Yellow jackets! Once before, a long time back, they'd got me bad. We was young then, living on the McCoy farm. Hadn't been married long and had big dreams 'bout how we'd better ourselves if'n we just worked hard.

Hmmph! All we done was better the ones 'at owned the land. After that we lived on the Patterson farm. Wherever we went Joshua always did fix the house up a bit. Ain't nobody else in the li'l houses on the Robbins farm got any glass winduhs. And ain't none of 'em got a kitchen cupboard like the one he built for me.

Well, I did at last make it home wit' my wounds and went straightaway to doctoring, and then settled in Joshua's rocking chair and set there and tole him all 'bout my day. Then I got to telling him how the li'l house sure missing his carpentry skills. Last downpour we had I was kept busy emptying buckets. They be two places leaking now. Lucky they ain't a leak over the bed. Sump'n gon have to be done. Reckon I could ask Sam to help, he wouldn't want his brother's widow suffering.

By midday I was swelled up wit' the yellowjacket stings and the rest of the day wadn't worth a hoot. More'n once I got to chuckling to myself, thinking how I musta looked scrambling under that fence. And then I got to thinking on fences. Hogwire fences, barbwire fences, split rail fences, even fences made of stones. But the kind I was picturing's the kind you can't see—but they sure as heck keep you fenced out. Never has tole nobody 'bout this kind of thinking. Maybe cause I don't believe they anybody can push these fences down. And they sure ain't much way to crawl under 'em.

The afternoon moved along and I done my best to shoo away this thinking. By the time I got to feeling some better, was almost dark and I decided I maybe could eat a bite. So I broke some stale cornbread in a bowl and poured some milk over it, then caught sight of the cabbage I pulled this morning. Some soon day I got to harvest the lot and get the cabbage in the crock. Wouldn't wanna face wintertime wit'out sauerkraut.

I take my bowl and settle in my rocker. Slim come to mind. He done come and took the lumber, but had to hurry along cause he had to take back the mule he'd borrowed. Wonder will he come again? Said he would.

That very first day I met that boy—yeah, I think of him that way cause he ain't far along yet on the road of life, I felt like I give some bit of myself away. Give it to him. Felt it go out of me. He 'bout the same age my boy'd be if'n he was walking this earth, and ever since Slim first said my name and stepped 'cross the threshold, I's felt a bit like he belong to me. Could be, in the long run he won't mean much a'tall. But I got my feelings on it, and I'd be just 'bout willing to bet that ain't the way things gon play out.

****

Planting the summer garden. A chore I always does look forward to, but this year I be getting a late start. Wit' all that talk I kept hearing 'bout me maybe gon have to move, I figured wadn't no point putting in a garden. Now it way past time these seeds shoulda been in the ground and I got a feeling we gon get rain, so I be making haste while the sun shine.

We always planted the summer crop on Good Friday. Joshua was set on it, so didn't matter how far behind I was wit' stitching up Easter dresses, had to lay 'em aside and pick up my hoe.

When planting time come round this year Ezra Dellinger, the best of our neighbors, come over and readied my spot. He plows up a big space for his fam'ly and say it ain't no trouble a'tall to bring the mule on over this way. Trouble be, cause some time's passed, the ground's done crusted over again and I gon have to get out there wit' a mattock and work it. Ain't gon be no quick and easy job.

I begged a bit of guano from Miz Robbins. He buy it in big sacks to fertilize the cotton fields, and I don't need much, so she let me get what li'l bit I need. Me and her, we got our li'l patterns worked out. She prob'ly figures I oughta get a little extra, since I always has to stay on the job till she say I can leave.

I set in to breaking the soil and give thanks for this strong body. And next thing after that I remember sump'n the li'l lady had to say one recent day. I'd just built the fire round the washpot. She come outside. "Hazeline, you know what? You walk with a long stride. I envy that." What she say surprise me, but I used to her surprises. Don't recall if'n I answered or not.

Cucumbers, yellow squash, half-runner beans, lima beans, and a few tomato plants I got from a neighbor. Too early yet to drop the seeds for cantaloupe and watermelon. This my part of the garden. They still a back portion yet to sow. Plant green beans and okra there, for Miss Kathleen to sell at the market. Don't have to plant corn. Get it from the big field, one the Robbins boys plants for feeding the animals.

Now the end of the day's come and I be's plumb tired out and way awful dirty. Wish I had enough water to fill my galvanized tub and get a all-over bath, but, just have to make do wit' a sponge bath. Gon put my head on my feather pillow soon as I can.

****

Sometime over in the night I come awake at the edge of a dream. And Joshua in the dream. Moonlight was coming in the east windows and me laying there looking thataway—and I spied his face. Didn't seem like was just a shadow.

I lay real still, careful not to move. Could it be him?

I held my breath. When I couldn't hold it no more I started letting it out easy, still watching close what I knowed wouldn't be there in the daylight. A minute more passed. I asked myself what it mean. And then I couldn't see it no more.

I put my hands to my face and pulled in a deep breath, then set in to speaking real soft. "Joshua, is yuh trying to say sump'n? All these times I been talking to yuh I's felt like yuh could hear me. Is they sump'n yuh wanting to tell me?"

Could be I wanted so bad to see him I just thought I did. But I lay awake quite a spell and after some while come on what I think it mean. Wadn't no words spoke, so the meaning up to me. I soon fell off to sleep, knowing I'd been blessed. Joshua was telling me what he'd be saying if'n he was here. To take hold of life and live it.

Was still early when I come awake. I lay a'bed, thinking. Time had come. That much was clear. Time to quit wishing things could be the way they was.

I climbed outta bed, washed a bit and got myself dressed. Then stood by the li'l mirror and said real low a promise to myself. "Whatever this day bring, I gon do wha's mine to do, and do it wit' a full heart."

Since then I's spent all the day long at my sewing. Warm today. Almost too hot to stay in the house, but got a good bit done. When I tired out I went and walked about a bit and spotted a wren perched on a bush. That li'l brown bird wit' her perky tail in the air. She was singing her heart out. And so close I could see the ball in her throat going up and down. Mighty big song for such a li'l singer.

Now it already late in the day and I carry my pruning shears and traipse up the edge of the field to cut me some rambling roses. They a nuisance, take over the place if'n yuh don't keep 'em cut back, but this time of year they sure put on a show. I lop off a few ends, bring'em back and stick 'em in a canning jar. They sure spruce up this li'l dark house.

All the daylong, this head o' mine full'a mem'ries. A widow woman, tha's what I be's now. So right often I gets to traveling down memory lane. Think this one mem'ry come cause I so needing some few dollars coming my way.

I r'members it clear. That day him and Sam went riding off to Shelby. Don't s'pect they ever been two brothers closer'n Joshua and Sam. Don't remember now why they went, but Sam was going and Joshua going too. He always did wanna go if Sam was going, but they was sump'n else that day. He wanted to tag along cause they'd be crossing the river. On a ferry.

We was a li'l better off then, wit' Joshua picking up a li'l extra work. I always been the one took care of our few dollars, see how far I could make 'em stretch. Joshua? Why he thought money in his pocket likely gon burn a hole in it. He come home that day wit' a roll of chicken wire—and a present for me!

I'd set my hopes on getting me a new hat. Awready had it pictured in my head. Narrow brim wit' a ribbon round it, so's I could change the ribbon to match my dress. But he come in grinning big and plunked down on the table a bi-ig black skillet. Didn't look much like a hat. I picked it up. Heavy. Big. But why would we wanna cook so much? What'cha cook don't keep long less'n yuh has ice.

I rubbed my finger round the inside edge. Joshua was still showing his big grin, so I said, "Sure is big. An' yuh thought of getting sump'n special for me, so I thank yuh."

He say, "Yuh don't like it, does yuh?"

"Sure I like it."

"No yuh don't, so go on and tell me what yuh thinking."

"This a fine cooking pot."

"No no—they sump'n else. Problem be, I got it in Shelby, so I can't take it back. And that fella wouldn't take it back no way." Then he started in telling 'bout the man. He'd knowed right away the man wouldn't wanna do business wit' colored folk, but Sam just marched right up to the counter and plunked down some money.

"Yuh know how Sam do, Hazeline. He just barrel his way through."

The storekeeper a fat man, rolling a cigar round in his mouth. First thing he say, "What you boys needin' today?"

Joshua was wanting to turn and walk out, but Sam be's Sam. He tole the man what he wanted and the man started getting the order t'gether. Tha's when Joshua noticed the chicken wire. Figured to fix up the chicken pen so's the foxes and possums couldn't get at his chickens. Then he spotted the skillet. On sale.

I stood there beside him. Put my hand on it again and say, "This pan so big it gon need least three chickens in it, so reckon yuh best get to working on that pen." By that time I was smiling big. How yuh gon stay mad when yuh got a man good as him?

We'd been saving quarters and half dollars, but sump'n was always stepping up and asking for a dollar. Joshua's big dream was to someday get hisself a car—cause Sam had bought hisself a ole car. Thing was, though, Sam didn't work on no farm. He worked a town job.

I was the one kept the bank, which wadn't nothing but a metal box wit' a latch. We kept it hid up in the rafters. In the first few days after he brung home that skillet, I'd sometimes think 'bout taking enough out 'the bank' to buy me a hat, but ever'time, figured against it. What I did do was pick out a pretty feed sack and cut me a piece on the bias, to make a ribbon to go on a old hat. Still don't think I coulda enjoyed wearing a new one more. And if Joshua hadn't bought that skillet, why I wouldn't'a looked for some way to make the old new!

I took the rest of the sack and edged a new collar—the kind I could put on a coupla my dresses whenever I wanted. Funny how it worked out. Went from big disappointment to huge bunch of pride—*pride in making do*! Anytime I pulled that collar out I felt good, and as time's gone by I's made a good many for the ladies I sews for.

Was a fine lesson. They sure do be more'n one way to skin a cat!

Chapter 7

Rev'rend Jones sporting a red bowtie. That man call hisself God's servant but he sure do have a devilish grin. I set in my place, down near the front on a bench at the right side. Our li'l wooden church been standing quite a few years now. Made of clapboard, and got wide plank steps and a shingle roof. We pushed some to come up wit' money for shingles and some of the menfolk nailed 'em on, cause wit' a tin roof if'n a hard rain come, yuh can't hardly hear the preaching. If'n a wedding going on, yuh wouldn't know whether the bride and groom had said 'I do' or not. The inside ain't so very big, but big enough, and they a podium for the preacher to stand at, and a corner for the choir. And rows of benches for the faithful.

Rev'rend Jones wearing a dark blue suit I ain't see'd before. Wonder how many suits that man's got. His voice still going. Up, down—and ever' li'l bit folks chime in with the Amens.

I keep my eyes on the Bible tha's open in my lap, but then I look up—and I r'members again. That day, he was wearing his gray pinstripe suit and a vest. She was in a bright red dress, tight round the bodice, and a hat almost the same color 'at fit close to her head. She jabbed her finger at his face and hissed at him. "Don't you dare open yo' mouth! Say one word, and I raise such a ruckus—"

She looked like she was 'bout to bust, and spun round and sashayed out the door. They didn't know I'd heard, and I hadn't meant to hear, but my ears couldn't help hearing. My ears heard cause tha's what ears does. His head dropped. I waited jus' a bit, then started bustling about, clunked my feet. He jerked hisself to attention and skedaddled right on out.

This 'bout a month ago when I got to church early one day so's I could visit Joshua's grave. I come on 'em in the back hallway. I'd been suspicious for quite a spell. So they was sump'n going on 'tween Rev'rend Jones and Shirley Grier. Later I remembered what the Bible say, how they ain't no place you can hide from God's eyes.

And soon after, when I was still thinking on what I'd see'd, some words Mama used to say come to me. 'You made your bed, now you has to lie in it.'

Most of the time I don't pay much attention to his sermon. Today I keep my eyes on the Bible open on my lap so it look like I be reading the text he preaching on. When I was on my way in, just 'fore the service started, I overheard another thing I'd just as soon not heard.

Was Sister Edwina. She say, "Do you mean to tell me?—why if'n I'd knowed I'd'a been glad to help." She a big gossip, usually got listeners gathered round her. I never has had no patience wit' gossip. Too many times I's see'd the harm it do.

He strong into his sermon now, making it a long one too, but I done heard this same one least a half dozen times. He talk it a li'l different way but it still the same. He getting a bit stout. Living too good, I reckon. What worry me be how the young folk cotton to him, like as if he the one can walk on water.

Hazeline

Far as I can see the whole bunch of us—him and Sister Edwina and me and all the rest, 'specially her close neighbors, we all shoulda done more'n we did for Maybelle Gudger. She was sick a long time. Maybe it was cause her sickness went on so long we didn't do more. We got used to it. She was sick, that wadn't no news.

She had trouble birthing her last chile and they called in Dr. Tom Craven and he had her took straight down to Good Samaritan Hospital. Mama and baby come home—but the little one never did seem strong and after a coupla years, he just up and died.

Wit' five chirren in the house and some of 'em 'bout growed, and all them sisters Maybelle had, I guess we just figured the fam'ly was looking after her. Word be, she grieved herself to death. They wadn't no other ailment.

After the chile died she took to her bed. Didn't surprise me none. Seemed the right thing to do, cause wit' that many in the house, the only way to get time to yuhself is go to bed and turn your face to the wall.

One afternoon I took two pies over there and set by her bed and visited for a while. On the way I thought 'bout how pretty she was when she was young. Maybelle was a small woman, 'bout the size I always wanted to be. I didn't think a woman tall and broad-shouldered like me could look so good as a li'l woman, but that notion changed when Joshua decided on me. He was a good-looking man, so from then on I figured the way I look be's just fine.

The day I went over to visit, Maybelle looked shrunk. Tiny like a girl and shriveled like a prune, and her eyes glassy looking. Had a rag quilt pulled up round her neck though it was a fine day in May—time when the wild strawberries be's ripe. Day be'foreI'd picked some 'long the edge of the cotton field by the wagon track that run 'tween the field and woods—berries so tiny they a pain to pick.

While I was picking I got to thinking 'bout Maybelle. Figured if I could get her outta the house and into the sunshine, she'd feel some better. But she just stared up at me when I stood there by her bed and in a tiny li'l voice she say, "Hey, Hazeline."

Looked like she had to work at getting the words out. I pulled a chair over and set down close. She tried saying sump'n else. The talking seemed a effort for her and I give up the idea of getting her out in the sunshine. I just sat by her bed and talked and talked—cause I didn't know what else to do. I talked 'bout the times me and her worked the cotton together. She always did make the work go faster cause she kept us laughing.

"Yuh r'member that year when we had to get out to the cotton field early in the year? When didn't look like we was ever gon get to the end of the last row? Chopping, chopping. Chopping that cotton! Working wit' the hoe, pulling away weeds from that young crop.

"And we was complaining 'bout our aching backs, remember? Say our backs aching so bad they might just break in two?

"And then, Maybelle, you said—never will forget it, now lemme see if'n I can get it right...you say, 'Hazeline, it won't matter none if'n our backs break, cause if'n they break then they be two of us—two o' you and two o'me—and just think of the look on our men's faces. They gon take one look—and turn they faces toward heaven and cry out, 'Lord God above, thank yuh thank yuh—yuh done doubled our women. Ooo-eee! Life sure gon be fun here on out!'"

I set there by her bed chuckling. Easy to laugh, cause I felt all over again the fun we had that day in the field.

But Maybelle just lay there. Kept her face turned my way, but didn't smile. I kept talking. Tole her how good the sun had felt on my back in the strawberry patch. And how I had went to pick one bunch of berries up under a leaf and almost picked a li'l green snake. Tole her how I yelled and snatched my hand back same as if'n it'd been a copperhead. And I laughed again, but no laugh from my friend.

For a minute I didn't say nothing more. Then I squatted down and reached for her hand. "Maybelle, your boy be's awright. He be doing fine. He's gone to be wit' Jesus."

She squeezed my hand and a tear rolled down her cheek. I knowed they was the words she wanted to hear and they'd give her some ease—so tha's what I said.

Maybelle's fam'ly say the doctor said was a fever 'at killed her. Maybe so. Maybe not. What I take offense about be the tone of voice the sisters was using outside the church when they was talking 'bout Maybelle. Whatever's said in that tone ought not be said.

That last day I visited her, one thing sure pleased me. Not once did I think of my own lost boy. Many a year's passed since that sad day. Seem now like it maybe happened to some other woman name Hazeline.

'The Lord giveth and the Lord taketh away.' I's reminded myself of that least a hundred times.

Rev'rend Jones be winding down now. I turn my eyes to Joleen. She sitting with the choir. Soon as I get her in sight words come: 'Pretty is as pretty does.' I remember telling her that when she was a girl. Reckon yuh has to live a good many years to reach that wisdom.

She say 'Amen' when the rest do. Look like she don't mind Rev'rend Jones. Look like she ain't caught on—and me being her mama she wouldn't likely b'lieve me no way, if'n I was to tell her he ain't no more'n a wolf in sheep's clothing.

Last Sunday when church was over, me and Joleen and Troy and a coupla others took off to see one of Mama's sisters. We piled in the back of the wagon and settled on the hay piled in there to make the setting a bit easier. Aunt Dora Lee. She still looking spry, and served us as good a rabbit stew as I ever did eat. Wish we was going visiting again today.

****

I decided to go on and do it. All I'd have to do would be open my mouth and let the words spill out, cause they was sure wanting to get out. More'n once I's had to hold 'em in my mouth. They like chickens—trying to fly the coop, wings just a'flapping.

I had my bundle in one arm, my umbrella in the other. A long way to go.

Fore I got there, my ease dried up, way a puddle do when the wind gets to going. Worried 'bout what I was gon have to worry 'bout after I said my piece.

Once I opened my mouth, might be I'd get turned out, not get to do no more work for Miz Black. And she a good woman to work for. Most of the time when she hand me my money, she add a li'l extra.

Now it the day after and I be telling the story to Henrietta, Sam's wife. She say, "So what'd she do once yuh tole her?"

I put a real serious look on my face. "Well, for just a li'l bit, a certain look cross her face. Wadn't a look to get yuh hopes up. She turned her head away for a bit and when she turn back, the look was gone—so my hopes went up again."

"And? Go on—tell me!"

"Well, by then I was holding my breath. Felt dang sure she was gon tell me she wouldn't be needing me no more."

"Hazeline, you keeping me in suspense. I can't even see in your eyes which way it went. But you don't seem too sad—so I b'lieve you playing wit' me."

Henrietta laugh then and head for the flour bin. I laugh too and watch her fill the sifter, thinking to myself, Uh-huh, that be the truth—having myself a li'l fun. Get Henrietta expecting the worst, then come out wit' the real story. If'n things'd gone sour I wouldn't be playing—I'd be moaning!

Henrietta spills a trail of flour from the bin. I has to hold myself back from grabbing the whiskbroom, cause cleaning be second nature to me. Lately, though, look like I been busting outta my nature.

Was when I was on my way over to Miz Black's I made up my mind. I'd speak up first thing, 'fore she even tole me what work she had for me. Otherwise, I might chicken out. When I said what I had to say, right quick her eyes showed her surprise, but just as quick she put back the face what hide her thinking.

I'd come a bit late, hoping to miss seeing her boy. Sure 'nough, he was already gone. Reckon he rightly called a brat. I doubt they's anybody likes him. They a place in the Bible 'at say, 'A foolish son be the heaviness of his mother.'

Twice now I been on my way to work for her and run into him. He look the other way when he pass by but he say—and say it real loud— "Here come that nigger woman. You be sure and get the work done right now, nigger woman."

So I tole his mama. Tole her if'n it happen again I won't be coming back to work for her no more. And I was almost fibbing, cause I needs to work, but I had to tell her.

She look the other way for a bit then clear her throat and say she'd take care of it. She even tell me she sorry it happened. Then she say she want all the winduhs washed, inside and out. Already had the rags and vinegar and bucket set out. I s'pect she maybe really was sorry, cause when she give me my pay she give me a extra dime.

When I finished up the story for Henrietta, she stopped her hand in mid-air and looked straight at me.

"Uh-huh," she said, "so you did speak up! Tha's the way to do it!"

****

I was tired out from washing all them windows for Miz Black, and the walk there and back. And first thing I noticed? The Gudger boy hadn't carried my water. So first thing, had to go up the hill and down again wit' my li'l wagon to get some.

That boy's big and strong and carries the buckets on a yoke. But young'uns can't always be counted on. I got all worked up, fussing and mumbling, but all the while I knowed the truth. Was least one other reason I was outta sorts. My Joleen. That girl of mine sure got a cussed streak in her. I don't understand it, and ain't likely to. We likely just gon have to make our peace outside it.

Seem like of late she been keeping her distance. If'n I had to guess, I'd bet she's got her head set on being 'a modern woman'—don't wanna be one bit like her ole mama. Downright peculiar, tha's how it feel...this distance 'tween me and my chile.

Late in the day I decided to stop what I was about and take a bit to calm myself down. Walked outside. Wind was up. I watched it. 'Course you can't see wind, but yuh can see what it do. And just that thought eased me some. I'd let a wind get to roaring down deep inside me.

Chapter 8

———— ⟶≈≋✦≋≈⟵ ————

Next day come and me still feeling not a bit like usual. So I got busy. And now the afternoon will soon be gone—and I done cleaned corner to corner. Way 'fore I got done that whirlwind in me had gone calm enough so's I could grab hold of some bit of good sense.

I's lived long enough to know how quick things can change. So this gap 'tween and me and my girl? Most likely, some one of these days, they gon be sump'n happen—and all this unease just float away on the wind.

Even swept the clearing. First, had to make me a broom. Cut some branches from a wild shrub 'at grow in the thickets, fastened 'em together wit' a bit of twine and set in to sweeping. I shoulda been too tired to tackle the job, but was already dirty as could be, so I went ahead and done it.

And now look! Sticks and twigs and leaves—gone! And iffen I say so myself, this l'il place look right good. I swept the dirt clean, so now inside and outside be looking spiffy. But reckon I can count on being tired tomorrow. I's felt today like I could tackle the whole world. Sure a puzzle how quick we go up, and down—and up again.

My eyes settle on my yard broom. A new broom sweep clean, so the saying go. And I bound and determined to do all I can do...to sweep away whatever it be tha's come 'tween me and my girl.

One good thing, Slim been coming by right often. Might be cause he likes my poundcake. And my damson pie. Might be cause he don't have no mama to cook for him. He say he lost her to pneumonia 'bout ten year ago. What he do have be a girl, and it easy as pie to tell how fond he be of her.

Name's Delia. And to hear him tell it, she likely the most beautiful girl ever was.

This last time he come by I learned his name. Benjamin Miller. Been thinking what I might make for him. A shirt, maybe. He's sure good to help out round here, and always in a good humor. Few days ago he took up the rotten planks on that tiny front porch that ain't much more'n a stoop, and put down some new ones. He couldn't've done nothing 'at pleased me more. Now I won't have to be watching close, so's to step over the rotted boards.

They's one other chore round here tha's way past needing done, but I gon be the one to do it. These rough walls. All of 'em needing fresh paper. I got enough newspapers saved for the job. Meant to do it early in the year. Now 'at springtime's come I just can't see the time.

Newspaper ain't fancy wallpaper, but it sure help wit' keeping the wind and bugs out, and I can change it no matter how few pennies they be in my purse. Last time I papered the walls Joleen helped and when we was moving some boxes of cloth she come on a mouse nest. Li'l mice so tiny they didn't even have fur yet—but off she went, yelling and skedattling like as if the devil wit' his pitchfork was on her trail.

That was the day I hung a piece of one of Mama's quilts. It be old and frayed, but I sure like looking at it and thinking of her hand making the stitches. Poor Mama, her life cut short. Wish I could set down wit' her right here at this table and make us some coffee.

I'd tell her 'bout this table, how Joshua built it. When we moved to this place, it was plumb trashy. The folks had lived here must not'a thought yuh ever s'posed to clean the house. So we got to cleaning, and Joshua got to thinking, and next thing I knowed he was measuring. Said he was gon build us a table.

Got one of his brothers to help him, and they took off to see a man close by what keeps wood tha's already cut and dried. Then they set to work. Joshua knowed zackly how he wanted it done. Put it t'gether wit' pegs what fit the notches he cut. All of it Joshua's idea. He made it fit this kitchen and said it wouldn't never be moved, said the pegs would hold so long as we let it be.

This mind of mine. How it do go on! My fingers been working too, wit' the shuttle. Making some lace to go on a good-as-new tablecloth. Gone carry it to Cousin Lavinia, in Mount Mourne—soon's I get the chance to visit her and her fam'ly.

****

Too early in the year to be this hot, but—weather's weather. Can't change it. Miz Robbins sent word for me to come. Say she got one of her headaches. I took my time getting here, cause ironing on a day like this'un ain't sump'n you get jumping up and down happy 'bout.

On my way cross the pasture I stopped to watch the white geese grazing on the green hillside. They got a easy life, look like, but ever' so often they a roast goose on the table. Miz Robbins 'specially fond of her feather pillows.

Always been a puzzle to me why she like to iron. Not often she call on me to do it. I let the backporch door slam so's she'd know I's come in. I know where she be—over in the parlor other side the hallway, holding a cold rag to her head.

I gon work in the big room 'cross the hall. It a sitting room and bedroom, and when cold weather set in, where they huddle round the fire. Right soon I gets a fire going in the stove in the dining room so's to heat the irons, and begins sprinkling wit' water and rolling up what's to be ironed, and here she come.

She wanna know if'n I remembered to check the eggs. And I says, "Yes'm, I gathered the eggs."

She keep a damp cloth to her face and walk this way and that in her bare feet. After a bit she say, "Hazeline, Luther tole me he gon let you stay in your little house. I been afraid he wouldn't, but I finally got him to agree with me. I don't wanna have to find somebody else to help out round here."

I fit a shirtwaist dress over the ironing board and don't look up. "That be fine, Miz Robbins. I thank yuh for letting me know."

Well now! That the news I been waiting to hear! I don't let on none, cause she'd have a fit if'n I said one word 'gainst him. She can fuss 'bout him, but ain't nobody else 'llowed to.

In my head I was jumping up and down. Wadn't much a surprise to me that it'd been the both of us waiting for his word. She hang around for a bit and gets to telling one of her stories. I's heard it a few times, so I knows how it end.

"Never heard anything like it in all my born days. I tell you what, Hazeline. If I never see that woman again—t'will be too soon to suit me!"

Next thing she gets to telling 'bout a argument wit' the mister. The end she give it surprise me. "My cousin Bessie said I oughta put my foot down." She rubbed a hand over her frizzy hair and dropped her voice low then. "No chance of that. I tried once. Luther always got to have the last word."

She shake her head side to side and head back 'cross the hall. Then she really surprise me. Was bout more'n I could believe. She say it so low, I wouldn't'a heard it if'n she hadn't been so near.

"Bless his heart. I know he means well."

All that was earlier in the day. Now the sun's done dropped behind the trees and I setting out here on Joshua's bench. This where he done his whittling. Most of the time he didn't carve nothing, just took his pocketknife in one hand and a piece of sapling in the other and whittled away. Seemed like the busyness in his hands give his mind ease.

What me and Joshua knowed t'gether was sump'n fine. Ain't no one name for it. Nor way to speak of it. But way I see it, it the most real thing of all.

I keep setting, watching the darkness come to finish off the day. The trees up on the hill go from green to gray to a deep shadow. And that too like the years wit' Joshua. He just ain't in the daylight no more.

They one thing I ain't said. Maybe could, to Ruby. Or maybe Henrietta. But it just about ain't possible to get Henrietta off by herself. Somebody always coming through, way it bound to be when yuh got chirren and gran'babies all in the same house.

Henrietta'd likely say, "What a strange thought, Hazeline." Then she'd start in to peeling another potato and say, "Tha's sad, real sad. But I see what yuh mean."

Ruby the one I likely to tell. Been thinking on it for a good spell. Guess it just the way life s'posed to be.

A breeze come through. It bring back memory—of the misery of the heat when I was there ironing for Miz Robbins. After a while, was 'bout more'n I could stand. Way too hot for ironing. Had to keep rags handy for mopping my face.

I felt a bit angry wit' that little woman. Why her sheets need ironing in this heat? A few wrinkles won't hurt none. I got so worked up I knowed I had to calm myself, so up under my breath I say, "Do unto others as you'd have them do unto you." That be one thing in the Bible 'at make good clear sense.

Was right after that, I decided. Gon sew up a summer houserobe for Miz Robbins. Got some extra material on hand, so I can make her a gift, cause I plumb tired of seeing her in the ole raggedy one she been wearing. Ain't usual for me to make her a present, so it'll surprise her.

Reckon I feels sorry for her. And it won't take long to sew up.

I still setting here in the dark, on Joshua's bench, and silly pictures playing in my head. First I hand Miz Robbins the robe, and then us talks for a bit and I tells her how I died. But of course I won't do no such thing.

It be's true, though. That day my Joshua left this world—why, in that same hour sump'n in me got cut away too. The Hazeline I knowed? She was gone. Plain gone.

****

Early this morning I stirred up a batch of sourdough bread. Always was Joshua's favorite. While I was at it, got to thinking 'bout sump'n 'at happened a long while back, when we hadn't been long living on this farm. I never told Joshua 'bout it. Miz Robbins was gone for the day. She'd left a pile of ironing for me and I'd been at it awhile. I leaned over to pull a shirt outta the basket and a strange feeling come over me. Was they somebody close by?

Hadn't heard nobody come in. I pressed the sleeves and the collar, but still that same feeling. Then caught sight of sump'n. In the mirror on her dressing table. Was a man. Standing just out the open door to the little pass-through from the dining room—a li'l passageway where now they be a big black telephone on the wall. His eyes locked on mine in the mirror, and quick as you could say "Jackrabbit" he was skedattling out the dining room door like a young'un caught stealing from the cookie jar.

And there I stood, like I'd see'd a ghost—holding my breath. When the backdoor slammed, I let out air in one big who-o-osh. That night I lay awake after Joshua went off to sleep. No doubt about it, that sly fox had come spying on me. Up to no good! The next Monday, when I went over to do the laundry, I found my chance. Miz Robbins had walked down to the mailbox and he come driving up in that shiny black car he got.

I was by the washpot and hurried right over to meet him—him not even out the car yet. "Mister Robbins, if'n you ever does such as that again, Joshua and me will leave this farm."

He say, "What you talking about, Hazeline? You talking crazy."

"Happens again, me and Joshua be gone. Mark my word."

I like r'membering that day. Surprised myself. Said my piece—I did!

For some days after that, my head kept making all kinds of pretty pictures. One, I r'member, showed a clear morning, not a cloud in the sky and the air so warm we didn't even need a sweater. We had us a mule and a wagon and was loading ever'thing we owned on that wagon and tying it down. One wagon could hold it all cause they wadn't no need to take things like tables and benches. Joshua was so good wit' a hammer and nail he could put that kind'a stuff t'gether in no time.

And where was we headed? I tried my best to picture Ohio. Or Baltimore. Some such place. I figured most any place'd be better'n this'un.

The picture looked so fine in my head I left my bread to rise and headed down to the branch. I was soon setting on what I awready called 'my rock.' I set right there by the moving water—and thought about leaving. Going north.

I'd heard tell how in Ohio, white folk and colored folk eat in the same restaurants. I wanted to see what it might feel like to be in such a place.

The water in the branch was low—so low it didn't make much of a song. I looked and looked at that water, trying to picture a stream in Ohio. Would take a lot of days to get there, and Joshua would sure miss his brothers. An' his mama. And Joleen'd miss playing wit' her cousins.

I knowed right then they wadn't no use even thinking 'bout it, cause whatever be in Ohio, it wouldn't make my sweet man and my li'l girl sing. I kinda hated, though, to let the picture in my head go. But, I knowed they wadn't no way to hold it. So I set right there by that singing water and tuned up a song Grandmama used to sing.

The world, it be full of sorrow.
The world, it be full of sorrow.
So what I gonna do – why
I gonna sing, and sing again tomorrow.

Never did tell Joshua 'bout that Ohio daydreaming. We'd talked some, soon after we was married, 'bout moving. I couldn't understand why he wouldn't go along wit' me on the idea. Was a sticking point for us. Him stuck on one end and me on t'other.

"Ah, go on," he'd say. "You know well as you setting here we can talk till next week and not see it the same way, so le's quit. Why don't you come on over here and give me some sugar? Tell me you love me anyway."

And I'm sure I did. Never could stay mad at him.

Chapter 9

―――――――――>⊰⊱⊰<―――――――――

This morning I lay abed a while. The house so often seem so awful quiet. Tha's what I was thinking. Nobody coming in the door. Nobody to say a word to. Had been awake a good li'l bit and still laying abed. I knowed I had to snap outta my bad spell, so I begun singing.

First, just humming, but by the time I was finishing my morning rounds and needing to move on to the day's work, my song was pumped up strong. "Way down yonder in the paw-paw patch...."

More times'n can be said, it been the singing tha's kept my people from giving up. Maybe Jesus save, but right here, singing can do the job.

Brevard Henderson just left. Seemed kinda funny how he showed up knocking on the door right after I'd been thinking nobody ever come by. I watched him when he started up 'long the edge of the path. He'd left his ole claptrap of a car up on the hill, 'fraid it'd get stuck in the mud.

He had to knock loud to make me hear. I was way down in Egyptland with Moses, telling Pharoah to let my people go—setting there at the kitchen table wit' the last of the coffee and singing at the top of my lungs.

I don't know Brevard well, but it did seem a blessing 'at he come by. He say he got a new job, working for a man what own a ferry and take folk to and fro 'cross the river. I tole him I got a cape to finish up for Miz Moore.

He lit a cigarette and blew smoke up over his head, then looked me in the eye and said, "Why you sew for that woman?"

That brung me up short. But I didn't have no trouble knowing what to answer. Cause she pay me to sew. Tha's why. She pay right away—and ever now and again she give me a little extra."

"I surprised yuh sew for that woman."

"Been sewing for her long time."

"Don't it bother yuh none? Don't yuh think on her and that fam'ly?"

"Cross my mind ever now and again. But the Moores don't own no slaves now. They ain't even rich no more."

Brevard had brung me some shirts to mend and was soon ready to leave, so I walked wit' him to the edge of the clearing. We stood near the big cedar tree and talked a little longer. I's wondered since then if'n maybe he don't like having the same name as one of Miz Moore's sons, the one 'at be a lawyer and live down in Charlotte.

She just a ord'nary white lady. A lonely widow, so far as I can tell. Her fam'ly don't seem to pay her no mind, and one of her chirren a huge grief to her. He just ain't quite right.

Talking wit' Brevard got me thinking again. Thinking how all this land on the Robbins farm used to be part of the Moore fam'ly's plantation—and it a property back then was so big it spread way out on both sides of the Catawba River. I heard it said that back in the beginning, when the king over in England *give* the land to a

Englishman name Moore, they was 5000 acres. That be the story, anyway.

Wish I knowed some of the stories of the slaves.

Then again, maybe not. Likely too sad. Folks say the reason we don't know the slave stories, cause soon as they was free they quit talking 'bout when they was slaves. Didn't wanna save the mem'ries, so they wiped 'em away, like wiping chalk off a blackboard.

Many a time I has wondered. Who was the slaves 'at worked right here on this patch of land? And how many was they? I can picture it, a great huge number, spread across the fields—bare feet moving down the rows, and they own sweat watering the ground. They woulda done same as we does now. Stand tall and stretch the back, try not to see how far that row of cotton stretch on ahead.

Well, right now, thing for me to do be get busy. Finish the machine sewing on this cape for Miz Moore, then set to turning those collars on Brevard's shirts.

While I work I think on my plan for Monday. Gon pull out my li'l wagon. Get it outta the shed, load it up, and haul my dirty laundry down creekside. Miz Robbins gon be away, visiting one of her sisters, and say she want me to wait and do her washing when she come back. So when Monday comes round I gon be down by the creek. It likely gon feel like a holiday. Been some while since I's had a chance to join the others. Sheets and overalls and such gets washed in creekwater. The spot ain't a far piece from here, 'tween here and the church. Where the creek's broadest.

I can get caught up on the gossip. Been quite a while since I's joined in. They'll be wives and daughters there, doing the fam'ly wash. Just thinking of going's got me feeling fine and dandy.

****

Creekside didn't turn out so fine. Only one other'n showed. The rest, I reckon, figured it was too cloudy, but I'd got a early start. Got my bedclothes washed. They hanging now on a coupla lines strung between nails. First I put 'em on the clothesline out back, but the sky kept looking darker, so I carried 'em in.

That was yesterday. This day a time for rejoicing. Ruby's coming!

'Fore she gets here I gon set myself down and sew a button on this old shirtwaist. Lordy lordy, how long has I had this dress? Joshua brung me the material. Pink cotton wit' blue stripes, a wove plaid design. He brung it home after one of those 'rides' him and his brother was so often taking.

I figured he bought it for me cause he'd been kinda short wit' me. There he come, in the door, wearing that grin and reaching out a package wrapped in brown paper. I say, "Wha's that?"

"Just a li'l sump'n for my woman."

The dress long been wearing thin, but I still wears it some round the house. Took a button off near the waist and put it where the lost one was, so now I gon look in my button box and find a odd one to go where the other'n come from.

So button box. Lemme see.

My o my...soon as I take hold of a button all a sudden seem like I ain't never see'd one. Two holes. Tha's what catch my eye. And right then, it dawn on me.

A button can't be a button if'n it don't have holes. I set there for a bit, and next minute I be saying, "Hmmm...now ain't that sump'n to think on?"

Right soon after, I peek out the south winduh—and there she come! My friend! Ruby Pharr. Hurrying down the hill. She such a little woman, but she sure make up for it wid' the big way she got. Laughs big. Talks big. Hugs big too.

I hurry out to meet her. She huffing and puffing, say her ride let her off out the Beatties Ford Road, cause the dirt road into this farm be's too muddy. And sure 'nough, her shoes tell the truth of it. They caked wit' red mud.

Ruby live on the Dellinger farm—few miles from here. Say she had to do a bit of finagling to get herself a ride, then laughs big. She a li'l woman wit' a big laugh, and that just one thing I loves 'bout her.

She hold the bag she carrying high and say, "Today be the day! Hazeline Morrison gon learn to knit!"

For some while now I been wanting to learn to knit and she say she glad to teach me. Least it a good excuse for a visit. Truth be, won't matter what we do. Time wit' my friend—that be's enough!

First thing we settle at the kitchen table and right soon she throwing her head back and beating the air wit' her arms. Least thing liable to set Ruby's tickle box going. This time it some lines she remembers from Amos 'n'

Andy, on the radio. We gets to laughing so hard we hold our sides—hoping we don't wet our britches!

She talk on and soon we laughing again and swiping at our tears. I make us a fresh pot of coffee, and the next hour and more we busy wit' our catch-up chat. Be on over in the afternoon 'fore we pull out the knitting needles. I'd been hoping she wouldn't, but she did.

First, she make a few stitches, then I give it a try and she brag on me, say I a fast learner. And a bit after that, somehow or 'nother, she open up that talk I didn't want her to get on.

Now, I ain't against the church. A good thing it be, surely—good for us to think on how we come to be here and why we was put here. But seem to me it jus' wrong-wrong to be so often looking ahead to 'the life to come.' I can't see no sense in so often turning to the next life. Seem like a easy way to turn aside from this'un we be living now.

I keep the knitting needles busy. Takes a bit of work to hold back a frown.

She saying, "Ever'day I think on the kingdom above. Where all my sorrow gon come to a end."

I pick up the thread and try to do like she showed me, but I ain't got the hang of it yet. Maybe ask her to show me again. That might hush her up. I open my mouth, but what come out surprise me.

"Ruby, you so often talking 'bout 'the life to come.' Why you always setting your sights thataway? I can't hold wit' it. Seem to me it this life we living now—this life...it the one we s'posed to be thinking on now."

She rear back in her chair. Her eyes go big. She don't say nothing.

We say a few more words, but ain't nothing the same. She soon say she best be going, got to meet her ride. I watch her go. Wanted to say I was sorry, didn't mean to hurt her feelings. But I couldn't say it. Cause I wadn't.

****

Up at Mister Stillwell's store I found some real nice material, a red plaid, and stitched up a shirt. Hung it on a hanger on the wall at the end of the bed and ever' so often, stop and admire how fine it look.

A few days later, Slim finally come by. He wadn't smiling like usual, but might be a new shirt would cheer him up, so soon as he stepped through the door I raised my arm and pointed. He say, "Miz Morrison, if'n yuh made it for me, I thank yuh."

Well, I didn't have to be too smart to see his mind wadn't on no shirt. "Come on and set yuhself down at the table. I'll pour us some coffee—if'n it still fit to drink."

"Thank yuh, ma'am. But I don't care none for coffee. If'n yuh got a glass of milk I'll take that. Or a dipperful of water."

I poured two cups of sweet milk, watching him out the corner of my eye. Same as usual, he took Joshua's place. Turned sideways, hunched over. Holding his hat 'tween his knees and turning it round and round.

I set the milk on the table and set myself down.

He looked up quick-like—and just as quick dropped his eyes to his hands again. Real low he say, "They took Delia. They hurt her!" Then real loud, "She had to get to the doctor and get some stitches—tha's how bad they hurt her!"

Tears welled in his eyes. He got a wide brow and a square jawline, and keep his hair trimmed close to his head. He rub at his eyes, still trying to hold back tears. My stomach had twisted up in a knot. Figured I oughta say sump'n, but didn't nothing come to mind.

He turn then and set wit' his hands on the table. He still don't look me in the eye. "They done it to get back at me, Miz Morrison! Done it to get back at me!" Tears crawl down his face and onto his hands. I reach for a clean kitchen towel and hand it over and he bury his face in it.

What I wanted to do was take him in my arms. I looked down at my own hands. They was limp in my lap.

After a bit he wiped his face wit' the towel and begun the story.

Coupla weeks back he'd had a run-in wit' some white boys. He walk by, they hiding 'round the corner of the store. They spit on him, call him "nigger." Then somebody coming, so they don't jump him, just threaten him.

And wadn't long after that, they dragged his girl inta the woods.

He soon took his leave and I watched him make his way up the hill. His strong young shoulders stooped, and him moving like a ole man. My chest was tight. I come on back to the table and set there some long while, then folded my arms on the table and put my head down.

After some while the mantel clock was striking the hour. My head had been making pictures. The girl. On her way home. Them white boys, calling to her—up to no good, having theyselves a bit of fun.

This sadness...our people's sadness. It run way deep in the soul. Ever since white folk figured they's better'n us this same kind'a thing's been happening. And still I come round again—come round to my same far-off hope. I b'lieve 'at anything 'at have a beginning bound sooner or later to have a end. And I standing by it.

Chapter 10

Coupla weeks pass. I say out loud, "I gots to do sump'n—by hook or by crook!" Say it again, say it loud...cause I can't rest.

Folk used to call one of mama's sisters 'obsessed.' Think they meant the devil got hold of her. If not the devil, sump'n she couldn't get leave of. And now they for sure sump'n in me. It won't let me rest. A way-deep feeling it be, and it stick close. Over and again it go: *Has to be sump'n I can do.*

I pull off my bib apron. Gon take myself out to Joshua's bench. They has been some few times I's felt like he could hear me. Can't say for sure, but I does know I has to talk this out. If'n anything can be done...well...awready done some praying, but didn't no answer come.

On my way out I grab hold a piece of cardboard for a fan. The air ain't stirring none, feel like thick soup. I look to see where Ole Dog be. He stretched out under the house. I settle on the bench and fold my hands in my lap and gaze out 'cross the pasture. I look beyond the tall grasses 'at reach to the top of the ridge. Ain't nothing stirring. All the stirring's in me. Uh-huh. And I plumb weary of it.

Tears come, so I pull a hanky out my skirt pocket.

Real low I says, "Joshua...oh my sweet Joshua—if'n you was here you'd know what to do. The girl was done wrong—hurt bad! And ever'body know it—white and colored. But ever'body just going on, same as if ain't nothing happened."

My tears keep a'coming. But tha's alright. It be a time for grieving.

This time mindful of when Mama passed. Ever'thing wrong. And me wit' no notion what to do. Shed tears then, shed tears now.

They for sure sump'n in me. Over and again it say, *You can't just set by and do nothing!*

What might it be, if'n they sump'n I might do?

Hazeline Morrison? What can she do? I set real still, waiting. Nothing come to mind. Yet the thought keep needling me, won't give up. And time keep moving on. I needing to know what that sump'n might be, if'n they be anything.

I drop my head then. I doubt I's brave enough.

Oh my. Moaning. Weeping. After some li'l bit I hear my voice crying, "O, my Joshua!—my sweet Joshua! If'n you was here...you'd know!"

More tears, cause now my heart's filled up wit' doubt. Plumb filled up. No reason to think I'd be brave enough.

At last the weeping dry up. I rub at my eyes and open 'em wide. And there the treeline. All them trees. They holding they place. They standing together.

I set a bit longer and it do seem they maybe some bit of peace settles in me. I don't tarry long. Says my goodnight to Joshua, wish him rest and peace, and head in the house. Needing some supper, but don't feel a bit hungry.

****

Next day come, and this worry the biggest thing in the house. Can't get shed of it.

Some of the neighbors pass along the path, and I does speak. But I careful not to ask nothing 'bout nothing, cause I don't know what they knows, and sure wouldn't be telling what Slim tole me. Wish I knowed where that boy be and what he's doing. Could be, he'd lose his head, think he can get back at them white boys.

Right this minute I 'bout to deal wit' another misery. Least it gon get me thinking on sump'n else. Sunday shirts for Mister Robbins and his boys, near wore-out sheets and pillowslips, four housedresses and one Sunday dress for Miz Robbins, and three tablecloths. And still got workpants and a petticoat and step-ins to iron.

Mister Robbins like a crease even in his workpants. Prob'ly cause he so often getting in his car and taking off for that store his brother runs. I ain't been to it but I know how the men likes to gather to talk and smoke. All of 'em smoking or chewing. They always a coupla red and white cartons of Lucky Strikes on the sideboard in the dining room, behind Mr Robbins's chair. Soon as the men at the table is done eating they set on for a bit, smoking they cigarettes, dropping the ashes on the bones left on they plates.

Got a early start this morning, hoping to beat the heat. Sprinkled ever' piece and rolled it up and set it in the basket. As a rule I don't mind ironing, but on a day like this'un they ain't no pleasure in it. Hot as blazes wit' the fire going in the woodstove to heat the irons. Wrapped a sweat rag round my head but still has to keep mopping my face.

My head ain't bothered much by the heat, seem like. It still keeping a heap o' things hopping around. Wishing Slim would get some word to me. And this other. Should I tell? Who would I tell? And then what'd happen?

I lay the iron down and take up a hot one, and soon circle back to the question I was asking when I ironed the first shirt. Wouldn't do one bit o' good. Would just stir up trouble. I could tell, uh-huh...could say I see'd the Rev'rend...well, I did see him. Saw him and Shirley Grier. But they'd deny it, and there I'd be, looking the fool, and all the gossips in the crowd happy for sump'n new to chew on.

So what I s'posed to do? Live my li'l life, say nothing, lay low?

I has a hard time picturing heaven, but if'n I ever should get to that gate, ole Saint Peter likely say, 'Why you keep your mouth shut when you knowed what happened was dead wrong?'

Then I'd say, 'Well, sir, I hadn't never before put my neck on no chopping block, and wadn't right sure I wanted to.'

Now tha's one thing I's done many a time—put a neck on the block! Wring the chicken's neck and wait till it stop dancing round the yard and fall to the ground, then put that neck on the block. 'Fore long, that chicken sizzling in my skillet! I always could kill one and clean it quicker'n anybody in my fam'ly.

A laugh begin welling in me and I fight to hold it back. Wouldn't do to have to explain to Miz Robbins why I busting out laughing. It be that preacher's head I sees on the chopping block. His head'd be gone and him still a'prancing round the churchyard in his fancy suit. He'd likely still be spouting a bunch of fancy words. Lately, he been wearing a new suit—likely cause he done outgrowed the other'ns. Look like he maybe living too high on the hog.

I finish up, put the ironing board away and head out. But Miz Robbins call me, say she got sump'n for me. I wait while she hurries back inside. She come carrying a paper sack wit' sump'n sticking out the top. Towels. If'n yuh can call 'em that. Rags, tha's what they be, and her giving 'em to the poor—her good deed for the day.

I thank her anyway and she say, "You welcome."

Maybe I oughta be grateful—but I ain't grateful not one bit! All the way down 'cross the pasture I steaming mad. Reckon she be feeling fine—she done her kindness for the day. I got going quick, didn't wanna look at her face, way my insides was all wound up in a knot.

I step on down cross the pasture, wishing I could trot right back up the hill and throw these ole wore-out towels in her face. She look like a witch—a skinny li'l dried-up scarecrow witch!

Could fling 'em on the ground and stomp on 'em, but somebody round would likely see, so I keep right on, holding the bundle and seeing in my head what I'd like to do. Like to tie the ends of these raggedy rags together and march right back up the hill and tie that li'l white woman up!

My feet keep going and after a bit I does ease some. Ain't no way I can tell her how she hurt me. And worst of it be, she thought she was doing good.

****

Next morning my eyes spot that bundle of rags. Right where I dropped it when I come in the door. Ain't in no hurry to get outta bed—likely cause the way I got so all-fired upset took sump'n outta me. I close my eyes and get a shock—remembering my dream.

There she be and there I be—the both of us. Can't get it all the way it was, but what we was about comes back clear as day. It was way back in some other time, 'fore all this crazy got going, and we was just two women, and didn't have no trouble getting along. But that sure ain't the way things be's now. Not by a long shot.

I says to myself I oughta get out this bed and start the day, but a mem'ry come walking by. So I take a look at it. Me and Miz Robbins, us both younger then, and me in the kitchen and here she come through the dining room door. She say, "Hazeline, I know now what you remind me of."

She'd give me a start. She move so light, little as she be. I turned and got a glimpse of her and kept on wit' my work. Her hair looked straggly, like it do so often. Sometimes I has to bite my tongue to keep from telling her to go brush it.

I was hurrying to finish up, wanting to get home 'fore Joleen come from school.

She lean against the cabinet behind me. "Uh-huh," she say, "done figured on it a spell, and finally come on the answer."

I knowed I may as well go along. "Answer to what?"

"What you be like. Was a coupla months back, if I remember right. I was watching you work, how you do this and you do that—and how it look like it come easy for you."

I say "Uh-huh," just to be saying something.

"So now I got it figured. You remind me of my Aunt Lucille. Now that woman could turn out some work, and you a heap like her, but they was something more too, and I couldn't quite figure it out. But now I know."

She had roused my curiosity, but I kept quiet, just picked up another pot to scrub. I knowed she'd keep going when she was ready.

She walk over and look out the window toward the woodpile. When she turn back she say, "You a lot like the woman I used to think I'd be."

Well, least that mem'ry was enough to get me out of bed. Might be, this the day I finish up a fancy dress I been putting together for one of her sisters. If'n so, I might carry it over there. She'd brag on my sewing, like she always do.

****

Time just a'passing on. 'Bout more'n I can b'lieve, but the calendar say the day has come—the day Hazeline Morrison turning half a century old. Never has knowed zackly what day I was born. Didn't nobody write it down, but Mama say she give birth to me in May, 1887. Fifty years. And look like I gon live a while yet!

Even wit' this loneliness for my man, I still looking forward to summertime. Slim and the girl...that still a worry, but so far I can't see no way to help. And right this minute I got my sights set on a celebration. Fifty years! That sure seem a fitting reason for celebrating.

Just so happened my special day fall on a Saturday, so I don't have to do not one blessed thing if'n I don't want to. Soon as the sun was up good I peeked in the little mirror over the wash bowl. Didn't seem like I looked any older.

A long time back I decided to count May 15 my birthday. Even the weather's turned out good. I'd'a sure been disappointed if'n the day had turned off rainy—cause I got me a plan. Gonna try sump'n special.

I r'member clear how Grandmama done it. First she filled the washpot with water, built a fire under it and waited till the water got hot—then throwed in some roots. I was just a li'l chap, but I was watching close—and that water turned red! Like magic, it was, right be'foremy eyes!

The missing part be what the girl looked like. One thing for sure. Her eyes was big and wide and set on her grandmama and that red water. I bust out chuckling. Why—course I don't know what I looked like. We can't none of us ever see ourselves. But I don't have no trouble a'tall remembering what I was feeling on that long ago day. Reckon the word for it be 'wonder.' *Big wonder.*

If'n I could make a birthday wish and it come true, I'd go right on back and see that li'l girl. Take hold of some magic, go on back in time and take a gander. I does know she was a skinny l'l girl wit' skin dark like chocolate. And her hair in pigtails.

At last, my special day's come and I's ready. Gonna ex-periment! Was a picture in the paper made me decide. A woman showing off her grandmama's quilt—a antique quilt, she called it. Say her grandmama used some roots to dye the cloth. What I needing now be somebody to guide me, but reckon if'n I had that somebody, wouldn't be no ex-periment.

Not long ago it was, I went down to my rock and walked on down a ways then up a slope some little distance from the branch—and come on a huge big patch of a little plant we calls bloodroot. I drawed in my breath. Ever'one was blooming, the whole bunch holding up they little white blossoms and nodding in the breeze.

The paper say the Indians used these roots for making face paint. Warpaint. Got theyselves riled up for a fight wit' it. I stood there in the woods gazing on all that beauty, thinking what a strange world this be. Ain't never understood war, but from what the paper say, some folks think that big war over in Europe 'bout twenty year ago gon be the last. They say it the war to end all war.

I blow out my breath and say, "Time to think on wha's right here. Time to celebrate!"

Uh-huh—yessiree! Time has come. Ever'thing's ready. I sorted through my stash of material and picked out two lengths of white cloth. Now be the fun time, see how it turn out. Will both the pieces take up the color? Will one take it better'n the other?

Time will tell.

If'n I end up wit' some decent-looking cloth, gon make sump'n special and keep it for myself. Problem gon be, how to keep it from fading. A vest maybe, cause it won't have to be laundered often. Uh-huh, that sound right. A vest wit' a briar stitch worked round the edges. Well, if'n it don't work, won't have nothing lost.

My head gets going then. Making pictures. Could gather up all kinds of plants for making dye. Could dye my cloth and sew up things special—things ever'body'd be wanting to buy! Get me a business going.

A chuckle starts up in me. Why, I awready in business! That skinny li'l girl done growed up and got her own business! She be's a seamstress!

I say out loud to my self, "Now whatcha think of that?!"

Got me a good stout pole for stirring. And soon as I pick it up I r'members. I b'lieve the trick for setting the color be a heavy brine. A good bit of salt in warm water. Least it worth a try. Be a ex-periment.

A bit later I's settled in a chair next to Joshua's bench, reading another ole newspaper. First thing though, I tole Joshua 'bout the fun I had trying sump'n new. And I reminded myself 'at this still my day, so wadn't no trouble a'tall deciding to steer clear of my sewing machine.

They one article in this paper 'at mention twenty-seven countries. I counted 'em, ever' one. Yep, a globe sure would be the thing, but likely cost a right smart. Another write-up say the folks 'at sell stuff be doing awright, while the farmers ain't making so much money. Say agriculture ain't the biggest thing in this state no more.

I read on, and doze off for a bit, but 'fore the day's done I get to feeling awful lonesome. A special birthday. But a wee bit lonesome. I didn't even mention my celebrating plan to Joleen. They stays busy going here and there.

Chapter 11

The next morning comes and moves on a little and me still laying a'bed. And ever li'l bit I let my eye stray to the rewards of my labor. Hanging on the inside line. Time will tell if'n the trick wit' the brine set the color. Problem gon be, when I wear that vest I got in mind, not to go strutting about and making a fool of myself. Gon have to be careful, so's not to look foolish—like that Rev'rend Jones do when he gets to liking the sound of his own voice.

Didn't sleep worth a hoot. A bunch of memories, too little sleep, partly cause the air was too warm. Might decide to sleep out on the front stoop if'n this heat wave keeps up. When I first crawled in the bed I was so wore out I dozed off, but then some dogs got to barking. And after that I got Slim and the girl on my mind.

Ain't in no hurry to get out this bed. I squinch my eyes shut and real low say, "What would yuh say to me now, Joshua? Say they ain't no use getting all upset? Say this kinda thing nothing new—been happening all along?"

After a bit my mind gets on to sump'n else, shows me pictures of the blow-up. A air ship, tha's what the paper say. A big balloon. A coupla weeks back now, it was. Caught on fire and crashed to the ground. *The Hindenberg*, it called. Made it all the way 'cross the ocean, and soon as it got here it blowed up.

A 'ship' they called it, up in the air and moving all that way. Say it eight hundred feet long, and that too more'n I could believe. I do wonder sometimes if'n these newspaper folk just make up stuff. Say they was close to a hundred people on that 'ship'—and a bunch of 'em died.

I still trying to figure out aeroplanes. Wadn't long ago the Charlotte mayor convinced the citizens—tha's what the paper say—the mayor *convinced* 'em they needing *a* airport. Mayor Douglas keep on saying, "Charlotte moving into the modern world."

Could make excuse, say I too tired to go to church. Just as soon skip it. If'n it worship we after, why we can do that anywhere.

Never has been able to picture no god up in the sky. Seem more like I got a god inside me, and it telling me wha's right and wha's wrong. Sometimes it give a hard yank on the bell rope to ring the alarm, so's to tell me I be's on the wrong track.

When the preacher or the deacon gets to talking too long, I start in to musing on such. Think 'bout Jesus. He say when yuh find fault wit' somebody else, that be just the time to look at yuhself. I's many a time thought on it, setting right there on the hard bench while the rest busy giving out the Amens.

I ain't inta shouting and ever'body know it, but I ain't one bit quiet when it come time to sing. The ole tunes stir my blood and I feels like I reaching out to Mama and her mama and all the rest—all the ones 'at come be'foreme.

More'n once I's had to hold my tongue when Miz Robbins mention the piano and the organ at they church. We ain't got nothing but our voices. So a time or two the devil's got hold of me and I fill up wit' envy. But it don't last long. It slip away soon as we joins our voices and makes a joyful noise. Seem like then 'at Gloryland's awready come.

If'n it wadn't for the music and the chance to see folks, I wouldn't trouble wit' going to church. Don't hold none wit' the notion 'at God be setting up in the clouds spying on us—ready to pitch us in a everlasting firepit!

And sure don't hold wit' what I's heard many a time, how it don't matter none if'n this life a misery cause in the next life they gon be pearly gates and ever'thing fine and dandy! Was the grandmama used to be a slave 'at planted the suspicion in me. Grandmama say it easy for the one 'at got all the power to say to the one that don't have none, 'Now don't you fret none. Your lot here may be hard, but heaven be a'waiting for yuh in the life to come.'

Ain't likely gon tell nobody all this in my head. And right now it past time to get myself outta bed and get on wit' the day.

****

It still kinda early when I hear a voice raised and stop to listen. Couldn't tell at first who it be, but somebody calling me. I hurried to the front door and there was Slim. Hadn't knowed his voice cause he didn't sound nothing like hisself. Just one look tole me he was powerful upset.

He come in the house and right away, same as usual, settled at the kitchen table. He always take Joshua's chair—and that fine wit' me cause ain't no doubt in my mind 'at Joshua'd like this young man.

He take off his hat, set his elbows on the table and cover his face wit' his hands. I stand by the cookstove and wait.

Soon as he lifted his head I could tell he was meaning to say sump'n but couldn't get the words to come. And his big dark eyes looked sad as any I's ever see'd. Was the kinda look at say they ain't no hope left.

He dropped his head in his hands and begun weeping. Was the second time I watched him weep at my table.

I didn't know what to do. Tears was flooding my own eyes. I stepped over and put a hand on his shoulder. "It Delia?"

Took him another minute or so 'fore he moaned, "She tole me to stay away!"

I had knowed he was planning to ask her to marry him. Not right away, but soon as she'd had some time to get over this. But what she tole him was, she ain't no good no more—since them white boys dragged her off to the woods.

After he bit he wiped his face wit' his hands and catch my eye and tell me his feeling for her hadn't changed none. I'd wondered a time or two if'n he wanted to marry her back be'forethem boys got hold of her. Might be, he was just wanting to make up to her cause he feels to blame.

He couldn't stay long, had to go on to keep his job. My worries for him keep me comp'ny. Such a *awful awful thing it'd be*—if'n this fine young man come on some notion of tryin' to get even.

****

Coulda been left to grow a bit longer, but I was glad to pull it. Be a few days yet 'fore the rest get big enough to go in my frying pan.

"So, li'l squash, you the first picking. Gon be just the thing to go wit' the dried beans on the cookstove."

Ever' year I looks forward to this day, when the first of the summer garden's ready to harvest. Awready had cabbages and turnip greens and radishes. But when yuh pick the first yellow squash, yuh know warm weather's finally settled in—the time of year when most ever'thing we eat be's fresh.

And I walk round barefoot. A fine fine thing, it be— wake of a morning and set yuh feet down on the floorboard and not shiver. Wild plums soon be ripe. And crabapples too. Time to make jams and jellies.

All the daylong that li'l squash keep me happy. On over in the afternoon I set myself down under the shade tree and read one of the old newspapers. Don't find much of interest, but the funnies good. And tha's where I find it.

A June mem'ry. Was the name brought it to mind. Verla. Right there on the comics page. Woman we knowed was called Verlie. I ain't never knowed nobody like her. Sweet as a angel one minute, then some little thing'd set her off and just that quick she'd change—like some devil spirit had got hold of her. Yuh see it first in her eyes, and wouldn't have time to clear out 'fore she'd get to yelling and cursing, her eyes just a blazing. Seemed like she'd gone mad.

One night at a fish fry—'bout 1920 or so, woulda been—sump'n set Verlie off. The women was mostly over near the picnic tables. The men was on the other side of the clearing wit' a game of horseshoes going, and likely placing a few bets. A coupla men wit' guitars and drums had come by and was tuning up.

Back then Joshua would take a woman's eye. Strong and healthy and good-looking, he was, and had a way 'bout him 'at made yuh notice. Wadn't much 'at got past him, and when yuh caught sight of him he was likely studying on whatever was going on, or else had that ear-to-ear smile on his face.

Verlie was new in the crowd. I was putting a lid on a jar of pickles when I heard the fracas. If'n I'd knowed what was coming I would've rushed over and put a lid on her.

First I didn't pay much attention, went on putting away leftovers, but then somebody punched my elbow and motioned. Wadn't dark yet, but almost—and standing by a big ole cedar tree was Joshua and this woman. She had her hand up, poking his chest wit' her finger. I'd already see'd her nails. Real long, and shiny red.

Looked like she was keeping time on his chest. And wit' ever' word she say her voice rise a bit higher. Folks begun gathering round. I didn't know whether to hold back, or step thataway.

Verlie had real light skin, coulda passed for white if'n she'd kept her mouth shut. But right that minute she was yelling at the top of her lungs. "You keep your hands to yo'self, you big black nigger. Don't be putting 'em where they don't belong."

The crowd opened up to let me through. I wadn't thinking nothing. I was watching—watching her and him, and me—to see what was gon happen. I woulda fought for him, no doubt in my mind then or now 'bout that. Verlie had her hands set on her hips. She backed up a step or two. The skirt of her red dress was hemmed a bit too short and fit real snug on her bottom. My body tall and got more angles 'an roundness, so I had sort'a envied how she look.

I studied Joshua's face. I could tell he was thinking hard, trying to figure out what this woman was up to. I waited. The crowd waited too.

Verlie kept her hands on her hips and her feet planted.

Then she start up again in that shrill voice, but she didn't no more'n get started 'fore Joshua took a step her way and she took one back and lost her footing. And down she went!

There she lay, sprawled on the ground, hollering at him to quit coming at her. The crowd started snickering, cause they all knowed Joshua. Didn't nobody make a move to help her. Joshua looked my way, and then he heaved a big sigh and stepped 'round Verlie and helped her to her feet.

The mem'ry got my face breaking out in a smile and I soon chuckling to myself. More'n once after that he come home laughing 'bout whatever was in his head, and wouldn't tell me 'bout it right off. First he'd tease me. "Wadn't nothing. Just thinking I might go visit Verlie, since you ain't been paying me no 'tention."

Hazeline

Now I setting here a'crying. O Lordy. Laugh and cry at the same time. Verlie don't have no idea how many good laughs she give us.

****

Joleen's birthday, and her and Troy coming for supper. Be the first time in quite a while she coming here long enough to set a spell. I's finished all the tidying up I gon do. While I been busy I been r'membering sump'n from long ago. T'will be a good tale to bring up while we at the table.

Joleen was just a li'l chap. We lived on the Patterson farm then and me and her had gone up 'long the edge of the woods—cause we didn't have no outhouse. She'd pulled down her panties and squatted, when I caught sight of sump'n moving our way. She hopped up and clutched at my arm—her britches still down 'round her ankles. Not far away was a dog 'at didn't look just right. Looked more'n just mean. I felt pretty sure it was a mad dog.

So what did I do? I froze. Couldn't think, couldn't move. Knowed it'd be dangerous to make any move a'tall. But right then a shot rang out—and that mean-looking dog went down!

I couldn't quit thanking the young white man 'at saved the day. Said he'd been on the dog's trail and was 'fraid to call out to us, so decided to just take aim and offer up a prayer.

I 'magine how to tell the story. Troy, Joleen's husband—don't b'lieve he's heard it. Could end wit', "Ain't never, in all my born days!—been so glad to see a white man show up!"

While ago, I set myself down in this rocking chair. And I still be a'setting. Almost June, but the weather done what it always likely to do. Change. Turned off cool, so it right pleasant to have the fire in the cookstove going. The beef stew one of Joleen's favorites. It tickle me to think of her and Troy coming over, but Slim...well, he stay on my mind. Don't seem right to feel so good and him feeling so bad.

This trouble of his ought never to've happened, but now 'at it has, how he gon protect hisself? Best be on his guard.

Ain't much he can do 'gainst a bunch of white boys. Not a chance in the world he'd come out right side up. But if'n he don't do sump'n, rest of his days he gon have to live wit' the shame of not standing up for his girl.

How many times has we knowed this? Has to back down, swallow the shame. Or end up dead—one or t'other.

Ain't hard to figure where his thoughts taking him. 'Fraid the girl won't have him if'n he don't show his strength. Sure a dilemma.

My most favorite preacher preached once on 'dilemma.' Say yuh got yuhself a dilemma when yuh turn one way and can't find no way to go, turn the other way and still don't find no way to go. So what yuh gon do? Make a move in spite of it, though yuh likely end up in more trouble? Or lay low, cause yuh rather see the sun rise the next morning?

Same as usual, when I gets to fretting, my hands can't rest. They been busy twisting up my apron. I gets to my feet. No sense setting and nursing worry when they plenty to be done. Better be checking that stew. I splurged and bought a bit of beef.

****

One more day over the washpots at the Robbins household. Stirring the clothes with my pole and keeping the fire under the pot going. First thing, diapers. Some of Miz Robbins's family visiting. Awready hung them on the line. They dry quick. Now the wash for him and her and they two sons 'at still live at home. And after all that, the bedding. A full day for sure. I gon be wore out, but I used to it.

Here come Mister Robbins and his brother-in-law, through the back screenporch and out the door. They wearing suits and smoking cigars, don't pay me no mind. They climb in the brother-in-law's shiny black car and get going. Wonder where they off to?

Soon's they drive off I gets to thinking again 'bout Joshua. Soon gon be the two-year mark since we buried him. Henrietta and Sam cried wit' me. Jolene wept so hard and long she got sick. Mama used to tell us crying don't help, but I believe maybe she was wrong 'bout that. It be the weeping 'at let the pain out.

My Joshua was fine. Big laugh. Big booming voice...tha's what I miss. How I'd like to hear it now, coming round the corner. And in the night, me and him together, that big voice go soft and easy. One lucky woman, I be—that for sure. To've had all them years wit' him.

Mister Robbins, walking 'longside the other fella to the car—he say good and loud, "When I kick the bucket I gonna take my money right along with me!" I's heard him say it more'n once.

Brung to mind when Joleen was a girl. She'd hear'ed somebody say it and come to me, wanting to know what it mean. 'Kick the bucket.' Can't remember now what I said. But ain't much way yuh can tell a li'l one 'bout a hanging.

My back done gone to aching, like usual. Bend over the washpot, scrub the dirtiest clothes on the washboard. The hardest part be's wringing the water out. I stand up straight, stretch my back and shoulders and stroll round a bit. And there go memory, flying off to that morning 'at Joshua passed. I wonders again what it be's like to die. All a sudden—and just that quick the breath gone. No more, like they only so much, and no more give to us.

I was twelve year old when Mama passed. She'd been sickly a good while. But when the end come, she went quick as lightning.

Too many squeezed in a li'l house. So they wadn't no way not to see. Seem like she didn't try to hold on. I was growed 'fore I figured that out. Our mama was wore out. Eight babies too many when yuh man can't stop drinking.

I was standing by her bed when her breath run out. She'd been breathing rough, and for more'n a day she hadn't opened her eyes. Lots of folk had been stopping by. Seemed like sump'n special was going on, wit' so many of the neighbors carrying in food.

Hazeline

I straightened the quilt over her and was looking at her face, wanting her eyes to open. Ever'body was outside, 'cept me and my eldest sister, Gertie. She was in the kitchen. And Mama pushed out one last long breath.

My own breath stopped, pulled back in my throat. I tried to call to Gertie and couldn't get no sound. I reached for Mama's hand. Guess I made some kind of noise cause Gertie come running and soon a whole heap of crying started up.

I didn't shed not one tear. Took myself out the door and down in the woods. Was on over in the afternoon when she left us. I set myself down cross-legged by a big poplar. Some long while went by. Seem like, when it was all done, 'at I'd set at the foot of that poplar a day and more. The sun was 'bout to go down.

I heard Daddy. Him calling me. "Girl, where is you? Come along now. Soon gon be dark."

Next day, Mama was put in the ground. Tha's when I done my weeping. I count it the day Hazeline learned to weep.

Chapter 12

Sunday morning. Been lazing about. So now I gotta hurry. Hadn't even fed Ole Dog yet, so I does that and take another minute to walk over and check my tomato plants. Got 'em in the ground late, cause of all that worrying I done about maybe having to leave this place. No ripe ones yet, but I be keeping a close watch. Guess they like the pot. More yuh watch, longer the pot take to boil.

I check the eggs then and head back in the house to pull on my Sunday dress. Now I heading out. Wit' a plan in mind. If'n the chance come—I gon do it. Dreamed last night 'bout Joleen. She was turned away. I called her name, hoping she'd turn back my way wit' a smile on her face.

It sure a grief. My girl, she be...but seem like she don't never even think of me. A locked heart ain't easy to unlock. Even the birthday visit.... That didn't turn out so good. Seemed all the while she was in a hurry to get along.

I got it in mind to push her some, make her least talk my way more'n her usual few words.

****

Evening now. Settled by the oil lamp wit' my Bible. It fall open to Ecclesiastes. And wonder of wonders, what does I find? Ever'body!

This ole prophet sure knowed people. He talk 'bout Rev'rend Jones, 'bout Mister Robbins—even Verlie! Look like maybe we had twins back in the prophet's time. He say some folks *own greed*. Tha's what he say. And say the greed take away the life of the one 'at own it.

Another verse say wisdom maketh the face to shine, and I sees the face of ole Miz Stephens. They sure a light in it. Been thinking 'bout going to see her. Wanna talk to her 'bout Delia and Slim—and those boys! It all stay on my mind. Might help some to talk to somebody wiser'n me. I just keep a'thinking how a wrong's been done—and nothing done 'bout the wrong!

Some verses bring to mind Rev'rend Jones. "Yielding pacifieth great offenses." I think on that for a bit. Believe it mean owning up to a wrong mean yuh likely get off easy.

A minute or so go by. And I rebuke myself. Say it out loud. "Hazeline Morrison, you ain't the cure of the world."

I was picturing going to Rev'rend Jones and telling him what I know. He'd deny it, of course. Then I'd say again how I know and I gon tell...so's to open the way for him to repent.

I shake my head side to side. Wouldn't happen thataway, not in a hundred years. A bit of time go by and I get another thought. "Yielding pacifieth great offenses." Hmmm. B'lieve this may bear some thought. Might be— if'n I could see wit' Joleen's eyes, I might see my own offenses. Has I done sump'n wrong?

I drop my head, but right soon raise it. And speak real low. "Well, daughter, one of these days maybe...some day ahead maybe, you gon tell me."

I sit quiet for a bit, then read another verse. It say the poor man's wisdom be despised, his words not heard. I lift my eyes. Best get out this chair 'fore I start boo-hooing. Past time for bed. A soft rain falling and the pitter-patter on the tin roof good as a mama's lullaby.

****

"Mama, can you stay in the nursery today? I s'posed to, but we been practicing a new song and I don't want to miss singing with the choir. Can you take my turn in the nursery?" She all but jumping up and down. Tha's my daughter. Just like her daddy when she get excited.

"What song is that?"

"Oh, Mama, I'll sing it for you later—I gotta go. If I'm late, somebody else'll take my part."

And off she go! And me left standing here wondering when it was I said yes.

By the time the preacher's done preaching and the mamas come for the little ones, I done been pulled a hundred dif'rent ways and spit up on more'n once, so ain't so sure I smell so good. But, I get my basket and carry it out to the tables on the grounds and set out my fried chicken and blackberry cobbler. This year's berries not ripe yet. These ones from the last jar on my shelf, put back last year.

Hmmph! Here she come. Strutting. Peddling her charms. If'n I was a man she'd catch my eye. That Shirley Grier's got some curves. And her skirt's flared, so's yuh notice how she sashay. She puts henna on her hair too, and wears dangling earrings.

Easy for me to find fault. Might be I envies her some. She got herself a man. And just that quick a mem'ry come racing through me and I has to turn away. Wouldn't do to bust out crying.

Soon as the dinner on the grounds is done, I set out home. They another round of preaching coming up, but thanks to Joleen I got me a good excuse to leave early. On my walk home my mind goes to Slim and the girl. One of the first things I liked 'bout him, cause it reminded me of my Joshua, was how he so often whistling. But I ain't heard him whistling in a while now.

I wonder how the girl faring. Wish I could see her, wrap these long arms round her and comfort her. I think of her mama. Oh my, that poor woman...the woe in her mother-heart.

Next thing I know—woe and woe! A cloud of gnats. I move fast and they keep up. I swat at 'em but that don't help none. I move quick, but I got things to carry—and has to keep my mouth shut and my eyes squinched up. I free up one hand and swat at 'em, but that don't help none.

Feel like I inside a bottle and the gnats in the same bottle. Ain't no way to get free.

But at last...they does move along. I hurry on to the house, shed my clothes and throw'em out the door and grab my hairbrush. Quite a few of them li'l devils come home wit' me. But at last the commotion's settled, and I settle my weary self in Joshua's rocking chair. I can count on it. Setting in this chair a comfort to me.

****

My visitor just left and I awready missing her. Wonder when time will come I see her again? Her and her fam'ly live in Concord, so it ain't often we gets to see the other.

Justine. Since long as I can remember, she been my favorite cousin.

I wanted ever'thing to be perfect, so yesterday morning I got up way early and first thing got a fire going in the cookstove and stirred up a battercake and throwed in some dried apples I'd put in to soak the night before. While it was baking I got ever'thing in order best I could.

'Bout ten o'clock I set to walking the coupla miles— and ever' step of it happy stepping, to meet Uncle Morse. Dressed up a bit, but had to wear my old shoes for the walk. He'd said he'd be glad to give me a ride after he finished his morning rounds.

I passed by Mr. Kidd's store and crossed the tall bridge 'at crosses the creek on the Beatties Ford Road. I always does hurry over it, 'case a car come along. Its big iron railings seem to reach up to the sky. The weather warm and sunny, and me sweating as I hurried along, but I made it. And didn't have to wait long till Uncle Morse was ready to set out.

I settled on the seat beside him and right off he say, "Hazeline, you sure looking fine today."

"Well," I tole him, "if'n happiness got anything to do wit' how a body look—reckon I prob'ly plumb beautiful today!"

We chuckled then and settled in for the ride. I was dressed up like Easter Sunday. And right then, on that wagon seat, it come to me how since Joshua ain't here I ain't been giving much mind to how I look. Dress I had on was a ole one, but I'd always liked it and wanted to wear it cause this a special day.

Uncle Morse ain't a big talker. By the time we got going good I fell in to watching the rumps of the mules. Like the way they keep a steady pace, moving easy down the dirt road. And like the way the big wooden wheels keeps turning, on and on. It feel sorta like I can feel them wheels working hard. They does a fine job.

After a while Uncle Morse start in to singing, first humming and then the words. "Git along home, home, Cindy, git along home...."

I was thinking 'bout Justine and me, when we was little. Had me a corncob doll named Justine and she had one named Hazeline.

Reckon I was grinning wit' the memory, cause Uncle Morse say, "Yuh got some happy thoughts rolling round in yo' head?"

I chuckled and patted my knee. "Uh-huh!—whole heap of good memories. Folks used to say 'bout me and Justine, 'Watch out now, here they come!'"

They was one spot 'long the way he had to pull back on the reins and wait for some hogs to get out the road. I was sure glad I wadn't down on the ground walking. 'Bout half a dozen of 'em. Oinking, grunting, scurrying 'round like they'd gone mad, but Uncle Morse give a few hollers and they finally did skedaddle. Wadn't long after that I caught sight of her. Waiting at the crossroads. I could tell it was her from the way she was standing. As we got close I spied a big shopping bag and a basket. Bag had red letters on it and the basket a red bow.

'Fore Uncle Morse could stop the wagon, him and me both had busted out laughing. Mercy, mercy! Justine had on a white dress wit' red polka dots, and my own was red wit' white dots!

Lawsamercy! Wadn't we a pair! Guess yuh might rightly say we hadn't changed much. Two peas in a pod.

****

The preaching today got me all riled up. Sure glad to get myself back home. Wishing I'd stayed home. How yuh s'posed to listen to a man yuh can't put no faith in? Yet there I sat. Listening. Getting more riled up by the minute.

The mem'ry of what I saw that day some while back still rankles. Ain't tole not one soul 'bout it, don't reckon I ever gon tell. Most preachers deserve a li'l respect, but mine for this'un's done gone sour as old milk.

He got going wit' his preaching, talking on and on. Highfalutin' talk. I figured likely wadn't none of us understanding the fancy words he was spewing. I got tickled and had to drop my head and cover my mouth to hold back my giggles. My head had throwed up a picture. I saw me marching right up to that pulpit—and sticking him wit' my hatpin. Let that hot air out!

He took his text from Jeremiah. Don't remember chapter and verse—just know I didn't understand it. But then, they a whole bunch of the Bible I can't understand. Like, why we need a sacrifice to save us. Never has made sense to my mind. But maybe I just ain't smart enough.

Hazeline

In the Old Testament they one place say the one what don't believe should be took out and stoned to death. And another place, say God complained cause the ones he sent to wipe out a town didn't kill ever' last living thing. Guess you gotta have a mind smarter'n mine to figure all that out, but one thing I does understand be what happen when a man and a woman come together. Tha's a power too, and I guess it been 'round since this world got going.

Most Sundays—praise the Lord, our deacons be's in charge. This preacher take turns, serve our church and two others besides. Got my fingers crossed 'at sump'n gon happen to bring on a change. Things always be a'changing. Might just happen that this Rev'rend Jones move on to some other place. I sure looking forward to the day we hear his last *Amen*.

****

Made it to the Robbins household early this morning, set on getting a good start and maybe finishing up a bit early. But first bit of the day was took up wit' her. That little woman was beside herself, likely cause they'd had some disagreement. She didn't even seem like herself. Like as if the best part of her had done gone into hiding.

So there I was a'listening—not getting my early start. She finally settled down some after a bit and I begun to get the fire going under the washpot. And now it won't be long 'fore I finish up.

Here she come now. She stand nearby for a bit and don't say nothing, then she up and say, "Hazeline, I been noticing how you always seem to know just the right thing to say. I was wondering how you come to know how to encourage the other."

I sure glad this li'l white woman can't see my face. Wouldn't want her to see how my mouth just fell open. Lucky for me I was bent over the washboard.

She keep on. "Been trying to figure what made you this way. Surely you've not always been so." Her voice not so whiney as it was but she still cracking her knuckles. Oftentimes that be a sign she ain't quite sure of herself.

"Miz Robbins, let me finish emptying these washpots, then we can talk a bit. I can smell rain a'coming. Believe we gon get us a storm."

That does it. Off she scurries to bring in what's dry. Was so much washing today it wouldn't all fit on the line so some's flung over the bushes.

Soon after that I spot her. A tiny li'l woman trying to carry a big load. They's times when her face look so white it makes me think of one of her dinnerplates, but right now it be's red. I hurry over to take the load and tell her to go get a cold rag to put over her brow and rest a spell.

A bit later I's finished folding the clothes and ready to head out, and here she come. She stand there on the backporch and start right in. I can tell by her eyes and way her hands stay on the move, she upset 'bout sump'n. She tell me it easy to talk to me cause I a good listener. It her youngest sister she got on her mind.

"Her time's on her, Hazeline. Going through the change—and she just ain't herself. Luther ain't wanting me to go, but I'm bound and determined I will. Just have to bide my time, till he comes round."

I s'pect she's right. A few days from now she will go. I ask a few questions 'bout Maddie, so's she can talk it out. That be what she needing. And sure 'nough, after a bit she begins to look a little more at ease.

I take my leave and head down the hill. Shocked me a bit, it did, her saying I a good listener. She said I one 'at encourage the other. That took me so by surprise you coulda knocked me over wit' a feather. I no more'n close the pasture gate and start up the dirt road than another surprise pops up. One I oughta be encouraging? Why, Hazeline Morrison! Tha's who!

I don't have to think twice to see why. Besides ever'thing else, I's plumb tired of working steady and never getting ahead. Always needing a few more dollars for sump'n, like what I owe at Mister Kidd's store. And getting a tooth pulled. And I think sometimes how nice it would be to buy a train ticket and just take off somewhere. Don't know where, don't even care, just wanna hop on a train and go. Seem like a body oughta be able to do such a thing least once in a blue moon.

Soon I be headed down the next hill and spot the li'l house and says to myself, "Well, for now, it gon be enough just to get myself home."

Chapter 13

Awready this morning I got my bread-and-butter pickles started. Sliced the cucumbers thin and layered 'em wit' salt and ice. Be a while 'fore time to scald the jars and get the spices heated in the vinegar, so I got time to go through these bags and boxes.

Hard to give any of it up. This fine dotted swiss, this brown corduroy. And here the taffeta. The mama of one of Joleen's schoolmates had me make a skirt for the girl to wear to a dance. Ain't much of it left, but look how it catch the light. If'n they was more of it I'd stitch up a curtain for the south winduh. That'd be sump'n—taffeta drapery! If'n I had a toilet in the house, I'd put the taffeta in it. Ever'body round would be coming over to see the toilet, so it'd be good to have it spruced up.

And here be the seersucker. Wonder how many times now I done come across these remnants and wouldn't let 'em go? Was a long way back, when we was getting ready for our first trip and I made him a jacket outta this seersucker. I give a sigh then, and think again how next week gon be the two-year mark since he been gone.

They was only that one time we got to go down to the coast t'gether. We didn't no more'n get there till we was walking out on the sand and taking a long, long look at that big water. I looped my hand round his arm, my fingers feeling the stripes on his sleeve.

Had to have me a new dress too, for sump'n that special, so I sewed one up. Joshua teased me, but I hadn't never see'd the ocean and hadn't hardly ever knowed so much excitement. When we got to where we could see that big water—and hear it and smell it too, I was glad I'd made a ceremony of it cause ain't often yuh gets to see sump'n that grand. It made me think 'bout the globe my schoolteacher had. I stood there wit' my feet on the wet sand and my eyes looking on into forever, wishing I could tell her I was standing at the edge of the Atlantic Ocean.

Looked like that ocean maybe stretched on to forever. Reckon that where Joshua be. I think of him in such a place—a place can't nobody imagine. It stretch way on past what we can see.

****

Few days ago it was, the button box tipped over. Buttons went ever'which way. And now here be another'n, up under the rocker of the chair. Joshua's chair. I be setting in it cause this the two-year mark—two long years since he been gone.

Still early morning. I'd just set myself down, ready to think on the past and feel sad. Time to be serious. And prayerful. Opened my Bible, rocked back—and there it went. Crunch! Got up to see what it was, picked up the pieces and set back down wit' the broken bits cradled in my hand.

Now, for some spell, I just been setting here. Ain't no doubt, this one of the buttons off his best dress shirt, one I made for him. He had a coupla store-bought Sunday shirts but they wadn't special, so I got the best white cotton to be had and made him a fine shirt.

I'd forgot 'bout saving the buttons. Was the only part 'at could be saved.

I still setting, holding these broke pieces. Had thought to read one of the Psalms and say a few words to Joshua, and end up wit' a prayer.

The buttons was bought special too. No doubt about it, this button used to be on that shirt. First he pulled on a clean undershirt, then buttoned up his new shirt, making a big show of whistling and buttoning, saying in his own way how pleased he was and what a smart fella he was gon look. And he sure did look fine—all spiffed up! And mighty handsome. He slicked his hair back wit' some pomade and stood there looking at me wit' a grin spread ear to ear.

He only wore it two times. That second time he spilled sump'n all down the front. The stain wouldn't come out. Just two times he wore it! I tried my best to get that stain out, but the cloth just wouldn't come white again. So I let him have it!

Said a few things I ought'n to've said. Then he say, "Now Hazeline, jus' think what yuh saying. Wadn't like I set out a'purpose to ruin it."

I turned my back on him, wouldn't say not one word—and he stomped right on out. I knowed I was in the wrong but I just couldn't quite say it yet. All that work! And all that saving! Took morn'n a few nickels and dimes—a bit saved ever' week, to get the makings for that shirt.

But, I never could stand to stay on the outs wit' Joshua long, so pretty soon I went on out and tole him I was sorry 'bout what I'd said. Tole him I knowed I shouldn't have let such as that come out of my mouth. Oh, I r'member it all, plain as day, plain as I be setting here now in his chair. Ain't read no scripture... ain't done nothing but r'member. And 'fore I know it I start boo-hooing. Not reading, not praying. Jus' weeping.

Some bit of time pass 'fore I can make myself move. I know I gotta take my mind off this sorrow. But then Slim come to mind, him and the girl—and my heart full of sorrow for us all. A girl wronged, and so far, ever'body just holding they tongue—like as though nothing ever happened.

But it did happen! Happened right here in our little neck of the woods. Sorrow and more sorrow. Somebody oughta make them boys 'fess up to what they done. Ain't right to let 'em go on like as though nothing ever happened.

I shed a few more tears. Joshua woulda been the one. He woulda knowed what to do.

****

Late that same day, for some reason, Chester come to mind. Ain't thought of him in a month of Sundays. That man was a reg'lar smokestack. Joshua liked his cigarettes too, but Chester kept a Chesterfield going 'bout all the time. That would rightly be his brand, of course.

They'd set out under the shade tree by Joshua's bench. If'n it was cold they'd build a fire and squat close by it. To my way of thinking, that man wadn't fit for nothing. Tha's what I wanted to say to Joshua. But I knowed better.

More'n once I had to hold myself back from sneaking up on 'em and listening. What was they talking on so long? Wadn't none of my bizness—'cept Joshua was my husband. And it did sometimes seem like he'd rather spend his time wit' Chester. Least a time or two I wondered what kind of spell that man had put on my man.

"Oh, go to the devil!" Tha's what I said one day when I spotted him coming down the hill. Seemed awful shameful later, when I wished I hadn't said such, even if it was the truth.

Joshua wadn't here no more when it happened. When Chester got hisself killed. I never did learn no details. What I did do was set right here and beg that man's pardon. I hoped he could hear me.

While my head remembering all this I been working buttonholes on a plain housedress made outta cheap material. And the money I gets for making it? Next to nothing. Yet it do take quite a bit of time to stitch up so many buttonholes. So why is it I keep making these cheap dresses?

Next thing I be mumbling, "Uh-huh. Now I see."

Look like I maybe be owing Chester a bit of thanks. He was killed in 'a bad accident.' Word was they was a gun involved, but far as I know, didn't nobody ever learn just what did happen. Could be, it his ghost I need to thank. I sure be's much obliged, cause thinking on that woe done helped me see my way.

Right away, my mind's made up! From here on out, ain't gon make no more cheap housedresses. This 'un in my lap the last of 'em. I just has to put the word out: Hazeline Morrison gon be taking in *fine* sewing.

I like to have to work a bit to figure out how. Or might be, I decide on a li'l sump'n different from the pattern. Change the pattern. Maybe even make my own pattern, then give it a trial run, use some cloth I got on hand 'fore I cut into the good stuff.

Well now. If'n I was wearing boots I'd have to say I's trembling in 'em, but I just ain't gonna think I can't find the work. And if'n I has to survive on beans and cornbread through the winter...well, done it before, reckon I can do it again.

****

Next morning, I wake up remembering. And my plan still feels good.

The day moves along wit' my usual chores, till 'bout midafternoon I go set out under the shade tree for a spell. They be sump'n else I wanna think on, so I carry along my embroidery. Seem like it easier to think if'n yuh hands stays busy.

I soon settle into thinking on how tired I be of worrying 'bout the book at the store up near the gin mill. It the bigger store. Got more to choose from. So sometimes I walks the coupla miles up the Beatties Ford Road to get there, when I need sump'n like needles for my sewing machine.

I been wondering how much *the book* say I be owing. Might be I just thinking bad of the storekeeper and his keeping track—but if'n I don't get to see the book, how I s'posed to know?

It come over me quick—and in a wink I done decided. From here on out, Hazeline Morrison gon do her darnedest not to buy what she can't pay for on the spot.

Well, no—can't do it just yet. But it sure be worth shooting for. That good sewing work I be wanting can come my way—I jus' has to put the word out. And I can fill a few more Mason jars wit' beans and tomatoes, and peaches and corn and blackberries and whatever else I can get my hands on, and make up plenty of jams and jelly. And thanks to Sam and Henrietta, I won't be running out of salted fatback and a bit of cured ham.

Uh-huh. It do feel right. Keep my buying to what I got to buy—flour and salt and matches and such. And kerosene for the lamps. And a bit of feed for the chickens.

Good thing I so like cornbread and beans. Grew up on 'em and still like 'em. And a good bit of the year I has a chicken to fry on a Sunday, and a egg sunny-side-up to start my day. I bet even the Queen of England don't set herself down to a meal better'n what gets cooked up in this li'l house.

****

Seem of late like I been under a spell. My head too often spinning, going round and round with this heavy thinking. On and on it go, like one of them toys the chaps plays wit', it spinning round and round till it fall over.

Miz Robbins been on my mind. I see me in the world, see her too. I the one got reason to be lonely, yet it just plain as day how she lonely too. And one thing I knows for sure. I much rather be living my lonely 'stead of her lonely.

Seem lately like this work's been give to me same as if'n somebody lay it in front of me and say *Do it*...this figuring how things be. I see him and her t'gether more'n most, so I see how they get along. Some days I feels sorry for her, and some days I wanna give her a good shaking.

Then they Joleen. How she doing? Wish she'd spend a li'l more time wit' me. She don't seem like she was when she was a girl. Back then she was easy, living the day through right as rain. Now, look to me like she mostly tries to impress folks. She like to tell folks how much she pay for a dress. I thank heaven for Troy. He do seem to steady her some.

And this living by myself...never once did the thought ever cross my mind I'd end up on my own. A lonely life, that for sure. What I'd give to see him coming in the door and hanging his hat on the nail. He'd call out, "Hazeline, they anything to eat in this house?"

And now this dreadful thing tha's happened.

Wonder how Slim be faring? How the girl doing? I pictures her huddled on a bed hunched up like a baby, her face buried in the covers. I crave to know how she doing, but most part of my thinking goes to this young man. And far as I know, ain't nothing changed. Not a word said 'bout punishment for them boys.

A mournful tune start up in me. First the humming, then the words. And I wonder how can it be, this sad song jus' as pretty as a happy one.

I be on my walk home and feeling downright hopeless. Ain't no reason to think anything likely to change. A few steps later I gets to wondering how much gunpowder it'd take to make a explosion big enough...for what?

I gets to chuckling then. But what if? What if we was to stir up a racket? Wha's happening now be 'bout as bad as wha's already happened, cause ain't nothing happening. Ever'body just playing hush.

I get to the house and pour me the cup of coffee left in the pot. Way too warm for a fire, so a good thing I like cold coffee. I get settled in my rocker and set there looking at the cold fireplace—and first thing I know I be wishing I had me a snuffbox. The thought sets me to giggling. Ain't never dipped no snuff—and sure wouldn't wanna start now!

When I gets to bed I's tired out wit' all the thinking I's done. So I tells myself I just ain't gon think on it no more. All my thinking ain't doing no good, so I gon give it up. Reckon the only thing left be's praying, and that much I can do, so I squinch my eyes shut and speak to the Lord.

****

I come awake and see 'at daylight's already come. Seem like I hadn't been asleep long, and don't take long 'fore I can tell I still all outta sorts. Ain't wanting to do not one thing. Don't even want no breakfast. Feel like the whole lump of me's done soured.

Before long I leave the house and take the path up the hill. While laying there in the bed I was wishing I could pull the covers over my head and stay a'bed all the day long. I wanted to close up, way some flowers does when night's coming on.

I don't walk far 'fore my feet stop. I stand still as a statue—looking and looking and looking. The tall grasses 'longside the fence holding up they seeds, and the rain 'at come during the night left ever'thing soaking wet, so now ever' li'l seed holding a drop of water—and ever' last one of 'em just a'sparkling in the early sunlight.

Look like diamonds! And me? Why I got eyes to see! I come on the sight right when I was thinking how ever'thing be's looking so dark. And now this glory. Sure be a marvel! Just the looking's done turned sump'n in me. And tha's when I know. I gon keep on keeping on. And send up one more prayer for justice.

Chapter 14

———————— ⤜⋙⟐⋘⤛ ————————

The sun up least a hour or more and here I be, still abed, wondering what day it be. I come awake early, but drifted off again and had a dream. Was a big square space wit' thick rows of trees 'long the edges, and me standing way off in a corner. I was watching and looking—but couldn't move.

Wadn't nobody else in sight. Had the notion I was s'posed to move to the middle of that wide space—but couldn't do it. And they was a feeling in me like maybe they was somebody else—and that somebody close by.

When I woke I could remember that much. And no more. Yet the feeling in me was strong, the feeling that they *was* sump'n more. Seemed maybe like that big open space had sump'n to do wit' the girl. Wit' Delia.

I does keep a'thinking and a'thinking 'bout her, though I ain't never even laid eyes on her. So reckon I shouldn't be too surprised if'n she show up. In spirit, if nothing else. I hope she can find some peace. Can she forgive? Nah. She ain't old enough yet. That'll have to come later—if'n it come.

Well, well! That thought sure jerk me up—cause truth be, I ain't had it in me to forgive neither.

Saw in the paper 'bout somebody 'championing a cause.' That might be what set all this thinking a'going. Cause it sure look like Delia be needing a champion.

Needing somebody to speak out, do it for her sake—and for all us.

That big rooster sure making a racket wit' his cock-a-doodle-doo. Sound like, *Get up-up-up! Get up-up-up!* I hear him, but I pull the sheet over my head and squinch my eyes shut. And whisper a prayer.

Soon as I get outta bed I see how the light seem strange. Wonder what the weather gon do?

Fore long I saying, "Okay, Ole Dog, come on over. Got you a fried egg and fried bread too. Yuh gon like that, I sure. Fill your belly, and you be ready for another nap."

I got a pale pink suit to finish for Miz Tessie—a lightweight nubby material. Gonna make up pretty. Miz Tessie be a sister to Mister Robbins—and one fine woman. Always friendly. She got a husband what make plenty o' money, so's she can afford to buy readymade dresses, but she say I make dresses 'at fit her better.

Ever' time she come visiting she stay a few days and spend a good bit of her time reading magazines. Some wit' stories 'bout out West, and detective stories, but mostly love stories. She sometimes passes a few of the magazines my way. They be's pretty good entertainment, get my mind on sump'n 'sides worry.

'Bout the time I be sewing up the jacket seams, a storm breaks. Rain coming thick, but I don't much more'n go for the buckets to catch the leaks 'fore it's all over and done. I take myself out the back to stretch my legs and sniff the clean air. On the way out my ole red and white housedress catch on a rough spot on the door facing—and now they sump'n else in this house in need of mending. It a ole dress, but still doing its job.

I gets to grinning then. Reckon the same could be said for Hazeline Morrison. She worn, but she still going.

Ever'day, seem like, they sump'n new to see. I stand by the field near the burnt woods. The field stretch on and on, far as I can see almost, and they rows and rows and rows of young cotton plants. They be one shade of green, while the tall cedars 'long the fencerow so dark they almost black green. They a new woman at church and Joleen say she paints pictures. Wonder how she'd paint this one?

I head back to the house, figuring on what I gon do 'bout my soup. Somehow or 'nother, I got too much pepper in it. Can't take the pepper out...so, le's see. What can I do to fix it? Potatoes prob'ly do the trick, but it be way too hot to be stoking a fire in the cookstove. Maybe some stale bread?

I break some in the bottom of my bowl and ladle on the soup. I gon eat it even if it do taste peppery, but I got my fingers crossed.

My eye catches sight of my peaches. Coupla days back I canned a half-bushel. Put most of 'em in a sugar syrup cause they one of my special winter treats. But a few of 'em I pickled. Done that for Joleen's Troy. One of the first things I learned 'bout him was what foods he likes, so I always does give him a few jars of pickled peaches at Christmas—cause that daughter of mine, she ain't gon do no canning! She a *modern* young woman.

Soon as the jars was out of the hot water I got away from the hot stove, went and settled under the shade tree wit' the Charlotte News. Right away a picture caught my eye. Picture of the chain gang boss. Paper say they been some question 'bout how he be doing his job, say he been accused of mistreating some of the inmates in his care. But the write-up didn't make it sound like he'd be getting punished.

I laid the paper aside. Didn't wanna see that man's face. He the one keeps men in shackles. Done heard too many stories too close to home 'bout his evil ways.

Most of the time the newspaper news seem far away, don't much concern me. I like reading it cause I always find sump'n interesting, but lately seem like the paper don't have nothing but bad news—and we got more'n a plenty of that right here. Got three boys getting away wit' what they done.

Right then a bluebird come flying by. Took me back to one of my earliest and happiest mem'ries. I picked up the tune.

> *Here little bluebird*
> *Through my winduh*
> *Oh, Johnny, I'm tired.*

A bunch of us chirren they was, playing in Grandmama's yard. We joined hands and wound round like a rope—round the one 'at was 'it.' That'un held his arms out and the rest of us moved under one arm and then the other.

Said the little patty man
Pat him on the shoulder
Oh, Johnny, I'm tired.

One patted on the shoulder was 'it' next go-round. Played that game many a time while the grown-ups was setting in the shade and gabbing.

I'd just started back to the house when the wind come in a gust and I took off running, after a piece of the paper it'd picked up, but right quick the paper was awready on the other side of the clearing. I got almost to it and passed right through a spider web. And it brung on a mem'ry. It happened at Grandmama's too, when a bunch of us was playing there in the yard. We was running and chasing and I fell and tore my leg. Don't remember what I fell on, but was a pretty deep gash. Grandmama covered it over wit' a spider web and tole me to keep still, let the web make the bleeding stop.

I bent over to grab that blowed-away paper and spied a shape up on the hill by the edge of the woods. Just wit' the way the shape move I could tell who it be. Speak of the devil! Leroy Patterson. Don't want nothing to do with Leroy. He be's plumb filled up wit' hate. Likes to tell how he despise all white folk. I reckon if'n ever'body was like Leroy we'd all be dead by now, done killed each other off.

Way awful ugly, he be. A good case for the ole saying 'at we end up looking like what we be.

When I come back in the house I checked the jar lids. Looked like the lid on ever' jar had done snapped tight shut. The jars sealed, so that fruit gon keep way on into next year. Seem like magic!

The stale bread did the trick, fixed my soup right up. Wish I could find such a easy fix for a few other things.

****

Another week go by and Slim and Delia still on my mind. That bit I see'd in the paper, 'bout somebody championing some cause or other, has sure stuck fast in my head. I does wonder...cause it do seem like sump'n in me's wanting me to step up and be that girl's champion.

This ain't the first time that notion's passed through. I been working hard to ignore it. I tell it to go on—leave me be! Ain't never done such a thing nor even thought of doing such—and wouldn't know where to start.

Hard work often a cure for wha's ailing you, so last few days I been working up a storm. Even took my ole broom in hand and swept the whole clearing, then took hold of the sling and cut back all the tall grass round the edges.

I like working a tough job, 'cept for how I tend to keep going till I way beyond *wore out*. Uh-huh, sure was tired out, so I went over and set on Joshua's bench. After a bit I started in to singing: *Gonna lay down my burden, Lord, down by the riverside, down by the riverside, down by the riverside....*

When day's end finally did come, I was glad of it. Washed myself a bit and slipped on my batiste nightgown and crawled in the bed. First thing, I stretched out my back and legs, all the way down to my feet, and just when I got stretched out, my head got to showing me one of my favorite stories. The prophet Samuel.

A voice called to him—and him just a chile. Bible say, was God calling him.

And Samuel? Why that li'l fella say right out, "Here am I."

Now a voice been calling me, seem like. And I still waiting to see what I gon answer.

****

Next day come and I set in again. Even clean the outhouse. Spiders had set up house, so was past time for a good cleaning. I put some lime and ash in the pit too, though I didn't feel like doing not one thing.

Trudged up the hill to get water, poured it on the sweet potato slips I'd set in the ground. Was at the clothesline taking in the few things I'd washed that morning and just slipping a clothespin in my apron pocket—when I decided. Time to set myself down and think.

And now it midafternoon. So out I come, to set under the shade tree. Sure seem strange setting here empty-handed. No beans to string, no peaches to peel.

Right off I gets to chuckling. Say out loud, "Okay, I be's ready"—like maybe some idea just gon fly right my way. I look up 'cross the rise of the land behind the house. Anybody looking my way would think I same as usual. But that ain't one bit so.

Deep in my soul, seem like, they be's a question. And it just keep coming round.

Is they anything Hazeline Morrison can do? If'n so, wish it'd pop right up in front of me—like a jack in the box. I gets to chuckling then—cause if'n it did, it'd most likely scare the daylights outta me.

After some while, I give up. Heave a sigh, head back inside. Got some darning I maybe can finish 'fore dark.

****

The days keep a'passing. End of the first week in June, but hardly seem like it oughta be. Been chuckling to myself 'bout my visitor. Wednesday it was. Tall, lanky fella. Got a long neck, and a adam's apple 'at bob like a turkey gobbler's.

There he come, stepping down the hill. All my pot plants was needing water, so I was dipping water out the rain barrel. Kept my eye on him, my curiosity bigger by the minute.

Pokey. Tha's what folks call him. Don't know his real name. When he got to the edge of the clearing, I stood and waited. I'd just swept the yard a bit.

He so thin his overalls just hang on him. He call out, "Hazeline! How you doin' this mornin'?"

I wait till he get a bit closer and say, "Doing alright, Pokey. Got a early start, soon gon be through wit' what I has to do." And soon's I said it, wished I hadn't. Had left myself wide open.

He had a cigarette going and started in talking 'bout the weather. I dipped a jar in the water bucket and begun pouring it on the penny plants I sowed in cans. The cans getting a bit rusty now, but that don't hurt nothing. And the blossoms pink and white. I'd saved the seed from ones I growed last year—and even built a cold frame so's I could get a early start with the planting. Hadn't never hammered together a cold frame, but looked like it was time to see if'n I could, cause the old one had rotted.

Pokey talked and talked. I didn't need to say much, just a 'Uh-huh' or 'Is that so?' He finished his smoke and ground it out under his boot. What he done then was 'bout more'n I could b'lieve!

That fool took a step my way—and offered to help! By then I was pulling off old blossoms, so I said I was 'bout done, thank you anyway.

He kept standing there wit' his thumbs in his overalls bib. I was doing my best to ignore him, and him talking on and on. And tha's when the mystery begun coming clear.

Strange, it was, him coming to call. But wadn't no sign he'd been drinking. I got to my feet and stood straight, careful to keep some distance 'tween us, him still talking on and on a like a monkey. I turned down his offer to help and made sure I kept my distance—careful not to warm to him one bit.

He kept talking, hands in his pockets, then pulled a pipe out and begun filling it wit' tobacco.

I'd been figuring hard. How to get rid of the fool. And then sump'n strange got hold of me. Uh-huh. The strangest part of all. What I done. Had to hold my hand back—it wanting to reach up—and pat my hair in place!

And there stood that turkey, his feet planted, still gabbing on and on. He rocked back on his heels and down again, and finally got round to why he'd come. His voice went low and soft. "Figured I'd come by and check on yuh. Ain't good for a woman to be on her own."

So I played pretend. Bent over a plant, pretending I'd see'd some other sprucing it needed. I pulled off a few blossoms still pretty as good be—wanting to look like I was busy and paying him no mind.

And some li'l bit after that, that fool did decide to be on his way. I stood out of sight, and watched. Soon as his straw hat disappeared over the hill, I set my hands on my hips and and had a fine good time, standing there a'chuckling. Why, that bony ole man had come a'courting! But the woman he come to see? Why, she wadn't one bit interested.

He did say one thing, though, 'at stayed wit' me. They was sump'n I'd said, I reckon. And he come back wit', "Sho you do—you that kinda woman."

So ever li'l while now I be thinking on it. What kinda woman I be, and what kind I wanna be. Or maybe, should be.

Chapter 15

————————⤖≋⬥≋⬥≋≪————————

This day come and go real quick. Tuesday, my own washday. Like a ice chip, seem like. That how quick the day melted away. Seem like time pass extra quick sometimes, and other times painful slow.

Got a early start. Hauled buckets of water in my wagon and figured on washing only what I most needed, but ended up filling the whole clothesline.

Truth be, I was trying best I could to stop this head of mine from bumping around. I got to talking out loud, saying whatever come to mind—talking to the only other'un round here wit' ears.

"What yuh think, Ole Dog? Your day bound to be easier'n mine—cause you never has to give a thought to time nor worries neither." I kept going, telling him I'd be done by now if'n I hadn't decided to plumb empty the dirty clothesbasket and wash out a ole blanket too. And all the day long, the trouble on my mind. Happened in May, and the more time pass the worse it gets. Sump'n in me done rared up and won't let me rest.

I started in to wondering one more time how come white folk want to make laws to keep Negroes down. Jim Crow laws, they call 'em. Next thing yuh know they prob'ly put up a sign telling us we can't breathe the same air. Say, 'Now you colored folk, you make sure you breathe this air over here—we not gon have you breathing our air.'

Greed. Uh-huh, that be the root of it all. Tha's why our people was brung here—cause rich white folk wanted workers they wouldn't have to pay. And now here come these boys. Ever since they been born they been soaking up this notion 'at folk wit' black skin ain't so good as folk wit' white skin.

Long as white folks making the laws, ain't much chance things gon get any better. Any fool can see that much.

All this thinking's got me real low. Vexation of spirit. Tha's what the Bible call it. Read it last evening.

I take the last of the clothes from the line and soon as I step inside a mem'ry show up. Why it come I don't know, but it jus' the one to cheer me up. Maybe twenty year ago...and me just coming awake. Was first thing my ears hear'd that fine morning. "Thank yuh, Lord, for this woman by my side."

I opened my eyes and there he was, propped on his elbow wit' that big grin. Wit' this sort'a mem'ry, how I not gon be happy? Ain't no white nobody nowhere can steal it from me.

While I was folding clothes I remembered something else. Miz Tessie said it. She say it my fate. Say for some reason I needing to spend some part of life on my own. I didn't believe a word of it, but I didn't let on.

****

Late in the day Saturday, and I got just one thing on my mind. Get my water heated so I can get my bath done. Won't be long now till time for the show, a high spot of my week. Most of the time I glad for the quiet, but ever since

Joshua got this radio I look forward to the Amos 'n' Andy show. Yuh can't listen to that show wit'out going "Heh-heh-heh!" Already checked the battery, to make sure it good.

I put the latch on the doors, push back the chairs in the front room, set the big galvanized tub down and pour in a few pots of boiling water, then get some cold water from the bucket—not too much, till it just right. And there it be, my bathwater.

All mine. Not like when I was a girl and a coupla my sisters got to get in first. Water was dirty by the time I got my turn, but Mama had her rule. The eldest went first, then the next born girl and the next. Then the biggest boys filled the tub wit' clean water and the boys took they turns.

I be's plenty dirty, cause the last few days has been awful hot. The heat don't keep me from getting my work done though. I picked a bunch of garden stuff for Miss Kathleen to sell at the county market. She the youngest in the Robbins family, married now and living out near the highway. For the picking I get a li'l money, depending on how much she sell—and she do seem to be pretty fair.

I lather up my washrag and right away wish my usual bath-time wish. If'n I was one could work magic, I'd shrink my body down so's I could sink all of me down in this tub. Sure would be fine, just laze in the tub till the water goes cold.

How I do love summertime! Me and Joshua was married in summer.

One night not long after we was married he got to teasing me at the supper table. Sopped his gravy wit' a biscuit, and wit' his other hand reached over and patted me on the arm. He say, "Hazeline, it a shame you not one of them high-powered lawyers. Or a politician. You could figure ever'thing out and make us a pile of money." Then he slap his knee and throw back his head and cackle.

Another time he say, "Hazeline, why can't yuh just do it and not think on it so?"

For the next li'l bit anyway, I can quit my thinking, cause I soon be ready to turn on that radio. But I does wonder, in time to come, how this summer gon look. Reckon that depend. It ain't over yet, so can't be judged yet. I's hoping and praying that 'fore it's done, we gon see somebody admitting to doing wrong.

Fore long there I be, at the kitchen table—turning the knob. Wonder how many folk gon be listening to Amos and Andy this Saturday evening? If'n things go like I s'pect, I gon be laughing out loud, and carrying that happy feeling wit' me for some good while.

****

Tuesday morning fairly early, Ole Dog got to barking and carrying on. I hurried to the door and found Ezra Dellinger. He'd done walked all the way over here carrying a towsack. His hound dogs had followed him. He set the sack down on the edge of the porch and pulled off his old felt hat and bent his head to his sleeve to wipe the sweat from his face.

I was noting the big patches on the knees of his bib overalls. He bent over and pulled the sack open. Green green green—tha's all I see'd!

He say, "Hazeline, you know how that wife of mine plants way more'n two or three fam'lies need. Keeps me busy trying to give the stuff away—when I aready tired out wit' chopping cotton."

I laughed wit' him and said, "Well, I sure glad you headed this way wit' this giveaway. I be's much obliged." That many fresh-picked cucumbers meant a lot of pickles would soon be filling some quart jars.

Ezra took off his hat and fanned his face. "Well, I figure if yuh can't use 'em all, yuh can feed 'em to yuh garden. Just dig a trench and bury 'em. 'Fore yuh know it, your garden gets to growing like the Garden of Eden, and yuh plant a row of beans and they ready and on yuh plate almost fore yuh can get yuh cornbread baked!" We both laughed big and I hurried to bring him a dipperful of water and ask him 'bout his fam'ly.

He grinned and started in telling how his wife grumbled on and on this morning 'fore she finally took herself off to the creek to do her laundry. Said she started the day complaining, saying all she wanted was to go back to bed, cause the whole houseful has been getting too li'l sleep since they's had to take in one of the gran'chirren. The little one has bad dreams and gets to yelling loud, so ever'body comes wide awake. I tole him the remedy I learned long ago. Take some sage and strew it on the floor and in the bed too. Grandmama called it 'the ghost medicine.'

He'd already started cross the yard when I remembered and called him back. Asked him to get word to Slim, if'n he can—tell him to come by his first chance. I been worrying 'bout that young man a right smart. What in the world would happen if'n he was to go 'gainst them white boys?

I come on in then. Wanting to get started right away. Just so happen I have on hand a good supply of vinegar and sugar and salt, so I pull out the crock and some jars. It occur to me then. Ezra's played angel, bringing my way just what I was needing. Work 'at has to be done right away. Now I won't be tempted to set around and fret.

First thing, go to the well and haul a good supply of water, and go again after while to get some more. If'n I had ice I could make bread n' butter pickles, but the iceman ain't coming no time soon, so I gon use the littlest cucumbers and leave 'em whole. Need enough water to wash up ever'thing and keep the jars hot till the lids seal.

On the way up the hill I watch some of the neighbor chirren playing ball. Reckon that what get the mem'ry going, cause soon's I start making the brine for my pickles I start seeing the past.

Joshua was sure excited. Him and Sam and some of the others was going to Raleigh, to a championship baseball game. The National Colored League. They knowed one of the players.

Joshua sat on the side of the bed and laced up his boots. "Our team win, Hazeline, I gon bring yuh back a present. Our team lose? Well, I tell yuh what, I still gon bring yuh a present!"

And he prob'ly did. I don't r'member. What I r'member be how dif'rent my man was when he come home. Low as I ever did see him. He come dragging hisself in the house and plopped down in his chair by the fire. I knowed better'n to set in asking questions. Did try to get him to eat some supper but he said he wadn't hungry.

Joleen was away that night. I busied myself by the light of the lantern wit' my needle and thread, just to be doing sump'n.

He set there a long time, slouched in the chair, his legs stretched out. Then he set wit' his elbows on his knees, his head in his hands. The silence growed louder and louder. I started a low hum. Wadn't uncommon for me to hum while I worked, but he didn't seem to know I was anywhere near.

Just 'fore it got dark, he got up and went out the backdoor. Wadn't gone long. Had gone out to relieve hisself, I figured. I wondered if'n he'd stopped to speak to the dog we had then, or the old sow in the pen.

When he come back and clicked the latch shut, I looked up, hoping to catch his eye. I could see the stiffness in his body and opened my mouth, but words didn't come, so I closed it. Woulda been like talking to a tree—a tree pushed this way and that in a storm. His eyes strayed round the room like as if the place looked strange.

I wished I could say, *Where's that present yuh brung me?* He hadn't even tole me who won the game. My hand went to my mouth to keep from crying out.

He tramped 'cross the floor and picked up the bat standing in the corner. Held it in his hands 'bout waist high, turning it, like he was studying it close. He give a big sigh and say, "Just a game. Just a game."

My breath eased. I hadn't knowed I was holding it.

My whole life had done lined up in my head. Hazelines parading on by. Later on, when I thought 'bout the strangeness of it, I figured that somewhere down in me I'd been scared life had took a turn. Might not ever be the same. So all the different mes had stood up at attention, getting ready to see that next turn. There was the chile I was long ago, and the growing-up-fast girl I had to be when Mama was dying—and all the rest. Maybe they was wanting to help me, trying to tell me I should be brave.

Joshua rubbed a hand up and down the bat then give his head a shake. I was afraid he was gon start in to weeping. Should I go to him? Should I wait? Didn't seem like he knowed I was watching. His shoulders slumped, his head dropped. He muttered, "Curse 'em all!"

I got to my feet and stepped toward him, still not sure if'n I should touch him or not. When I laid my hand on his arm he looked up and his eyes was bright wit' tears. I moved close and folded him in my arms. He blowed out a bunch of air and let me hold him.

Once he begun talking the words spewed out and I knowed we wouldn't get much sleep that night. We'd knowed other nights like it. Nights when they's work to be done in the dark, a fitting time for bemoaning injustice. Again.

The man that let Joshua and the others stay overnight invited some of the other ball players over. They talked 'bout they dreams of joining the big leagues. But they knowed it wadn't no more'n talk. No matter how good they played, wadn't not one chance those dreams'd come true. Cause, to play big league ball, yuh has to have white skin.

My man spent most of that night reliving his heartaches. And more'n once he got up and paced the floor. If'n he'd been a violent man...well, I don't know what woulda happened.

I finish packing the pickles in the jars and start putting on the lids, but no more'n get started 'fore I drop my hands to my sides. Heck!—ain't these lids I be's mad at!

I breathe in deep, blow out air, and says real quiet, "Joshua, my sweet—sure wish I could tell yuh things be's dif'rent now."

****

Early in the day Saturday, Joleen and Troy come by and stay a few minutes. That 'bout long as they ever stay. She set and painted her fingernails. Say she be glad to paint mine.

"Nah," I say, "these be working hands. I don't aim to keep 'em shiny, just tries to keep 'em clean."

I was s'posed to be going over to help Henrietta ready things for the fish fry and Sam s'posed to pick me up. He wadn't coming till a good bit later and me just busting to tell Henrietta 'bout all tha's been happening.

As it turned out, Troy say he glad to take me—and surprise surprise!—that girl o' mine went along wit' the plan. I did wonder what woulda happened if'n she argued 'wit him. Would Troy've give in to her? Could he vote her down? Sorta wish I'd got to see how that woulda played out. If'n I was a betting woman, I'd'a put my bet on Joleen. Look like most o' the time she gets her way.

I left a note for Sam, but soon as I got here I spotted him, busy in the backyard readying things for the crowd. Henrietta seemed glad to see me, like she usually do. They my favorites in Joshua's fam'ly.

Henrietta use my showing up for excuse. Say she ready to set down and rest a spell. She pour some lemonade and we carry it out on the front porch. They got a good-size house, and it painted white, wit' a porch 'at reach all way 'cross the front.

She take a hanky out her dress pocket and mop sweat off her face. She be's settled on the edge of the chair, so's to let the air stir 'round her. We cool our faces wit' paper fans 'at show pictures of Bible stories. The funeral homes gives 'em away.

She turn sideways to get the hanky in her pocket and I notice again what a li'l nose she have. She ain't what yuh'd call pretty, but she sure be pretty in how she act. Almost always in a good humor. Big round brown eyes, and now she turn 'em my way. "Reckon yuh heard 'bout Eli?"

"Hunh-uh," I say, raising my eyebrows.

"Twice now, we's heard tales of Eli Cooke and some of his drinking buddies showing up where they ain't invited and stirring up a ruckus. They come late—when they drunk as skunks." She give a sigh and say almost like saying it to herself, "Don't know why hard-working folk has to put up wit' such *no count*."

She talk on. Been a while since I's see'd her so riled. But I be hoping too—hoping the whole day and evening gon move along wit'out a hitch—and not one sign of Eli and his friends.

We sip our lemonade, and I say, "Tell yuh what—you hunt up some rope and have it ready, and if'n Eli show up, I'll help yuh catch him and we'll tie him up in that rope! That'll slow him down!"

We has us a good laugh then and soon thereafter get busy. Late afternoon, folks start showing up, and 'fore long the young'uns get a ballgame going. By sundown, only complaint I'd heard was how the fish and hushpuppies was so good 'at some was saying they felt like a stuffed turkey.

They was one time just after we'd finished eating when somebody mentioned Joe Lewis, and others joined in, wondering how he been faring since he become the boxing champion of the world. It was then my heart went to grieving, same as it done day of the fight. A whole bunch of us gathered 'round Sam and Henrietta's big radio, ever'body jolly and happy, but seemed to me like it just wadn't fair. Joshua ought to've been there, yelling with the rest, cause one of ours had done won the championship.

Just 'bout the time it got good dark, three men wit' guitars and some kinda horn showed up. I don't know if'n they was invited or not, but ever'body seemed glad to see 'em. The crowd was pretty good size and all seats filled, even the upturned buckets, so Sam and a coupla others took off to the woodpile and soon come rolling some big chunks of oak, the firewood 'at hadn't been split yet.

Seats for the music folk. They settled in and chimed up. Ain't many things better'n settin' and listenin' to music played right close by.

Like usual, I helped Henrietta clear up. Put the leftovers in the new 'lectric icebox. The 'lectric lines awready run down here, closer to town, so I wadn't one bit surprised when Sam went out and bought one. He say it ain't his yet, cause he be buying it on time.

The icebox at home just a wooden box. The ice man set a big block of ice down in it and wrap it good so's it don't melt quick. When I wanting some ice I take the icepick to the block and chip some off. Comes in handy for keeping milk and butter, so's I don't have to take 'em all the way to the spring—or do without.

But this icebox they got? It *make* ice. All you gotta do be fill the trays, and that water turns to ice. Like magic. While I was putting the leftovers away, I thought 'bout what Henrietta said 'bout Eli. Brung to mind what I read in the paper this week.

The gist of it clear enough. 'Bout sump'n called opium. Paper say it do what liquor do, but harder'n liquor to quit once you try it, so then yuh end up a trouble to other folk. Eli like that. A bother. He done been too long on the liquor, maybe don't know right from wrong, can't tell the difference.

Make me think of mistletoe. It can't live on its own, got to hook itself to a tree. Eli's mama makes sure his brothers and sisters pitch in so he don't starve to death.

'Cept for one. He flat out refused—say Eli should just lay down and die if he can't look after hisself.

The paper say China execute the ones what can't quit the opium. Whoever wrote the piece made fun of the Chinese. But I wondered. Made some sense, seemed to me, to make the punishment for not carrying your own weight least big enough 'at folks'd maybe think twice 'bout what they do.

But then I thought 'bout what the Lord say, 'bout the li'l ones. I always has thought he wadn't talking 'bout chirren. He mean the li'l ones—no matter how old they be. He mean folk like Eli, ones needing help. And who they be to help but the rest of us?

Chapter 16

I stay the night at Sam and Henrietta's. When sleep don't come right off, I start in to remembering our fam'ly witch. All the time I was growing up I heard passed-down stories from long ago. Our people used to b'lieve the spirits of babies lived in trees, and used to pray to the ancestors— even left sump'n out for the ancestors to eat. We was good at casting spells too, and working a li'l magic.

In our fam'ly, was Grandmama's eldest sister worked the magic. Had her a backroom full of boxes and jars, stuffed wit' herbs and bark and such. I never wanted to know what was in that backroom, cause I heard some of the other chirren say Aunt Susie was a witch.

She bent over the fire and said some strange mumbled words then throwed things in the fire to make it smoke. Then raised her eyes to the sky and sang out some strange kind of tune.

Some of the chirren spied on her, but I kept my distance. The ones 'at watched told tales. Said the air shivered when she spoke. Next day she'd be back to ord'nary, just Grandmama's sister, bringing in a armload of roasting ears or scalding a chicken and getting one of the girls to help her pluck it. I wouldn't go nowhere near her.

When I was 'bout fifteen, word spread 'at a young man on a farm some few miles away had died cause Aunt Susie worked one of her spells. Don't have no idea whether what was said was true or not.

I like staying over in this house cause I can feel the welcome. In this room they a iron cot, where I be stretched out, and a big bed with three grandkids, two at the top, one at the bottom. They's finally asleep, thank goodness.

Moonlight's shining. I lay here looking up at the boards of the ceiling, wishing I hadn't never thought of trying to do sump'n to help—well, not just the girl, but all us. Time just keep going by, and ain't been no good idea pop up yet.

If'n I knowed Aunt Susie's magic, I might least scare them white boys, make 'em think twice. Lord knows, sump'n needing to be done. One of the young'uns over at the Robbins house the other week spread out a jigsaw puzzle.

Reckon tha's what I be doing. Working at a puzzle. Difference be, I got to find the pieces 'fore I can put 'em together.

****

Ain't like me, this ain't. But reckon it time to snap outta my usual, cause somebody I cares about be's hurting.

The day moved on like usual till on over in the afternoon Miz Robbins say she can bring in the last of the clothes, and tell me to go on. So I don't tarry. I get started home and right away that picture come again.

I'd already see'd it more'n once. They a bunch of us, traveling which-ever-way we can. In a buggy, a wagon, a car or truck. We make our way down the Beatties Ford

Road 'bout fifteen mile or so, all the way to the courthouse. Cause tha's where the sheriff be.

We ain't overly scared as we ride, cause we going t'gether. We get to the sheriff's office and I says to him, "Thank yuh for the chance to speak to yuh." Then I clutch my handbag tight and keep talking, tell the sheriff wha's happened. "Sir, they a young man out our way, and him like a son to me. Ain't got no son of my own cause I lost mine when he was born."

I know tha's just a made-up picture, cause I wouldn't be saying all that—and the sheriff wouldn't set there and listen neither. And why would I be the one talking?

By the time I's walked far as the gate, I be shaking my head and saying, "Tsk tsk—all this just daydreaming foolishness!"

But idn't it the right thing to do—go to the law? Wouldn't the sheriff see us if'n all of us was to go?

Would be easier to get there if'n we had help from somebody wit' money, but only body I know what got money be awful miserly. Ole man Richey. They say he been stashing money away all his life long. For many a year he drove a ice house wagon and after that a ice house truck. Only other bodies what might have more'n a few dollars put back is white, and I can't even picture asking any help in that direction.

I walk on, humming a few bars of 'Amazing Grace'—and pretty soon, a idea settle in. Awright then. So what I can do be the one thing I can think to do—the one thing what seem like it might do some good.

I gets to the crest of the hill and spot my li'l house. Stop there, stand still. Promise myself I gon do it. Start at the first house out near the highway, work my way back this way.

At one or two places, won't be no need to stop, cause ain't nobody there tha's able nor cares. Yep, if'n all goes well, by this time tomorrow I gon get word to the coloreds on this farm and the ones close by. Then they know somebody else to tell.

What I needing now's for time to move quick—so's I don't back out. I says to myself, "Whatever happen, yuh gonna end up right back at this spot, and it'll all be over and done. Only thing left now, be wait and see."

I hadn't no more'n said it till somebody hailed me from behind. One of the neighbors. I was sure glad she was a ways behind. Don't know what I'd'a said if'n she'd asked why I was talking to myself.

I be almost home when I gets to chuckling—and glad to have sump'n to laugh about. Happened this morning when I was at the washpot. I'd stepped in the kitchen to get some bluing and heard Miz Robbins in the front room.

"Luther!" she cry out. "Don't you come near me with that thing!"

She went to shrieking like she was dying. I wadn't sure what was going on. She be the shrieking kind, so probably not much, but I stayed right where I was and listened close.

She cry out again. "You gonna be the death of me!" He was cackling and carrying on, so I knowed he was up to one of his tricks. I was just about to head out the kitchen door but drawed myself back when he come onto the backporch from the dining room. He was chuckling to hisself and sounded 'bout as merry as I's ever heard him. They was a black snake curled round his arm.

Reckon it ain't funny. But I chuckle anyway. Good to have sump'n to think on 'sides all this other in my head.

****

Don't know what made me think of this. Ain't it the farthest thing from my nature? Ain't never done nothing like it. Ain't wanted to. Now Joshua, he'd be the first one to step right up and say, "Listen to me! They sump'n going on! We can't just set back and do nothing!"

Then the body he speaking to object and Joshua go right on, speaking his mind, looking the other'n in the eye. "Anybody that can set back and do nothing, why that fella ain't got no heart—or no courage, one or t'other."

Way on over in the night now and so far I ain't slept a wink. O Lordy Lordy—Lord help me! I got to do it, I gon do it. Tomorrow. Either do it, or face many a sleepless night. A voice start up. What yuh think gon happen? You say your piece and ever'body line up and listen? Maybe you oughta start wit' Brother Jenkins—see what he think.

Now this a voice I can talk to. It be speaking in my head, but I ain't gon have it. Quickest way to give up be ask Brother Jenkins what I oughta do. That man good at standing up in church in his ole gray suit and reading the scripture, but I ain't 'bout to listen to much more'n that from him. He got a pleasant reading voice, and sound like he b'lieve what he reading. But ever'body knows he ain't so good to his wife. Nah, I wouldn't go to him for nothing.

My hands take hold of the sides of my head. I got to get some rest—cause I gon do this thing tomorrow.

****

Knock on a door, then what I say? Ain't got no idea—but I on my way.

A good piece to the first house. While I walk a mem'ry come and it a surprise. Was Joleen, trying to keep up wit' the big girls. She wadn't more'n five or so. I stood and watched her—little legs a'flyin, but the big girls was way out ahead of her. She come back to the house crying.

Ain't hard to figure why this pertic'lar memory come along now. But it ain't girls I be chasing. I got to go after the big boys. Tha's how I see 'em in my head—cause all the law people be's men, and all of 'em white.

If'n I was a girl I'd know better'n to go running to 'em. But look like now I done moved on into some other kind of sense.

A strange thought come then. Uh-huh, just plain strange. This change tha's come over me be cause of some girl I ain't never even laid eyes on. But I do know what to do when I gets to where I be going. Know just the thing. The trick gon be to act like Ruby. That woman ain't never at a loss for words.

****

The black birds rouse me. I been setting here in a stupor. I come out in the shade and brung my work along. Inside not the place to be on a hot afternoon. Was the crows. They started cawing and I come to. My work was laying in my lap and me all in a muddle.

Hazeline

Played the fool—tha's what I done. Plowing on ahead, like I knowed what I was doing. Like I the one could make ever'thing right. But look like all I done was poke a stick in a hornet's nest.

I knowed why I was willing to go knocking on doors. Since Slim first come here with his sad news, it has hurt me to see him hurt. Thing of it be, I's always been one to watch what happen, maybe think on it some, but no more'n that.

They was one big surprise. Once I got to knocking on doors, I wadn't even scared. This a small community. Most ever'body walk to school and church, and ever'body'd heard 'bout what happened.

So why wadn't ever'body upset? Why come the white folk wadn't speaking out? Least in public, they was keeping they mouths shut—like as if to say, 'Don't talk about it and they ain't no problem.'

I made it round to most of the little houses my feet could carry me to. More'n once I reminded myself, "Don't count your chickens 'fore they hatch."

Some places, one I needed to talk to wadn't home. And a coupla times I got tole right quick how I best forget trying to rile folks up. Even Ezra Dellinger's wife say she wouldn't want me to mention it to him, cause she didn't think what I had in mind could help none, all it'd do was stir up trouble.

I aready knowed, no matter what I done, wouldn't amount to more'n striking a blow or two at a big strong oak. How yuh gon knock off its feet wha's been standing so long the roots running way deep?

One visit I keep r'membering. Bud Wilson fam'ly. He a bigshot—least he think so. He wadn't home and I was glad of it. His missus, Frances, she open the door and we say our greetings and I go in. I didn't want to get settled in, wanted to say what I come for and get on my way.

"Set down," she say. She a puny little woman but almost tall as me. Had on a fancy dress, so I figured she was getting ready to go out, but she didn't seem in no hurry. Four chirren was clinging close 'bout her knees and they sure wadn't dressed up—was dirty and ragged. Why didn't she tell 'em to stay away, not soil her good dress?

I set down in a dirty ole raggedy chair. She set on the edge of a straight chair and I noticed her eyes. They looked funny.

But I said why I'd come. "Guess you heard 'bout what happened some weeks back, to that girl some white boys took down in the woods?"

Frances nodded her head but still she didn't seem right. Did this woman even know what I was saying? I went on anyway, tole her the rest, and mentioned my fears for Slim and the way things might go—"if'n we don't speak up."

Frances's eyes got bigger and bigger and her hands started working, her fingers twisting and pulling like they was fighting. She brung to mind a rabbit I saw once, caught in a trap. Still living, but doomed.

She blurted out, "Time I was getting supper started." She bobbed her head and said it again. "Time I was getting supper started." Her big round eyes like to bore holes in me.

When I got out the screen door I stood there a instant, shocked at how quick she turned me out. I heard a scratching behind me and took it to be her latching the screen. She needn't'a worried, I wadn't 'bout to go back through that door. I heard the whimpering of the chirren and got my feet to working and set off.

For a minute then I come close to turning round and heading home. But I knowed that Frances Wilson's troubles, whatever they might be, wadn't no reason to call a halt to my mission—cause fact was I did feel like I'd set out on a mission.

Reckon tha's why I didn't feel scared. Like that young woman I r'member reading 'bout in a schoolbook. Joan of Arc, she was called. Lived way, way back—long time ago. That girl said a angel tole her to lead a army—said tha's why she done it!

I had my reasons too and my mind made up.

What I didn't wanna think on was how that young woman died. Wouldn't do, right in the middle of my mission, to let myself get to thinking on that. Even when I was reading her story, I wondered where that angel had got to when the townfolk set Joan on fire. The book had a li'l drawing. It showed the people gathered round to watch her in the flames, like it was some circus show.

The puzzle 'bout Frances Wilson didn't get cleared up till I had a chance to talk to Henrietta. Was two things going on when I knocked on Frances's door. She lonely, and for a woman to come calling—well, tha's okay. But once I started telling her why I come, fear got the best of her. That good-for-nothing husband of hers wouldn't have his wife even listening to talk 'bout what I had in mind. All his wife s'posed to think on be his needs, what he want, and she sure better have herself dolled up and ready when he hit the door. That explain why she had on her good dress. I just hope she learns how to keep from filling the house to overflowing wit' babies.

That mem'ry 'bout Joan of Arc. It made me look at myself. I hadn't heard no voice from above. But I knowed it a fine thing what Jesus said, to do unto others as you'd have them do unto you.

Chapter 17

I think 'bout not going to church. Been a rough week. If'n yuh a pious kind of person yuh might want specially to take yourself off to church when the week yuh just lived been awful hard to bear up under. But I rather go listen to the water running. 'Cept this time of year they not much water to run.

Still, it do be quiet down there. And nobody catching my eye.

Ever'body round know by now. Saying, 'That Hazeline! Wonder what come over her? Too bad Joshua ain't here to take her in hand.'"

I put off getting dressed. Keep moseying round the house. Straightening this, stowing that. Undecided, I be, like a chile has to choose 'tween a whupping wit' a belt or a whupping wit' a switch.

But, we all us got to face up to consequences. And ain't that the truth!

'Consequence' was a word our Aunt Beulah used to say right often. She was Mama's sister 'at took the most interest in us after we lost Mama. Half the time that woman opened her mouth she was talking 'bout consequences of one sort or other.

I start to take the ashes outta the cookstove. *What yuh doing, Hazeline?!* That ain't sump'n for a Sunday morning. Would need another bath if'n I done that chore, so why my hand reaching for the ash pan? Cause I ain't one bit wanting to face the fire in the faces bound to turn my way.

Even my own mind throwed up doubt. More'n once I wondered if'n what I planned on doing would end up wit all us outta the frying pan and into the fire.

I stand straight and blow out air and says, "Well, doggone it! I done what I could!"

Wit' my next breath I stand straight and tall and tell myself to quit all this thinking—just shoo it away! Then I begins to get myself dressed. And as it happen, I make it to the church just at the right time—late enough, and not too late.

The congregation be's singing. Making a joyful noise. The sound of it so fine I wouldn't mind just settling here on the ground and listening, but I change outta my walking shoes and slip on my two-tone heels, and soon thereafter I setting in my place, on the right, four rows back. I push my bag under the bench and listen, ready to join in, when the song ends.

For some li'l bit they ain't no sound and my blood begins to rush. The silence seem long. I stare down at the hanky I be twisting in my lap. Wouldn't surprise me none if'n Rev'rend Jones'd call my name, tell ever'body to have a look at Sister Hazeline—but praise be!—he start in to reading from the Old Testament.

I pull in a breath, pull my shoulders up and fix my eyes on a spot just over the top of his head. Now I can rest easy. All I gotta do is wait him out.

But just when I get all that worked out, he start in to praying, so I bow my head, wondering if'n all the rest got they eyes closed. Sure feels like they maybe a few eyes boring holes in me.

I awready saw Sam and Henrietta and they brood, in they usual spot. Joleen ain't here cause her and Troy's gone to visit his fam'ly. Some time go by, and all a sudden I come to. My eyes on my hands in my lap.

Seem to me like the preaching going on extra long. I start to squirm, tired of setting so long on the bench. Johnnie Mae in her place right ahead of me, and now she step off the bench wit' her hand in the air and tiptoe out. Her hand up mean she alright, just needing to go out, prob'ly headed for the outhouse. Crossed my mind to fall in behind her, but I stayed put.

****

By the time I got myself home I was feeling so low I was wishing night would hurry and come. Wanted to go to bed and pull the covers over my head. Many a time I's said this li'l house ain't much. But lately it's seemed a bit like a cocoon. Much as I can, I stay put, so's not to get those stings sure to come my way when I get out in the world.

Soon as I change outta my good dress I take myself out and settle in a chair next to Joshua's bench. Tell myself some days just be time to feel bad. I'd tried to reach the highest apple on the tree, but my ladder wadn't tall enough.

Sure strange how you can do a thing and it turn out not one bit like what you thought you was doing. Sorta like when you pick the first of the summer's blackberries and make your pie—but the fire be's too hot and your pie burn slap up. There yuh be, set on tasting that precious goodness, and yuh has to throw it out.

They only one thing right now I can see clear. Just cause I be wanting things to go a certain way don't mean tha's how they gon go.

I shake my head side to side and blow out air. Pshhhhh!

Some li'l bit of time goes by and I set up straight and squinch my eyes tight shut. This ain't no time for wallowing about. Goldarn it! Done the best I could—and that wadn't good enough.

I open my eyes and stare at the blue sky. Sure as the sky's blue, and sure as I be settin' here, I already know I gon start all over—looking ever'which way. The thing for me now? Just keep on believing they can be some way or other.

The afternoon take its time, move slow seem like, but at last the sun do be dropping below the treeline. Soon afterward, I be reaching into the kitchen cabinet Joshua built and catch sight of a jar. One Joshua brung home after some trip, I reckon, maybe one of his fishing trips wit' Sam. Must've meant to give it to somebody. S'posed to be some 'fine stuff.'

Prohibition come to a end some time ago, but don't matter if'n they a law 'gin it or not, they somebody gonna be making homebrew. Joshua learned when he was young 'at he couldn't handle it. Praise be, I never did—not once—have to see the monster he told me he become when he got to drinking.

Ain't never tasted liquor. Seem to make some people happy, least make 'em think they happy, cause they sure gets to talking big. I wipe the dust off the top and unscrew the lid. Whew! This stuff don't talk—it shout!

I dip my finger in and put the finger in my mouth. Ugh! Awful tasting stuff.

I turn the jar up and take a swig. Al-l-l the way down, it burn. I take another swig. A chuckle start in my belly and work it way up. It keeps on coming—till I's 'fraid I might wet my pants. And right quick then, I start feeling like a fool. I carry the poison out the front door and picture myself pouring it on the potplants. They'd prob'ly start in to dancing—if'n they didn't fall over dead. Ole Dog comes and stands there looking up at me. I set the jar down and set myself down wit' my feet resting on the step. I don't no more'n get my arms folded over my chest and tuck my hands under my arms than it start. Boo-hooing.

And more boo-hooing. After a bit the tears does ease up and I hear myself moan. "Joshua...oh my sweet, sweet Joshua. How I needs yuh here—needs yuh here wit' me!"

****

Her eyes open wide and her head jerks my way. "Mama, has you done lost your mind?!"

This ain't a good time for this chile of mine to come busting through the door screeching. Her head jerks up and she say all in one swoop, "I-don't-know-wha's-come-over you!"

"Hush, Joleen! Don't you come here talking thataway!"

She spread her arms wide. "What else I s'posed to do?!" Then her voice go low and slow. "Pretend I don't know wha's happening? Why the devil did you have to go and stir up a ruckus?"

She blow out air and for some bit don't say nothing—then come at it again. "Ever'body saying you a fool! And they talking 'bout my mama! And I says to myself, 'Why, that ain't sump'n my mama'd do. Can't be talking 'bout my mama—must have her confused with somebody else.'"

She drops into her daddy's chair and covers her face with her hands and bursts into tears. I ain't in no mood to baby her. This been a hard enough time for me. Even Miz Robbins give me the cold shoulder when I done her washing this week.

Joleen wearing a chartreuse green skirt and top. That yellow-green don't flatter her none. I stand there beside her, listening to her bawl. But after a bit—on they own, seem like—my hands reach out.

Now I be comforting her, but thinking it sure woulda been good if she'd come here to comfort me. I stoop and put my arms round her and pat her on the back. After a few minutes she sniffle some and stop the tears. I go get a clean cloth and dampen it so she can wipe her face.

I hand it to her and she mumble, "I'm sorry I hollered at you, Mama." She sets back, blows out her breath and moans, "But I just don't understand." I try to think of what to say, but she rush on. "Cause if what people is saying's true—you sure has changed!"

I lean over and push her hair back from her face. "Well...guess I don't have no answer to that. Come on in the kitchen and try the coffeecake I made this morning. I'll tell yuh what I done, and you can tell me if'n it's what you heard."

I don't even touch my slice of cinnamon cake cause I so busy talking. Joleen gulps hers down so quick I doubt she even tastes it.

I tell the story short as I can. She don't say nothing, so I just have to guess what she be thinking. She reach over and cut another hunk of the cake. I can see she done put on some weight. Might be cause she stuff food in, trying to find ease when she gets all upset.

I ask her if she want sump'n more. "I got some good hoop cheese."

"No, ma'am, the cake's fine. I wouldn't mind a glass of milk. You got any?" She glances up when she asks for the milk and it seem to me then that since she come busting through the door, it prob'ly the first time she's really see'd me.

"Sure do. Got it fresh this morning. I miss having a cow, but Miz Robbins usually let me have enough milk to do me—and if not her, then my good neighbor." I go to the box wit' the block of ice and pull out the jar, set a glass on the table and start pouring.

"Mama! Look at your hands!"

"They doing okay. I rub 'em wit' Vaseline."

"You need to quit doing their washing. It's too hard. You oughta quit and just make your money sewing."

"Can't do that. The washing and the other things I does for Miz Robbins is what 'llow me to stay here. This little house ain't much, but it be keeping a roof over my head."

I think of the bucket in the corner of the front room and decide not to mention the leak. "I just thankful I got to stay on here after we lost your daddy."

My fists clench and unclench. I hold myself in check. Not gon complain 'bout this li'l house. If'n I was to tell Joleen how I dream 'bout a roof 'at don't leak and a well right out the backdoor…well, that wouldn't help none.

She still ain't said nothing 'bout what I tole her. Now she get to her feet. Guess she ready to leave. No, she ain't turned thataway. She stops at her daddy's chair. Stands wit' her hands resting on the back.

She don't look at me. She say, "What I heard 'bout you, Mama? It sure be's true. You has changed."

****

Reckon when yuh take on sump'n yuh don't know nothing about, yuh likely gon make a mistake or two. Was they sump'n I coulda done dif'rent? Well, one thing. Coulda talked it over wit' *somebody*.

Right now I gots to quit thinking, turn my head to this measuring. Late in the week already. And I sure running behind. Has to sew up a bolero jacket to fit a big woman. Real big. Glad I thought to ask for a shirtwaist that fit her. If'n I got sump'n to go by I likely get it right.

Ah-ha! So tha's what was missing. Didn't have nothing to go by. Just set out all on my lonesome and stirred up a mess.

Delia often coming to mind. Some li'l while back I learned a bit more 'bout what happened. Was passing by some of the ladies huddled t'gether talking after church, and one of 'em grabbed hold of my arm. She say, "How Slim doin', Hazeline? Ain't seen much of him lately."

I thought it strange, her asking me, and tell her I don't know. Then all of 'em gets to talking at once—words gushing, like somebody'd primed the pump.

Essie had on one of her wide-brim hats. When she talked a big bunch of red cloth flowers bobbed ever'which way. She say, "Delia's aunt tole me, so I know it be's true. That poor girl been staying in, won't see nobody. The aunt say she could be out and about if'n she wanted, she ain't so bad hurt."

Clara shook a finger at Essie. I noted the ring on her finger. A big green jewel. "No," Clara say, "that ain't what I heard—the girl was hurt terrible bad."

Essie come back wit', "Who done tole you that?"

Then Louella popped up wit' her soft li'l voice. "Well, may be, the aunt trying to keep the truth hush-hush. Just natural, the fam'ly trying to make like things better'n they is."

Emma Mae say, "Whether this girl can be out or not— why, look to me like that ain't the question to be asking." I stare at her hair. She's getting on in years and her hair thin and gray, yet on and on she still tryin' to straighten it.

Inez Moore say, "Question I keep comin' back to? Why the girl out in the woods by herself anyway? She oughta knowed better."

Essie Mae jumped back in, saying the aunt tole her the girl never woulda gone in the woods by herself. "Was the boys—them boys. They got her into the woods. They tricked her."

Now I was listening hard too. The aunt say the boys come running up to Delia when she was 'bout halfway home. She'd stayed late at school, helping the teacher, and had her arms full of books. When the boys come trotting up—the aunt wadn't sure whether they was three or four of 'em—they yelled out, "Hey, girl—you better come quick! Your little brother's hurt. He's hurt bad!"

Delia dropped her books 'longside the path where the Moore property ends and this farm begins, and took off running. The boys was leading the way and when she got a li'l ways in the woods they grabbed her and tole her they'd hurt her li'l brother if'n she screamed or yelled.

I was more'n ready to take my leave, but Joleen come over and Inez got to admiring her dress. Joleen say she got it at Mr. Belk's Department Store. Was 'bout the same color as this bright blue material I be working wit' now.

I's bent over the table so long my back's aching. I stand up straight and stretch my arms high over my head.

Was while I was listening to Inez and the others 'at I got to feeling more'n a li'l bit stunned 'bout my own self. Bout what I done. Wadn't one bit like me. Never has been one to put myself forward thataway. But way it happened—way the sense of it come on me, sure seemed like the thing to do.

I drop my hands to my sides and blow out air. Pshhhh!

What happened in the woods...can't just be over. Cause it happened. And whatever happen make sump'n else happen.

The girl won't never be the same. And I ain't so sure I will be neither. And Slim, that dear boy. Most of my prayers I been saying for him, cause I so wanting him to keep his self out of trouble. If'n my boy had lived, I coulda see'd him tall and walking around looking so handsome— and me pitching my care in his direction—but that wadn't the way things happened.

****

Woke up this morning set on one thing. Lay by my troubles. Put it all away. Might go mad if'n I don't soon get some rest from it.

I be aiming to set my sights on wha's good and beautiful. And then maybe, by the time the end of such a fine day come along, I maybe can sleep the sleep what don't bring on bad dreams.

Done decided to skip church. Stay right here. The one thing I was set on was going down by the branch to set for a spell. Tell the water and the rocks and the trees how glad I be to visit wit 'em. One thing was fairly certain. They wouldn't be giving me no bad news.

And tha's zackly what I done. And by the time I woke up from a afternoon nap, I was feeling almost a hundred percent better.

Was putting my li'l bit of leftovers on my plate for supper when I heard a noise and hurried to the door. Most of the time this boy's stopped by, his mouth's been curved in a big smile. He never do say so, and I ain't one to say such things neither, but I do b'lieve he usually 'bout glad to see me as I is to see him. That didn't look like the case this time. I stood back, waiting for him to cross the threshold. He stopped just inside the door, standing stiff-like wit' his hat in his hand.

"Come on in, Slim."

I was 'fraid he might bolt if'n I didn't get him on in the house. I didn't have nothing cooked up, but I offered to open a can of pork 'n' beans and a can of sardines to go wit' some soda crackers.

He still hadn't moved. His head and shoulders was bent low. "Thank yuh, ma'am, but I ain't hungry."

I decided to forget about my supper. I stepped over to my chair and set down. He took Joshua's chair, leaning forward wit' his hands on his knees and turning his hat round and round. I let my breath out easy.

"Miz Morrison..." He said that much and no more.

My stomach was tied in knots. I decided to wait him out—likely cause I wadn't in no hurry to hear whatever it was he was gon say. My fingers was working, rolling up my apron.

His eyes still down, he say, "You been going to the neighbors."

Took me a bit to answer. "Uh-huh, I did. Didn't have much luck though."

"But, Miz Morrison—" His eyes turned my way wit' a earnest look. "Don't you see? I don't want yuh to have no luck. Making a big fuss 'bout what happened—why, that won't do no good. One to think about be Delia."

He stopped for just a bit then kept going. "I know yuh wanting to help, but it scares me to think what the outcome might be—wit' this thing yuh done, I mean. Cause folks just be talking and talking."

My hands come up and covered my mouth. A sound come outta me. Like a laugh. But wadn't no laugh.

I'd been so all-fired up, wanting to help him, wanting to keep him. It had turned into some big thing, me dreaming on and on 'bout Justice. Why, I'd been living in a dream world, and not once thought 'bout the girl's feelings.

I put my hands in my lap and willed 'em to stay still. My words come out, but just barely. "I see."

I looked up but reckon I was 'fraid to look straight at him. I just stared at his hands. They was on his thighs and his fingers spread out. Big hands, like Joshua's.

He lifted his face. His eyes was wet wit' tears, like my own. I leaned to him and said, "I tried to help, but it wadn't no help, was it?"

"I dunno, Miz Morrison."

"I stirred up a mess...an' all the while feeling so proud of myself for trying to help. Somebody oughta—or so it did seem to my mind."

His head dropped again.

"Could I meet the girl? I don't know as she'd want to see me, but it comes to me now, that what I done—well, I'd like to tell her—" And there I sat. Not knowing how to finish.

His head still hanging, he moaned, "She won't even talk to me."

My hands was working, twisting my apron tight and straightening it again. When the mind don't know what to do, the body gon do sump'n on its own. I was surprised to hear myself say I wanted to meet Delia. Hadn't give it no thought, just popped out of my mouth.

Sump'n Joleen say come to mind. She say I must be getting addled, that I shoulda knowed better'n to think they anything can be done 'gainst "the powers that be."

Chapter 18

————◄═══════►————

Sun sure getting hot. I be ready to take me a shade break soon. Got six rows of green beans to pick. Miss Kathleen gon take 'em to the county market in the morning. She usually sell 'em all, so they gon be a few pennies for me.

I always has liked picking beans, 'specially young fine ones like these, but when it hot as blazes and the sun shining down, I can't think on much 'cept the heat. I still be thankful for beans to pick, though. And sure be glad the boy carried my water this morning, cause wit' all this sweating I gon stink to high heaven. A good wash 'bout the time it gets dark be sump'n to look forward to.

A bit later I be setting in the shade and Ole Dog come over and set down close by. Soon as he gets settled I say, "One come right on the tail of the other'n. Want me to tell yuh 'bout it?"

Sometimes I gets so full of thoughts I has to say 'em, and he the only one to talk to. He ain't the only other breathing thing around, but he the only one wit' eyes that look like they care.

"Uh-huh, now you sleep already. You ain't even listening."

He lift one ear. Might be he's smarter'n I think. Reckon I maybe a bit smart myself, cause I done learned a few things these weeks just past. Joleen thinks I's crazy—come and give me a scolding. And Slim come by and done the same.

I don't rest long 'fore I stand and stretch, then go inside to get me a dipperful of water. Soon as I come in the backdoor I spot the new oilcloth on the table and just has to stop and admire it again. Sure a pretty pattern, wit' the crisscross blue and yellow.

The afternoon moving on so I head back to the bean patch, carrying another basket. Ole Dog's already done moved hisself up under the porch. Sure glad I got most of these stringbeans picked already. Gon have to hurry now cause they some thunder in the distance.

I bend over a vine, my hands busy, my mind busy too—same as usual. Thinking 'bout all that time I spent 'magining what we could do. All them pictures 'at played in my head.

Lawd, lawd! Look now like it all come to nothing. Since that day when Slim showed up wit' his sad tale, till now, when he come over here and shut down my scheming...why, that ain't been more'n a few weeks, but seem like a heck of a long time.

After he left I set myself down at the table. Stayed right there a long time wit' my head in my hands. No matter how I looked at it I had to admit I'd been *wrong wrong wrong* not to think 'bout the girl's wishes. And I wondered again what she look like. And if'n she be fine enough for a young man like Slim.

The house was quiet, me still at the table wit' my thoughts. And rain threatening that day too. A crack of thunder and lightning rung out, then a hard rain begun pelting on the tin roof. A big noise, but I could hear myself think. And pretty soon I knowed they was sump'n I was needing to admit to myself.

When I went knocking on doors I was all hepped up wit' some idea 'bout us banding t'gether, standing up for ourselves. I heard it said 'bout some government man 'at he just a bunch of hot air. Reckon that was me, when I put on my hat and set out. Had me sump'n important to do! And all the while my plan just dead wrong.

Another thing I figured out was news to me too. Remembered way back, when Joleen was growing toward her womanhood, how I 'bout worried myself sick. I knowed they wadn't much chance she could grow to womanhood wit'out some boy or some growed man getting after her. They all seems to want the young girls.

So there was one reason for my getting so all-fired hepped up. That old-as-Methusalah worry, the kind 'at any mama'd have for her chile.

Not sure I ever did b'lieve what I was set on doing would change things. I acted bold. But all the while I was dead set on not looking not once at the picture right there in my head…one that had us showing up to see the sheriff and him laughing at us: Heh-heh-heh, ha-ha-ha!

Ain't no sheriff nowhere round gon pay us no 'tention. I musta been crazy, way I got all fired up. But, right 'longside it I can say the other. They was sump'n good, sump'n almost fine, 'bout my crazy.

That thunder getting close now. And where they's thunder they's lightning, so I give it up. Pick up my basket and head back to the house. I get almost to the backdoor and a verse pop up. I read it recent in the book of Proverbs. "Where there is no vision the people perish."

The rain started and soon slowed to a steady drizzle. I'd settled at the table, my hands folded on that new oilcloth. I heard myself ask myself what it was I was wanting. No sooner'n the question come than a answer come a'running.

To honor what it was in me 'at was so determined to do something.

I hadn't never counted on ever'body jumping high just cause I made a move, but did seem like they coulda done a bit better'n they done. Seemed to me like they was disloyal to the good they be in all us.

Ain't hard to figure why. We all of us scared, the whites and the colored. And on both sides they some tha's disloyal to the holiness God give 'em. They done squooshed it down so far they can't feel it no more.

Seem like a long time go by 'fore I get up from my chair and go to the east winduh and look out on the wet world. Cloudy and misty, can't see no distance. And it come to me then that if'n I coulda see'd what was gon come of it, I wouldn't have set out to go knocking on doors. Guess tha's the right way of things, though. Cause we ain't meant to see ahead.

I 'magined a few years down the road. If'n I should live say, maybe, twenty years. I'd be looking back then. And what would I say?

'Just look what yuh done! A fine thing!'

'Yuh tried, but what yuh was up against was just too firm in place.'

'A fool, tha's what yuh was.'

I blow out my breath. Look to me like what happened was, a bee got stuck in my bonnet and stung me good. I still smarting from it.

Well, least I got most all the beans picked 'fore the rain come. No sense bemoaning what yuh can't help. And no sense crying over spilt milk.

****

Sure 'nough, Uncle Morse won't take no money for the ride, say he going over the Sandridge way anyway. And he insist on going the half mile or so out of his way to drop me at the top of the road down to Ruby's. Now I got my fingers crossed she gon be home. Ruby live wit' her sister, Irene, and a ole aunt 'at must be old as Methusaleh.

Right then I spot somebody heading up the road, coming my way. A man, look like. I squint, trying to make him out. Down in the ditch and 'long the bank, they some wildflowers putting on a show. I slow my step to admire 'em. Didn't stand more'n a minute or so till I heard, "Oh-ho! You the one!"

I turn quick and see who it be. The last body I'd wanna see. Eli Cooke. Joshua said once 'at Eli 'mean as a stripe'd snake.'

He be thrashing his arms in the air. The clothes he wearing ain't much more'n rags. "Ho ho ho!" he cackles. "You comin' ovah this way now, gon start up some of yer foolishness?"

Do he be drunk awready? This early in the day? May be, he's too tottering to do me any harm. But he sure give me a start and I stumble a bit and drop my bag. Right quick I stoop to pick it up and while I'm bent over I reach behind and grab hold of a stone.

He so close now I catch his scent. A rotten smell. I be thinking quick, figuring to speak to him calm-like and keep on walking. Ignore him—tha's prob'ly the best way. He staggers a bit and I step back. My foot catches and down I go. My bag hits the ground first and the rock drops outta my hand. I yell loud as I can, "Eli, you get on up the road!"

He still froze up. I shout again. "Go on! Get on your way!"

He shake his head like he be tryin' to clear it, then turn and start off—but 'fore he get out of earshot he start making a hissing sound. I gets to my feet and bend over to brush my clothes off and sneak a look, see if'n he still on his way. Yeah, he be heading in the right direction. I take in a deep breath and keep moving, knowing Ruby gon like this story. While I walk I think on Eli, him headed 'in the right direction.'

No, can't say that 'bout him. Wish I could, but somehow or 'nother that man be's crippled in his spirit. If'n I had to guess I'd say he can't get over nursing some wound he suffered, sump'n long back in the past—so it just ain't in him now to do much dif'rent 'an what he does.

****

"Hazeline? That you? You sure a sight for sore eyes!" Irene spots me when I come tramping through the dust to the house. She say Ruby not home but expected soon. "Help yo'self, Hazeline. Take the dipper and get yo'self a drink. The water's cool, I just brung it from the well."

I thank her and soon settle in to wait, which mean doing my best to put up wit' the ancient one. She a wrinkled-up ole lady. Her skin dark like mine and she still dipping her snuff. She reach for her spit can and Irene tell her again who this visitor be.

'Bout a hour later Ruby come in. I rejoice in my heart—cause I get to see her, and cause I plumb tired of trying to understand the jibber-jabber from the aunt. The ole woman seem to know what she saying, but from what I can tell it all be in the long ago and far away.

When I get home I gon start up my praying in earnest. Don't ever want to get to the place where I done lived so long I ain't able to do for myself. Might not tell Ruby this thought. She'd tease me pretty rough, I s'pect, cause she think she the one 'at prays.

I wait in the kitchen while the sisters care for the ole woman. Finally they come in. Ruby heads for the flour bin but Irene say "Anh-anh-anh!" and shoos us out the door, say she'll have dinner on the table 'fore long and for us to go on out and be t'gether.

The day 'bout good as days get. Mild, and real bright. We come to the chairs in the shade but keep walking. I start giggling like a girl when I tell Ruby 'bout my 'encounter on the road.' To my surprise I spice up the story.

"He was coming at me—an' I was trembling scared!" She knows I didn't come to no harm, so she laugh wit' me.

We lean on a pasture gate and get quiet, looking out on a pond and some ducks. And in that quiet I come on two things. I really was in danger. If'n me and Eli had been a li'l younger...well, I wouldn't wanna know what might'a happened. And second thing, how I got so bold and yelled at him like I done. Sure surprised me! Reckon Joleen right, I has changed. But then, when yuh live alone, yuh ain't got much choice. You the one has to do whatever needs doing.

****

The morning dawns. I's had too little sleep, but the day ahead looking fine anyway—cause it so much a pleasure to think on my visit. The mem'ry keep me comp'ny all the daylong.

Me and Ruby—we forgot the rest of the world. We just set in the shade and talked on and on till Irene called us in to eat. She 'pologized for not having dinner ready at noon. I understood why she was running late when she set before us a feast. Me and her and Ruby, we talked and talked—while the ancient one pushed her food round her plate. I ate till I was stuffed and happy. Chicken'n dumplings, sauerkraut wit' bits of spicy sausage, cucumbers in vinegar, sliced tomatoes, and a reheated apple pie what tasted fresh baked.

I let out a belch and was 'shamed of myself, so I begged pardon and then headed in to praising Irene for the feast she'd shared. She looked kind of bashful when she said, "You welcome."

The kindness showed me done me a heap of good. Soothed my wounds, least for now. And one thing I knows for sure. A few good friends worth more'n a ton of money.

I went to Ruby's thinking to talk wit' her 'bout all tha's been bothering me. I ain't used to a world 'at feels so turned upside down. But I didn't more'n touch on what was on my mind. Seemed enough to be away for the day and in the comp'ny of kind folk.

Was late in the day when I got back and checked on the chickens and Ole Dog. Figured I'd sleep like a angel after such a fine day, but that wadn't the case. I lay awake in the dark, seeing Eli's face leering at me. If'n it'd been wintertime, wit' a fire going, I'd'a got up and mixed some bee balm leaves in a cup of hot water. But I didn't have no hot water, so I just took me a BC Powder.

The morning come and I still feeling groggy, in no hurry to get up. Keep seeing Eli's face. If'n safety what I be wanting, guess I best stick close to home. That'd be the safe way.

A few days back when I was setting at my machine all this was on my mind, and even though I was setting down, felt like I was moving. Had to stop what I was doing and get still. After a bit I got to chuckling. Seemed like maybe they was some mules inside me, one pulling one way and the other'un the other way. Couldn't get nowhere.

I said out loud, "Whoa! Hold on now!" That give me a good laugh and I begun to feel some better.

Right now it past time to get outta this bed, so I throw back the sheet.

A hour later, I still be dawdling time away. Setting at the table, chiding myself. Why I setting here when they so much to be done?

But I knows why. Done decided to call a meeting. What I need now be a chairwoman, and a few good folks on the committee, to come up wit' some ideas. Then we take a vote.

Wish I could see inside this brain of mine. They for sure more'n one voice in it. And least one of 'em ain't willing to give up. It done already voted.

Well, look to me like, I gots to either let the notion go and not think on it no more—or pick up the best of the ideas this committee can think of, and go marching on.

Next thing, I gets to chuckling again. So just where might I march to? If'n I should set out marching I'd have to be invisible—cause if'n the folk hereabout catch sight of me I likely get shot. Done stirred up too many feelings and too much fear.

I drop my head in my hands and whisper a few words, sump'n like a prayer. Then I get myself up and get busy—shoo away all that thinking!

It late in the day when the idea comes. I be sewing on a button, content with my labor—and it just settles in me. Right away, it feels right. Wonder if'n it still gon feel right after I sleep on it?

I whisper, "Lemme do the best I can."

****

I spend the next morning in the kitchen. Peel and chop, sift flour, beat egg whites to a froth. Was putting a dishtowel over my dough, ready to leave it to rise—and it come to me then, how oftentimes when I upset I starts in to cooking.

Made a potful of soup wit' ever'thing I could find to put in it. Cabbage, potatoes, onion, squash—even opened up a Mason jar of tomatoes and okra left from last year. Then a pan of soapy water and another'n for rinsing, and soon the kitchen clean and I got more food cooked up than any one body need. I wouldn't'a made such a big pot of soup if I hadn't been expecting the iceman.

I spend the afternoon working at my sewing, but working half-hearted. Maybe ate too much. And all a sudden I r'members a day long back, the day I decided lying be bad for the digestion. I tole a whopper that day, and right soon after had me a awful stomach ache.

Joshua had come home sick at heart. He didn't zactly say so in so many words, but my man was feeling like he'd failed. Sam, his brother—and best friend—had done a heap better for hisself and his fam'ly, if'n yuh judge by money.

When Joshua finally got round to talking, 'stead of just setting out there on the bench wit' his whittling, I said what wadn't no way true, and done it wit'out giving it a thought. The lie just popped out easy.

I had give him some time to hisself but after a spell I went out to where he was whittling—on his bench, arms on his knees and the knife sending flakes down between his feet. I tole him supper was ready anytime. He grunted. I stood there, looking out 'cross the field.

After a bit he say real low, "That man works me hard and I does him a good job—I knows that for sure, but he don't never have a good word to say. It'd prob'ly split his tongue if'n he say, 'Mighty fine job yuh done there, Joshua.' And if'n he did, it'd prob'ly be, 'Mighty fine job, boy.'"

I squat down beside him. I say, "Maybe he don't brag to you, but he do to her. Miz Robbins sometimes tell me she hear him brag on the work yuh turn out."

I heard myself say it, and wondered. Where a lie like that come from? Sure slipped out easy enough. And that was scary, cause if'n I'd done it once, likely do it again.

Wadn't hard to figure why. My man was needing comfort, so I served it up. He'd been clearing ground. Cutting trees and digging out stumps and hauling rocks— overseeing the job too, with the other hands. Mister Robbins woulda liked it finished the week after they started. Ever'day, he'd drive by in his Ford car. And then he was gone for a week, him and some other farmers off touring farms in Virginia. Joshua pushed hard to finish the job 'fore he got back. Had the mules helping too, like usual, and all the while picturing how pleased Mister Robbins'd be.

Joshua the kind what love to see a job done right and see it through to the end. So Mister Robbins come home and didn't tarry long 'fore he head for 'the new ground.' Joshua was expecting him. What Joshua didn't know was 'at Mister Robbins'd have a guest wit' him—one of the farmers from the trip to Virginia. The two of 'em stood over on the edge and pointed this way and that—and never said not one word to Joshua.

I couldn't blame my man for wanting to walk away and never see his boss again. It was one day I prob'ly coulda talked him into moving, but we'd heard 'bout some of the other farms and knowed we couldn't be sure we'd be better off if'n we did move. At least on this farm Joshua was the one in charge—got to see the work done wit'out somebody looking over his shoulder, and feel the pride of knowing it was done right.

I was careful that day not to mention Sam, cause I knowed how it bothered Joshua—Sam working a job in town and buying a ole house and a ole car too. But Joshua couldn't do the work Sam done. It woulda killed him to have to work indoors. My man loved working the land— rather be out under the sky in most any weather. But, still and all, a li'l praise woulda gone a long way.

Chapter 19

———————⟫⟫⟫⟫⟫⟫⟩⟨⟨———————

Dadblame it. Can't carry 'em in, don't wanna wait till they dry. So what I gon do?

The missus over in the front room resting, so I decide to take myself on home, come back after while. Least I can hope that be the way it work out.

Me and the missus got a paper tablet we keep in the cabinet drawer. She be over in the front room nursing one of her headaches, so I leave her a note, tell her I be back after while. I ain't even emptied the washpot yet. One minute sun was shining, next minute cloudy and the rain come quick. And soon after that, sun out again. If'n God be setting up on His cloud deciding when it gon rain, reckon he be having a bit of fun—out to catch us by surprise.

The shower didn't last more'n a few minutes, and most of the clothes on the line was 'bout dry. But sure ain't dry now. The shower come so quick I couldn't get 'em all in.

I head on down through the pasture, headed home. Maybe take me a nap 'fore I come back this way. And like usual, my head's a'working. Saying what I don't wanna hear. Telling me tha's how quick change can come. But I push the thought away, cause don't seem likely they ever gon be much change in these parts. People just too stubborn. Or ignorant, one or t'other.

As the week wear on, I think on it more'n a few times. And finally chastise myself. What a way to think. No hope, none a'tall. Sure didn't like the feel of that.

And then, praise be—at last, come this morning we all been looking forward to. I swung my feet to the floor and soon as my head tried to pick up that kind'a thinking again I tole it I just wadn't gon listen. Got to humming instead and was soon singing at the top of my lungs. Run through 'Camp Town Races' three or four times. "Doo dah doo dah, camp town races sing this song, oh doo dah day."

Out the backdoor I went, calling, "Come on over here, Ole Dog—we gon eat good today."

I'd just cut up a chicken. This the Sunday of our homecoming. Gon be a big crowd at church, so I gon wear my favorite dress, one wit' the yoke cut like a dress I saw readymade. Night before I took out the shoe polish and shined up my shoes.

Feel awful good as I set out. Wearing my old shoes, carrying a bag over my shoulder wit' my high heels and my pocketbook, and a basket full of food in the other hand. Homecoming mean we gets to see folks we don't see often. They one cousin of Joshua's always brings damson pies. My mouth water just thinking on 'em.

****

It do turn out a fine good day, yessiree!—but sure moved along quick. On the path home now, and my load not so heavy. I wadn't the only one 'at ate like a pig. Might not even need any supper. Ruby the one I was greedy to talk to. Kept wishing I could get her off to the side and chat a bit, but wit' such a crowd that couldn't happen cause she the kind wanna talk to ever'body there.

Slim tipped his hat my way and said, "You sure make a good pie, Miz Morrison." That was it—nothing more. He spent his time wit' the other young men, so I didn't get to say no more to him. Soon as I get home and change outta my good dress, I gon have to walk right back up the hill to fetch water. Took me a good bath last evening, didn't spare the water none. The galvanized tub ain't quite big enough, so water splashes on the floor, but last evening that didn't bother me none.

By the time I was done I was feeling fine as any queen.

'Fore I put myself to bed I walked out and looked up at the sky and right away a night earlier in the year come to mind. The air was cold then and I looked one way and spied the Little Dipper, turned the other way—and there was the Big Dipper! I wadn't used to seeing 'em both at once, so the sighting did seem a blessing. I stood there plumb filled up wit' wonder, grateful for eyes to see.

****

The next coupla weeks fly by. They so much to do I can't keep up. And now we got Fourth of July. Time to set off some firecrackers. For some folk anyway, that be the thing. For me it be blackberry cobbler.

Mister Robbins fond of saying this a important holiday cause this 'the land of opportunity.' But this year the Fourth fall on a Sunday, and that mean lots of folks won't get no opportunity for a day off. When the holiday fall on a weekday, most ever'body get a day off. Only work done then be milking the cows and feeding the other animals. Thank goodness Miz Robbins ain't expecting no comp'ny.

This be's Saturday, day before the holiday. I gather up my boots and my pail and a long sleeve shirt, and pull on a ole pair of thick stockings to keep the chiggers at bay. I gon take my opportunity in the blackberry patch. Know right where they's two good patches. Prob'ly get enough berries to can a few jars too.

I might eat just cobbler for my dinner. Cobbler—and nothing else. Bake a big one to carry to the dinner on the grounds, and another'n just for me—if'n I finds enough berries tha's ripe.

One thing 'at please me most 'bout this creation be how ever' season be's dif'rent. A whole heap of the joy in life be this looking ahead to wha's coming round again. Come autumn, it be apples and pears and persimmons, black walnuts and hickory nuts. Muscadines too. When winter come, ain't nothing I like better'n snowcream. And sometime 'fore Christmas, Mister Denny Stillwell take hisself off to Florida to pick up a truckload of oranges. Miz Robbins always do get a half bushel and she let me have a few. Now a fresh orange—tha's a fine thing. If'n they's angel food in heaven, I s'pect some bit of it's oranges.

Day after day of late, I been thinking on when Slim come here and say he don't want me to try to help. Strange thing of it be, him saying it seem to've stirred up this brain of mine. It sure been a'stewing.

Oftentimes it do be the womenfolk 'at eases the wounded and poor in spirit. I sure wish I could ease

Delia's way a bit. Most likely me and her both would get to weeping, and I could wipe her tears.

****

Wednesday awready. And I be wondering how long it gon take to hem this wide skirt. If'n I ever does make it all way round, I gon set out for my rock. Done promised myself.

But after a bit I give it up and set the skirt aside. That singing water and my sitting rock be right down the hill, waiting for me. 'Fore I set out my stomach begins to rumble, so I spread a bit of my fresh blackberry jelly on a thick slice of the bread I baked yesterday. Then I set out. But as it turns out I don't stay long, cause even my rock seem to be telling me, *Don't try to help.*

I talked back—and right away got to chuckling, cause lo and behold my rock tole me *why* I be wanting to help. Cause I got a big heart! And that kept me chuckling for some li'l bit. I sure wouldn't mind a big heart. It be my favorite thing the Bible say. 'God looks on the heart.'

On my walk back I stopped to pick up some trash somebody'd throwed down. When I come on it I'd just been wishing I could take myself off to my pastor. Ask his help. But not this preacher we got. Far as I can tell he ain't no better'n trash. Don't trust him—not one bit!

I settle in wit' wha's mine to do, and 'fore I know it suppertime's done come round. Here the skillet, here the eggs. Didn't eat much earlier, so I decide to make me some fried bread too.

'Fore I get started I has to do a bit of work wit' the flyswatter. I do so love summertime, but yuh does have to put up wit' flies. Reckon though, that be the right way of things. Wouldn't do to have paradise here and now.

The rest of the week go by quick and soon it Sunday again. I rise early to cook up sump'n to take to the missionary program. Gon be some visitors coming. Wish the limas was ready, I'd stir up some succotash.

Once again, the tables out under the trees gon be piled high wit' some mighty fine eating. This the time of year when our gardens be giving us a bounty. Hard to keep up wit' the canning and preserving, stowing away our food for the wintertime.

I start the fire in the cookstove. Gon make the quickest thing I can. Muffins. And fresh corn seasoned wit' a bit of fatback. That be all I gon do.

Day 'fore yesterday I headed over to the great big cornfield the Robbins boys always plants. Took a burlap sack and pulled as many ears as I could carry, so now I got ten pint jars of corn put back for the winter.

Ain't much of anything better'n corn straight from the field. While I was there I walked on out into the field a bit just to feel what it feels like to be in the middle of all them tall stalks. Sure was a green world—a different world, and the stalks so thick and high I couldn't see the sky. And sure seemed a long, long way from our ordinary world.

Was at the church yesterday too and thought again how this world must surely be haunted—cause of the way things happen. Sure strange, way one thing happen on top of t'other. They was a ballgame going in the field by the church and that same morning I'd read in the paper 'bout somebody's reputation.

When I come on it I chuckled to myself and said out loud, "Uh-hunh—kinda look like Hazeline Morrison's done built herself a reputation!"

I'd knowed they was talk going on, but I done lived long enough to know how folks be. Talk 'bout one thing don't last too long, cause sump'n else bound to come along and then ever'body be talking 'bout it.

The ballgame was almost over so I headed inside to get some big spoons for dishing up the fresh peach ice cream. When I come back out I was headed for the churns but passed by a wagon still hooked to a mule, and setting on the ground on the other side they was a coupla men. My ears perked right up. One of 'em said sump'n 'bout 'reputation.'

They was turned the other way, didn't see me—but the other fella say, "She wouldn't'a done it if'n Joshua was here."

The first one say, "She oughta have sense enough to leave well enough alone."

And what did I think? That they was right. Wouldn't have done it if'n Joshua'd been here. I wadn't the same then. Never woulda even come to my mind to do such a thing when he was at my side.

Well, right now, I got to get these muffins in the oven. Awready got my Sunday clothes laid out. While the oven do its work I gon step out the backdoor and say good morning to the world—and not give not one thought to my reputation.

First thing, I breathe the morning air. Take it in deep. Then speak to the chickens. And the trees and the sky. I sure love this time of day. But muffins bake quick, so I best remember to get back inside soon.

Once in a while at the fishfry over at Sam and Henrietta's, they a man folks calls 'the philosopher.' He the kind like to spout fancy words, and the kind 'at go for the drink and the women too, but he don't seem such a bad fella. I was standing close by once and heard him say, "Jus' as easy for a strong man to be strong as it be for a weak man to be weak."

Uh-huh, them was his words. So I stand tall this morning and says to myself, "Uh-huh... and same can be said for a woman."

Guess I ain't never been more surprised 'an that day I took myself off to go knocking on doors. Some kind of strength sure showed up in me. Could be, was there all along.

Thursday morning early I gets to making bread. Turn the dough, push, turn, push again. Been a habit wit' me long as I can r'member, this working the dough when my head get so full o'thinking it be weighing me down.

Still don't have no idea worth a hoot. Least half a dozen crazy ones done come and went. Like maybe, walk round wit' a big sign on my back. It say, *Where the justice?* Lord knows, that wouldn't do no good.

I see my hands work. And a mem'ry come. Was wa-ay long back. Joshua say, "There she go again, Joleen. Cooking up a storm. Watch her now, see how her arm go round and round? We might not get to eat that pound cake—cause your mama beating that batter to death!" He laugh big then and slap his knee, and right quick set his hat on his head and get hisself out the door—'fore I could give him a piece of my mind.

Late in the day I take the paper out under the tree. I gets to reading, but ever so often, glance up and watch the light fade. Ole Dog come over and settle close by. Been a lazy afternoon, maybe cause I ate too much buttered bread.

Can't seem to make no sense of what the paper say, cause of what happened some few days ago. Was in the kitchen. Heard sump'n 'at sounded like a car. Was a car. And him in it.

I made it to the screen door just in time to see him drive close up to the house. Didn't get out. Just poked his head out the window and called to me.

Didn't say much, neither. But what he meant was, *Hazeline best lay low.* I didn't know what to say, but didn't matter none. Soon as yuh could say 'scat' he turned that big black car around and skedaddled.

I knowed what he meant. Telling me I best stay inside the fence. I knows how his mind work. He'd likely said to hisself, 'Let me just run on over there and tell Hazeline not to go getting no ideas 'bout busting down the fence. She best be behaving herself, like a good mule.'

By bedtime I'd pictured them fences ever'which way. They be fences yuh can't see. But they gon scratch you up bad, same as if'n yuh get tangled up in a barbwire fence.

My people come up 'gainst the bound'ry, give it a shove...might move a inch. No more'n that. Cause what holding it in place be's powerful strong. Reckon they ain't much sense in thinking it ever gon come falling down.

Late the next morning I go out to the clothesline to hang up my few things. Was a make-do washing in a bucket. I'd already used the water once. Always tries to make a bucketful go far as it can.

I reach in my apron pocket for some clothespins. Ole Dog come over and I start in to talking. He my best listener. "Yuh know them fences, Ole Dog? No, don't reckon yuh do. You sure used to go romping and tearing in all directions." I reach down and scratch behind his ears. "Fences I talking 'bout yuh can't go running under— nor jumping over neither."

Was yestiddy I got to thinking 'bout the way bound'ries change if'n they pushed and prodded. But now I got the picture dif'rent. Us colored folk in a inside pasture. White folk in a outside pasture. They got more space for moving 'round, but ever'body's fenced in.

When I read the paper I look at wha's playing at the picture shows in town. Randolph Scott maybe in one, or Gene Autry. Maybe Shirley Temple or Dorothy Lamour. One was called, 'The Road to Glory.' I ain't never see'd one of 'em, but somebody told me the pictures on the screen always end happy.

Wit' this story I be worrying over, don't look like they ever gon be no road to glory. And no happy ending...less'n white folks comes to see how these fences be fencing them in too.

I takes the clothes basket back in the house and round up a few leftovers for my dinner. While I'm at it I get to wishing I could get away, put some distance 'tween me and this Robbins farm. And blessed be—no sooner think it 'an a idea pop up.

Distance. Why, they be's more'n one way to come on distance. And right then I decide. Tomorrow morning I gon take myself off to see her. She the only body I know can maybe take this good intention I got stirring in me—and turn it 'round to some good sense.

****

Yessiree, on my way. A long walk, 'specially in these shoes. Shoulda wore my ole shoes.

Soon's I spot the place I begins to wondering. They sump'n wrong? Don't see not one soul, and that sure ain't like usual. They quite a few live in that big house. I hurry my steps and soon lifting my hand and knocking at the frame of the screen door.

After a bit they a sound like somebody moving around. Yeah, somebody shuffling about. She call out, "I'm a'coming, I'm a'coming!" It be her, one I come to see. Miz Ida Mae Stephens.

"Just me, Miz Stephens—Hazeline."

She hobble into the kitchen and say, "Come on in the house."

"I was 'bout to think ever'body's gone."

"Whole bunch of 'em, gone fishing. T.K. talked Suzy into going along too. But she cooked up some beans and cornbread 'fore she left—case you hungry."

"No'm, thank yuh just the same."

She point a finger at the water bucket. "Get yuh a glass off the shelf." I take the dipper in my hand and offer to pour a glass for her too.

She say, "Nah, I don't need none. Come on back here to my room. Yuh picked a good time to come. Keep me from sleeping the afternoon away. Took me a while to get to the door cause I'd dozed off."

She still a pretty woman, but so thin now yuh think yuh might see right through her. For some years now I's been fond of Miz Ida Mae. Look like she still sharp as a tack, and like usual she got her white hair plaited and coiled in a li'l topknot. She goes to her old upholstered chair and says to me, "Pull that straight chair outta the corner. You can dump wha's on it on the bed."

The room's big, like all the rooms in old houses like this. She sleep on a metal cot. Close to hand she got a whole basket full to the top with yarn. I wonder what she be crocheting now. "So, what yuh making—?"

She jump in. "Reckon yuh come to talk 'bout yuh troubles."

I start in to laughing and laugh for a good li'l bit. She joins in and finally I says, "You sure don't miss much, huh?"

She giggles, and she begins to feel easier'n I has for some time. For sure, I done come to the right place. After we been talking for some li'l bit I ask her what she thinks I might could do.

She shakes her head side to side. "Hazeline, I hears what yuh asking. But I don't have no answer—and wouldn't wanna answer if'n I could."

The time moved on quick and I stayed quite a while, but figured she'd need her rest so took my leave 'fore the afternoon got too far along. Sure done me a lotta good, just setting nearby that wise old woman.

On over in the afternoon a quick thunderstorm come through, so on my way home I got to noticing the way the light had changed. The rain cleaned the air, made ever'thing brighter and fresher. And it come to me then. That be the kind of change to hope for.

Ain't no reason in the world to think things gon turn right side up from here on out. What can happen, least I b'lieve it so, be some bit of change for the better. Like that light. Change enough so's yuh notice and get hold of some hope 'at maybe a bit more just might come along.

Just being round that dear old woman made me feel like a young'un again. I got a lotta years to go 'fore I make it to her age. Doubt I ever do make it to her wisdom.

She reminded me how long it'd been since we'd set together for a long talk. Said she remembered the early cucumbers and squash I carried along, first little'uns of the season. Last year. I'd got my seed in the ground early and figured theirs might not be ready yet. I'd plumb forgot that, but once she spoke of it I r'membered— r'membered how proud I was to get my garden in the ground so early, taking a chance on it surviving—and it did!

That be my kind of gambling.

Got home just 'fore nightfall and went straight to chopping down some tall weeds and briars. So what I needing now be a good bath, but I gon have to make do wit' a sponge bath. The night so warm I ain't even gon' heat the water.

Finish my wash and reach for a clean nightgown. One that comes to hand's my best one. May as well wear it. Nothing special to save it for.

Would like to settle by the kerosene lamp wit' a magazine Henrietta give me. But the light draws bugs, so I just set quiet in my rocking chair wit' my hands resting on the arms. Not often I set and do nothing.

A strange feeling come over me. Somebody...? Nah. Ain't nobody here 'cept me.

Sump'n back behind me creaks, but they always such noises in this l'il house. Still, I peep over my shoulder. Nothing.

Another sound. Real soft. My name. "Hazeline."

I under a spell now surely. Ever' bit of me done come to full attention. The voice come again. "Hazeline, yuh doin' jus' fine."

I feels froze to the chair, goosebumps all over me. The words ring in my head. I whisper, "Joshua?"

I don't move, jus' wait, holding my breath. But nothing else come. I keep on setting, still under the spell.

What seem like a long while go by. When at last I crawl in the bed I don't care if'n I don't sleep none a'tall. Wouldn't wanna try to convince nobody, but I b'lieve my man spoke my name. I pull the sheet up and lie real still, wanting to keep hold of such wonder.

****

Next morning, I be pushing the flatiron cross my gabardine skirt when the wind gets up. It come whistling round the corner of the house. I'd been walking the famous mem'ry lane till the wind got to calling. The mem'ry from way back. Joshua and Joleen here—his friends coming by, her friends coming by. Even then I worked for Miz Robbins and picked cotton ever' autumn, but most of what I done was for my man and my girl.

I finish my ironing and stand by the winduh. The wind jus' whipping the limbs. The chinaberry tree bending low, and the oak limbs thrashing all about! I like watching the wind work. They a ole saying, 'the wind of change.' Soon as I think it I says, "Uh-huh, even back then, the wind of change was a'blowing. And me so busy I didn't have time to notice."

Ever since my visit to Miz Ida Mae, my head's been a'spinning. She tole me to think wide. I come away so excited I felt kinda dizzy-like.

I can set back and watch the wind blow, or do what I can to make it blow a li'l different way. Could write a letter to President Roosevelt—maybe send it to Eleanor. Could talk to the people at WBT radio. Could hitch me a ride to Raleigh and march right in at the Capitol—tell 'em wha's going on in these parts.

But thing of it be, Slim don't want me to stir up nothing else. Still, more I think on it, more the ideas keep a'popping. I know now my wise-woman friend was right. Ain't no end to the possibles.

****

"Ruby, yuh shoulda see'd me. All I could do was laugh and laugh some more. Done me so much good!"

"I hear yuh, Hazeline, but you best be careful..." Ruby laughing so hard she can't get her words out. "Best be careful...cause the neighbors might decide to cart you off to the loony bin!"

We both laugh so hard we bend double. When we straighten up she throw her arms in the air and I throw mine up and we touch our palms t'gether. I wipe tears from my eyes and usher her in the house.

She sure a sight for sore eyes. I been wanting to see her—and lo and behold, she show up! She look awful good. Wearing a pretty blue and white sundress and got her hair pulled back from her face.

She can't stay long, so soon's we get inside I start blurting out all I been saving up to tell her. After a bit she throw her arms wide and say, "Whoa! Slow down—you gon run outta air. I ain't never knowed yuh to talk such a running spurt."

I take a deep breath and blow it out. My hands fly to my breast. "Reckon you right. Can't tell yuh ever'thing."

She say, "Tell yuh what. Let me get the stove hot and make us some coffee, while you get yuh mind in order. Think 'bout what two-three things yuh most wanting to tell."

A short while later I be setting in a straight chair under the shade tree and her behind me wit' scissors in her hand. While she trim my hair I fill her in on ever'thing. But I don't tell her 'bout Joshua speaking to me. That mem'ry too close to share. Kinda like my own skin. Can't give it up.

She leave a good while 'fore dark, 'case she end up having to walk the whole way home.

Chapter 20

><del>>>≋≋≋≋≋≋≋<<</del>

The next morning I'd just got started seaming up some curtains for Miz Robbins's sister-in-law when lo and behold Joshua—his voice, got to talking. Was late morning already. I had my dinner cooked and waiting. A pot of fresh lima beans, potatoes and onion, a black iron skillet full of crusty cornbread, and a fresh-picked tomato.

The words what come to mind was some Joshua said way long back. A evening it was, and Joleen busy at the table wit' her homework, but I could tell from the way she was making li'l noises and hunched over her paper that she wadn't getting much done. She always was good at reading and writing—but 'rithmetic didn't come easy. So that evening she push her book away and set up straight and say in a good strong voice: "I'm quitting this stuff—giving it up. Cause I can't do it."

Now Joshua didn't get much chance to go to school. He knowed how to read a little and could sign his name, but he was bound and determined his chile would be at the school reg'lar. So that night he say to Joleen, "Wrong thing to do, girl. Quitting? Huh-unh! Don't you be letting your head tell you it awright to quit."

Wadn't hard to figure why this mem'ry show up in my head now. Ever'body high and low telling me to give up. Tell me I oughta mind my own business.

I filled my machine bobbin and dropped it back in place, and next thing I heard sump'n. Might be a car. And sure 'nough it was, coming real slow.

When I saw who was coming, thought crossed my mind 'at what I needing be one o' them signs they got at hotels. At the fish fry last week, K.T. tole a story 'bout staying in a hotel. He say, "If'n yuh wanna be left to yuhself, all yuh gotta do's hang the sign on yuh door. *Do not disturb.*"

I played wit' the idea of staying quiet. Could just not answer the door. But this place too li'l for hiding. My heart was in a panic when I put my hand to the door latch. I mumbled, "Oh, Lord," and pulled in a big breath of air and held myself up straight and tall.

The man in a fancy suit on the other side of the door wadn't worth me getting upset—and I figured the quickest way to get shed of him was to let him have his say. I knowed how he wants ever'body to think he a important man, 'man of authority.'

One thing in my favor, I was dressed. Not in my ole housedress. I'd spruced up some cause time was drawing near when I'd set out walking to the Moore place. I'd be carrying two dresses for the woman of the house to try on.

He come through the door and right quick it dawned on me. He mustn't take Joshua's chair.

I scooted cross the room and moved a pile of cloth from a straight chair and motioned for him to have a seat. Tole him I didn't have much time. It's only now I see how rude I was. Didn't even offer him sump'n to drink—like I woulda done wit' anybody else, but I guess it be hard to act civil to a man you think might sprout horns.

He set his hat on one knee. I hadn't even offered to take it. All I was wanting was to hurry along the time for showing him out. He got a long face, and eyes what smile but don't smile. The devil prob'ly got eyes like his'n when he be shoving folks into that Lake of Fire.

Many a time when the church service be over I figure Rev'rend Jones has done shouted hisself hoarse, but today he wadn't one bit hoarse. He set hisself down, pulled out a cigarette and flared a match to light it. I hurried to get the ashtray Joshua used to use.

He take a deep draw, blow out smoke, then clear his throat. "Sister Hazeline, they been some talk—whole heap of talk!"

I wadn't wearing my apron, so soon as I set down I pulled a hanky outta my pocket and started rolling it up. After a bit, when that didn't help much, I just shut my hands tight and waited to see what all he was gon say.

"A number of the brothers and the sisters"—he clear his throat again—"well, they thought I should come and have a word wit' you. P'haps we could pray—ask the Good Lord what He would have us do in, uh... at a time like this."

I held my tongue and kept my feet flat on the floor, all of me caught up tight. I needed to swallow, but I just held myself real still. Didn't want him to see how upset I was.

Right soon after he left I took off walking—and chuckled and giggled most all the way to the Moore place.

Tickled me pink. A plumb good feeling it was, to be a speaking-out woman!

There I was, setting right here where I be setting now, but long as he was here didn't nothing seem the same. Wadn't the same! Felt a bit like the devil's den. And him just keeping on, filling the air wit' words, marking out what I'd done—and that much he got pretty much right. But he wadn't paying no 'tention to me—not one bit. I s'pect I could'a stood on my head and he'd'a just kept that booming voice of his a'going.

I thought 'bout making some excuse, go to the kitchen maybe, leave him setting. He was so caught up in what he was saying he prob'ly wouldn't'a noticed.

I waited for him to run down. But he kept on. Seemed like he was talking to somebody 'at wadn't there, like they was somebody else nearby and him looking at that one, not paying me no mind.

"...You trying to help. But you trying to help where help ain't wanted." He stopped for air then and say a li'l softer, "The girl's fam'ly asked me to come speak wit' you."

I gripped the arm of my rocking chair. Maybe even gritted my teeth. But I said, "I awready know how they feel 'bout what I done. So—does yuh have any other news? Did they send any pertic'lar message?"

His eyes looked like they might start shooting sparks. He leaned my way. "Did you stop to pray? 'Fore you took yourself off to the neighbors' doors—did you stop to think what you was doing, what it would mean to go stirring things up?"

My teeth clamped tight and my backbone reared up—all of me wanting to be rid of him. "Rev'rend Jones—"

"Look'a here, Sister Hazeline. I just be reminding you that the Lord God on High—reminding you, how the Lord God be the only One knows wha's best—"

I'd dropped my head, thinking how I'd like to spout right back at him, but he caught his breath and hurried right on. "You shouldn't'a done that meddling—should'a stayed out of it. Best leave things be!"

He stopped for breath, and then he say, "Let the Lord take care of it."

Then I heard myself talking. Surprised myself. "And what we s'posed to do? Be longsuffering while we on earth, wait till we get to heaven for happiness? Wait for that heavenly place, where we gon have joy and life everlasting? It all jus' setting up there waiting—that what yuh be saying?"

It all come in a rush. I wanted to grab hold of the fool and shake him good.

I musta looked like what I was feeling, cause merciful heaven!—he nearly jumped outta that chair. Slammed his hand down on his leg and spouted sump'n or t'other, and quick as yuh could say, 'There go a rat!'—that fool had done skedaddled out the door.

Rest of the day went to my liking. I come home wit' money in my pocket.

****

All that was yesterday, and today I been wondering why I even bother going to church on his Sundays. Could stay home then, just go when our deacons in charge.

The answer come quick. Cause of Joshua. And Joleen. And Henrietta and Sam—and all the rest! Ever' Sunday I picture Joshua at my side just like he used to be, and right often I even feels like he really do be right there beside me. This thought gets me to chuckling. Dif'rence be, nowadays they ain't no need for me to give him a look when he sing out too loud, nor nudge his elbow when he starts dozing off.

I still be feeling mighty good 'bout talking back to the preacher man. And seem like maybe the feeling good done spread to cover ever'thing else.

A ole saying come to mind. 'Yuh made your bed, so now yuh has to lie in it.'

This bring on a chuckle, cause now they a picture in my head of this bed I done made. Was sure scared to make it, but now, look like it might just be a right good place for me.

The wind's up today. Sure glad I don't have to be out in it. Done fed the chickens, gathered the eggs, fed Ole Dog. And emptied the slop jar. Keep it handy, cause I ain't much fond of going outside to do my biz'ness in the dark of night.

Facing off wit' Rev'rend Jones seem to've stirred up my appetite. He sure riled me. Still, might not be fair to blame my gluttony on him. Early morning, I kept the cookstove going. Cooked some white beans and fried out some fatback good and crisp. Baked a apple cake and deviled some eggs. When I was ready to eat, all I had to do was slice up one of my ripe tomatoes.

As it turned out, had to carry Miz Moore's dresses back to the sewing machine. She'd lost some weight, so now I gon have to make some tucks.

I worked at that for a spell, but didn't seem to wanna stick wit' it, so I give it up. The lady didn't ask me to hurry wit' the sewing, so seemed awright to lay it aside. Ended up reading a magazine or two while it was still good daylight. Felt kinda rich to set and take it easy on a workday.

That picture of Rev'rend Jones hightailing outta here's come to mind again and again. Tickled the fire outta me!

Now the day coming to a close. I settle in my chair wit' my Bible in my lap.

And wouldn't yuh know—first thing, I come across a verse 'at sound like it was wrote wit' that man in mind.

In Ecclesiastes. 'Dead flies cause the ointment of the apothecary to send forth a stinking savor: so doth a little folly him that is in reputation for wisdom and honor.'

****

Slouchy. And grungy. But here she come! Moseying my way.

Too late now to turn and run. Sudie Duncan. If'n ever'body was like Sudie, may as well go ahead and light the fuse, blow this world to pieces.

Now she yelling. "Oh-ho-ho! There go that smart woman!" Her words come slow, mushed t'gether like her mouth maybe full of molasses. She plant her feet and set her hands on her hipbones and look up at me from under the wide brim of a ole straw hat. Her dress be's awful thin. Wouldn't surprise me none if'n she been wearing that same one a week or more.

Her voice screechy. "Wonder what next—what that woman...woman...gon think up...next?" Now she close enough I see's bubbles trickling out the corner of her mouth. Might be this woman's done gone mad.

Ain't nobody else in sight. She dances about some on her bare feet and swipes at her mouth wit' a raggedy sleeve. I ain't said nothing but that don't bother her none. She go right on. "Anybody else, and somebody'd be going after 'em. But don't nobody wanna say a bad word 'bout Miz Morrison. Hunh-uh! That Miz Morrison such a *go-o-od* woman!"

I put on a wide smile. "Sudie, how yuh been doing? How yo' fam'ly?"

Her eyes blazing. "Don't be trying to sidetrack me! Ever'where I go folk saying, 'Why she do that?'"

More spittle. I begins to feel a bit uneasy. I knowed I didn't have to answer her questions, but I had my own. What was I gon do? Run? Fight? Felt like spittin' at her! Then she'd start pulling at my hair and there we'd be—two fools, going at it!

But right then my fortune turned. Another fool show up. I didn't know it yet, but that was a stroke of good luck. Tha's what saved me.

Sudie had just took a step closer and me a step back when somebody yelled out and she took her eyes off me to see who it was. I was facing away from the store so I couldn't see him right that minute, but turned out was

Leroy Butler, a big slovenly fella. Joshua said once how Leroy ain't got the brain of a gnat.

Early in the morning I'd come close to ruining a fine fabric cause my machine needle was dull. So right away I set out walking to the store. Was when I was leaving 'at Sudie come along. But soon as Leroy Butler give a holler that skinny gal forgot all 'bout me, and I didn't waste no time, set off home quick as I could go.

Didn't no more'n get going good till I got to chuckling. Easy to laugh when the danger's over and done. When at last I topped the hill at the well and spotted this li'l house, I slowed my steps and just stood there a bit. And got to giggling. Reckon that the kind of happy folks calls *bittersweet*.

Come to mind, it did, how I be like a fly—a fly they's a flyswatter after. Ever corner I head to, here it come again, that flyswatter still after me.

Midafternoon now and I's chuckled a few more times. Feeling fine now cause it such a pleasure to work wit' such fine material. Feels like silk. When I get this blouse done, I gon hang it on a hanger so's I can keep looking at it, admire it again and again.

By the time tomorrow come and the woman come walking over here to pick it up, I might not wanna let her have it. All the while I been sewing, been playing at how I might tell today's story. Gon be fun to tell it to Ruby.

If'n it'd been anybody else spouting off thataway, I'd still be a'fretting. But that Sudie? Why she ain't worth getting upset over. All the while she was a'carrying on, right close by they was a post for tying up a horse or mule. Why I'd sooner hear what that post had to say than what come outta Sudie Duncan.

Well, time to quit my brooding. My work's done, so time now for my treat. A Nehi grape soda. Got just enough ice left in the box to chip a bit off and fix me a tall glass. Gon take it outside and visit wit' Ole Dog. Reckon I better find him some kind of treat too.

****

Traveling! Tha's what I been up to. Now my head's done set me back down here and I spot my machine needle, sewing up a long seam. My foot kept the treadle going while I was far away, standing wit' Joshua where the water coming in, going out, coming in again. And my feet sinking in! The sand kept washing out from under me. I remember asking Joshua how many miles we had rode from Mecklenburg County to get to the coast.

He tole me and I stood there by the edge of that big restless water trying to figure how much farther it would be to get to the other edge. And if'n we was to go straight across, where would we come out? I pictured the map on our schoolhouse wall. North Carolina, Atlantic Ocean, Europe. I knowed we wouldn't come out at Africa, cause it on the low side of that line round the middle.

Ever chance I got I looked close at that globe. Belonged to the teacher, her prize possession. She wouldn't leave it at school, just brung it in ever so often. I studied 'bout the planets too. I can see that picture too, me in my feed-sack dress Mama made, staring at that globe, trying to picture this world hanging in the sky.

Hazeline

And now here I be settin' at my machine—while my mind off at the beach. And right after that, stop by the schoolhouse to see Miss Hinson's round map. I can go any place. Wouldn't mind dropping in somewhere to meet somebody famous. Booker T. Washington come to mind. But I'd have to stop by heaven to see him.

One teacher we had showed us his picture. Say he was born a slave but while he was still a boy freedom come and he set out to get hisself a education, and then he begun preaching. And kept on preaching—saying how all Negroes oughta get a education.

They was one day he lived I sure wouldn't wanna visit. Don't r'member where it was, but some church and him getting ready to speak, and some of the seats upstairs and some of the folks up there arguing 'bout finding a empty seat. Somebody say 'fight' and another'n think that'un say 'fire'—so right off a bunch of folks got to hollering 'fire'...and the stampede begun. Pushing! Shoving! Ever'body wanting to get down those stairs. More'n a hundred people died that day.

I was pretty young then, but I remembers hearing 'bout it. That kind of news the kind 'at spread fast. And when Booker T. died, all us mourned his passing. That man had spent his life trying to help our people. Me and Joshua hadn't long been married then and I thought often of our hero, Mister Booker T—and pictured him taking his seat in heaven.

He tole us education would help us better ourselves. I don't guess my learning to read and add a few numbers helped us much, but the reading has made me a traveler.

A magazine, a newspaper—and off I go! Never got a chance to be a real traveler. Think I might like it, though, go a thousand miles or more! And I could bring home a souvenir.

That one time was the only chance I's had to see 'the big pond.' We'd been married a coupla years then. He'd awready see'd the ocean, so right away he showed me how to catch a ride on a wave.

Most of the talk 'bout heaven don't feel right to me, yet and still I got a feeling 'at someday I gon see my Joshua again. And I got me a suspicion...that when it come time to leave this world, it gon be a right smart like catching a wave.

****

When day's end gets here I gon be tickled pink, cause I be keeping a promise to myself. Awready on the way. Moved all the dishes and pots and pans—washing this kitchen down. When I get done it gon feel brand new, top to bottom. 'Bout too hot for this job, but I done made up my mind. Gon put fresh newspaper on the walls too.

In the corners I find bugs and bugs—bane of my life! These ones is dead though, praise be. This li'l house so crude built, bugs don't even have to work hard to steal they way in. Ruby say she be glad to come help so's we could paper all the walls pretty quick—but today be's the day! Way long past time to see this job done.

It cross my mind how glad I gon be next time Slim come and set hisself down here. I won't be looking his way and seeing this faded picture of Groucho Marx. It always do remind me of the day he set right here and wept like a chile. He dropped his head to hide his face. And I set waiting, my eyes fixed on Groucho.

Strange how li'l things like that stick in yuh mind.

The clock strikes three jus' as I finish putting up the new paper. I'm hot and a bit weary and a lot thirsty. But ain't time yet to quit. Got to put ever'thing back in place and hang the clean curtain, and put my new oilcloth back on the table. Then I prob'ly gon want a bo'quet too. I don't doubt I can get it all done, cause my steam's been so high today I's had trouble keeping up wit' myself.

Now this ole black skillet, and this other black skillet. Wonder how many meals they done held for us? Here yuh go, skillets. Back up on your nails, so's yuh be ready for the next cooking—in a clean kitchen!

Cake pans. And this ole black biscuit pan. I s'pect they been 'nough biscuits baked on it to feed more'n one army.

What that noise? Must be hearing things. No—there it be again, somebody at the door. I sho' don't look like receiving no comp'ny. I push my hair back and straighten my apron. That'll have to do.

Surprise, surprise!—Slim! And me just thinking 'bout him!

He admires my labor and we soon settle in at the table. I set aside the few things I hadn't put away yet and tell him how good he be looking and how I hope he be feeling fine.

"Yes'm," he say, "I got some good news. But they some bad news too."

"Well, ain't that the way of life? I guess it be's just in songs and poems 'at ever'thing's rosy. I r'member some lines our teacher had us recite—r'member 'em after all these years! 'The lark's on the wing, the snail's on the thorn, God's in his heaven, all's right with the world.'"

Slim give a li'l chuckle and set his glass of milk down and swipe at his mouth wit' the back of his hand.

I wait a minute and when he don't say nothing I says, "So yuh come to tell me good news."

His eyes twinkle. "Yep—can't hardly b'lieve it, but the news I come to tell? Since day 'fore yesterday, she been talking to me!"

I look on his smile, as fine a one as I s'pect ever has crossed his handsome face. Ain't no wonder she decide to open up to him. That smile's enough to lasso many a girl.

I smile too, and next thing I know I be wiping a tear at the corner of my eye. This young man. Healthy, handsome. Helpful and kind. Since the day he first knocked at my door I has felt attached to him.

A wonder how the heart work. Coulda been some other young man come here wanting that ole lumber, and if'n so I wouldn't even know Slim, but now here he be, setting at my table.

And the bad news? Wonder what it be?

I say, "Come on out back and lemme show yuh my new laying hens." I aready on my feet, heading out the door.

He brag on my big fat hens. I's raised 'em from the time they was li'l biddies and so far has kept 'em safe from possums and foxes. I been selling eggs ever' week at the market. Lately, Miss Kathleen been letting me ride into town wit' her, help wit' the selling. Been doing me a lotta good to go inta town some, not to mention how it pad my pocket a little.

The extra money help me face the coming of winter a bit easier. And I like riding through the streets to get to the market. They one or two streets got what they call shotgun houses on both sides. I like looking at all them chimneys lined up in rows. A time or two I's had the chance to visit some distant kinfolk down there. And tha's all it took to make me certain of one thing. I don't never wanna live so close on to others.

Slim saying, "If'n you aiming to keep on keeping the varmints from getting at these chickens, reckon I best be getting over here soon and take a hammer and nail to a few spots."

"Well," I say, "I be much obliged. I know you can do a better job of it'n I can."

He kicks at a dirt clod wit' the toe of his boot, keeping his eyes down. He say, "I need to be getting on over the way. Don't want to let a day go by and not see Delia—now that she'll see me."

When he lift his head they a wide grin on his face. He say, "I figured yuh hurried me out here to keep from hearing the bad news."

I give him a grin back. "You could tell that, could yuh?"

"Uh-huh. Wadn't too hard to figure." He stretch a hand to a corner post of the pen and lean on it. "In the long run, if'n Delia'll have me for her husband, the bad news won't be so bad, I reckon."

"You mean...she carrying a chile?"

"Yes'm." He holds his cap in his hand, turning it slow. "I didn't know till last night. She thought telling me would mean she'd see'd the last of me. But that wadn't what happened. I stayed awake most of the night thinking on how I'd been—I mean, when we was spending time t'gether."

He lifts his head and catches my eye. "Why, I'd been 'fraid to show my feelings! But now I done passed that. And the other thing I figured, was how easy it'll be to love the chile—cause it her chile."

I move close and lay my hand on his shoulder. "Slim, they one thing I can see for sure, see it clear as day. You love this girl."

He nod then set his cap on his head. We walk side-by-side round to the front and say our goodbyes. He start cross the yard, me watching. Then he stop and turn back like maybe he forgot sump'n. "Meant to tell yuh," he called across the little distance. "Bout that verse yuh learned in school. Our teacher had us say it and a bunch more. One thing I didn't like was, only one of the poets we studied was colored. Paul Lawrence Dunbar. I won't never forget his name. The lines you said? They by a Englishman. I r'member cause his wife wrote verses too— 'bout how much she loved her husband. Right funny 'at you happened to say 'em today—of all days, huh?"

He wave his hand and start off again. '

Fore he get outta earshot, I call after him. "Guess yuh gonna bring her this way someday soon?"

He throw his hand up in a salute, then pick up his pace. Ain't long 'fore he over the hill and outta sight, but not outta mind.

I finish up the loose ends of my task and stand there gazing on my handiwork. Ever'thing's clean and in order. Sure a fine feeling, to get done what yuh been putting off doing. Then that same day, such fine good news!

The night's just beginning to set in when a storm comes through. By the time the rain starts the wind's eased up so I go set under the lean-to. Watch the lightning in the far distance. Long, jagged flashes in the sky out 'cross the field.

A light rain now, spilling off the roof. The wind's moving easy, and row after row of raindrops coming off the roof. I watch and I watch. The air feels awful good, and the falling raindrops be like a sheer curtain. They sway easy, moving to one side.

Soon the daylight's gone. Can't see my rain curtain no more, but I stay put, sniffing at the washed-clean air, listening to the rain's soft music. Seem a fitting way to end such a day.

Chapter 21

───── ⊰⊱ ─────

"Ain't so easy all by my lonesome, Joshua. Go to bed by myself, get up by myself. Nobody to whisper to in the night. I just plain lonesome for yuh...sometimes I wonder if'n it be lonely where you be. Most of the time I picture yuh sleeping. Guess that wouldn't be so bad. Sure wish you could talk to me, tell me what you think 'bout wha's going on here. I wanna b'lieve what some folks says they b'lieve, that those 'on the other side' can help us."

I pull the sheet up to my chin. Oughta be getting some sleep.

"Ain't no doubt in my mind you'd like Slim. He be's happy again now. But I ain't so happy. They still a injustice been done and nothing done about it. I keep thinking on the ole saying, 'A stitch in time saves nine.' I think it mean, what can be done now might keep us from the same trouble in days to come."

That gets me to chuckling. Reckon I know 'bout as much 'bout sewing up a ripped spot as anybody in these parts.

My mind roams a bit longer, and a surprise thought comes round.

"If'n you'd been here, Joshua, I might never woulda become so fond of Slim. He woulda talked to you when he come by asking 'bout the hog pen. Well, no. Cause if'n you'd been here, they wouldn't'a been no lumber for him to get and he wouldn't have come by."

A big sigh come out of me. Talking to Joshua just make me miss him more. Feel like I been cut loose. Used to belong to somebody.

Grandmama used to say, 'Let bygones be bygones.' But Joshua ain't no bygone. He still real to me. Wish I'd paid more attention when Grandmama was talking. Who was she talking to, and what happened 'at need to be a bygone?

Next thing I know, the clock on the mantel striking four o'clock. I stretch out on my back, rest my hands by my side and lay still as I can, listening. In case my Joshua can speak.

Another thought come. Heard somebody say it recent. *Temporary.* My ears perked up. And I wondered why. I knowed the word, but wadn't no reason to use it. But now I see! Hope so anyway. *Temporary.* Tha's how I gon think of this sad bit of life I be traipsing through now.

****

Another night, and this'n too, me just laying here. Thinking 'bout how folks been calling me a crazy woman. Musta been dreaming. When I come awake my chest was tight and my head running on and on wit' awful thoughts.

Folks was telling me I oughta mind my own bizness. And in the dream I yelled back, yelled way loud. "Well, just tell me what it be—if it ain't my bizness!!"

Just laying here a'bed, I get plumb mad. My hands ball up, like they ready to knock somebody up 'side the head. And so the night goes. Till at last the sky shows the first light. I go over to the winduh and watch for some little bit, and tha's when it come to me. *No matter what happen, the sun still come up.* Seemed a lesson I was needing, but I wadn't ready yet for the day to get going. What I was feeling way down deep wadn't like usual. Didn't feel like me.

After some while I get outta bed, still thinking on it. Seem like some wicked spirit done crawled in and set up house in me. Jesus say that in one of the Bible stories.

Huh-uh, this feeling ain't like me. But they still enough me so's I know I got to find some ease. I speak it to the air. Maybe God will hear, or an angel. I say it out loud. "Help me."

Thing was, I'd got mad as a hornet! And that sure ain't like me. Was the folks I'd tried to rouse 'at I was thinking on. Was they just plain dumb? What else you gon call folks 'at ain't willing to see things as they be? Ever' word 'at come outta my mouth wadn't no more'n the plain truth.

What a long night. Ever' once in a while I heard the clock striking again. When the anger got going in me, I got scared and drawed back—pulled back on the reins. What fools, I thought—talking 'gainst me, 'stead of listening.

Uh-huh. A long night. But reckon it maybe needed to be long, so's to make me look at myself. Thank goodness it happened right here, where can't nobody see this fool I be.

Somewhere on over in the dark of night I become like Cain, feeling just the way he musta felt when he set out to go kill his brother. My body was rarin' to go—go do sump'n! If'n daylight hadn't come, I does wonder what woulda happened.

I couldn't get up right away. Needed a li'l rest after all that going-on. When at last I dragged myself outta bed I gulped down some water, pulled on my housecoat and headed out here to Joshua's bench. Soon after I set down Ole Dog come ambling over. And here we still be a'setting.

He can't figure why I out first thing and ain't brung him his breakfast.

S'pect I'll remember this night long as I live. Cause I wanted to kill. Wadn't them boys. Not really. Hard to say for certain. I was wanting to be rid of the way things be. So if'n they'd been only one guilty, 'stead of three, might be I'd'a been fool enough to set out and stir up big trouble...make a real fool of myself.

****

Sunday evening—one of my favorite times. Just pulled on my ole sweater. Weather all day long's been cool, and I don't wanna build no fire. Ain't done much of nothing this day. Set wit' my hands empty. Sure glad of the commandment 'bout no work on the Sabbath. For supper I stirred up some mush. Didn't want none of the leftovers. Wanted sump'n simple. Sump'n soothing.

Ever since I left church I's had Joleen on my mind. She had that chewing gum working—same as usual, and the way she act the same too. Speak to her mama, but that 'bout all. She was too busy showing off her ready-made dress.

All I could think of, the words shouting in my head, 'I coulda made that dress!'

She like to tell 'bout where she buy her clothes. Sometimes she hardly seem like my chile—leastways, not the same chile she used to be. 'Where that girl of mine?' Tha's what I'd like to ask her. I done played wit' all kind of pictures of me asking her sump'n like that.

I settle in my rocking chair and stir butter in my bowl of mush. Feel good to eat this humble food. Corn ground up, so we can eat it any time of year.

Corn be our main food. Corn mush, grits, cornbread, corncakes, corn on the cob, creamed corn, whole kernel too. We save some for winter in canning jars, and add it to the soup mix we can too. Corn keeps us alive, and it do the same for the chickens and all the animals. When we hardly has anything else, we's got corn.

I soon setting my bowl aside, and ease my upset mind by reminding myself how quick things can change. One of these days Joleen just might come to and stop that trying to impress ever'body. Then maybe she have some time for her ole mama.

Not s'posed to work on Sunday, and I try to abide by the commandment, but I can't sit so long by myself and do nothing. So I pick up my tatting. Late summer now, but the weather's turned off cool, so setting here working the shuttle be a pleasure. The threads come together and there the pretty lace—easy as pie!

Worked hard this past week. Coupla afternoons I picked lima beans. They a heap of trouble to pick and shell, but sure worth it. Ain't nothing from the garden I like better. Well, reckon fresh corn rank right up there. And if'n yuh throw in a ripe tomato fresh off the vine, and fry up some okra—yuh got sump'n fine and dandy!

Hazeline

Awready got a good many quart jars of my garden stuff put by for the winter. And got a second crop of some things coming on—if'n the bugs and rabbits don't get to it first.

Last week Ruby come and stayed overnight and I talked my heart out. For a long time that woman's been a good friend. But what she say this time sure had me upset.

I ain't quite over it yet. Was early Saturday afternoon. I heard her call and rushed to the door and she was awready coming 'cross the yard, carrying a bundle over her shoulder and a big black pocketbook on her arm. When I went to embrace her I knocked her straw hat off.

We set in to giggling, so glad she'd found a ride and headed this way. She'd walked from the Beatties Ford Road. I poured her a cold glass of lemonade, a treat I'd fixed for myself, not knowing she'd come. As luck would have it, I'd got a block of ice the day before.

While the sun was moving west she filled me in on wha's been going on over her way and I tole her all my grievance. I had some hope. Might be she'd say just the right thing, help me see my way.

But what she said come more like a wallop. Same as if she'd hauled off and hit me one. I'd made us a pan of biscuits to go wit' my late tomatoes. I took the scraps of the dough and rolled it thin and spread it wit' butter and sugar and cinnamon. Stickies. And I said what Grandmama used to say. "A li'l sump'n sweet to put up on."

The cookstove had warmed up the house so we put our supper on trays and carried it outside. They ain't nothing better 'n buttered hot biscuits for a tomato sandwich. The juice ran down our hands and we licked it off and said, "Hm-mmm, yum-yum!"

I coulda eat anything and it taste fine, I s'pect, cause my friend was visiting.

While we ate the daylight begun to fade and there we was, bellies full, the night air cool and pleasant, and the tree frogs getting they chorus started. For some long bit, didn't neither of us say nothing.

As it turned out, was a good thing we was setting in the dark when she decided to say her piece. The words come all in a rush, like she spewing venom. "Turn your trouble over to the Lord, Hazeline—and all will be well!"

At first, I didn't make a move. Couldn't think of nothing to say noway, but once I had a handle on what she was saying I almost let out a chuckle. Throwed my hand over my mouth to hold it back.

Then she say it again, a li'l dif'rent. "The Lord'll take care of any troubles yuh turn over to Him."

By then I was holding my breath and tears had sprung to my eyes. This woman, my friend—what was she saying? She mean what we do don't count? She think the Lord gon come down here and undo the wrong done to Delia?

A long time past bedtime, while she was sleeping, I lay awake. If'n all we had to do was let the Lord handle ever'thing, hadn't enough prayers been said awready? If'n prayers make ever'thing right, the world oughta be like heaven by now. Didn't my slave grandmama pray? My mama sure did. She wanted more'n anything for our people to be treated fair, and wanted them ridiculous Jim Crow laws wiped off the books.

The morning come. And Ruby took her leave early. Just as well, since she was still into her preaching. I was glad she went, though the house seemed a bit empty. There was plenty to be done, though, like usual, so I tied a kerchief round my head and got busy.

Late afternoon now, and a wide bank of clouds moving in. I go out back and watch 'em floating high up over the hillside. The changing sky often seem to my mind a sign of hope, a little reminder how don't nothing stay the same for long.

****

By the east winduh, embroidering. Putting li'l flowers on the bodice of a christening dress. Just get started, and humming a ole blues tune, when I hears somebody.

Well, doggone—it Skunk Man! Ain't see'd him in a coon's age.

Lester be's called Skunk Man cause way on back he got sprayed by one and nobody'd go near him. Him and Joshua used to pass a few words from time to time. But I don't remember him ever saying more'n a word or two to me.

"H'lo Hazeline, how you doin' today?" He say it through the screen door. He's
holding his hat in his hand. He always has seemed a harmless fella so I ask him in. Judging by his overalls, I

figure he's come from his work and it was awful dirty work.

The daylight was starting to go so I crossed the room and lit the kerosene lamp. Lester's a short stubby little man and always do have a goatee, which I s'pect takes some care to keep in shape. He was still standing near the door. He say, "I sure misses Joshua. Know you must miss him terrible bad."

I don't say nothing to that, and he keep going. "Weather's been good lately. But I guess we 'bout to need some rain."

Why this man come? Sure wadn't to talk 'bout the weather. I'd already had one suitor I didn't want. Was Lester gon be the second? I sure hoped not. Any woman wit' a man so fine as Joshua ain't much likely to figure on such luck a second go round.

He cleared his throat. "I almos' didn't come. Started to, and backed out, and now, well..."

"You trying to say...?" I was 'bout to ask if'n he'd brung bad news. But then I had the sense to hush and wait for him to tell me why he'd come here.

I pulled a straight chair over for him and turned my rocking chair to face him. We both set down and he dropped his hat on the floor. When he straightened up he caught my eye and cleared his throat again. I clutched my hands tight in my lap, readying myself for whatever I was 'bout to hear.

He clasped his hands and started in. "Yuh see, I figgered it was time for somebody to say thank-yuh—I mean, folks round here, they's just kept on saying all yuh done was stir up trouble—but seemed to me you was the only one trying to sort things out."

All this pour out in a rush, like he'd memorized it and was 'fraid he'd forget 'fore he finished. He shocked me so I didn't know what to say. He looked down at his lap, then put his hands on his knees and looked straight at me. "I 'preciate what yuh done, Hazeline. Least, what yuh tried to do."

I think I kept my surprise from showing. How strange that this man, of all people, would be the one to say what I'd longed to hear.

I took care to keep my voice even, tole him it was awful kind of him to go to the trouble of coming by to tell me this. And when he left I stood at the winduh and watched him go, wondering if'n angels sometimes take on the shape of short li'l men wit' goatees.

****

The next afternoon I come back from taking my stuff over to Miss Kathleen and feel chilled to the bone. Don't often get weather this cool this time of year. Evening come and I get a fire going in the fireplace. Now I ready to do sump'n I been wanting to do. While my hands busy, I start in talking.

"Joshua, you shoulda see'd my dolls. You'd'a prob'ly give 'em all names, cause when I embroidered the faces I made 'em all a li'l different. A dozen dolls, made outta socks. The caps was fun to make too. Miss Kathleen was tickled pink. Say she much obliged to me for coming up wit' the idea, cause having 'em at her booth make people stop by and that way she sell more of her stuff. She bought the socks and the stuffing, say she gon give me my bit of money when the dolls sells."

I keep on, telling him all I been doing while I make up my dough. Gon put my biscuits down in the Dutch oven and bake 'em in the fireplace, way Grandmama done. Grease the inside of the pot good wit' some lard, take hold of my rolling pin and roll out the dough, then the biscuit cutter—and they ready to go in the pot. Hold the pot by the handle wit' my big potholder and set it in the fireplace close to the fire and shovel some hot coals over the top, then set myself down in my rocker.

Wait and watch. After a bit the pot gon need another helping of hot coals.

Been a tiring day. Guess it was the hurrying tired me so. Hurried to finish the dolls and get 'em delivered. Least while I was hurrying my mind didn't go to thinking on them boys and why they ain't see'd no recompense.

I watch careful. Not wanting my biscuits to burn. Be some fine eating, slather some butter 'tween a top half and bottom half. But it sure getting too warm in here now.

Wish I had a ghost I could count on. Could send it over to haunt them boys. The ghost'd rattle things, and blow papers and stuff round the room. The boy'd get real scared. The ghost'd talk—talk so's only that one could hear. It might say, *You beating a path to damnation. Better look to your heart now, 'fore it get too late.*

All it would take would be one of 'em to come out wit' the truth. Wonder whose ghost be up to the job? Best to have somebody from round here, I reckon, somebody tha's been wronged. That'd be best. Maybe...uh-huh, that young man—one they lynched a few miles east of here a coupla years back.

What kind of justice could happen?

Well, Delia could get over this and live a long and happy life. And them wayward boys? Seem like, if'n they the kind 'at do this now—when they still young'uns, more'n likely they gon do it again. And it bound to work against 'em. So less'n they repents now, ain't likely gon live no happy life.

After a bit I's almost dozed off—but right quick rouse up, grab my thick potholder from the nail where it hang and pull that black pot onto the hearth. Got to work careful, get the lid off so's not to let ashes in—and there they be!

'Fore long, I done finished off two biscuits stuffed wit' a bit of leftover meat, and one jelly biscuit.

Now I full as a tick. I get up and move around some, then take hold of one of the li'l short-handled brooms Joshua made outta broomstraw and sweep up the hearth. Soon's I finish up what has to be done, I crawl in the bed.

But sleep don't come right away. Talk starts up. One o' them voices talking in me say, *Don't give it no room*.

This part o' me can't see no sense thinking on and on 'bout justice. It say I be thinking crazy, if'n I be thinking anything round here can change. Yet and still, they a part of me 'at still think sump'n can be done. Trouble be, that'un ain't near so big as the other'un.

I lay still and quiet, flat on my back, hoping to clear this head o'mine. After a bit a ole saying comes to mind.

Where they's a will they's a way. I always did take that as true, long as yuh ain't thinking pie in the sky.

The weeks has just kept going by, and all the ideas 'at come to mind soon fade away. Like a rainbow. Look real fine...but don't stay long.

I plumb weary of it all. But yet and still, they this deep-down voice in me. It keep saying, *Has to be sump'n. Has to be.*

Chapter 22

———————— ➤≥≋≋≋

Plenty of work waiting to be done. But not today. I in the mood for whatsoever I wanna do. Now, wonder what that might be? Lemme see. Ole Dog ain't no help. He up under the house, fast asleep.

If'n Henrietta lived close by I'd hang onto her close— close like a tick on a dog. She'd have to pull me loose. If'n she din't, I'd talk her ear off. But ain't nobody near to talk to, least nobody I cares to talk to. Less'n...well...and so I might!

Now what can I carry along? Won't do to go empty-handed.

I soon head out. The walk just long enough to help me settle down some. First thing, I tell her I sorry to be bringing jus' half a coffeecake. "Come on the spur of the moment—so wadn't no time to bake a new one."

Miz Ida Mae grin when she take it from me. "Mine," she say. "All mine. If'n yuh'd brung a big one I'd have to share it wit' all the rest, but I gon keep it for my own nibbling. Much obliged to yuh."

They do be quite a few live here. Good thing it a big sprawling house. I's been through here when Suzy was cooking and could hardly believe how many dried beans she cook in a day.

A good thing Miz Ida Mae's son's worked hisself up to a good job. He a mechanic. And they always wagons and cars and trucks lined up waiting—even tractors and sewing machines. That man blessed wit' a gift for fixing what need fixing. Sure wish he could fix people. Squirt a little grease here, a little there—get things to running smooth. I don't tell her my thought, but I wouldn't mind seeing them boys get a little fixing.

The little woman leads the way, moving awful slow, headed for the big maple out front. She send me to the other side o' the house to get a chair. Must be 'at when she under her maple, the rest of 'em know better'n to bother her. A couple of 'em pass by but don't even look our way. And I guessed right. She say this her own setting place, say she don't always feel like putting up wit' so many.

We start out talking 'bout the weather and such. After a bit she lean over and spit in her can and put another pinch of snuff in her cheek. We keep talking a good li'l spell and I surprise myself. Don't even mention wha's been bothering me.

All the way home I rejoice. Time spent in that wise woman's comp'ny be pleasant as any holiday. I coulda been fifty miles from home—no troubles nowhere round!

Now I settled out here under the shade tree wit' the paper. Ole Dog come over. He rest his head on my knee. I know what he want—wanting me to scratch behind his ears. I ain't so sure he can hear but he do seem to like my talk, so I set in.

"I been looking, but musta been barking up the wrong tree. Needing to find some way to do sump'n. So what you think 'bout it? Is they sump'n I can do 'at won't get folks all riled up. I done upset a right smart of 'em, even that no-good Eli. Wonder if'n he was named for that fella invented the cotton gin? I tell yuh what we be needing now. Need a invention 'at pick cotton. But I can't see that. Don't b'lieve there'll ever be such a thing."

I quit rubbing his ears but he don't move, so I keep on. "Newspaper say some farmers thinking 'bout turning away from cotton. Prices down, soil wore out. The landowners finding other things to grow. My guess be, me and you both be long gone 'fore that happen on this farm."

****

Saturday morning. And I hear the call. To Tucker's Grove! The cotton's done laid by, so now be the time to get away for a bit.

I come out the door to throw out some scraps and the morning air so fine I's just kept a'lingering. I lean over and say to Ole Dog, "Just look 'cross that pasture. Yuh see it? The clouds a'racing. And the light? Why, it just keep a'changing!"

Pretty a sight as yuh could hope to see, and here it be, right here. But right now, time for me to get busy. Get ready for tomorrow. Big Sunday at camp meeting. Most ever'body gon be there. Some folk been there all week long.

Camp meeting come round same time ever' year, early September, when the cotton bolls busy getting ready for the picking. I gon be riding in Mr. Harry Lawing's truck, squeezed in wit' a bunch more. Gon need a bit of money to pay him for the ride. Like a reg'lar taxi, it be, back and forth 'tween here and Denver. We hunch up close in the truck bed. He a white man, and look like ever'time our camp meeting come round he do awright for hisself. Another thing that man do to earn a bit of money be making the big baskets—ones 'at stow the cotton when we's picking.

Camp meeting. Uh-huh! A long-time tradition—and loads of fun. We gets to see folk we ain't see'd all year. Been many a fine time at Tucker's Grove. When Joshua was by my side it was fun enough for me just to follow along and watch him. He'd slap folks on the back and laugh that big laugh of his.

Like one big party it be, wit' people coming from miles around. Snow cones and popcorn. Hot dogs and fried fish. Sawdust on the ground. Preaching too, but I s'pect most folks same as me—mostly goes just to see ever'body. The first camp meeting after Joshua passed I couldn't go. Knowed it'd be too sad. And it surely did end up a sad day, but least I wadn't in the crowd wit' my weeping.

Gon get to see some of my folk. And most all Joshua's brothers and sisters and cousins be there. A lot of 'em look a lot like him. The thought put a smile on my face.

"Ain't none of 'em handsome as you, Joshua. Yuh know I always did say so. And sure as heck ain't no need for you to worry 'bout me wanting any of 'em. Furthest thing from my mind."

I know I gon feel lonely for him, maybe even feel like he be there, so I gon wear the dress he liked best on me. A bright blue, real bright. I still r'member how he looked up when I first put it on, followed me wit' his eyes and say, "Well now...."

Wish I knowed what the weather gon be like. Best take along some rain gear. I gon wear Sunday shoes, but always do end up kicking 'em off. Gon get me a hot dog wit' onions, and stroll along in my bare feet. Walk one end to the other—and stop at the spot where they be selling *ice cream.*

The big arbor in the middle. Tha's where the preacher gon be doing his hollering and raising a joyful noise. Praise the Lord, it won't be our preacher.

Won't get back till late. And then soon be time to start that picking. Bend over them long rows. Four fields to pick—way wide and way long fields. For sure—I gon be doing my share, 'cept for the days I works for Miz Robbins.

****

This one time I ain't in no mood to be heading off to Miz Robbins and her dirty clothes. Had a heap of fun at camp meeting, and come home late. Now this day. Well, I be going—but I sure ain't jumping up and down happy 'bout going.

They was one at camp meeting I was sure glad to see. He real old now and don't always make it, but there he was, holding to the arm of his eldest boy. DeWitt Kelly. In his time, he was a spunky fella. Tried to stand up for the rights of colored folk. Don't know as it done any good, but we all loves him for it.

DeWitt joined the Army and got sent to France back during the Big War. When he come home he had aged so much was hard to b'lieve and had all kinda tales to tell. Joshua said he tole horror stories 'bout the fighting, but what he tole far and wide was how the black man ain't treated over in France same as he be's here.

I s'pect when DeWitt come back he found it kinda hard to get used to the ways here. I heard it said once that only reason he come back was cause of his chirren. Otherwise, wouldn't'a been a hard decision to make. Ain't many of us would choose to come back if we could get to a place where we treated like we just usual folk.

Well, best quit delaying. Get on 'cross the way. If'n I still got any get-up-and-go when I come back, thinking I might write a letter to my cousin what moved to Philadelphia. Ain't heard from her in a coon's age. Wanna tell her 'bout this year's camp meeting. She can't read, but she always find somebody to read for her and send back least a few lines. Been quite a spell since I took out my fountain pen and my li'l ink bottle.

I trudge along. Still early morning. When I gets past the well and turns east, the sun a'shining through the few trees and the light coming right at me. Straight as can be! I can see the lines. They be light rays! And they stretching my way. Just one more wonder!

The day move along, me bending over the washpot. And 'fore I know it, Miz Robbins be ringing the bell. That her main job while the pickers in the field. Watch the clock, ring the bell. A big bell, on a tall post out by the corner of the house.

Right on time she ring it. Now the hands gather in the shade and eat the biscuits and whatever else they brung along. One hour, tha's all. And if'n it look like they some chance of rain, don't get that much. She ring the bell again and it time to get at it again.

If'n the threat of rain big, most ever'body gets to picking. Coloreds and whites alike. Course, the Mister and Missus, they don't pick, but the Robbins boys and Miz Kathleen too, they likely come to help if'n they dark clouds lining up.

Be my turn tomorrow and days to come, following 'long them rows wit' my sack over my shoulder. Keep on till it so full of snow-white bolls it drag the ground.

That ache – and this bending over the washtub? They 'bout the same.

Oftentimes that bell gets me to thinking 'bout my man. I see him clear. Bell go *ding-dong ding-dong ding-dong—* and Joshua throw his hat in the air and hurry over near the woods at the edge of the field. First thing, he'd lay flat, stretched out, easing his back 'fore he filled his belly.

Funny how the men and the women most often set in dif'rent spots round the edge of the field. Me and Maybelle always did set t'gether. The other women close by, but me and her'd commiserate. Swap our lists, we would—'bout what part of us aching worse.

A bit later I be wringing out some towels and another mem'ry come along. Hunger in the field. A long time back that was. But I still r'members it clear. Night before I'd been so tired I couldn't sleep. Didn't sleep none till toward morning, and woke up late, so they wadn't no time to fix breakfast. Had to make-do wit' pulling some dry bread from the breadbox and munch on it on my way to the field. Way long 'fore time for that noon dinner bell I was so hungry my stomach was hugging my backbone.

****

Didn't have 'nough water to rinse my supper dishes. And too tired—way awful tired, to fetch water. Reckon I gon have to face the truth. I be getting older. A day in the field take ever'thing outta me. Nothing I can do 'bout it, though. Picking time's here and they ain't no way to get round it 'cept do it.

Used my li'l bit of dishwater to wash my feet, and had enough water in the washbowl to sponge down a bit. Don't b'lieve I ever has been so tired. Aching tired. Gon take me a BC Powder and tuck myself in.

They was one thing 'bout this day 'at was fine. All the while I was filling my bag wit' bolls of cotton, I was off a'wandering. Got to picturing ones 'at used to be here. Maybelle. Joshua. A coupla others. Tried to picture 'em— picture where they be's now.

And all a sudden, sump'n come to mind. Sump'n I heard once.

Some far-off cousin to Miz Robbins had come to visit and I happened to overhear what he say. Hadn't never see'd him a'fore. Miz Robbins got all nervous—say he 'big' company, a 'highly educated man.'

He was setting at the dinner table wit' the rest and me waiting in the kitchen. I still remembers it clear. He say, "They a other side to this life, and it's like a undiscovered country."

All I know...can't find it in me to b'lieve they a place where folks is burned alive—and burned for all the rest of time! I tries to stay clear of such thinking. Ain't gon b'lieve it—no sirree!

At last I crawl in the bed. Ooo-wee! I knowed I was tired, but this beyond tired—way beyond! A few weeks from now, when all this cotton picking's behind us, I gon give myself a day off. A whole day! Start to finish!

My day. And not one blessed thing I has to do less'n I want to.

****

Sunday. Our rest day, praise the Lord.

Late in the day I decide to get out the house, give the ghost some room. Ain't never see'd a ghost, though some folk say they has. Couldn't shake the feeling, though, so decided to go on out 'fore dark, give it some room.

I chuckled as I headed out the backdoor. More'n likely I be 'magining things. Night before I'd stayed awake a long time. Seemed to me like things in this neck of the woods was way past any fixing. So far as I knowed, ain't nobody called them boys on what they done.

Just 'fore I climbed off my straw mattress this morning I said out loud, "May as well quit."

When I had the fire going in the cookstove I went out and did the outside chores quick, then got the coffee going. Soon as it boiled a bit, I poured me a cup and set myself down in Joshua's chair.

Did seem like I may as well quit. I been thinking on it a heap and ain't come up wit' not one idea worth looking at a second time. I thought of talking to Joshua some, but didn't. All I done was just set there quiet. After a bit it seemed like maybe I was pouting. Yessiree, pouting! Like a young'un 'at didn't get some candy. They just wadn't no idea had come along 'at felt right. Not a one! Why, I coulda kept setting there till tomorrow or next week—and wouldn't likely come up wit' no idea.

But they was one thing I knowed for sure. The remedy—uh-huh, the remedy—it has to fit the wrong. And it has to stand some good chance of working. And there I set, and just set right on, till after some long while wit' me staring at a knothole on a board by the fireplace, the clock chimed. I chuckled a bit and tole that knothole I might be coming back to set near it again, cause they was one thing 'at had come to me clear. I wouldn't again be thinking on giving up.

I tole that knothole, "Just gotta be patient."

And right soon after that, a strange feeling come over me. Like they was maybe somebody else close by. And the feeling didn't leave me. I tried, but couldn't shed the notion that maybe they was a ghost close by. And might be the ghost was Maybelle's. I sure miss Maybelle Gudger. And if'n she knows what I been going through, I wouldn't be surprised none a'tall if'n she come along. She'd be just the ghost to help me and encourage me. Lord knows I been needing some help, so maybe tha's what happened.

Walking 'long the path now, edge of the field by the burnt woods. I pull my sweater close and tuck my hands up under my arms. Sun's already dropped below the ridge of trees up on the hill but they still some daylight left.

I keep thinking 'bout Maybelle. Sad, sad, sad. My friend grieved herself to death. Ain't none of the other women on the place ever been a friend to me like Maybelle. When they was burying her, I had to work hard to keep from falling down and weeping. I was thinking 'bout her and her boy. And 'bout when I lost my boy. The cord caught round his neck. Never had a chance to get his breath—no chance a'tall.

Maybelle saved me, way back then. She just kept coming, reminding me time and again, how I had to get back to life cause my girl was needing her mama and Joshua was needing his wife, and all that while all I could see was the picture I'd made in my head. My boy. Buried in the cold ground. No life for him. And him there all by his self, curled up in that box they built for him, and it cold and damp. No comfort for him, no comfort for me.

But Maybelle come again. That time she knelt down beside me and took my hands and we cried together. And after a li'l time had passed, I knowed I had to quit going wit' the dead, had to turn my little one over to the Lord Jesus, let him look after my boy.

Maybelle was right. My place was right here. It be a hour I won't never forget.

My friend. And then she the one left this world cause *her chile* didn't live. My tears come. And oughta. Maybelle worth more'n a few tears. I be hoping we gon be side by side in the next life. Next morning come and I get up and get started, like usual.

Started the fire in the cookstove, dipped some water into the washpan so's to wash my face and hands, put on a workdress and tied on my bib apron. When the fire got to going good I set the coffeepot to boiling and my mind got going too—same as usual. Thinking on the day ahead and me bent over the washpot.

I opened the backdoor and put my head out to sniff the morning air, and just like that, quick as a bee-sting—it got me! Wadn't no more'n a thought buried in a mem'ry, but I wouldn't soon forget it.

How it come so sudden? Just showed up outta the blue.

I was hanging 'tween the kitchen and the outside, wanting no more'n a whiff of fresh air, when the mem'ry stepped right up and spoke. Wanting to look at it close, I took myself back inside, poured my coffee and settled by the south winduh. And ever since then, here I been.

Happened 'bout the time Mama died, so I was still pretty young. Happened in church. We had a ole Rev'rend then 'at ever'body loved, and sump'n had happened—happened not too far from us. All I knowed 'bout it was 'at some white man had brung charges 'gainst one of his workers. A colored man.

White and colored—ever'body all stirred up. I was too young to understand much 'bout it. Didn't know the people, and hadn't never been more'n a mile or so from home, so didn't try to learn no details.

Even so, I r'member zackly how I felt when Rev'rend Wallace stood before us—me on the bench next to my sisters, and him saying the same word again and again. So I got to listenin' close.

Now many a year done passed and I still see him standing in front. White-headed, in his black suit wit' his arms raised over his head, just standing there, like he'd run outta words. His arms dropped then and he looked 'round, and when he spoke again his voice was soft.

"Justice," he say. And again then he didn't say a thing for a bit. Then he raised up his arms and pointed a finger toward heaven. And say it louder. "Justice. Tha's the prayer. Pray for justice. And may the Lord God grant our prayer. Amen."

Then ever'body was saying 'Amen.' But I just set there, not moving a'tall. Like as if I was froze. I wadn't sure I knowed what 'justice' meant. But I knowed the word had struck deep in me.

I get outta my chair by the winduh and head for the kitchen. On my way I hear myself say, "So, Rev'rend Wallace. You alive in this house today. Speaking to me again."

Strange the way that picture from long ago come when I was standing in the open door. Like a echo. Like his words in the wind. All I needed do was stick my head out the door to hear 'em.

The day good and started now, and *justice* the word for this day. Rev'rend Wallace still saying it. And whatever I do, I gon do it for him. Cause way back yonder, he planted a seed in my heart.

Chapter 23

———————•>══════<•———————

Wearing my boots, got my shoes tucked in my bag. I go wit' the firm belief that they hope for us all—least all us living in these parts. Don't know 'bout the rest of the world. I see in the paper 'bout troubles in faraway places, but they always seem just that, faraway.

We's hit a rainy spell, so they ain't no picking cotton. And that give me the chance. I decide to go ahead and make my move. Been quite a few days since I promised myself. I be looking to 'take aim.'

Get to chuckling then. Sound like I maybe figuring on picking up a gun.

Mud and more mud. In some spots the road all but can't be passed. If'n I had me a telephone I coulda called and made sure the one I on my way to see's at home and willing to receive me. It be this not-knowing 'at make me uneasy.

I ain't wanting to think tha's so, but my body be telling me—way it be all tensed up. I know she ain't gon invite me to come in and sit in the parlor. But I'm going. On my way.

Had a bit of trouble deciding what to wear. Wanna look decent, but this ain't Sunday, and I ain't heading for no fancy ball. I heated me some water and washed myself good and pinned my hair back close to my head.

What was most on my mind was getting out the house 'fore I changed my mind, so I hurried up quick. If'n I'd lolly-gagged, mighta quit 'fore I got started. When you ain't got but a li'l bit of time you has to make the best decision you can. Think I might try that trick more often.

The few times I's been in her presence, I's felt a peacefulness in this Miz Stillwell. Reckon maybe it what yuh call *serenity*.

My guess be, she a li'l nearer to the angels'n most other folk. Miz Buford Stillwell. Lottie, her name. She one of the white women ever'body like. Ain't never heard nobody say a bad word 'bout her.

She knows how to think things out—look at one side then the other. A coupla years back, she got two women was near 'bout ready to kill the other'n to set down in the same room and talk. I doubt they ended up friends after that, but didn't neither of 'em do no harm to the other.

The Lord God say, 'Vengeance is mine.' That seem pretty plain. He saying, 'Leave it to me.'

And since He the one give me a mind and hands and feet, He prob'ly won't be too surprised 'bout what I be up to now. Sunday last, that rascal of a preacher say again how when the world end, the Lord gon crown us wit' *a full reward*. He didn't no more'n say it till I was thinking again how I ain't willing to wait for heaven.

What I wanting to see? Why, a better place right here. If'n I can picture it so—don't that mean it can be so?

What we count *real* be's the way things is right now. So look like maybe a better way got a good chance of being real too. I done made up my mind to b'lieve it can be so. It be like hot and cold—just two sides of the same thing.

Last time I set out on 'a mission' I went wit' high hopes and a head chock full of happy-ever-after pictures—and not one dadblame thing turned out one bit like them pictures. Tha's why I be so set and determined now. Ain't gon let no picture set up in my head and tell me I oughta just head home and forget it. If'n such a picture do show up, I gon throw it in the ditch, right by the side of this Beatties Ford Road—and keep a'going.

A verse come to mind. 'Love your enemies. Bless the ones 'at curse you, and do good to the ones 'at hate and despitefully use you.' Saying it now seem like a good reminder, since ain't no way to tell how this thing I got my mind set on gon turn out.

One thing for sure. Vengeance ain't what I be's after. And this Miz Stillwell, she ain't the kind to want that neither.

****

There the house, got it in my sights now. Not much farther.

I get almost to the backdoor and hold to a tree and pull my ole rubber boots off and slip on my shoes. Leave the boots under the tree. Wet as the ground be, I ain't likely to forget 'em.

By the time I get to the railing by the steps to the backdoor, my shoes plenty muddy. I find a stick and start scraping. I's bent over and chuckling to myself, picturing that young woman I used to be. Why, she wouldn't 'bout to b'lieve what I be up to now. Here I is—'bout to call on a white woman!—and wha's more, planning to speak my mind! Land sakes! World prob'ly be getting ready to end.

The door open and I give a start. Not ready yet for talking, but least now I know the lady of the house be's home.

She saying, "Don't you worry none 'bout getting mud on this floor. Come on in. This just a enclosed porch and I sometimes wish we'd left it as it was. Now it's the place that catches everything we don't know what to do with."

A small room at the back of the house wit' winduhs all way round. First thing, I notice how cluttered it be. By the wall, they a table wit' a metal top and on it almost more pots full of African violets 'an it can hold.

She pulls out a chair and dusts the seat off wit' her hand. I begins to say who I be, but she starts in to laughing and I hush. First she giggles a bit. "Yes, Hazeline. I remember you—and if I didn't, I'd sure know you by now. Why, you've become rather famous in these parts!"

I can't think of nothing to say to that. She say, "Be right back."

This li'l room opens onto the kitchen—a handsome kitchen. Red and white. Up high they a row of cabinets and a wallpaper border wit' black and white hens and roosters. They be running and chasing, having fun up there. I spot one thing I covet—and that be the light. They a big winduh over the sink.

My hands in my lap. Making fists. Opening, closing.

She comes carrying a tray wit' two glasses of iced tea. Holds it out for me to take one. I thank her and she say "You're welcome," and pulls out a chair and sets herself down. "Now," she say, "tell me why you've come."

She a fine-looking woman. A li'l younger'n me, I s'pect. Got real dark hair. A few tendrils of it hangs loose but the rest be's braided and coiled up in a bun. Her dress made from a good quality wove cloth, a plaid tha's dark navy crisscrossed with li'l red and white lines.

Spiffy. Tha's how she look.

I take a sip of the tea, not knowing how to begin. Then I start in telling her how I agreed wit' myself to try to help, and done my best to stay ready for any idea wanted to find me.

She wear her spectacles low on her nose. She look over 'em when she look my way. Nearby they a clock. It strike the half hour. I pull in a deep breath.

"They sump'n I wanna ask yuh."

****

Soaking wet, like a near-drowned cat. The clock striking four when I come in the door. Was halfway home when the downpour started. My ole umbrella's tore to shreds.

Right now I needin' quick to get myself warm and dry. Good thing I took time this morning to stock the woodbox wit' dry kindling. I build the fire in the cookstove so's to have sump'n hot for supper. Soon's I get myself dry and wrap my ole robe round me I set close by the stove, waiting for the heat—and says to myself, *I done what I set out to do.*

The mystery be, how I come to do it. Sure a surprise to me!

The water in the pot gets to boiling good and I stir in some grits. By the time they done I got my butter ready and one of the last of the year's tomatoes. All the while I be a'wondering. *Who'd ever believe I'd do such a thing?*

Was like sump'n come over me. Touched me. So I could lay aside my fear and just set out and do it.

I got myself dressed and took off. Dressed careful, knowing it was a important meeting I was off to—if'n I found her at home. Soon as I got to tromping through mud 'longside the highway, I begun to wonder if'n I was just wasting my time. Might get there and find nobody home. Or maybe some of the fam'ly, but not her. Or might be she'd turn me aside. Or maybe I'd get there at a time 'at didn't suit.

But that minute when the will to do it come over me? Seemed to me like a miracle, like in the Bible when somebody be's anointed.

Don't think I wanna tell nobody such thoughts. Best pour these grits in a bowl and eat. Too early for supper, but I gon eat anyway. And let the thoughts go. That be easy enough, cause I feel 'bout as good right now as I has in a month of Sundays. 'Sides that, this bowl of grits and ripe tomato a fine mix. A coupla leftovers too, and I got me a feast. It do be time to celebrate!

That storm 'at come through on my way back? Why that wadn't much. Real storm be wha's been going on round here, and just might be it gon soon come to a end.

****

The new day come and I start out feeling tired. 'Bout seven of the morning and me dragging. Not sick. Just weary feeling. So I decides to take it easy.

Thursday, and rain just a'coming down. That suit me fine, cause I ain't in no mood for heading to no cotton field. Figuring on doing whatever pleases me. And since they ain't nobody else to do it for me, first thing I gon do be fix myself a fine good breakfast.

Mr. Rooster outside crowing. He can just keep on making a racket. I gon feed myself first. Eggs over easy, and finish up wit' blackberry jam on a hot biscuit. Gon be a leftover biscuit, but tha's alright. Split it, pop it in the oven for a bit, then slather it wit' some of that butter I churned yesterday.

Yum yum. I eat hearty. While I eat I remember what Miz Stillwell said 'bout knowing my name.

Miz Robbins mentioned some woman wit' a name I hadn't never heard. Sump'n like Biddy, or Liddy, or some such. I always was glad I didn't get Gertrude. Or Lottie, or Puella. Hazeline got some ease to it. Always was glad it was mine, cause 'fore I'd lived long on this earth I'd already see'd some hard women. Loud-talking, fussing 'bout ever' little thing, didn't nothing satisfy 'em. Was likely 'bout the time I started talking, I already knowed I didn't wanna end up thataway.

Wish I could hear Joshua, him saying my name least once more.

Well, time to feed the chickens and Ole Dog, then clean the kitchen and make my bed, and then I gon set a spell wit' one of last week's newspapers. Let that dress on the sewing machine wait a while longer.

And tha's zactly what I do. Don't seem like I been setting long when the clock strike half past the next hour.

Still, I don't feel like doing nothing. Might even take me a nap this afternoon. Been pushing hard and worrying too, so now my git-up-and-go done run out. Left me behind. Reckon it shouldn't come as no surprise when I collapse.

I gets to chuckling then. Uh-huh, tha's just what it feel like. I done collapsed.

That idea 'at come along 'bout me calling on some white woman sure took me by surprise. And then, lo and behold, I done it! But it ain't easy to believe I done it.

I pick up my tatting and work at it a bit, but soon lay it aside, lean my head back and remember how it went. The kindness of that woman gon be sump'n I remember long as I on this earth.

I said, "Yes'm. Figured when yuh see'd me at the door you'd know why I come." Soon as I said it I begun to giggling—nervous I reckon. But it *was* sump'n to laugh about. Wadn't it? So I went ahead and said it. "Guess I has been building me a reputation!"

She laughed wit' me, and I set to staring at my hands in my lap. When I looked up I see'd the kindness in her eyes. She was waiting for me to speak my piece. I sucked in my breath and opened my mouth, set on letting the words spill out however they come.

"Miz Stillwell, I come to yuh cause I couldn't think of nothing else to do. I know you the sort what listen—and might be tha's all tha's really needed. Some speaking. And some listening. Yet I do wonder if'n sump'n even that simple can happen."

I looked again at my hands in my lap. What I'd just called simple wadn't simple. I knowed it wadn't.

"It's communication you're wanting. Am I understanding right?"

"Yes'm. How can that be so hard?"

"Well, first of all, people tend to hear...I guess we could rightly say they hear what they're set to hear—in other words, what they're prone to hear due to their backgrounds and experience."

"Miz Stillwell, I sure those boys know what they done was wrong. It was hurtful. And they knows the wrong of it."

"I hope you're right. If they don't, we're in bigger trouble than you and I think."

"You know 'em well?"

"I figure there's one of the three that pulled the others into doing the wrong. Based on what I know, I have that suspicion. And I have thought on it—and figured that perhaps two of the three might welcome a chance to admit the wrong, maybe even say they're sorry."

I took a sip of the tea and clutched hold of the glass and stared at it. I didn't know what to say. Seemed like a miracle to be setting near her and drinking her tea. I heard her clock strike. And knowed the silence had got long. I was certain I wadn't wrong in coming to see her. But what now?

I did tell her my thought, and my thoughts the past weeks. Told her how it seemed like the more I sought a answer the farther away a answer got. Like a stick far out on the river current. It there, but may as well not be, when they ain't no way to get at it.

I told her 'bout my prayer too—how tha's when her name come to mind.

"I don't have no plan. Don't know what to do—nor what can be done. I just know I can't rest for thinking on it."

She nodded her head and sucked in her lips. I gulped down a big swig of the tea 'fore I went on. "And yuh know wha's strange 'bout it, Miz Stillwell? I ain't even met the girl."

"That is a surprise," she say. "But I understand there's a young man. You know him."

"Yes'm. His name's Clement Wilson, but he go by Slim. He visit now and again, and always good to help out wit' whatever's needing done." I drop my head again. When I look up I say, "He make me think of my boy, one I lost when he was born."

Was hard for me to b'lieve I was telling her that. It sump'n I don't never say out loud.

But right off my mouth was opening again. "The white folk. And the colored folk. Tha's what we got. Right here. All us living in this same l'il part of the world. That much I know. What I trying to figure out...where the brains, where the souls? Ain't we all got brains? Ain't we all got souls? Don't look like it—cause if'n that the case we all us oughta be speaking out—saying, 'Tha's wrong. Wrong wrong wrong!'"

Oh my. Had all that come outta me? My hand covered my mouth and I s'pect my eyes showed my surprise. Miz Stillwell shifted in her chair. And then she giggle some. I had done startled us both!

She picked up her glass of tea and when she set it back down she looked up wit' a twinkle in her eye. "You got strong feelings, huh?"

She pulled her shoulders up and brushed back a stray bit of hair. She say, "You are right, I think. The whites and the colored. Neither group is loyal to the best that's in us. A sad fact, but a fact nonetheless."

I's been over and over it, ever' word we said. And they one thing surprise me. Seem to me like, Miz Stillwell could hear even what I didn't say.

Chapter 24

———————⟫⟨⟨⟫⟨⟨⟪⟨⟨⟨⟪———————

Early morning, I begin drying some apples. Don't have many, but figured to get 'em saved. They come from Miz Robbins's brothers, up in Wilkes County. I much obliged to her for 'em, and gon be obliged again come a cold winter day when I fry up some turnovers.

I put the slices on a big flat pan and set it out in the sun wit' a screen over the top to keep the flies off. Then got to wondering what I was gon set to next.

Could go fishing! Lawsamercy! Last time I held a fishing pole was back in the spring. Course, in the heat of the summer the fish'd likely keep to the bottom, not take the bait. Least I can think so, so's to make me feel some better 'bout not getting out there and dropping my hook.

Saturday afternoon now. Up till midday, had to pick cotton.

I be just ready to go dig some worms for bait when I hear somebody calling. Sure 'nough, one of the neighbors from 'cross the way. Wanting me to read sump'n for him.

Had to read it, and tell him what it mean, and tell him again. So now I finally ready to go find me some worms. Usually be plenty up by the well where the ground stays wet. Take my spade. Take a tin can. Won't care none if'n the fish biting or not. Just wanna set by one of the deep pools in the creek and hold my pole.

I head out the backdoor—and almost stumble and fall. That dog right by the step. Soon's I catch my breath I say,

"Ole Dog, wha'cha think? Wanna go along, help me catch some fish?"

He hobble to his feet. But when I head out, he don't follow.

On my way up the hill so's I can head down the hill toward the creek I gets to wondering again. Has Miz Stillwell had a chance yet to make some headway on our plan?

I begins muttering to myself. And listening. "Could be, them boys gon get struck by lightning—the wrath of God!" That gets me to chuckling. But if'n ever' word the Bible say be's true, reckon it could happen.

****

Another day in the field. End of the day come and I slap wore out. Didn't go till midafternoon, but by then I'd awready done a day's work. Right now I got my aching feet soaking in a pan of hot water with Epsom salts. Sure wish I could soak my back too. Most of the time of late I been looking down the long row—the distance still to be picked. And all the while the world's kept on a'spinning and done turned up one more misfortune.

Was early this morning Miz Robbins sent for me, wantin' me to do her ironing. I looked at that pile she'd laid out and wanted to turn myself 'round and head back from where I'd come. But she'd awready sprinkled some of 'em—so I heaved a sigh and set to.

'Bout a hour later I was swiping at my sweat, trying to keep it from my eyes—and here she come. First she just stood by the door. I knowed she wadn't gon stay long where the stove got to be kept going to heat the irons.

I knowed too, more'n likely she'd come in just to talk a bit. I the one she count on to do the washing and cooking and cleaning, but it ain't no secret to me. They another reason she want me coming over here. And that be, cause I listen. If'n I could charge for the listening, maybe could earn me a fifty cent piece.

"How you been feeling, Hazeline? My shoulder's been acting up again."

And she start in. Set herself down on the arm of a chair and lean my way and clear her throat. I could tell she was waiting, wanting to be sure I was listening good, so I looked up and caught her eye.

"Guess you heard the latest."

"No'm. Ain't heard no news."

"Them boys—ones that harmed the girl you was concerned about?"

I set the iron back on the stove. She say, "Somebody beat up one of 'em. And he won't tell who done it."

I come close to saying, *How you talk, Miz Robbins!*

I drawed in my breath. Careful. Not wanting her to see my feelings. Truth be told, I couldn't'a said right then what I was feeling. Ever'thing in me was all a jumble. I turned the shirt and begun pressing the yoke.

She dropped her voice low. "Hazeline...you know anything 'bout this boy they call Slim?"

Goosebumps popped out all over me. And even wit' all that heat coming from the stove, a chill run through me. I tole her I hadn't heard nothing lately 'bout nothing going on, and let it go at that. Sure wadn't gon say Slim's name.

Wouldn't want it said in the same room wit' her talking thataway.

Was when I was leaving, a strange thing crossed my mind. Real strange. It jerked me up.

Where'd such a thought come from? Was sure a surprise, but I did think on it. What would this day be like if'n I was the white lady, and Miz Robbins the colored? Well, first thing, I wouldn't be on my way to no cottonfield.

I kept thinking on it. Round and round the bend I went. Look from this side, then that side.

But thing of it be, if'n everything else the same, why I reckon things'd be same as they is right now. One body'd still be white and the other'n colored, and if'n I was white I'd be like her—cause tha's the way of things. Long ago it be's now, since the white folk took up this wrong thinking.

Guess things'd still be 'bout the same, though. 'Cept I'd be living in the big house, and her in the shack.

Chapter 25

Well, it's come at last. The time of year all us look forward to. The cotton on this farm's done been loaded up and hauled to market. Our young'uns can get back to a reg'lar schoolday, 'stead of getting out at noon so's to spend the rest of the day in the field.

What we pick don't go far for the ginning, but I often does wonder where it end up. Ain't never had the chance to go along and see.

I know the trip be's slow, wit' mules pulling the wagons and the bales piled high. I's heard tell of a place in town 'longside the depot where the cotton gets loaded on the train. Say it like a big party, cause ever'body so glad the harvest over and done.

Food and drink for sale—ever'body lively. But might be it ain't such a happy time this year. The paper say cotton prices still down.

End of the day now, and for the most part I been just taking it easy. Reckon tha's awright. Time for catching my breath after the long labor's done. So why I still feeling so tired out?

Ruby been on my mind. Right after the sun come up I got the fire started in the cookstove, then headed outside. Wanted to feel the morning air. Soon as I said 'good day' to the day, I begun thinking of her. Wadn't nothing pertic'lar brung her to mind. She just showed up.

I come back in after a bit and cooked up some eggs and biscuits, and all the while r'membering times we's spent together. Like that day she showed up wit' a basketful of biddies. Least one of the hens scratching out there in the yard now from that brood.

Then they was the time she got all fired up, couldn't talk 'bout nothing else, ever' other word she say crowing 'bout some man she'd met. Can't recall his name, but I sure r'member how she couldn't get enough of talking 'bout him. On and on she'd go till I was sick of it and had to grit my teeth to keep from telling her to hush.

Now he long gone. Reckon his name faded from mem'ry cause I didn't want to hear it no more. Any man a woman go slap-dab crazy over...well, I don't b'lieve no good likely to come from it in the long run.

The day hurried along and by the time I was setting down to eat my cold supper a thought come that surprise me. Why it be? Why it be I so fond of Ruby?

I finished up my cornbread and milk, still studying on it. Since the first day I laid eyes on that woman I has loved Ruby Pharr. She got a spark in her 'at bring out a spark in me—like as if she the piece of pinewood and I the cold log laying up on the andiron. I just be waiting for that kindling to get me going.

Bedtime come and I stretch out on the straw mattress, but sleep won't come. Ruby still on my mind, for no reason I can put a name to. She keep on staying on my mind, so after a bit I figure must be past time to think of getting over that way. Go see her. The week moving along and Miz Robbins don't have nothing special planned, so if'n I can get a ride I might just go on over to the Sandridge and surprise her.

If my luck's good, she'll be home. And glad to see me.

****

What a sight! Bleary-eyed and lifeless. Now I know why I come. This where I s'posed to be right now.

The ole woman in the back room. I peep in. She look like she sleeping so I go on back to the kitchen. Ruby setting at the table wit' her head in her hands. I drop some wood in the cookstove and go out to the well to pump some water. The well here ain't far from the door. I come back in and put some water on to heat. Ruby's dropped her head down. Look like maybe she done fell off to sleep.

She knowed who I was, I could tell that.

Wonder if'n a doctor can be found. Need to ask the neighbor. A racket come from the back room. I hurry that'a way and find Ruby's ole aunt stumbling outta bed. The smell in the room way past awful, the slop jar needing to be emptied, no doubt.

I get the old one settled down, then gets Ruby tucked inta bed. I's just about to slip over to the neighbor's to see if'n she know wha's been going on—cause Ruby ain't up to talking and the ole aunt's addled—when the neighbor shows up.

I get to the door quick and put my finger to my lips to shush her. She say real low, "I sho glad you showed up." She old and a bit crippled, her gray hair a frizz round her head.

I take the pot of beans she brung and set it on the stove and motion to the door. We go outside and stand near the chinaberry tree. She say Irene been gone more'n a week, and Ruby, when she first got sick, didn't tell nobody. "I noticed I hadn't see'd her in a coupla days. Wadn't natural—nobody going in and out."

We talk a li'l longer and I tell her I best get back inside.

I play nurse and housekeeper and another coupla days go by. All the while I keep thinking Irene gon show up. Ruby still way too sick to be left on her own, but she don't seem to get no worse so I back off trying to get a doctor. That'd be just one more bill to pay.

I end up asking Miz Dellinger, Ruby's boss lady 'bout half a mile down the road, if'n she can get on her telephone and let Miz Robbins know I might not can be there to wash when Monday come. I been worried 'bout Ole Dog too, so I start in to adding more to my message, when Miz Dellinger tell me to come on in, she'll ring the number and let me talk. That sure surprise me.

I ain't used to talking on no telephone, but I get it done, talking loud inta the big horn you pull off that big black box on the wall. And Miz Robbins promise to get word to one of the other tenants 'bout where I be and get somebody to feed my dog.

Finally, late in the morning Monday, Irene comes home. She's shocked to learn wha's been going on and goes on and on thanking me—thanking me too for the dozen jars of scuppernong jelly. I made it cause the neighbor lady had fruit going to waste.

Late in the day I go to Ruby's bedside to say my goodbye. "Okay, Ruby—be heading home now. Yuh had me plenty scared, yuh sure did, so now I counting on you to eat good and get your strength back. Then I gon be looking for yuh over my way one of these first days."

She grin and say, "Uh-huh, I awready looking forward to it."

She still not herself, but her eyes got more light in 'em now. She give my hand a squeeze and say, "Go safely, my good friend."

I awready took my leave of Irene. And the old one. She thought I was just getting here so I let her go on thinking it. If'n I have to walk all the way home, that gon be okay, cause I needing some time to handle this big load of thanksgiving on my heart. Ruby gon live!

****

This year the November leaves seem brighter, like they got more color'n usual. Sure a glory to see. I walk along the edge of the field where one of the Robbins boys has run the cultivator. They gon plant a winter crop here, so's to plow it under later. It be a way to build up the soil—or so the government man that come round been saying. He been teaching the farmers some new tricks.

I cross the plowed ground and hear my footsteps crunching the crust. Since the summer thunderstorms ended, we been awful dry. A bit of wind gets to going and picks up some of the loose dirt.

Makes a li'l whirlwind. I stop in my tracks, watching.

I's read 'bout the dust storms they's had out in the middle of the country, wit' the wind blowing so hard, loose dirt come right through the house walls. One storm was so bad they called it Black Sunday. That was hard 'nough to 'magine, but what I couldn't picture was what they called a 'mud blizzard.'

Next thing, I be kicking at the ground cause I so like the smell of fresh-turned-up dirt—and lo and behold!—I spy something. Why it sure is! A arrowhead!

Some folks round here's found bunches of 'em, but I ain't never found but one other'n. I hold it in my hand and wonder again, how the Indians did live. One of 'em shaped this rock, and I do wonder what that one was like.

This land's knowed a lot of people. I close my eyes and think on it. And now here I be, standing in the same spot.

Wadn't long ago I was wondering again, 'bout the big rocks here and there 'at jut up out the ground. Hard, black rocks. Bunches of 'em. Wonder how long they been here?

All this thinking back brings on a thought 'bout wha's to come. Here we all be, living right here. And a few thousand years go by, I reckon, then somebody else still gon be standing here a'wondering.

It do seem a blessed day. Even 'fore my good-luck find, I was feeling at ease, cause I got a chance to ask Slim 'bout the news I had from Miz Robbins. He say he heard it too, and when I ask him 'bout it, he put his hand to his heart and swore he didn't do nothing to that boy.

I slip the arrowhead in my pocket and keep going. Pretty soon I come to the wire fence and turn right and follow 'longside it. If'n I keep straight on, after a li'l while

I'd be at the creek. But I won't go that far. Gon be getting dark 'fore long.

Guess it was yesterday, or day before maybe, when a old question sneaked up on me. 'Bout our grandmama on Daddy's side of the fam'ly. The question be, how she got her freedom. She was freed 'fore Mister Lincoln put a end to slavery—least that the story 'at was told. So I always has wondered, did she buy her freedom? But how could she a'done that? Ain't no way of knowing—but I like to think she done some courageous thing, maybe saving some white body's life. That coulda been the case, cause the stories I heard made it sound like she was the kind that woulda risked her life for somebody.

A idea pop up—just jump right up in front of me. Why not go see Cousin Lavinia? In Mount Mourne. If'n I can get a ride...well, I got a notion to just go. I'd have to stay the night, and she wouldn't know I was coming, but I could go. But then I'd need a ride back.

Oh me. How can I get a ride all the way to Mount Mourne? Well, won't find it if'n I don't look.

The idea seem a wild hair, but more I look at it the better it look. Lavinia love visitors, and her husband real easygoing. One of the Gudger girls maybe come over and make sure the chickens fed and watered, and see to Ole Dog. Reckon he'd be the only one at'd miss me.

Lavinia the only one of Daddy's people I's kept up wit' much and it's been a long spell since I see'd her last. After Joshua passed, I didn't care to go nowhere. I was the grieving widow, so it was alright for me to stay close to home. But now it seem high time for me to branch out, sprout some new leaves. It ain't springtime, but I got a spring kind of feeling.

****

Well, couldn't get away near so quick as I wanted. Took a good bit of time to find a ride, and me already figuring my plan was doomed.

I figured she'd be home and glad to see me—least somebody'd be home. I wouldn't get turned away. And now I riding in style, watching the countryside go by.

Looked like I was gon have to make the trip in the back of a wagon. But then I learned 'at Mister Stillwell—husband to my white-lady friend—was heading to Statesville on business and glad to give me a ride. He gon come by and pick me up on his way back too.

When I was ready to leave I hung my apron on the nail in the kitchen, same as u'shul, but this time I stood there for a bit and looked at it. Seemed a bit like a ceremony, me telling my apron to wait for me—telling it I'd be coming back. I reckon it still hanging there now. Waiting.

Don't know much about cars, but this one sure big. It be squared off at the back, and real shiny black, and got a wide front seat and not-quite-so-wide back seat. Yessiree, I be riding in style! Likely the envy of all the poor folk—white and colored. Mister Stillwell gon catch hisself a train in Statesville and head on over to Asheville. Good thing I wore my sweater, cause the wind coming in the winduhs is right cool. Noisy too—and I glad of that, so's we can't talk none. They ain't much we'd have to say one to the other. I wonders if'n his wife tole him why I made a visit her way. But I sure don't ask.

We pass more'n one big two-story brick church. Wonder if'n the prayers in them big churches goes up to the same god as the prayers said in our li'l church. And what about our people, 'fore they was brought cross the ocean?

Many a time I's wondered what life was like for our people 'fore we was brung here. Did they pray to the same god we praying to now? Reckon so, if'n they only one. But it ain't hard to see, 'at not ever'body ever'where pictures God the same.

What catches my eye when we pass these big churches be's the cemeteries. Big stone markers at the graves. Our li'l cemetery got mostly rows of upended flat rock. Or a piece of wood wit' some words carved on it. If'n I had the means, I'd go right out and buy Joshua a big fancy marker. Was Sam 'at took care of that, got some man he knowed to chisel a nice squared-off slab of stone. Ever so often I get at it some, trying to keep it standing straight.

Sure feels good, this riding along and watching the countryside go by. I spot a huge persimmon tree at the edge of a field and wish I could come back later, cause that tree's loaded. Orange fruit, hanging thick—'nough to make quite a few persimmon puddings.

Sure looking forward to seeing Cousin Lavinia. I got a lot of respect for that woman. She know how to do—and how to make do.

Here I set, looking out the window, riding in style—and come close to laughing out loud. I be remembering one of my favorite stories 'bout Lavinia. She was in a shoe store once and found out the man was going outta business and wanting to close up quick. So she hurried home and got the money she'd been saving one dime and one dollar at a time and went back and bought up a bunch of shoes. Got 'em home, put the word out—and folks from all round come to buy at her 'shoe store.'

She never would say how she fared on that deal. If'n she'd been born white she'd prob'ly be a rich woman by now—maybe even 'filthy rich.' She ain't much good at sewing, though, so I took some of my lavender I harvested early in the year and sewed it up in li'l satin pouches and edged 'em wit' some of my lace. Pretty li'l things, to freshen up the drawers in her bureau and sideboard. And I brung the tablecloth too, one I fixed for her some while back.

Got my fingers crossed 'at somebody gon be home when Mister Stillwell drop me off. If'n none of 'em home—well, I just have to set and wait.

****

Lavinia the kind what tries to have dinner on the table right at noon, so she scurrying around. And won't let me help. Tell me to have a seat and keep her comp'ny. The sun's up bright and the weather just perfect for this time of year.

Sure a pleasure to be here. Ever since I got here yesterday we been talking up a storm.

Lavinia's built like Daddy's people. Like me. Tall, and kind of squared off. We got big bones and a heap of angles. She got a face like a bird. Her nose a beak, and her chin hardly there, so yuh can't call her beautiful, but yuh does have to say she one fine woman.

She tell me our sweet gon be wha's left from a cake she made day before—and that remind me. While she taking off pot lids and tasting and adding a bit of this and that, I take my chance and begin, tell her 'bout a time not far back when I was determined not to be traipsing off to the store and spending my dime, though I was hankering after sump'n to please my sweet tooth.

"I got to thinking on what I might make—but wadn't much on hand for making. So I got to looking around. Had plenty of sugar. And a wee bit of flour, and one batch of my dried apples left. I kept scouting round, looking before and behind, see if anything was hiding."

Then I wait a minute, till she turn from the cookstove and catch my eye. "And guess what I found?"

She guess molasses and a coupla other things and I say, "Nope. Ain't no way you gon guess, so may as well tell yuh. A chocolate bar. Joleen must've brung it over at some point. Was pretty well dried up but I figured it wadn't rotten, so I chopped it fine and added it to the batter of my apple cake. Now yuh know, Lavinia, how any cake wit' fruit in it better if'n yuh let it set a while, least till the next day?"

"Uh-huh. So did yuh wait? Thought yuh was all fired up and ready to eat your sump'n special."

"Well, I put my nose down to that cake when it come outta the oven and took a whiff and just the smell was 'bout good enough. That helped me wait a bit—so's I could look forward to it a li'l longer. And I'm here to tell you, it was fine! I called myself eating it after my noonday meal, but truth be, I didn't eat much else. Ate all I wanted of it and called it dinner, and sure was a fine one."

She laugh wit' me and I say, "Now I thinking 'bout stocking up on chocolate bars and letting 'em go stale." We laugh again and I tell her I know she the queen of making-do, but I done signed on as her 'prentice.

When the food's ready her husband and four more show up. A bit later they's all gone and the two of us set on for a spell, still catching up, and I find myself reaching for another bit of gravy. I sop it up wit a biscuit and say, "Hmmm, that's good, Lavinia. You one fine cook."

I couldn't'a told her how fine it was to be her guest. Not often I gets to be a guest at any table, but this one 'specially good.

She washes and I dry and we soon got the kitchen clean. And then she pulls a envelope out of a drawer. It so old it's beginning to fall apart. She squeeze it and it opens at the slit on one end.

When she pulls the pages out my throat goes dry.

She had tole me she had sump'n to show me. A letter, she said. A letter wit' answers—answers 'bout what I been longing to know. Said Ida, her sister, had found it. So what was this feeling that'd come over me? Dread? Might be I didn't wanna know. Might be, it a story so sad it beyond bearing.

I always did love Grandmama so. She always was good to me—treated me fairly and wit' respect.

But what about her early life? A heap of times I'd tried to imagine it. A slave. But then sump'n musta happened, cause Grandmama was set free. I still setting at the long table where we ate. My hands in my lap. Clenched tight.

****

Lavinia's in the chair 'cross from me. She clears her throat and pushes her spectacles up on her nose.

I don't wanna show Lavinia these feelings. I be wanting to cry out, *No no—stop! Don't read the letter!* But that won't do. I's come this far, so I's bound to see it through.

I chew my lip, but Lavinia don't notice. Her eyes be on the page. A glimmer of light catch my eye. On a little table near the winduh. Sump'n shiny. Some kinda ornament. Look like a brooch, maybe.

She say, "The ink's faded, hard to see. Let me just read it through first."

The letter was found in her mama's things after the funeral. Aunt Josie was Daddy's sister. She was the kind you don't much mention after she's gone. Nobody saying, *I miss her.* I s'pect her close fam'ly feel like even her mem'ry sump'n they wanna keep at a distance. She was a hard woman. Real bitter.

This good Cousin Lavinia ain't one bit like her. Lavinia kind and generous—tha's why I knowed I'd be welcome. Somehow or 'nother she missed being one bit like her mama.

After a bit she shift in her chair and start in. She reads all the way through then turns and points at that jewel I'd noticed. She say, "There the brooch. You can help me decide who should have it."

****

Right that minute, her folding up the letter, I didn't care not one bit 'bout no jewel. All I wanted—what I longed for deep in my heart, was to be off somewhere by myself. The letter set up a pain in me so big I couldn't speak. I got to my feet and took a few deep breaths and did manage to tell Lavinia I just needed to get off by myself.

The afternoon clear and not too hot, best kind of weather for a walk. Mount Mourne a tiny community, only a few houses scattered about. I headed for the woods.

That letter. What a long time it took to get there. From the hand of the one what wrote it, to the hands at the post office, and somehow or other passed on to Aunt Josie, where it stayed all those years till she died and Cousin Ida—Lavinia's eldest sister—found it.

How Aunt Josie come to have it we don't know. Now Lavinia got the letter and the jewel too. And what Grandmama wanted us to know has done come to light.

I can't help wondering what woulda happened if'n Lavinia hadn't been there when Ida found it? Where would the letter've ended up? Would Ida have passed it along? She a right strange bird too. Never can tell what she likely to do.

The letter was enough. Answered my questions. But the jewel be stealing the show. No, that ain't it. Ain't no show. What happened to Grandmama ain't no excitin' tale. It a story what pull up a heap of hurt and sorrow, but yuh can't deny how the story make the jewel precious.

That story in the paper come to mind, 'bout that lady in Washington at the New Year, wearing the Hope Diamond. That jewel really really famous—but this purple stone in this old brooch at Lavinia's, it be's special for only one reason. Our grandmama's story.

It be a token of the sacrifice our Grandmama made.

My heart aches and aches. *O, my poor grandmama, how you did suffer.*

These woods full of old trees tha's way big around. I stop by a big oak and rest my palms flat on the bark. This tree real old. Woulda been alive when our grandmama was living.

The letter left out one thing I'd sure like to know. How many? How many chirren was it she birthed?

My heart be aching for them too. Those little ones. Tore away from they mama—and sold away to strangers!

I slip down onto the ground by the trunk of the old tree, draw up my knees and bury my face in my hands. After a bit my arms move up and reach round me. Like they trying to comfort me.

Ain't no way of knowing who the chirren went to. And no way of knowing who they was, or where they chirren and grandchirren be. I hold still, my arms wrapped round me, my head buried.

Don't wanna look, don't wanna see even in my mind what happened, but somehow or other I does see pictures. Real young little ones, sent off to grow up and become slaves. And where was it they was sent? Ain't no way to know.

I start in to humming.

That always our way. Music. It be's the music 'at help us bear our sorrows.

After a bit I get real quiet and still. Wondering. What tunes did Grandmama's chirren sing? And how was it my sweet Grandmama could bear up under her sorrow and not lose her mind?

And what about the mating? How it happen? Wit' what man? My dear grandmama—forced to breed chirren for sale.

The letter tell why. Say the law put a stop to trafficking in slaves, couldn't no more be brung in from other lands. So what then? Why, they just come on sump'n else, start breeding slave chirren. Breed 'em for sale! The letter say the chirren was sold when they was real young, mostly to farmers other side of the Mississippi.

O, my sweet Grandmama. So good to me yuh was. Maybe you was trying to give to us the love you didn't get a chance to give the ones they took from yuh. But reckon they ain't no sense in weeping now...nothing to be done for it now.

However long my life run, I still gon be remembering that minute. When Lavinia opened that letter.

Chapter 26

Come home to more sad news. Strange thing was, the feeling I had 'fore I started home. Seemed like I awready knowed sump'n was wrong—knowed it while I was waiting for my ride. Mister Stillwell had said he'd pick me up 'bout noon, so I'd said my goodbyes and walked up to the end of the road near the highway.

Got the news right away. The Robbins barn was gone, burned to the ground. It set a good piece back from the house. And word was the fire was set. And big suspicion 'bout who done the deed. Wouldn't surprise me none if'n it was him.

It be the mules we grieving. Babe. And Jenny. Both of 'em died in the fire. Ones 'at got to the barn first tried to get 'em to come outta the stalls, but they just kept backing up and pulling hard, wouldn't come out. Been some days now since I heard all this news, yet ever' so often I gets teary again. Ain't no doubt in my mind 'bout one thing. If'n Joshua'd been here he coulda saved the mules. They'd'a done what he wanted.

The fire come during the night, so by the time anybody knowed what was happening was too late to save the barn. Good news was, most of the animals was out in the pasture.

The afternoon moving on now and me and my new broom getting acquainted. A new broom sweeps clean, so the saying go. Quite a few things I'd like to sweep away.

I pull out a coupla mousetraps so's to r'member to set 'em 'fore I goes to bed. Glad I got a bit of cheese on hand for bait. Them doggone mice done gnawed at some of my best cloth.

The suspicion be that the barn was set on fire, and only took one rat to do the deed. He showed up last summer and right off I said to myself, 'There goes a scoundrel—best not trust him, not one bit!'

He showed up on foot. Took hisself right over to the cast-iron pump by the Robbins backporch and started pumping the handle, and bent over and gulped down some long swigs. When he come up, he let out a big belch.

I was dipping dirty water from the washpot into a bucket, fixing to scour the backporch, and he come right up on me. Give me such a start I had to catch my breath 'fore I could call for Miz Robbins. She come and stood on the porch and talked at him through the screen wire.

Mister Robbins hired him, but 'fore long anybody wit' any sense could see he'd made a mistake. Hired the kind 'at lie and do shoddy work and stir up bad feelings. Took Mister Robbins a bit longer to figure it out.

Gossip flying ever'whichway, but problem be, how yuh gon prove it?

A curious thought cross my mind. If'n he do get charged, and end up in a courtroom, he gon swear on the 'white' Bible. I heard tell the judge keeps two. One for the white hand, one for the colored. That just might be the silliest thing I's ever heard.

They even got rules 'bout the parks in town. No colored folk allowed. We sure in a bad way. I can cook food for white folk, but can't set down and eat at the table wit' 'em.

Bout a year ago, President Roosevelt come to Charlotte to make a speech in one of the parks. Reckon they wadn't no colored ears listening, less'n they was chaffeurs, or watching some white woman's chile.

****

Another week fly on by. The sky pouring rain. Look like it might be the kind 'at settle in and stay awhile, so I decide to take my opportunity—do what I been looking forward to. Sortin' scraps and cuttin' scraps.

Chilly today too, so I got a fire going. By end of the day I s'pect I gon have a good start on a rag rug. First thing, cut a whole heap of cloth strips and sort 'em by color. Long 'bout January when it too cold to work outside, and yuh has to set right by the fire to keep warm, tha's when I gon be settled in and hooking this rug.

Getting a start on sump'n yuh been wanting to do feels mighty good. Right quick I see how the center of my rug gon shape up and how the colors gon come t'gether. Once I get the pattern going, won't have to think much. Tha's why rug-hooking such a satisfying thing. The mind stays free and flies ever'which way—anywhere it wanna roam.

They some folk nowadays really does fly—just ride along, setting up there in the air. B'lieve it or not!

Flying be one thing I'd try if'n I got the chance. Can't even picture what fun it'd be to ride through the sky. Ain't been so long ago, sad news come 'bout that woman. Big story, front page it was. 'Amelia Earhart.' I still think on her from time to time.

The picture showed her ready to set off. Dressed like a man, but looking like a pretty woman. She'd already crossed a ocean in that aeroplane. Now she was gon fly all the way round the world.

Sure wish she'd made it. Paper said she just disappeared. That was some months back now, and she ain't been found. I still feels sad for her. Wish I coulda knowed her. Looked to be a tiny woman, but for sure her courage wadn't one bit tiny.

Once in a while I catch sight of a plane. They a airport—tha's what they call it—in Charlotte now. Was a big to-do 'bout it, all kinds of celebrating. Built what they call a runway. And now they say they be airplanes making reg'lar trips, New York to Florida and back again.

I does get awful excited 'bout this notion of flying. This been the case ever since I first heard 'bout them two brothers, when they got they flying machine to working. Happened right here in this state. Done the impossible was what folks said—though quite a few said they didn't b'lieve it.

I b'lieved it—likely cause them brothers tried so long 'fore they got it right. All that trying! And it finally paid off.

My mind sometimes seem like a aeroplane. Go on long flyings. And where it come down? That the surprise. Might stop some place I ain't had no reason to think on. Some bit ago my head flew round and landed on the giraffe day.

Joleen was almost growed then. Even now, I can see Gaither ducking his head, bashful-like, while we all bragged on him. He did finally get to grinning wide—like a possum that'd caught hold of a hen.

We hadn't even set down to eat yet, but Sam couldn't wait to show us what his boy had made. He'd took a block of wood and ended up wit' a giraffe. When we pressed Gaither to tell us how he done it, he pulled out the picture he had to go by.

The boy was painful shy, so was good to see him in the limelight. His giraffe was 'bout a foot tall and looked real—though of course hadn't none of us ever see'd one. Seemed to me I could see the forest that giraffe was in, right there on the table—a forest in Africa.

Oftentimes the name Africa seem to put a spell on me. If it hadn't been for them dadblame slave traders, we'd be there yet—wit' giraffes for neighbors!

If'n Mama'd lived longer I woulda asked her more. Did she know who it was in our fam'ly come from Africa? And what was it like when Mr. Lincoln freed the slaves? When I was young, people still remembered the War 'tween the States.

Mama was just a girl then. Way I heard it, our folk didn't know what to do once they was freed, cause wadn't like they had a bunch of money put back, ready to strike out on their own.

What I wanted was real stories. What'd he do? What'd she do? What become of 'em? Best I can figure, the slaves was shamed to talk 'bout slavery once they was freed. But that don't make no sense, to be 'shamed of sump'n you couldn't do nothing about.

I's done a heap of thinking on slavery. It come to pass cause of just one thing. The love of money. Once yuh gets to craving money yuh won't never get enough of it to suit you—least tha's the way it looks to me. The Good Book say it harder for a rich man to get into heaven than it be for a camel to pass through the eye of a needle. Now that be saying it plain.

One thing for sure, ain't no amount of money gon keep Mister Misfortune away. He likely show up any ole time.

I stretch my arms over my head. Tired of setting now. And this head of mine's done enough traveling for one day. I lean over and give a pat to my stack of cloth. A pile of strips cut and ready. Gon be many a fine hour spent hooking my rug. Fine hours!

And at the end of my labor? Sump'n new from sump'n old. Glory be!

****

The mules still coming to mind often. Such a awful thing. Coupla times I's talked to Joshua 'bout it.

Surprised me to hear the way things went. Was Mister Robbins 'at hurried in the barn and tried to get the mules out. But they just backed up in they stalls and wouldn't budge. A mule stays round a long time and helps wit' many a thing. Gets to feeling like part of the fam'ly. Doubt I the only one still grieving for Babe and Jenny.

Got a fire going and wouldn't mind just setting by it.

Another good thing Joshua done for this li'l house was put a door at the back by the lean-to, so's to carry in dry wood and not have to go all the way round the house. And thanks to the neighbor men, I has firewood to stack. My guess be, they does it for him—cause we all misses Joshua.

Wish I'd hear sump'n from Miz Stillwell. Ever'time she come to mind I says to myself, "Just take it easy, hold your horses."

****

My head goes to remembering. A bit more'n a week ago it was, the sort of autumn day tha's *just right*. Was a good crowd gathered too, over at Sam and Henrietta's. Most of the afternoon I'd been helping get ready for a fish fry.

I wanted to set myself down in a out of the way spot and rest a bit 'fore the crowd gathered, and it was then I got to looking at a magazine. Usually a word easy to figure out, but I always wanna make sure if'n I got it right.

So some hours after that, wit' ever'body gathered outside, I mentioned it to Henrietta and one of her neighbors. Henrietta opened her mouth to answer but Jacob Gudger popped up out of the dark behind us and say, "*Ardent*? Why I know zactly what that mean, Miz Morrison. That the way I feels when I set off to see my sweetie. I be the ardent lover, you better b'lieve it!"

He hooted and hollered, so we figured he'd been hitting the moonshine.

That was some few days ago, and now I done come on the same word again. Happened yesterday, when my boss lady got a bee in her bonnet.

Settled in at home now, praise be. Just poured myself a cup of cold coffee from the morning's making. We in a spell of warm weather again, like the weather can't make up its mind, so I decide to settle my bones out by Joshua's bench. Still need a sweater, but the sun out and feels good to be out.

Feeling plumb wore out cause of all I done yesterday. Why that woman decided all the bedrooms needed cleaning top to bottom right then, I don't know. I knowed the upstairs rooms where the growed sons live would be awful nasty dirty and the task wouldn't be one I could do quick.

So there I was. Moving furniture, scrubbing, waxing, changing sheets. I finished the upstairs and come down to the main room.

It a big wide room. On one side they her dressing table and the bed. Then they's lots of chairs and a stove too. It a real big room they call "the house." Tha's what Mister Robbins say when comp'ny comes. "Come on in the house." When the weather's warm they entertain guests on the front porch, but in the cold season ever'body gathers in that big room.

She said clean all the bedrooms, "downstairs too," so I took that to mean I didn't have to bother wit more'n the bedroom side of their room. It be the room at the front of the house. One window look out onto the front porch. Couldn't move the big bed him and her sleep in, but got behind it and under it best I could.

Miz Robbins had bought a new counterpane. That seem to be the reason she got such a bee in her bonnet. Was in a bit of misery, I was, cause we was in a warm spell in November. Had to look up some ole rags and make me a few more sweat rags.

And while I was cleaning I got to wondering what the big room downstairs be like in the middle of the night. Him. And her. Together. I picture him getting up in the night to put more wood on the fire. But maybe he tell her to get up and do it.

Does they sleep sound? Does one lay awake and think ill of the other'n? Does either of 'em plan any kind of spite? Might be one of 'em snores and keeps the other'n awake. Think what I was trying to see was some sort of tenderness 'tween 'em. Seem to me, if'n yuh at odds when the sun's up, likely gon be at odds when the sun go down. I finished polishing her dressing table and moved it and the stool back in place and stood there admiring how good it looked, then caught sight of me in the mirror.

Don't have no big mirror here at home. Some of the silver had wore off on that one, but if'n I stepped back a bit I could see almost all of this good strong body I got. Surprise was, how the picture I carry in my head wadn't much a'tall like the picture I was seeing in the mirror.

Was right after that, when it happened. I was taking the stuff off the li'l table by her side of the bed, in the back corner. A big ole Bible slipped out of my hand and hit the floor. My heart come up to my throat.

Might be I'd broke the spine on it. I held my breath and bent to pick it up. It looked to be awright so I let out a big sigh. Thing to do was straighten the papers in it and set it back same as it was. But then one of them papers caught my eye.

I set out here in the yard now, wit' my cold coffee, and almost wish I hadn't never opened it. I know better'n to ramble and meddle in what ain't my bizness, but what I was looking at was just a clipping from a newspaper. Was a 1927 writeup from the Charlotte Observer. 'Bout the Moore fam'ly.

Started off telling how the Major Moore come here from Scotland, a way long back, and then come right on down the line till it get to Mister Baxter Moore. We all know some 'bout him. He got hisself a law office in town, and he the one had the rock wall built round his fam'ly's burying ground.

I took the page over to the winduh facing west and stood there in the afternoon light and read ever' word. There they was, the names of the Moore boys what went to war in 1865. Headed off soon as the war begun, that paper say, but way it said it was that they daddy—one of the richest whoever anywhere round—sent 'em to the fighting. Two of 'em come back. The other'n was took captive and put in a prison camp in New York, and didn't live long after that.

Was what it said near the end 'at upset me so.

'Bout the two 'at come home from the war. Richard Moore and John Springs Moore. Then them words, right there. And me standing there reading. Said both of 'em become "ardent supporters" of the Ku Klux Klan.

I held to the winduh frame. Shivers run through me. What bothered me most was how the paper made it sound a worthy thing to belong to the Klan. Wadn't no reason, of course, to s'pect this white folks' paper would say otherwise, but knowing that didn't lessen the hurt none.

The feelings come back now, though I'm just setting here looking out cross the hill up toward the woods where the world a pretty sight. What I keep remembering be the work I does year after year for the Miz Moore 'cross the way. 'Fore she married she was a Alexander, the fam'ly I made them heavy drapes for. Both fam'lies been living in these parts many a year.

So this Miz Moore's husband come from the same line as them boys what joined the Klan. And when I takes the sewing I does for her over her way, I be stepping along in the same place where them men in the Klan walked.

My coffee's gone and I just be setting here wit' all my sad thinking. Somehow or 'nother, I gotta push it away. Sure as I be setting here, I knows how dwelling on it won't do me one bit of good.

****

Some days pass. Wish I could say I done pushed all them thoughts away. 'Bout the Moores, and the Klan. That all happened some while back—but thing of it be, the Klan still going strong.

This land right here was once part of the Moore plantation. And right here, the slaves working. Back then the Moores lived in a big fine house. Three stories high and a cellar too, but sometime soon after the North and South stopped fighting, the house burned down. Word was the fire was set, wadn't no accident. Still today they a few ruins standing.

This morning, praise be! They ain't no slave master here telling me what I has to do.

I stop for a bit and admire the material for this dress. Sure feel good to the touch. Real soft cloth, pretty shade of lavender. I bend over the table to cut out the facing. And right then the button on the waistband of my skirt pops off. I ain't wanting to stop and sew on no button right now, so I hunt up a safety pin.

This not the first time I be sewing up sump'n I wish I could keep. 'Bout as pretty a piece of fabric as I ever did see. I reach for my needle and thread and start the next buttonhole. The house nice and quiet. Just me here, and my needle going in and out.

Some li'l time go by, and a face come to me. Her face. I can hear her too, same as if she be talking here and now.

How many years done passed? Well, I was almost growed. She prob'ly wadn't old, but seemed old cause we was so young. And in a just a few years that good woman'd be gone from this earth.

Arthur Henderson, I remember, was setting at her right hand. He was sweet on me then and had a habit of catching my eye ever' chance he got. I wadn't a bit interested in him, but he turned out all right and still live hereabouts. And he the one sent Slim my way, so guess I oughta thank him for that.

I finish the buttonholes and start gathering up the skirt. Wonder why the mem'ry of Miss Maude show up now?

Next thing, seem like I under a spell. I can see her clear and hear what she say.

When I come from under the spell I still working buttonholes. And ever'thing else look the same. A bo'quet of goldenrod nearby. In the kitchen, the dish of fried-out fatback wit' another bowl turned down over it, and the pattern on the new oilcloth on the table still pleasing to my eye.

Miss Maude Barnette. She was a old woman by then. Hadn't never married. I was always happy just to be in the same room wit' her. Our Sunday School teacher. Close by her I could feel... well, reckon yuh'd maybe call it strength. It was coming off of her, like heat.

The morning I remembering, they was maybe fifteen or so of us. She looked us in the eye, one after the other. Next thing, she touched a hand to her heart, rested her hands in her lap, and begun speaking. I can here it like it was yesterday—least the most of it, or the gist of it.

"They gon come a time...a time when each of yuh gon be called on to come into yuh own self. And I can tell yuh, it won't be easy. They gon be sump'n yuh wrestle over, same as Jacob—in the Bible—him wrestling wit' the angel. When the angel come, might not have no wings—or none yuh can see.

"I know it must sound strange to yuh, cause yuh ain't old enough yet to understand—but when trouble comes, the trouble just might be the angel.

"They gon be some wrestling, and the wrestling be right inside yuh. The angel tell yuh what yuh need to do, and likely as not yuh say, *Hunh-uh, I be too scared.* Or maybe yuh say, *I don't know how.*

"And so it be, the angel wrestle wit' you. And you the one gon have to decide. This 'at I be telling yuh be the same as prophecy—that zactly what it be! Prophecy.

Cause the time gon come—ain't no doubt—when yuh has to wrestle wit' your angel.

"But what I telling yuh—main thing I telling yuh, be's this: if'n yuh give up and let go, just go on your way and ignore the angel, that be's natural. So don't be too hard on yuhself, if'n that's what yuh do.

"Cause thing is, yuh gon get another chance. That angel ain't gon quit, it gon come again, give yuh another chance and another'n after that—and a good many more after that.

"The last thing I got to say, be a warning. So I want all of yuh to hear me now. And take heed. You young now, and all I saying likely still ahead of yuh. But here the thing yuh need to be mindful of...that angel gon be patient wit' yuh just so long. Just so long. Cause after yuh done said no so many times, the angel maybe gon quit talking to yuh.

"And when that happen, yuh become one of the hard-hearted. Tha's what the Good Book call 'em. The 'hard-hearted'—wit' hearts hard and dry like rock!

"And once that happen—yuh heart's turned to stone, and even that angel won't likely get through to yuh."

She quit talking then. I still see her clear. Her shoulders went slack and she slumped back agin' the chair. Goosebumps had broke out all over me. I r'member it clear as if'n it happened Sunday last. But why it be—that mem'ry show up now?

I put away the pretty lavender dress, and the thimble and thread. Reckon, wit' all the strange dreams I's had lately, ain't no wonder I's conjured up a wise woman.

Chapter 27

Soon's we got to the last amen, Sam and Henrietta and me set off, driving all the way to Charlotte. Sam asked me along cause this fam'ly got a 'lectric washing machine.

Hard to b'lieve all the fancy stuff in that house. Li'l knick knacks scattered all about—and the woman of the house set on telling us 'bout ever last one, looked like. Eustace, her name, and her going on and on while me and Henrietta rolled our eyes behind her back.

"Bought this teacup in Atlanta, and this little glass bird, it come from Philadelphia. Now that vase, it look expensive—but George won it throwing darts at the county fair and it so pretty I decided to add it to my collection."

And on and on. The men was outside, squatting on they haunches by the fancy automobile. Sam's car good enough to haul us here and about, and he mighty proud of it, but Eustace's husband had the latest model right off the fact'ry line.

Heard a story once 'bout a city mouse what visit a country mouse. No, b'lieve it other way round. Whichever way it go, the one making the visit wasn't one bit happy wit' what he found at the other'n's place and just pined to go home. I listened on and on when Eustace was carrying on and right quick knowed which one o' them mice I was like. I was wanting to get back on the road home.

That woman just talk-talk-talk! But right now, praise be, I be setting in the quiet. Monday morning, and rain done set in, so I just setting and crocheting. The dirty clothes over at the Robbins place have to wait. I be making a bedspread for Miz Moore. A pretty thing it be— a rose pattern, pink on white. She hiring me to make it.

Wish Miz Stillwell would be in touch. But right after the thought I tell myself again 'at what I has to do be hold my horses.

On the sewing machine they a Butterick pattern waiting for me—pattern for a three-piece linen suit. For that artist lady at church. I doubt Eustace, that woman in Charlotte—doubt she ever made anything. Her husband the brother of the man 'at own the shop where Sam work. I won't never see 'em again, but it wadn't them I was wanting to see. Was the machine.

The house on Graham Street—not far from the courthouse, Sam said. When he said it I felt my face flush. I was thinking of all that big daydreaming I done 'bout showing up at the sheriff's office and demanding justice. That all seem awful foolish now. If'n we'd gone, they'd have laughed us outta town—if'n they didn't shoot us.

Eustace showed us the machine and tole us how it work. I coulda done wit'out the other thing she said. One more tale 'bout some woman getting her hand caught in the wringer.

I wanted to stop by Efird's, see the shoes and hats, but all the stores closed on Sunday. What I need be a garter belt and some heavy stockings and a brassiere. Got to get the have-tos 'fore I can get the wannas.

Hazeline

****

Woe and more woe. Seem like ever'thing going wrong. Least I made it home alright. Late in the day now and I done finished another washday for Miz Robbins. Wonder how many times I's done they wash?

My back got to aching sump'n terrible when I was bent over the washboard. And then when at last I was crossing the pasture on my way home, the sole of my ole work shoe come loose. Still had most of the way to go so just had to hobble on, one shoe on, one shoe off. And bless pat, just 'fore I made it back I stumped my big toe.

Don't have no choice now. Gon have to spend a bit of my little savings and get me some sturdy ever'day shoes. Maybe get a ride wit' Uncle Morse over to Mister Wash Davis's store. Reckon I shoulda done it 'fore now, but what I been aiming at's keeping a tight hold on my li'l bit of money.

First thing, deal wit' this toe. Wash it good and douse it wit' alcohol and put a bandage on it. Got maybe enough water to do that and wet my whistle. I give the Gudger boy his dime reg'lar, but he ain't always reg'lar wit' his side of the bargain.

I slice a apple and flop down in Joshua's chair. The apple for holding back my thirst, and his chair just the spot for me when I be's in need of comfort. Don't no more'n get set down 'fore a sad mem'ry pop up. Was a li'l white boy lived nearby. Bout six year old he was. Curtis Kidd. That chile stumped his big toe and it swelled up big and a fever come on him. Wadn't long after that till that chile left this world. Word was it was sump'n called lockjaw 'at killed him.

Some while later, I come to. Didn't mean to drift off to sleep.

I reach up and rub my aching neck. Soon as I get to rubbing, I r'member my idea. It come in a dream. If'n I take the idea I gon do sump'n I don't usually do—but, do seem like I been doing a right good job of getting used to new things.

A wonder and a wonder, how these ideas come along. This'un soon got my head in a spin. Look like maybe—uh-huh, just maybe, I gon be doing some entertaining.

What I got in mind's a luncheon. The table gon have to be boards set on sawhorses, and the weather have to be fine—cause sure ain't enough room in this little house to set up tables.

The newspaper always speak to what kind of weather we can expect, so I'll be sure to check it. And beyond that, all I can do is plan and keep my fingers crossed. But what if...?

I grin then, and says out loud, "Well, look like the thing to do be wait and see." Miz Robbins says that often. Huh! Look like that woman maybe rubbing off on me.

So...time has come. Gotta decide who to invite. Ruby, for sure. And Henrietta. Prob'ly ain't no need to ask Joleen, she wouldn't wanna come. Next thing, I thinking of Miz Stillwell—how I'd like to have her come. And if'n she wanted, she could bring along another white woman.

No, can't do that. Wouldn't no white woman wanna come to this li'l house. And if'n I did ask 'em, I might get carted off to the loony bin. It do be some picture, though. White ladies and colored ladies...at the same table. Now wouldn't that be sump'n?

I keep hoping to hear from Miz Stillwell. I tells myself to hold my horses, but I sure wanting to hear from her. She gon get a message to me somehow or other, that much I be sure of, and I does try to keep a hold on b'lieving some good's soon gon come to pass.

****

Was yesterday the magic happened, when this li'l radio opened up my day. Made the day a heap bigger'n this li'l spot of land 'at hold us in its hand. Was late in the day. And my good fortune. I got to hear 'The Blue Danube.' A marvel, it was. Sump'n so divine as that coming right to my ears—from out that li'l box!

Joshua bought it when him and Sam was off gallivantin' one Saturday. Come home all excited—saying he ready to dance! It run on batteries and I ain't had none of late, so now that li'l box seem new all over again.

Thing of it be, a waltz not the best kind of music for when you lonesome. My wonder at the beauty of it didn't last long. A big bunch of loneliness come right up and settled in my lap and I couldn't make it go away. Took it to bed wit' me, and 'fore sleep finally come, shed a few tears.

Most of this day the tune been in my head, keeping me comp'ny while I's busy doing this, doing that. A fine humming tune it be—way it swirl and twirl and jump up and down. More'n once I got to sashaying 'round the front room a bit.

Close to suppertime now. While I deciding whether I gon eat leftovers or pour some milk over some cornbread, I get to r'membering the chirren at the fish fry last week. They had caught two junebugs and tied 'em to strings. We used to do that when I was a chap.

I watched 'em let the bugs fly, but of course the bugs couldn't go no farther'n the string reached. And tha's when it come to me. Tha's 'xackly what I been like. Junebug on a string. Flying 'round in this head of mine—and getting nowhere! Been thinking on and on 'bout my Joleen.

The string I caught on be's the one folks call *Sorrow*.

I switch on the radio again, but this time wha's playing not much to my liking, so I switch it off and begin crumbling my cornbread in a bowl. A idea starts playing in my head. Joleen wouldn't like it, I pretty sure of that. But I might do it anyway. Gotta do sump'n, one way or t'other.

I'd bet a bunch of money—if'n I had a bunch of money—that that girl of mine make her way through a whole week and don't once think of her mama. The very thought grieves me. They's been a few times I been thinking on my girl and begins to hurting in my chest, like maybe I's weeping on my inside.

I wash up my supper dish and hang the dishrag to dry—and hear myself say, "My land! Speak up, why don't yuh? Tell her how yuh be feeling! She your girl—so ain't no reason yuh can't just talk to her."

But tha's the problem. Tha's just what I can't do. Done thought on it and thought on it.

I head out back and stand looking 'cross the field, all the way to the treeline, watching the darkness fall. It do seem strange. And don't make no sense. A mama wit' just one child—and that mama 'fraid to talk to her child.

"Humph!"

After a bit I heave a big sigh. Soon be dark, best get on back in the house. But still they some piece of me 'at just keep standing, and it then I hear it clear. It say, "Don't give up yet. The darkness, it do fall. But the sun bound to come following along."

Way it happen, seem like maybe they was some other Hazeline down in me. Felt like all them words showed up on they own. Wadn't me 'at said 'em. So if'n it wadn't me, who was it?

I turn back toward the house. Been a good while since sump'n surprised me so. But more'n likely, the words was my own. Or maybe God give 'em to me. Don't reckon I need to know. Wha's come to mind now's what I was reading in the Bible a day or so ago: "Ye of little faith."

Well, don't reckon I wanna be setting long with that bunch.

****

Next day come and first thing, I put my big idea to rest. Thought 'bout maybe making a dress for that girl of mine. That'd be a way to show I can make a dress good as any she can buy. But I back off the notion. Got 'bout more sewing than I can do, and she likely wouldn't wear it no way.

And where would that leave me? Worse off'n when I started.

All the while I's getting the morning chores done, memories keep parading by. One evening she was setting at the kitchen table doing her homework and kept scratching her head, like maybe that'd help her think better. I bent over to look, on the lookout for lice. Had heard tell of a fam'ly where lice got started and they 'bout had to burn the house down to get shed of 'em.

Didn't see no lice, but put my hands to her head and begun pulling at the scalp, this way then that. Felt good, I knowed, cause I sometimes pulls at my own. Real soft, I said to her, "Now just think. Right up under my fingers and this li'l bit of skin and bone, they a brain. Joleen Morrison's brain! Now whatcha gon say 'bout that?"

Course, she made fun of me, say she didn't wanna think 'bout no such thing cause her brain wadn't helping her none. O well, past time to quit all this r'membering. Time to get a start on the day, see wha's mine to do this day.

No sooner'n I get started and my brain takes me back to that idea I had 'bout entertaining. Fix a special dinner—what well-to-do women call 'a luncheon.' I can host a luncheon. I can invite special guests. But sure would mean a heap of work.

This morning I be working wit' tucks and gathers, and a lining too. A fancy suit wit' a jacket what fit snug then flare out below the waist.

My mind go again to Miz Stillwell. I knowed wadn't gon be no overnight miracle, but sure seem like the wait's dragging long. Or maybe it just seem so.

Oh my! Sump'n ain't right. Done let my mind roam and....

I stand there looking and looking. Can't b'lieve it. The back lining piece be's too short. I lay it down and pick it up and lay it down again. Still short.

I comes close to busting into tears. A good cry might help.

I stand up straight and tall and take in a deep breath. Well...they only one way to make it fit. Piece it. Won't make no difference in how the jacket wear, and the woman wearing it ain't likely to pay no mind...but it sure don't set right wit' me.

I set down at the kitchen table, in Joshua's chair. And breathe deep. Hold my head in my hands and shut my eyes.

After a bit I come to.

I know right away at sump'n big's happened. This sump'n big ain't no more'n a thought. I close my eyes and look at it again. How come I ain't see'd it a'fore now? All the way through me I got a real strong sense—strong so's it don't leave no doubt, 'bout what I has to do.

My girl.... My girl's been grieving. And me caught up in my own sorrow so's I didn't see. Joleen her daddy's girl—and him gone so sudden she didn't even get to say good-bye. I always has been glad she wadn't there when he left us. Glad she'd stayed over wit' her cousins.

No wonder my sweet girl been staying away from here. She can't wanna come here—cause her daddy ain't here. Now, at last, I finally seeing what I couldn't see.

I set there in his place a wee bit longer, then blow out my breath and get up and go to cutting more of the lining material for this fancy jacket. What I gon do, cut two short pieces to make one tha's long enough. What worry me be how this material ravel so. Gon have to cut the pieces wit' wide seams and make it up a way I don't usually do, but in the end, should work fine.

While I labor to fix my mistake, I figure on how to make up for this other'n. The answer do come to me, a bit later. Same as in a dream. The Bible got stories of people gathering up wisdom when they dreaming.

I see now why the seam 'tween me and Joleen's raveled and frayed. It been for some while now a seam in need of some mending. And if'n anybody round knows how to work seams, it be's Hazeline Morrison.

Soon thereafter the lining's stitched t'gether. Made French seams, so's they won't ravel. While I done it I kept on picturing my girl.

A growed woman, chomping her Juicy Fruit gum. Don't look very ladylike. And how many times I done warned her how chewing all that sweet gum gon rot her teeth? But next time I see her chewing I ain't likely gon complain none. Gon have a few other things to say.

My heart full now. Full to the top. I start in singing. "A-maz-i-ing Grace, how swe-e-et the sound…"

Chapter 28

This the big day. Don't know when I been so excited. 'Fore I got outta bed I wondered again if'n Miz Stillwell's had any luck at working out our plan.

And counseled myself a bit. Guess a few weeks ain't so long if'n yuh looking at changing the world.

Henrietta said why didn't I invite the one I been admiring from a distance. The artist woman. Robin James. So I did ask her. And Henrietta asked one of her neighbors, and I invited two more from church.

I be all fired up, so wanting ever'thing to go just right. They sure a heap of work still ahead. The trick gon be to get it done so's to have time enough to get myself ready. Don't wanna look all flustered when my guests arrive.

Didn't sleep much last night, likely cause I couldn't quit thinking on how early I was gon have to get myself outta bed this morning. Yesterday I 'bout worried myself sick cause the ice man come so late—so late I'd 'bout done give up on him.

My pies soon be ready to go in the oven. The chicken salad and deviled eggs been on ice for a while. Been thinking of all this like a distance to travel, so won't be long now till I gon get to my destination.

My dress ironed and ready to slip on—and not my usual style, but this ain't no ordinary occasion! A full skirt and cowl neckline, and the material real fine, deep rose wit' soft pink polka dots. Wish Joshua could see me wearing it. I can hear him now. He'd take one look and give a whistle.

Right now I got a fork in hand, beating egg whites to a froth. First I made the crusts and baked them, then cooked up the chocolate custard and filled the crusts. Now the pies in the oven for just a li'l bit while I get the meringue whipped. Then I spread the meringue over the custard and set the pies back in the oven and watch close—don't want the meringue to get too brown—and that be all they is to it.

Ever'body always rave over my chocolate pies, but just in case I baked cherry pies too. Had two cans of cherries on hand and wanted to try out the cookie cutter.

The other day Miz Robbins had me polishing up the silverware and there in the cabinet was this star cookie cutter, so I asked her if'n I could borrow it. She say, "Huh, didn't know I had such a thing. Just take it on."

Now it look like I's maybe done the wrong thing. Decorated the top crust wit' stars, and now the juice done bubbled up and my pie not so pretty as it was. I get to chuckling, thinking of the fun I can have. Tell my guests, 'That be the way of it. The juices of life keep a'bubbling and a'bubbling, till 'fore yuh know it we just don't look much like we once did.'

But that won't do. Ain't no kind of talk for such a happy occasion, but just the prospect of these guests coming my way's got me bubbling over. I be feeling mighty fine.

They still a plenty to do, but first, I best take myself up the hill to the well. Let my little wagon carry another coupla buckets of water.

****

The morning moves right along. More'n once I offer up my thanksgiving cause the weather be's so fine. Any day now we could get some real cold weather. November like that. One day warm, next one chilly. I ain't even had to use my flyswatter much.

I be unfolding the tablecloth when I hear sump'n. Sound like a car.

Somebody here early? I hurry over and peep out the winduh. Uh-huh, sure 'nough—they a car coming. This ain't no time for a drop-in visitor...but that car...b'lieve I know it.

My my! Yes it is! I watch her get out, glad the clearing's swept clean and my pot plants all spruced up. But look at me! Still in my ole work dress and this raggedy apron. I brush my hair back wit' my fingers and hurry to the screen door. It be all spruced up too—thanks be to Slim.

"Why, Miz Stillwell! I ain't used to seeing a woman driving a car."

I push the door open and she step inside. I hurry over to open the shutter so the light can get in on the north side, and I don't say nothing but I feels awful proud of Joshua's winduhs.

She take a look around and say, "You've a good eye for color, Hazeline. I expected your place'd be attractive."

I s'pect it the touch of red I added 'at she be admiring. Seat cushions on the rockers, ruffles on the curtains. I heard it said once 'at all rooms need sump'n red. Least the place in tip-top shape, and I hurry on to tell her why it a little more in order'n usual.

She got her hair swept back wit' a pretty comb and a white collar framing her face. She points to the fireplace and looks a question at me. I know what she's meaning. I just put it there today.

Don't usually keep it up there, cause when a fire's going day after day they just too much heat and smoke, but while I was sprucing up the place I decided to set it up on the mantleboard. The picture of Joshua and me. We had a man in the business of taking pictures make it while we was on that one trip we got to take to the beach.

I tell her this, and she say she glad I have least one good photograph and say how we sure look happy. Then she say, "Sorry I've come at an inconvenient time, but I have news I know you want to hear."

****

She didn't stay long. Soon as I watched her make her way up the hill and out of sight, I set right quick to work. Would soon be time to get myself dressed. My stomach was a bit nervous, so I was 'specially glad when Henrietta got here a bit early. Was busting to share my news, and she just the one to tell.

When I got to telling it, I called Miz Stillwell a angel. The words popped right outta my mouth, and made me stop a bit—me calling a white woman such! But I didn't let on to Henrietta. We went on out back where I had the table set up and while she was admiring it I decided they wadn't no reason not to call Miz Stillwell a angel. She a good woman. And goodness ain't got nothing a'tall to do wit' the color of a body's skin.

Henrietta had news too. She say, "You stick to yuh'self so much o' the time 'at I wondered if'n yuh'd heard the latest."

I come to attention. Didn't say nothing, knowing she'd go on.

"So I was right. You ain't heard. Sure come as a surprise. One of ours, 'at went up north, has come back. Say he ready to be back wit' his own people."

Think I can guess who, but again I don't say nothing.

She hurry on. "Wade—tha's who I mean. He staying somewhere over close to where Ruby live."

I say sump'n or other, but don't let on none. Ain't so sure I wanna see Wade Simpson.

The day moved along wit' me 'bout happy as a body can be. All my guests come. And if'n I say so myself, was one happy party! I didn't tell Miz Stillwell's news to the rest, but to my mind, her coming here this day did seem a bit like a benediction.

Ever'body talked and ate a'plenty, and all us laughed a heap. A colorful bunch too, round the sawhorse table, and 'bout ever' color of the rainbow. A coupla shades of blue, a fire-engine red, sunny yellow—and Robin, the artist, she had on a mix of colors swirled all together. So there I was, admiring her again.

But much as I loved having comp'ny, even then somewhere deep down I was looking forward to this minute. Wadn't 'at I wanted to hurry my social along—no sirree! But the quiet part in me...why, it was already looking on ahead, knowing how fine I'd feel wit' the chance to think on all tha's happened.

So right soon after the last of my guests headed out, I went straightaway and carried myself down to my rock. Felt a bit like I'd won some big prize. And on top o' that one, another'n—my bundle of joy so big I could hardly keep hold on it.

Been back at the house now some little bit, just standing here. The feeling in me so big it wanting to shout. But all I does is stand still and look, just inside the door. Then my arms comes together like a cradle and I begins rocking back and forth, my heart plumb full-up— and rejoicing rises up in me and I stand there just inside the door, singing my thanksgiving.

****

Wouldn't even hear of my guests helping wit' the cleanup. But now that I's standing here looking, I be figuring it maybe gon take two or three days—to get this kitchen back in order. Way too tired to start now, though it ain't one bit like me to leave it.

Thing of it be, if'n I tackles it now, I has to trot back up the hill and haul water *again*. The other day I was bent over the washtub and Mister Robbins and some man I hadn't never see'd was standing over by the man's car. Couldn't hear what they was saying, but just happened 'at I looked up in time to see the man throw his arm in the air and shout, "I know the truth of that!"

And I hear it now. Me, Hazeline Morrison, shouting at the top of my lungs. "I sure knows the truth of too little water!"

For some little bit I just stand there by the table. My arms come up and wrap 'round me. Hadn't knowed I was gonna yell out thataway. But it sure be's the truth. It often a misery, this trying to stretch water far as it can go—make it do two or three times. If'n I was rich I'd have me a spigot right to hand, so's all I'd have to do would be turn the tap.

Tha's what that woman down in Charlotte do. The water already there, waiting. Tha's the kinda rich I be dreaming on. A spigot right here in the house!

I can wish for it, uh-huh—least do that much. And for right now I gon do the best I can. Wipe these dirty plates wit' a rag and stack 'em in the oven, and make sure whatever else the bugs and mice might get at be closed up in a pot wit' a heavy lid. Then I gon settle down for a long rest.

****

On over in the night, rain set in. Drumming rat-a-tat-tat on this leaky tin roof. Kept on raining. The noise so loud it'd wake me, then the music of it'd send me on back to dreamland.

Was raining so hard I got up a coupla times to check the buckets under the leaky spots. Then morning come and some little bit after that the rain stopped—stopped all a sudden, like maybe God put his hand out and turned off the spigot.

Ain't even thought 'bout going to church. Too wet, too muddy, and me not wanting nothing more'n to be quiet and thankful. First thing, wash up all that pile of dirty dishes.

Would'a been a big disappointment if'n the rain had come sooner. As it happened, wadn't not one sign of rain till early evening. Reckon I gon be counting yestiddy a red-letter day for some while to come. My guests here!—and Miz Stillwell too! Her driving up in that automobile...a sight I won't soon forget.

What mostly on my mind be all the heap of thanksgivings I gon be saying. Done said a few—but I's planning on sowing my thanksgiving deep.

This a special day too, and it moving along fast as the one before. Now the middle of the afternoon's come and the sun's out. The air's a bit chilly, so I pull on Joshua's ole overalls and start moseying down the path.

I so love the little stream's music—the water rushing over'n round the rocks. That might just be my favorite of Mother Nature's music. I gets to chuckling then and say out loud, "Hazeline Morrison, yuh said the same thing a short while back 'bout the wind soughing through the pines!"

Soon thereafter I's settled on my rock. I set real still. Listening close.

A heap of water racing along, so the music's strong and clear. Tha's why I hurried to come on down here. I prop my feet on a flat rock and gaze down at the water. It be rushing on so I can't hardly see it 'fore it's gone already—gone round the bend.

It a hour so fine I whispers, "Icing on the cake."

Oft'times, that mean a body be's complaining. But not now! This glory a fitting icing on the news Miz Stillwell brung. I shut my eyes and listen. Down under the water sound they a gurgle 'at fit itself in ever' few beats.

Reckon tha's what yuh call 'the music of the ages.' Reckon tha's what Miz Stillwell brung. Music of the ages—the hallelujah news we all been waiting to hear. She say she went and talked wit' her preacher, and he went to see them boys what hurt Delia. And wonder of wonders!—if'n two of 'em didn't say they was willing to repent of what they done, and say they wanted word of the repentance delivered to the girl.

Hard to b'lieve. Sound 'bout too good to be true. One part of the story wadn't so fine. The white preacher picked Rev'rend Jones to be the one to get the message to Delia. It the only part of what Miz Stillwell said I wish had been dif'rent.

I stay on a bit longer, then take the path up the hill and get to thinking 'bout Ruby. Wish she lived next door so I could run over wit' the good news. But more'n likely, she be hearing it soon. Good news or bad news, it travel quick.

****

My curiosity was growing bigger by the minute. Slim had sent word he'd be coming by late afternoon.

Surprised me when he set a pertic'lar time. Usually he say sump'n like, 'I'll come on over some morning soon and see if you done any cooking lately.' What he really mean, he coming to see if'n they anything round here needing fixing.

Five minutes 'fore the clock was gon strike four I was right curious. Would he get here on the dot? I stood watching out the winduh. Wadn't like him to come so late in the day.

I'd started early that morning. Made a big pot of soup and a blackberry jam cake with caramel icing. They was other things to be done, so I wanted to make sure I got the important stuff done first.

And then, law's a mercy, there he was! Yessiree, on his way—and on time! I stood at the winduh watching. Joy swelled up in me and my arms crossed over my chest. They was two of 'em! Her holding to his arm and looking up at him, and him looking down at her. A wonder they didn't stumble. The first I'd laid eyes on the girl, but wadn't hard to see why Slim was so taken wit' her.

They didn't stay long—but by the time they headed out I was plumb filled up wit' happiness. Even now, seem like the happiness bubbling out the top of my head.
It sure a time for rejoicing! And I know just the thing to do. Gon settle for a spell on Joshua's bench—and tell him the news.

Chapter 29

———— ⟫≔≋≕⟪ ————

Was early morning and me s'posed to be headed over to the Robbins household, but my head had got to hurting awful bad. Don't usually suffer headaches, but I did have some BC Powder and took some, and set down at the table and rested my head on my arms. The pain eased a bit, but even so I didn't feel like cutting no cartwheels.

I got myself ready and set off. Dragged myself up hill and down hill, and was still dragging when I opened the gate to start up 'cross the pasture. Miz Robbins had fam'ly coming the next day and I'd promised to show up bright and early.

Was wishing I could turn right around and head on back to the house. The walk to the backporch seemed mighty long, but at last I did make it and plopped myself down. Didn't see nor hear nobody, so I set on the rock step and rested my head in my hands. Was time to get started churning the butter, but maybe if'n I just closed my eyes a bit I'd feel some better.

Next thing I knowed Miz Robbins was saying, "Hazeline, you sick?"

Her voice startled me so I brung my head up quick. Felt dizzy, and that was the start of it. Now some days has gone by and look like I gon make it. They was least one time when I did wonder, cause I didn't hardly feel alive—'cept for the pain.

I remember, for what seemed a awful long time, laying flat of my back, and I remember a tiniest thought passing through to say 'at life might be getting ready to stop. And then what, I wondered. Why, I'd see Joshua. There he'd be. But what would come next?

Most times, when I was awake enough to know I was still among the living, I felt stuck in the middle of a thick fog. Ever'thing hazy. Strange thing 'bout it was, the fog seemed a pleasant thing. When I first begun to come out of it, I still wadn't clearheaded, but I did r'member being on the step and Miz Robbins, her asking if'n I was sick. What I couldn't recall was walking home. Figured I did. Surely didn't fly home.

Now I be getting a bit stronger wit' ever' day 'at passes.

Joleen and Troy, they just left. They brung food, but I ain't got much appetite. Spend my time in my rocking chair or stretched out on the bed. Watching time go by.

Was the Gudger boy 'at spread the news. He brung my water a second day and saw I hadn't used what he'd brung the day before. The neighbors got word to Joleen and she got word to Henrietta, so they been checking on me. This the first day I's felt anywhere near like myself.

Joleen brung some Campbell's soup and saltine crackers. Henrietta brung some good homecooking. But so far I ain't had much appetite.

The house quiet now. I been wondering what day it be. And I's curious to know what happened after Miz Robbins asked me if'n I was sick. She wouldn't'a felt of my head to see if'n I was running a fever. She wouldn't'a touched me,

I pretty sure of that. Guess she could see I wadn't up to helping her that morning. More'n likely she got herself in a tizzy and was going round in circles getting ready for her comp'ny.

Guess I gon have to wait till Monday to find out—if'n I able to work by then.

****

Troy shows up on a Saturday in his ole car. Say he took Joleen by the beauty shop, and come on by here to tell me to be ready this afternoon when Sam planning to pick me up. Him and Henrietta planning a hot dog supper, then ever'body gather round the big RCA radio and listen to *Amos and Andy.*

If'n they anything might perk me up, likely be our laughs when we set close by that wooden box and listen to the funnies. That show a lot like the funny paper, but better, cause yuh can listen wit' your family and friends—and ever' body gets to cackling!

Right now I needing to rouse myself, wash myself. And iron my dress. Been cooped up way too long. Feeling a heap better wit' just the prospect of getting outta the house for a spell.

Now I remembers something else was on the radio recent. A show 'at kicked up a big stir. I didn't hear it, but I reckon ever'body round heard 'bout it. Sure stirred things up. A lotta folks took it for true—thought the world really was 'bout to come to a end.

But turned out, wadn't nothing but a show on the radio. B'lieve the man that set it up was named Orson. I still remember for sure his last name, cause it like the 'well' where we draw up our water. Well, that Mister Orson Wells sure drawed up sump'n—drawed up *panic*. Tha's what the Charlotte paper say.

Bout four o'clock, Sam show up. He so much remind me of my Joshua. Look like him and act like him too. I no more'n get in the car 'fore he start in to talking—same as Joshua, both of 'em big talkers.

Sam's all upset. Fussing 'bout what happened to him early in the day. He went to town, to the Sears Store on North Tryon, and was on his way down the steps to the basement. On the landing, they be two water fountains.

The sign by one say *White*, the other'n say *Colored*. A white woman was there wit' her l'il boy—begging his mama to let him drink colored water, but the mama telling him, 'No no, not that one, we drink outta this one!' But the chile stir up a racket, wanting to drink water tha's colored. Then the mama notice Sam and give the chile's arm a yank. The chile didn't get no water, and Sam decided he could do without it too.

Tha's the first thing he tells when we start our ride.

Soon as he gets that off his chest, he r'members what he's meaning to tell me. I be setting all comfy in the passenger seat, and he begins giving me the answer to what I been wondering 'bout. Can't hardly b'lieve my ears! Maybe he just fooling me, but I know him good, and they ain't no sign 'at he be telling anything but the truth.

After he tells it, he keep on talking—but I don't hear. The car keeps a'moving and I set there like stone—plumb lost in wonder.

He say after Miz Robbins saw I was sick that morning, she helped me in the house. Tha's what Sam said. 'Helped yuh get inside and lie down."

Lie down where, I wonder. Not on her bed, nosirree. Musta been on the cot in the corner. Or maybe on the floor. Anyway, he say she got on the telephone and called Dr. Tom Craven. And say the doctor come pretty quick—and she paid the bill!

Sam still talking. I turn my face to the winduh. See the fields and woods go by. I be thinking, *Wonders never cease.* Tha's all I can think. *Wonders never cease.* And I get goosebumps. Laws a'mercy! It do be true—miracles does sometimes happen!

****

Out of butter, and don't have no milk to churn, so I decide to carry my empty basket over to the neighbor's place. Ezra and his family maybe got a bit of milk to share. I can ask for the clabber milk left from the churning, cause it plenty fine for making cornbread or a coffeecake.

While I be walking, my head begins to line up all that happened this summer. Some of it—like Eli, just plumb funny. Hollering and stumbling. Couldn't even walk straight—but knowed how to put me down.

Then Mister Robbins, showing up here. Him on his high horse! Acting the big man. Would be a good thing if'n he could see hisself way other folks sees him —the ones of us has to put up wit' him!

And there was Sudie, up at the store. She sure had me scared! Thought maybe we was 'bout to start rolling round in the dirt, pulling at the other'n's hair. Praise be, the bell sounded, just in time.

I grin and I chuckle. Now it's all over and done with, do seem funny. And sure as I be walking down this hill they gon be sump'n else happening, sump'n new 'at make a good story. I reckon it wouldn't be far off the mark to say life just one big show.

This new story—'bout Miz Robbins coming to my aid—why it 'bout more'n I can take in. They has been one time when me and her spoke of it—me trying to tell her I 'preciate it and don't know how I can pay her back.

But she surprise me. Say she don't want me to feel indebted to her. Said if'n the tables'd been turned, I'd have done the same for her.

Way she said it was, "You'd've done all you could to see to me." Reckon I ain't soon gon forget them words.

****

He left 'bout a hour ago. Was the last thing I expected. Folks was mentioning him Saturday at the fish fry. And now he done come by here.

That man always was a talker. Might be he wadn't quite at ease wit' me neither, cause he sure talked a blue streak. I couldn't get a word in edgeways—but wadn't like I wanted to. Wouldn't'a knowed what to say. He talk and he talk, and ever so often I put in the refrain. "Uh-hunh...yuh don't say."

Way it happened was, he come riding up on a handsome black horse and didn't even get off at first. He just call out, "Hazeline!"

I knowed the voice. Knowed it sure. My hands flew to my mouth. Couldn't be! But it was.

I'd just started getting outta my Sunday clothes. While I was changing I thought on the week to come, figured it was maybe 'bout time to dig me a mess of turnips—but all a sudden I was buttoning up again. Slipped my vest back on too, that special one from the cloth I dyed.

Right off, same as ever, he start in to talking. Seemed strange, him talking and it sounding same as those years ago. Ever' now and then he'd throw in a cuss word, and that the same too.

"Lemme tell yuh sump'n, Hazeline. This part of the country—right here? It the best—best of the whole damn creation! I been living up north a helluva long time, and wadn't one year went by I didn't miss the lay of this land—and this ole red clay dirt too. And yuh know for sure I missed the weather! By now, up north, it already cold. I'd be wearing my longjohns—and still my ass freezing!"

He laughed big and I laughed too, and he kept on. We was settled under the maple. The afternoon light was golden and the air not too chilly. I was glad of that. Wadn't sure I wanted to invite him inside.

When a breeze come through I wished for my sweater, but I didn't go after it. Mostly, I just listened at him. The maple leaves would soon be falling. Looked like maybe a angel had flew by and painted the leaves gold. A sight to behold!

Wade Simpson. He a sight to behold. Still looking good. Tall, but not gangly tall. Look to be still good and solid, and holding his shoulders straight. He always was one to stand tall, and didn't take long 'fore I could see 'at his eyes still got the same spark. Course, he's aged some. Hair cut close to his head, same as he used to keep it, but showing a bit of gray now.

I was glad I'd braided my hair that morning so it was pulled away from my face. I was giving some mind to holding myself up straight too, and couldn't help but wonder how his eyes was seeing me.

He talked some 'bout the way things used to be when we was growing up. They a lot he could've talked on and I breathed a prayer of thanksgiving 'at he steered clear of most of it. After a while I kept thinking he was surely ready to leave—cause I wadn't at ease. But then he'd start in on sump'n else. Tole 'bout the jobs he'd worked. One in a steel mill in Pennsylvania.

I did r'member my manners, thought I should offer him sump'n to eat or drink, but 'cept for coffee in the pot since morning or a dipperful of water, they wadn't nothing much to serve a guest cause they wadn't nothing left of what I carried to church.

Then all a sudden he quit talking. I'd been readying my apology 'bout not offering him least sump'n to drink, but 'fore I could gather my words he say, "I never did forget."

My heart flip-flopped. What was it he didn't forget? I sure wadn't gonna ask, wadn't going down that road. Think maybe I stuttered a bit. I said sump'n like I'd always hoped he was doing well and any time I heard mention of him the report sounded good and I was glad of that.

"Well," he said, "I done what I wanted, and made a heck more money'n I coulda made here. But now that I'm back I's wondered a time or two if'n it was the best thing—staying away so long, I mean."

I couldn't think of nothing to say to that, so I looked at my hands. Think they was wishing I had my apron on, wanting to roll it up.

Wade's Joshua's cousin. I wadn't more'n fifteen or so when he begun showing interest in me. He had a loud mouth, liked to show off, and was awful proud of his light skin. I sometimes thought he acted uppity, like a colored man what couldn't get over wishing he was white.

He got up outta the chair and walked past me and on over to the oak tree. I caught his scent when he went by. Like tobacco mixed wit' some store-bought scent. He was clean-shaven, and wearing trousers wit' a crease, and a shirt open at the neck. He leaned forward and reached his arms up and put both hands flat on the treetrunk. And he kept on standing, not moving one bit.

The evening sun put him in shadow so's he looked like he was cut outta paper.
He turned back my way and rubbed his chin. I looked down again.

"Woman," he said, "you a sight for sore eyes. You know that? Law me! Many a time you come to mind. And all I could do was grin and bear it—say to myself, 'Cousin Joshua sure got hisself a good woman.'"

I couldn't help but look up then—cause I knowed he was bound to be grinning big. I crossed my legs, glad I was wearing my new two-toned shoes wit' the strap round the ankle. A smile crossed my face too. I was feeling plumb foolish.

Wade be's my age, but that just one thing I know 'bout him. How he be now, I don't have no way of knowing. Do he ever get drunk? If'n so, what kind a drunk do he be? I sure ain't likely to ask.

He stayed a good while. Till I was waiting for him to leave. I got to my feet. And praise the Lord!—the man had sense enough to see what I was trying to say. Was right then 'at Ole Dog come from under the house and Wade reached down and rubbed him a bit and tole him to look after me, then a goodbye and he was on his way.

Been a while since I see'd such a handsome horse. I stood watching as he left, but hid behind the oak tree, out of sight case he should look back.

The day would soon be over and the air getting chilly, so I put some kindling in the fireplace and soon had me a fire going. Ever since then I been setting here staring at the flames. That man sure stirred up a bunch of mem'ries. And seem to me like he maybe said a bit more'n he should've, but likely I just reading too much in what he say. More'n likely, he was just putting t'gether words what sound good. Doubt he ever thought of me much when he was living way off up yonder.

****

Slim went dashing up the hill. Just watching him made me feel good. Don't reckon I ever could run like that. He was racing along cause his energy so big it just bubbling over.

I'd just finished my morning rounds—all the li'l things 'at has to be done ever'day, when I heard him call out. I knew soon as I heard his voice he was feeling fine. I got to the door in time to see him come leaping over the step and onto the li'l stoop porch, holding to a basket of muscadines and not spilling a one. I held the door open and he crossed the threshold. I hadn't see'd him this happy since—well…since before.

His grin spread ear to ear. He set the basket on the floor and raised his arms high over his head and give a cheer: "Ah-ha! Hoorah!"

His arms dropped to his side then, his eyes just twinkling wit' merriment.

"Miz Morrison." He'd dropped his voice low. Later I thought on it many a time, how he tried to make what he said sound official. "I come to give yuh a special invitation. I do beg the pleasure of your presence on the day I become the husband—of Miss Delia Tompkins!"

His voice rose high 'fore he finished, then he crossed his arms over his chest, so full of hisself he was 'bout to bust. And he say, "Will yuh come?"

All that was yesterday. This morning, I be thinking maybe this a good day for picking some muscadines. One year long back, Joshua and me was walking through the woods and had just rounded the bend where we knowed they was a good vine up in a tall tree, and soon as it come in sight we spotted 'em. Raccoons. Looked like maybe a whole family of 'em up in there, feeding on muscadines.

We knowed what would happen, so we just kept moseying along, and once we got just beyond the vine we turned around and saw just what we knowed we'd see. Ever' one of them critters had froze, not making not one move.

Been thinking on what I gon wear to the wedding. I tole Slim I wanna make Delia's dress—my gift to her.

Got a few jars of muscadine jelly and damson preserves lined up on the shelf, ready to give to the new couple. And might be I'll come round to deciding to part with least one or two jars of my blackberry jam and crabapple jelly and strawberry preserves. Gon pack the jars in a box and make a fancy bow to dress it up.

Ever since Slim left here, ever' once in a while my heart perk up. It say, *Hot diggity dog!*

This the day I be set on doing what I been putting off. Not gon put it off no more. I say out loud, "Got to remedy the dullness."

Well now...that a fine sounding bunch of words. Sound good to you, Ole Dog? Just popped outta my mouth. *Remedy the dullness."*

Out by the shed, I got two big blocks of firewood 'at ain't been split yet turned up on end. One for a seat, other'n for a table. If'n Ole Dog could talk he maybe could tell me how to do this chore, cause when Joshua was out here working he'd be stuck right by his side.

I say, "Does yuh know how? Or is yuh just gon sleep on and pay me no mind? I don't blame yuh. Be hard to help a somebody so unhandy wit' tools as I be."

Soon as the words outta my mouth, my mind jerk me up. *Hunh? Why you wanna say that?* I stop then and think for a bit. If'n I pretty good wit' tools in the house, might be I could be good wit' this tool.

I blow out some air and say, "Alright then."

First thing I turn the whetstone and look at it good, then hold it a li'l dif'rent. Got my knives and scissors lined up on the block right by me, so I reach for a knife, ready to give it a try. Maybe 'fore long I gon have knives and scissors what cut good. Trick gon be not to sharpen too much and wear the blade away.

Guess this a catch-up day. Already done one thing I been meaning to do. Pulled out my savings and counted. Ever'time I get paid for a sewing job I put just a li'l of it back. And if'n they's too little, I still try to put back least a few cents. Was disappointed when I opened the box and counted. Nickels and dimes and quarters and half dollars don't add up quick. Wadn't much folding money.

A picture pop up. Folding money. I was emptying the water from the washpots last Monday when a white man pulled up in a car. He didn't pay me no mind. Went up to the porch door and knocked so hard the door rattled. In a minute Mister Robbins come out and the two of 'em go over and stand beside the man's car. I couldn't hear what they was saying and wadn't trying to, but I did happen to look thataway just when Mister Robbins slid a hand down in his pants pocket and come out wit' a whole wad of folding money. My mouth prob'ly dropped open, but they wadn't paying me no mind.

I still don't have enough saved yet to go inta town. Wanting to go to Belk's basement. And Efird's. Soon as I get a few more dollars saved, I gon ask Joleen if'n Troy can take us into town to do some shopping. Need to get in some supplies. Thread and elastic and embroidery transfers. And maybe shoes, and least a look at hats. T'will be a disappointment if'n I go wit'out a bit extra in my pocketbook. Sure would be fine to bring home sump'n extra, sump'n at just take my fancy.

Well, least these knives gon work some better. The scissors gon be harder to get at, but no sense delaying, may as well get on wit' it.

"Yuh see here, Ole Dog? Hazeline Morrison ain't too old to learn new tricks." He just waking up. Prob'ly getting hungry. He wobbles to his feet and heads for his water pan. Poor thing. Look like he in pain.

****

Troy outside. I asked him to go out back and do a small chore for me. It be sump'n I could do, but I wanting a bit of time wit' my girl—have her all to myself for a bit.

She look like she be dressed for sump'n special, but that just the way she always look. A pretty blue dress wit' a flared skirt. Say she got it at Mr. Belk's store. Bet she paid least $6 for it.

She say, "I'm so full I could bust. Daddy always did say you the best cook anywhere 'round." She pats her tummy. "I shouldn't'a had that second slice of pie."

I was relieved. The meal had turned out awright, though I'd had to jump a bit to turn it out on time. Got caught up in some embroidery work and plumb forgot to r'member the time. "Oh my land!" I said out loud. "Look what done happened. My comp'ny likely to arrive 'fore I ready for 'em."

I'd been so busy of late I'd give the place no more'n a lick and a promise. When I tucked the embroidery away I said to myself it was just family coming, no use getting upset. But thing of it was, this daughter of mine and her husband come here so seldom they seem more like important guests.

Then right quick I said out loud, "Well, 'course they important guests!"

Good thing was, I'd got a block of ice. The iceman had come just at the right time. And that a mighty important detail, cause my girl crazy 'bout iced tea. I made two pumpkin pies. And early in the day walked up to Mr. Henry Stillwell's store and bought a slab of beef, cause roast and gravy's Joleen's favorite—same as her daddy.

And all a sudden I was saying out loud, "Oh my land! Don't let me forget the surprise!"

Now here she be, setting at her place at the table. And I says, "Wait just a minute. I got sump'n for yuh."

I hurry to the chifferobe and pull out a li'l brown case. When I get back she sipping at her sweet tea. She wipes her hands dry 'fore she picks up what I set in front of her, and tears springs to her eyes—but her smile spreads all the way 'cross her face.

For a minute or so we don't neither of us say a word. She turn the gift in her hands then hold it to her breast. And next thing, she put that harmonica to her lips and play a few notes. Soon as she gets warmed up she start in on the tune Joshua played more'n any other. "Take me out to the ballgame."

She play it through a coupla times. And tears fill her eyes and mine too.

"Mama, you remember when Daddy played that before one of the championship games? I was maybe 'bout ten then, and him all fired up, putting on a show—playing the tune, and a crowd gathering round him."

I start in to chuckling. "My land yes! I sure do—and then, after all that—you r'member what happened?"

She cackle big and say, "They lost the game!"

Wadn't just that they lost, but how bad they lost. We both still laughing big when Troy come back in. I notice again how broad my son-in-law be in the shoulders. Fine looking fella. He asks what we be carrying on about. Joleen and me reach 'cross the table and clap our palms t'gether—and laugh some more.

She my girl. She a good girl. A lot like her daddy. I was glad I remembered the harmonica. Couldn't have bought her anything she'd want more.

Chapter 30

---❖---

I so tired I don't want no supper. Did get the fire going in the cookstove and heated some water. Soon as it was good and hot I poured it in my foot tub and dropped in some Epsom Salts. My feet likely think they in heaven. Even my hands resting easy. They deserve a rest too.

A few days ago the weather turned off chilly and Miz Robbins sent word. Time to kill the hogs.

I come home so tired I could hardly make it through the door. We been working steady, a bunch of us, and hardly any chance to rest. Got the smokehouse cleaned out, the streaked meat and hams ready for curing, the sausage made and the chitlins cleaned. My back and legs aching, and my feet past hurting. They done gone numb. But, I don' t much mind the pain, cause they gon be times ahead when I be saying, "Mmm-hmm!"

The lard, the salted down fat meat, I'll get my share of that. Won't get none of the pork chops. Don't want no pigfeet. Couldn't get 'em if'n I wanted, cause they Mister Robbins's favorite. Don't want no chit'lins neither. Would if'n Joshua was here, but way back when I was a chap I decided chit'lins ain't to my liking. Don't like the smell of 'em. Give me a country ham biscuit, or a piece of meat from 'long the backbone and baste it wit' my barbecue sauce—now tha's some good eating!

Wit' the room so warm and my feet so happy I be just 'bout to doze off. Pictures start coming, like dreams—

though my eyes be wide open. Long ago, tha's what I be seeing. I wadn't even full growed yet. Back then I thought my future was gon be wit' Wade. All he had to do was look my way and a smile'd start in my eyes and spread all the way through me.

Late one afternoon he come by the house when me and my sister Ellie happened to be standing t'gether. We watched him stride 'cross the field wit' them long legs and that hat set on his head just so.

Ellie say, "Can't you see what he like, Hazeline? He so full of hisself he can't even think 'bout you. He just wanting you to think he be sump'n special."

Was that day 'at me and him walked up the dirt road a piece. I thought to myself then 'at he had a wicked look in his eye. But he sure knowed how to talk nice. Reckon I'd'a set off wit' him and gone anywhere he wanted to go— woulda gone clear the other side of the world. But he didn't ask me. He just stopped by once in a while and got me all stirred up, and then he left. I never did quite figure him out, but I was certain I'd sized him up right. Underneath all that putting on airs, they was a good heart.

When he come by to tell me he was taking a job up north, he made out like he'd be back 'fore long. I had it in my head I was waiting for him. Wadn't long 'fore he sent me a letter. And after that, not another word.

I wouldn't let nobody say nothing 'gainst him, though. And didn't let on none 'bout how I'd been expecting him to come back for me. But now, I can't help wondering. What would I be like now if'n I'd lived up north, if'n I'd been wit'

Wade? Him and Joshua was cousins, but not much alike far as I could see—'cept they both talked a whole heap.

Since that Sunday when he come by he's been at church a coupla times, and always give me a look and tip his hat. Look like he might even bow! And I thank the Lord for small favors. No bowing, please! The thought gets me to laughing. It sure worth a laugh!

I wouldn't wanna tell how much time I's spent wondering what his life's been like. And what was his woman like? I'd bet money they was more'n one. No matter how often he come to mind I always end up wit' the same thoughts, like as if I got 'em all tied up wit' one ribbon.

They be one thing I sure 'bout. That man's got a good heart. Even so, they sump'n else too. Seem like I maybe just a bit afraid of him.

Wit' my very next breath I get a surprise. *Huh-unh! That ain't it!*

No, that ain't it a'tall. No sirree! One I be's scared of? Hazeline—tha's who. Cause she ain't none too sure what she'd do if'n he come close.

Most ever' time I read the paper I come across some word 'at sticks in my mind. Just recent, the word was *noble*. And right quick, it brung him to mind. No matter what he done nor what happened while he was living up north, look like it maybe done all come t'gether for him. And who woulda thought it, if'n you knowed how all-fired stuck on hisself he was when he was young?

The water in my foot tub ain't warm no more. And tha's a good thing. Make me get up outta this chair and quit all this thinking.

****

Don't have to go nowhere today and sure glad of it. By midmorning I wondering what I gon eat, so I take a look around. Find potatoes and carrots. Uh-huh, so I can make one of my specialties. Ain't see'd nobody else do it, but I like doing 'em up together, in one pot and one bowl. Since I been by myself I tends to fix things in one pot. Else I cook one new thing and to go wit' it grab whatever be easy to grab—maybe peanut butter and soda crackers, maybe a tin of potted meat.

I cook the potatoes and carrots in a li'l water and not one other thing. Put the lid on and cook 'em on low heat till they done. Then lift 'em outta the water inta a bowl and use my long-handled fork to mash 'em, then add a li'l of the cooking water, a bit of cream off the top of the milk, a bit of butter, a li'l salt and pepper—and maybe some green onions, if they's any to be had.

I eat a huge helping. They so good I don't want nothing else. I like the way the carrots don't mash up smooth, leave li'l chunks. Sure good.

I'd need a li'l more to hold me if'n I was gon be working outside this afternoon, but my work for the day be's easy. Shelling pecans. One of Miz Robbins's sisters bring a heap of 'em ever' year 'bout this time. I do all the shelling, so I gets to keep a share.

On over in the afternoon I rake a few leaves to ease the setting too long. After that I settle in and read the paper till suppertime. The Ivey's Store be running ads wit' pictures of dresses 'at say they come in ever' size, from 12 to 20, all the same price. $6.95. They in the budget department, but I s'pect the style the same as in the highfalutin' part of the store. Likely just the fabric and the buttons dif'rent.

A swing skirt come just below the knees, and the shoulders big and puffy and look like wings. Wit' wings like that on yuh dress, look like yuh might oughta get to flying. The thought gets me to chuckling. I s'pect they quite a few women wearing such dresses 'at find a way to fly!

I gon fly right on inta making one. Use the same pattern I been using for a long time, just alter it a bit—and end up wit' this same dress. Have to make a belt too, one tha's wide and fits snug. I ain't fond of working wit' belting, but I can do it once I set my mind to it.

The ad say, "See these new frocks today."

Well, can't see the one I be picturing till I make it. Gon have to get a ride into Charlotte, to Mr Belk's basement store, so's to get just the right material. May be I get it right and may be I won't, but it be all the planning and trying and maybe another go at it that keep me feeling fine.

I work my way from the back of the paper to the front and come on a interesting bit of news 'bout Florida. Say they planted 90,000 acres of cotton, and first of July harvested 32,000 bales. Was the date 'at surprised me. All that crop picked and harvested that early? Round here cotton don't get picked till autumn—and I sure glad of it!

I be already ready to put the paper aside when a strange thing happen. First I spot the word 'sacred,' and right soon after it, "defiant." Felt sorta funny, way they come t'gether, and way they seemed to speak to me. I stopped for a bit and studied on 'em.

And then it come to me. They fit. First, all that thinking I done 'bout seeing justice done—that push in me! Reckon yuh might call it *sacred*. Sure felt thataway. Come hell or highwater, I had to do sump'n!

But first, they was the fear. A whole heap of it! I sure done some work to defy it.

Now here these words, right on the page—saying the truth of it. Ain't no doubt in my mind. They was sump'n in me pushing for justice.

'Sacred.' And 'defiant.' Doubt they any better words for it. But I sure wouldn't wanna go round telling it to nobody. That'd be a sure way to get run off.

I set still for a bit, feel a kind of wonder. After some bit I lay the paper down and see wha's piled up and waiting. Can't help but laugh. First the high thinking—then Miz Robbins's underwear! A waste of time putting new elastic in these step-ins. Monday morning, hanging the clothes on the line, I was thinking these wore-out step-ins oughta be throwed away. So I mention it. And she say she been holding 'em on wit' safety pins, could I put some new elastic in 'em?

How come she don't just buy new ones? Might be cause he won't give her money. He always saying how he like to put his money on sump'n gon make more money—maybe a new plow or another acre of land. He don't b'lieve in spending to make the house fancy, nor top-o-the-line clothes—but he sure proud of that automobile. He get ole Abraham's boy, one 'at cuts they firewood, to keep it shined up.

Won't be long, I 'spect, 'fore Mister Robbins get the house and barn hooked up to 'lectric power. And then a 'lectric icebox. And 'lectric cookstove too. Maybe even a 'lectric pump to bring water right in the kitchen. And that washing machine I be dreading.

Joshua never showed no patience wit' my worries. "Laws-a-mercy, woman! That machine gon do the worst of the work—make your job easy!"

What I looking forward to be pushing a button on the wall and a light come on. When the white folk round here gets that, they won't need kerosene lamps no more. But if'n they smart, reckon they'll hold onto 'em, just in case.

****

Soon as Slim come in he go to joking 'bout how they just come by to get sump'n to eat. I had to tell him he was out of luck, cause I been too busy of late to cook more'n just enough to get by. Some fresh greens and turnips, and a pot of beans, that much I had, and not much of that left.

He stood near the fireplace wit' his arm round Delia, and then he dropped his arm and took a step forward, 'tween her and me. I could see he was making his face stern. He say, "Now Delia, it won't matter none if'n you not the best cook—cause this woman here, she the best in the whole world, so it'll be alright with me if you come in second."

He let out a holler and hooted wit' laughter then, and her grinning big. Her face round as can be. Don't think I ever has see'd anybody wit' such a round face. Her nose flat and wide. It be her eyes what make her pretty. They gleam and they twinkle. And her belly showing good. I'm betting she be carrying a boy.

Slim change his tune then, take on a serious look, say they got to be getting along. Her daddy had give 'em leave to get married and they'd decided to do it real quiet, so they was awready man and wife.

This hit me real hard. I'd been so looking forward to making the wedding dress. Had to work hard, so's not to show how disappointed I was, cause there stood Slim 'bout to bust wit' happiness. His feelings was so big they was getting the best of him. He dropped his head and swiped his sleeve 'cross his face, then glanced back up at her.

He turned to me and said this was one of the stops he'd insisted on. They'd come to tell me they was leaving. Gon move some li'l distance from here. Not too far, he say, just down 'bout Monroe.

Took all my strength to keep from busting out in tears. Might as well be California for all the distance it be to me. He wouldn't no more be stopping by from time to time.

He had his cap in his hand, turning it round and round, same as usual. "Monroe not so far from here, Miz Morrison, and I can make my way. Shoot, you know I a good worker—so won't be no time 'fore I get me a job—and 'fore yuh know it I'll have me a car. I know how to keep it running, too, so we gon be coming back to visit. Gon take you for a ride in that car!"

He slapped the cap on his head and took her hand and led her toward the door. When he turned back he say, "They be one thing to keep in mind."

Now he had that smile in his eyes again.

"That car ride gon cost yuh. We be trading rides for pies!"

I give 'em both a big embrace and bid 'em farewell. They leave the yard and start the walk up the hill. I stand on the stoop and watch, my hands rolling up my apron.

****

Woke up feeling stiff, so decided first thing to go out walking. Cooler weather's finally come along. First thing, went by the gully, where so many things gets dumped. More'n once I's found sump'n there I carried home, but not this time. I kept on and soon decided to go all the way to the river—and now here I be, standing on the bank by the willows, watching the water go by.

Wonder how old this river be? And where it start? And wonder if'n it know folks has give it a name?

Catawba. A Indian name, I know. But wonder why this water called that?

Our school teacher tole us 'bout how some long while back the business men in this part of the country got the notion they'd connect the rivers, so's they could haul goods cheaper. But the plan didn't work. Don't know 'bout the rest of the rivers, but this'un—in this stretch anyway, be's way too shallow and rocky for boats.

Wish I had my fishing pole. Could make a day of it. Oughta plan to do that soon. I get to watching some ducks. They pop they heads underwater and pop up again, looking for breakfast I reckon. My stomach starting to talk to me 'bout food too.

A picture starts up in my head, folks down here by the water, some in the water. Fishing, playing—laughing and calling out. The slaves that was in these parts. Likely a Saturday late in the day, a bunch of 'em gathered here. A picnic—maybe spread right where I standing now.

It come to me then. This the place where I belong. If not on this Robbins farm, somewhere in these parts—cause my people's been here a long, long time. We's suffered more'n can be told, suffered it right here. I guess we done become part of this land, even if we don't hold no deed.

I stand real still right on the bank. See how the morning light make the water shine. Watch for a good little bit, then figure I best be getting on back. Need to get started on this day. Most likely it gon be a good one.

What seem to help be this adding in a li'l sump'n dif'rent. I ain't used to walking to the river of a morning, so it serve the same I reckon as adding a bit of spice to my cooking. That li'l sump'n sure make a big dif'rence.

In the summertime this path too growed over. I won't walk it then. But this time of year the frost done killed back the tall weeds and grass, and I can step right along wit' not one worry 'bout Mister Copperhead.

One reason I come walking today, cause I needing to get over my aggravation. That washing machine I spent so much time dreading do make the work easier—whole heap easier! But all the while I scared I gon get my hand caught in that wringer.

Miz Robbins was bound and determined I'd put the dirtiest clothes in the ole washpot first, so's to scrub 'em on the washboard 'fore they go in the machine. I had to bite my tongue. Wanted to flat out refuse. But, ain't my place to balk when she say what she wanting done. I just the hired help.

The thought gets me to chuckling. Feels good just to think it. Yep, Hazeline the hired help. She ain't no slave! She don't even have to stay on this farm if'n she don't care to.

They a crow close by. In one of the big pine trees. There he go again—making his call. I spot him now, setting on a limb. I look his way and say, "Mr. Crow, it be the truth. Hazeline ain't no slave. You got anything to say 'bout that?"

And bless pat, if he don't give his 'caw' again. I chuckle to myself and keep walking. Then it dawns on me that I been down to the river and not once thought 'bout 1916. The Big Flood, wit' the river way up over the banks. Water just a'racing along, carrying cows and houses and all sorts of things. Was like nothing we'd ever see'd before—and hope never to see again!

When I get to the top of the hill and my li'l house come in sight, I start in to singing. "Gonna lay down my burden, down by the riverside, down by the riverside...."

I finish that one and pick up the Swannie River— "...far far away, and old folks at home." Then I bust out laughing. Reckon now that I's turned fifty, I be getting on in age too. Thing of it be, I ain't feeling none too old. Feeling like they's maybe a bit o' life left in me yet.

'Fore I get back to the house that washing machine done come to mind again. Reckon we just gon have to become friends. I s'pect my back and my hands and arms gon be thanking that machine. Least that's what my Joshua said, and I b'lieve maybe he was right.

****

Next week Thanksgiving, and Miz Robbins got a crowd coming. Wish she'd plan ahead a bit, so's I'd know just when she gon be needing me. But that ain't her way—not her way cause she don't have to do no other way. Nobody to call her on it.

I's settled myself by the south winduh. Shelling pecans again. Sure take a long time to pick out so many, but I don't mind—cause ain't nothing I like better'n pecan pie.

On her special occasions Miz Robbins counts on me being right there anytime she say. Oftentimes they long days. But I reckon I ought not to complain, cause I be beholden to him and her—for a place to live. Still, it just don't seem quite right. I has to keep the hours she say, but she don't say. I won't know till the time come when I has to be there and when I gets to leave.

One thing I sure be thankful for. Miz Robbins convinced that man of hers to hold off on buying a 'lectric cookstove. She reminded him that a crowd's due to come, most of 'em from his side of the fam'ly, and don't me nor her know a thing 'bout cooking on such a stove.

Ever since the workers hooked up the 'lectric lines, Mister Robbins has been all fired up and excited—same as when he got a new car. He had a Model T and it still running good, but he went off and got hisself a new Buick.

Much as he like new things, wouldn't surprise me none if he took hisself off to Mayor Douglas's new airport and got hisself a ride in the sky. I been thinking on this flying business. Don't understand it none, tha's for sure, but back in the summer I watched one of Henrietta's gran'chirren wit' a junebug flying at the end of a string. I decided right then that if'n a bug can fly, it do make some sense that a aeroplane can fly.

If'n a flying machine was to land right out here in the field, I s'pect I'd hop right on. The thought surprise me.

Reckon I would? Well, no matter. Ain't likely to get the chance, and no sense wishing for what yuh can't have. But just look what I got right here. A whole big pan full of nutmeats, and the hulls to scatter in my flowerbed. And come Sunday, I gon make three pies.

Chapter 31

This be the third day of rain, and my work for the Robbins's Thanksgiving feast all over and done—praise the Lord! One of the Robbins boys give me a ride to the top of the hill. Wouldn't come no further cause o' the mud. I wadn't plumb soaked by the time I got here, cause I got a reliable old raincoat that come almost to my feet. Tired and hungry I was when I come in the door. Ain't much pleasure in setting in the kitchen and eating by yuhself while a crowd of folks be gathered in the dining room.

I carried my share home and ate turkey and dressing and giblet gravy right by the fire in the fireplace, all by my lonesome—but didn't feel a bit lonesome. I don't mind my own comp'ny. Kinda like it. And that thought gets me to chuckling.

Rain and more rain. Good thing 'bout that be, my buckets outside the front door be filling wit' water. Won't have to go to the well. A few nights ago I went late in the day. Hadn't realized my buckets was so near empty, so even though it was already pretty dark, I set off. Turned out a blessing.

I turned the hoist, listened to it creaking, and when the bucket come up they was moonlight shining bright on the top o' that water. Took my breath away. Soon as I caught my breath I said a few words of thanksgiving for all the beauty they be in this world.

Glad I don't live near the creek. By now, the water bound to be flooding over the banks and into the fields and pastures. Only thing getting done anywhere round here now be milking the cows and putting out feed for all the farm animals.

Sure glad I got dry wood stacked under the lean-to and another pile of wood ready to be split. When the first cold rain sets in, it awready past time to have plenty of dry wood put by, and I pity anybody 'at don't, no matter what they color, cause one thing be's certain. Mother Nature treat ever'body the same.

My woodpile a reason for thanksgiving. Since Joshua's been gone I's had help from three or four directions, mostly Ezra Dellinger. In return I does a bit of sewing for his fam'ly—but it ain't a fair trade and Ezra always quick to say it don't need to be.

I best go check my buckets. Got two of 'em catching the roof leaks. Long as I can stay dry I got plenty to do, but first off I gon finish my new dress.

Wade say he gon be at the fishfry at Sam and Henrietta's. If'n this rain don't ease up we gon be sloshing round the yard, but I got it in mind to wear this dress. Making it from a piece of material I had put back and styling it like one I made for a rich white lady. When I spotted the fabric I couldn't figure why I was so bound and determined to buy it. Cost a right smart more'n I usually spend for a dress length, and seemed perhaps a bit too fancy for me.

But come the day of the fishfry, if'n things go the way I got in mind, I gon be wearing this new dress. And this time I s'pect I gon feel a bit easier when he come round. Cause I done been figuring on sump'n. Ain't gon be asking him no questions 'bout his life up north. No reason to. All I need to know, be what he be's like now.

Ain't gon be telling him 'bout extra special moments 'tween me and Joshua, so I gots to let Wade keep his mem'ries too. That way, we be meeting at the same spot.

He was by here a few days ago. We set at the table and he dipped a spoon in the jar then looked up at me. "Ain't had no damson preserves in many a year, Hazeline. They always was my favorite."

He didn't have to tell me that. I r'membered it from more'n thirty years ago. Soon as he said it my stomach tightened up and tears started. I choked 'em back and left the table, went and stood by the east winduh. I was looking out but I wadn't seeing. My arms was holding tight round me, and tears was crawling down my cheeks.

He come up behind me. I knowed he was there, but he didn't say nothing. After a minute or two I turned to face him. "Wade, the mem'ries is too big. I look at you and I see so much of Joshua." I swiped at my tears wit' my hands. More words tried to get out but my throat held 'em back. All I could manage was blowing out a bunch of air.

It crossed my mind how he was doing a mighty fine job—him being such a gab mouth, of keeping his mouth shut. The thought tickled me and I laughed some through my tears. His shoulders eased then and his face broke into a smile. I reached a hand out like I meant to push him away but he took hold of it.

I didn't pull away but I said, "When you around, they always seem to be sump'n 'bout you 'at bring Joshua to mind. It just too much for me—I can't help it."

I pulled my hand back and stared down at the floor. "I done decided I reckon I could put up wit' the talking—I mean, you a big talker, and now I be used to quiet. But Joshua talked a heap more'n me too, that ain't no secret, so I figured I could get used to your mouth running on."

I looked up at him then, seeing him through my tears. And said real soft, "But now, seem like the mem'ry of him be's just too big."

The clock tick-tocked. Hadn't neither of us said another word. Was prob'ly just a minute or so passed, but the time seemed long. I'd looked down at the floor again so after a bit I lifted my head to see what he was doing.

He looked like he was waiting. He reached out and took my hands in his. He say, "Hazeline, the talking I do—I give yuh my promise—gon be the only way I touches you. The only way. Lessen you decide yuh want that to change."

He grinned real big then and said, "Le's go finish our toast. We can talk to Joshua 'bout what good taste he had—in damson preserves, I mean."

We both laughed a bit then and headed back to the kitchen. My eyes was running over wit' tears—but I couldn't help smiling.

****

Ezra Dellinger come by and brung me a possum, and it dressed for cooking. Said he'd been hunting and could hardly b'lieve it hisself but in one week he got three of 'em. He'd already had the one he brung here penned up for a week, to let it eat clean so's to get 'cleaned out.' I thanked him, but all the while I was figuring who I might give it to.

I don't fancy eating possum. Rather eat beans.

Some bit later I remembered last winter. I watched a woman eating dirt. She'd been sickly, and word was she wadn't getting some kind of mineral we needs in our food. She didn't live long after that day I see'd her. And she left behind three young'uns.

So I cooked up that possum and carried it over there. Didn't know if'n they'd like possum or not, but figured it'd do me good to take sump'n their way. Just so happened I had on hand some sweet potatoes. Yuh always roast a possum wit' sweet potatoes to soak up the fat. Couldn't carry just a roasted possum, so I cooked up a coupla other things and packed my basket and carried it over.

When I come back the afternoon was almost gone. My feet stopped. I was at the edge of the yard. Just the day before I'd been out there raking the yard free of leaves, but now it seemed like I was under a spell, my feet stuck to the ground. For some li'l bit I thought 'bout Paul, the apostle. He was stopped in the road, and ever after his life was changed.

I didn't see no bright light, but sump'n was telling me to go to the back yard. Didn't seem to be no reason not to go on in the front door, like usual, but I stood real still, looking and listening. There was the house, and seemed almost like I hadn't never see'd it a'fore. The li'l house where I be living. Where Joshua'd lived, and Joleen too.

Woulda been my boy's home too, if'n he'd lived. A li'l shack really, compared to some big fancy house. But just the same, been home for quite a few years now.

I stood there, like as if a spell had come over me. Pictures from way back filled my head. Joshua. Setting on the bench, whittling. Setting under the big tree wit' his Mama and his sister. Joleen and one of her li'l friends, making mudpies for they dolls.

I thought 'bout Ole Dog, and the dog we had soon after we come here. My feet turned me again. I had the notion they was some reason to go round back. Whatever could it be? Ever'thing looked as usual. Chickens scratching in the dirt behind the chicken wire. Joshua's bench. A few clothes hanging on the line. The ole shed weatherworn.

By the backdoor. Tha's where I find it. A packet wrapped wit' a string. No name on it. I take it inside and lay it on the table. For some reason I don't open it right off. Wanna save the opening. I pour a dipperful of water from the bucket and set myself down at the table. Sip at the water, keeping my eyes on the packet.

After a bit I build a fire, get out of my work clothes and sponge my body a bit. Wish I could take a good bath but they ain't enough water.

When bedtime come, I knowed I couldn't let the packet go unopened no longer. My guess was Wade had left it for me. Couldn't think of nobody else who might've left it. But what was in it? And why all this delay in me 'bout opening it?

I finally decided it was just another sample. Of how Hazeline Morrison does too much thinking. Better to take action.

I was awready in my flannel nightgown. I went and got the packet, still right where I'd put it. I picked up my scissors and went to my chair by the fire. Soon I had the string cut and had took off the brown paper wrapping.

Inside, a shiny red satin cloth. Folded just so. I pulled it open and there lay a brooch. A sparkling ruby-like jewel wit' li'l clear stones set round it, and the casing like antique silver. I don't know much about jewels, but this one real pretty, and prob'ly old. They a note too. Not many words, wrote out in pencil.

Hope you accept this. A token of my affection. Wade

He'd scrawled his name out big. Somebody else done the writing I guess and he copied it. He never was much good in school.

I think 'bout the fish fry. Was planning on wearing a ole necklace wit' my new dress. If'n I wear this brooch, Henrietta gonna be asking where it come from. If'n I don't wear it, Wade likely figure I don't want his gift. Oh my.

I don't get in bed straight away, just keep setting by the fire. Watch the flames, hear the cracking and popping, and get to thinking on one of the church words. Fallible. Means we awready fallen—did our falling in the Garden of Eden, and been falling ever since—cause we human folk. We ain't none of us angels, cause we fallible.

All this thinking. Over and over I has to get through my long thinking. Guess it a habit. Cause I's sure—sure as I be setting here by this fire, that my heart and my whole self—'cepting my head—done awready said *Amen.*

Sure 'nough, no doubt about it—we all be's fallible. But that don't mean when we fall we has to stay down. Hunh-uh! Gotta keep getting up one more time.

And so at last I see the truth of it.

It awright—more'n awright, for me to pick myself up and get on wit' life. cause the life I had wit' Joshua, it ain't here no more. I didn't want it to end, but it sure do be gone—for some while now. And if'n I ever did feel like I was falling, was when I lost him.

But time has come now. Time to move on to a new life. The one closed out and left me when I was still living and breathing. Look like maybe a bit of rejoicing's in order, cause another way's done opened—and it a far better way'n I coulda thought up.

Hallelujah! Hallelujah!

The clock strike. Way long past my bedtime. I stir the fire and put on another log, and next thing, start in to singing. "We-e three kings of Or-ient are."

That song always been one of my favorites cause it got such a happy rhythm. I sing the verses, then chuckle a bit. Now why in the world? Why that song? Why sing 'bout some kings of long ago—when I celebrating my prospect of happiness?

But it ain't hard to figure. Ever since December come, I been letting myself picture Christmas. This one ain't gon be so full of sorrow.

"We-e three kings of Or-ient are, bear-ing gifts we traverse a-far..."

When I was just a li'l thing I liked looking at pictures of the three kings and the baby Jesus in the manger. The kings brought gifts, so that mean it a fitting tune for right now. My heart going to Wade, his coming to me. Can't be no better gift 'an that.

A Christmas gift. Need to come up wit' sump'n to give to this dear man tha's done come back after all these years. Who woulda thought it? Laws-a-mercy, wonders never cease!

Well, time to wind the clock and crawl in the bed. Might be I'll have some happy dreams.

****

The sun high in the sky and I be on my way. The ground slick wit' wet leaves and the tree limbs bare and sun shining, but the air's cold. I'm looking to set on my rock and speak what I be feeling in my heart.

Sunday today, but first thing when my eyes come open, figured I wouldn't go to church today. 'Fore I set out I fried up a chicken. Wouldn't seem like Sunday wit'out a hen in the frying pan. Most Sunday mornings I kills one. Was my job at home long 'fore I was full growed.

The old sycamore come in sight. Sure a glory to see! The bare limbs stretch high and the white bark shine in the sunlight. I brung along a burlap sack. Gon spread it on the wet rock and set myself down.

For some li'l bit I jus' listen. The water's deeper'n usual this morning and sure making a fine music. Can't listen long or the cold will have me plumb stiff, so I clasp my hands in my lap and start in, speaking real soft.

"This year soon be coming to a end. It sure been a year for me...a year when I's tried to do what I thought best. And most of what I done most folks said was foolish. May be it was. May be it wadn't. I can't say for sure."

A cracking noise...and I jump. Other side of the branch a fairly big limb's come crashing down. Now it be just laying there on a bed of brown leaves.

"One minute still a limb on the tree, next minute on the ground."

I gets to chuckling then. Was what coulda been said 'bout me. Sure did feel like folks round was doing they best to push me down. But I didn't give up, kept on believing sump'n could change—and sure 'nough, some of the change I was wanting did come about. And who woulda thought it would come wit' the help of a white lady?

They one thing I's kept wondering about. Whatever was it made me think of asking her? And how was it I got up nerve enough to go knocking on her door?

One thing in pertic'lar I come here to say, what I most wanting to say. So I start in. "If'n such a idea can settle in my head, and if'n I can get myself out my door and go knocking on her door...well, ain't like we's see'd the last of injustice—so what 'bout times to come? Is I still gon have to go knocking on doors I scared to knock on? Is that wha's gon come to pass?"

The cold's got me rubbing my hands t'gether. Shoulda remembered my gloves.

Cold out for sure, but beside the cold, sump'n else. A peacefulness. Might be these woods feels peaceful. Mother

Nature gives us spots like this'un, where we can go to find peace.

I button the top button and pull my ole coat close. A gust of wind comes ripping by. The wind working hard, but somehow it ain't scaring me. It gets loud so I gets loud too.

"Wind, I feels yuh! On the move—tha's you. And I sure knows what that mean. Mean yuh be bringing on change."

The cold deep in my bones now. Best be getting myself on home, stir up the fire and set by it.

And right soon after that I does head up the path. When I gets to the top of the ridge I turn and look back, and whisper, "Let me...let me be like this wind...a wind what bring on change."

****

Strange it was. Was on my way home. Had carried a dress I'd made to a woman out on the Beatties Ford Road, and some words popped up. Was like somebody stepped up in front of me holding a sign.

But wadn't no sign, was a mem'ry.

From when I was a girl...playing ball wit' my cousins. Don't know what made me think of doing such, but I climbed up on a fence post and tried to stand on it wit' one leg—and soon come tumbling down. And turned my ankle. Well, 'course I shed a few tears—cause it hurt, and cause I didn't wanna be no cripple.

Uncle Percy, one o' Mama's brothers, he come hurrying over and took a look and said he thought it'd mend ok. He was the one in the fam'ly who'd studied some on doctoring, but all I cared 'bout was how bad my foot was hurting. So I cried some more cause I didn't figure I could make my way home.

And Uncle Percy say, "Lean on me." So tha's what I done. Hobbled home wit' him holding to my arm. And now, this day, them few words come back.

Lean on me. Seem now like it might mean I can count on my own strength—the strength 'at's already been give to me.

And now I be coming home this day. Come in the door and first thing get to building up the fire in the fireplace. And right soon I settle by the fire and start saying my thanksgivings, cause I know for certain they sump'n been growing in me.

And got a feeling I gon sleep mighty fine, 'cept for getting up to feed the fire.

CPSIA information can be obtained
at www.ICGtesting.com
Printed in the USA
BVHW082046260921
617557BV00001B/2

9 780578 903460